CHERISH

Sherryl Woods

Prologue

Brandon Halloran had never felt so rich, and for once in his sixty-eight years it had nothing to do with the money or the possessions he'd amassed. Squaring his shoulders, his eyes misted over as he caught sight of his beloved Elizabeth at the back of the old Boston church he'd been attending for his entire lifetime. There was no denying the passage of time, but by God, she was a beauty still.

Petite, vivacious and with an undimmed sense of mischief in those twinkling blue eyes of hers, Elizabeth Forsythe Newton radiated joy as her gaze met his. Her pace picked up just a fraction—one beat ahead of the wedding march—as if she couldn't quite wait, after all this time, to be his.

Oh my, yes, Brandon thought, his own heart filling with anticipation.

The wait had definitely been too long. Nearly fifty years had passed, during which he'd married another woman and raised a family. He'd seen his own grandson wed to a spunky girl who'd reminded him so much of his precious Elizabeth that his heart had ached.

Life had a way of making amends, though. Finding Lizzy again after all this time had made Brandon feel twice blessed. When he'd finally convinced her that they weren't a couple of old fools for wanting to get married at this stage of their lives, she'd tackled the plans with the enthusiasm of a young girl. She'd even drawn his beloved daughter-in-law and granddaughter-in-law into the celebration and convinced them to share the day by renewing their own vows.

His heart full, Brandon watched his son pledge to honor his wife. Kevin had almost lost that woman—twice, in fact. There'd been a time when Brandon himself had put obstacles in their path—one of his few regrets.

He'd been convinced that Lacey Grainger wasn't the right woman for his son, that she'd been responsible for his rebellion against everything the Hallorans stood for. Only later had Brandon come to realize that Lacey was the mellowing influence, the gentle force that brought out Kevin's best instincts. To Brandon's everlasting relief they had mended their marriage, and after today's ceremony of renewal, he expected it would be stronger than ever.

Now, impetuous, full-of-life Dana Roberts was another story. She'd led his grandson on a merry chase, starting things off by slugging Jason in a quiet, respectable tavern. Word of the ruckus had spread far and wide, to Jason's chagrin and Brandon's own delight. My, but Dana had been a breath of fresh air with her feistiness. She'd been a little rough around the edges, but Brandon had spotted the life in her right off, and he'd watched with glee as Jason struggled against the pull of her offbeat ways. Now they were expecting his first great-grandbaby—any minute by the looks of Dana.

Yes, indeed, he'd had a full and blessed life, Brandon thought. Maybe he'd been missing Elizabeth all this time, but the years hadn't been wasted if they'd all led up to this moment. Maybe Brandon and Elizabeth had come to appreciate what they had just a little bit more. Their path to the altar hadn't been easy. They'd had to learn all over again about trust and forgiveness, but he didn't have a doubt in his mind that it would be worth it.

When the minister turned to him, Brandon clasped Elizabeth's fragile hand and held on tight to quiet an unexpected attack of nerves.

"You are the light of my life," he told her. "We have missed so many years and yet it is as if they never were. What I feel for you today is as strong and as deep as it was on the day I first told you I loved you so long ago. Perhaps those words have even more meaning now that we have known the sorrows of loss, the strife of living, the meaning of forgiveness and the joy of rediscovery."

He raised her hand to his lips and kissed it. "I, Brandon, take thee, Elizabeth, a woman I loved and lost and have been blessed to find again to be my wedded wife. I promise to cherish thee all the rest of my days."

To his surprise there were tears in just about everyone's eyes when he'd finished. He wanted to whoop with joy himself, but knew he didn't dare.

He'd caused the rest of them enough alarm over the past few months with his impetuous courtship of the woman who was now, at long last, his wife.

Brandon couldn't hold back a chuckle, though, as he thought of the way he and Elizabeth had shaken things up. By God, they had had a fine time.

God willing, there was more to come—for all of them.

Chapter 1

It had been an absolute bear of a day, with one last wintry rain to cast a pall over the promise of spring. Exhausted, Brandon Halloran poured himself a stiff drink and sank into his favorite leather easy chair in front of the library fireplace. As he stared into the dancing flames, he tried to empty his mind of all the problems that weren't up to him to solve. Unfortunately he didn't seem to be having any more luck with that now than he had over the past weeks.

He'd spent the whole day worrying anew about whether his son and daughter-in-law were going to patch up their marriage. A few weeks ago a divorce had seemed all but certain, but after Kevin's most recent heart attack, Brandon had seen for himself how much Lacey still loved his son. He couldn't imagine why the two of them were so darned blind to something that was clear as glass to him.

Brandon's hopes had risen when his son left the hospital. Kevin and Lacey had traipsed off to Cape Cod together. Brandon had been reassured that things were finally on the right track for the two of them. Then, just today, he'd found out that Lacey was back in Boston—alone.

He'd confronted her earlier tonight, only to have her remind him that he was butting in where he shouldn't. But if he didn't make them see sense, who would? He was family, dammit, to say nothing of being older and wiser.

It was nights like this that Brandon missed his wife the most. Grace had been good to him, loving and gentle. Given his mulishness, she'd also had the patience of a saint. And she'd known when to exert that iron will of hers to keep him from making mistakes he'd regret.

If he and Grace had lacked a certain passion, well, that wasn't the worst thing in the world. Before she'd died so suddenly two years ago, they'd raised a wonderful son and seen their grandson grow into a fine young man. Maybe it was good she hadn't seen Kevin's marriage hit this rough patch.

Her heart would have ached just as badly as Brandon's did.

He and Grace had always been able to talk things through. That was the quality he missed the most. She would have understood this empty feeling in the pit of his stomach better than anyone. She'd always known what trouble he had letting go of anything, whether it was putting an end to the meddling in his son's life or walking away from the textile company he'd inherited from his father. How did these young people today say it? Get a life! That's what he needed to do, let go and get a life.

There was certainly no denying it was time to let go of the business he'd spent a lifetime building. He was sixty-eight years old. Thank goodness he still had his health. He could carry on at the helm of Halloran Industries another decade—at least that's the way he felt in the mornings with the whole day stretched out ahead of him.

The truth of the matter was, though, it was past time to give his son and grandson their chance. He'd first taught Kevin and then Jason the best he could, and now it was time to turn over the reins.

Maybe if he had a different personality, he could keep a hand in, stay in the background. He knew himself well enough, though, to realize that as long as he entered that building, he'd never be able to keep still about the decisions being made inside it. The only way for Kevin and Jason to put their own stamp on Halloran Industries would be for Brandon to walk away and not look back.

Damned if he knew how, though. What the devil would he do with all those long, lonely hours? Travel? What was the fun in seeing the world if there was no one to share the experiences with? He could read, play a little golf, but that would never fill up enough hours. His mind would atrophy in a month without the daily challenge of running his company, without the fun of finding some new fabric to design and work into Halloran Industries' line of quality textiles.

Brandon's "whims," Kevin and Jason called them. Yet those whims had kept their company thriving. They'd given him a reason to go on during the bleak days after Grace's death. He'd had some dandy adventures searching for ways to upgrade fabrics so that designers the world over would seek his company out for their richest, most sophisticated customers. The thought of giving all that up left Brandon feeling lost.

Well, he'd just have to make it work. It wasn't fair to hang on forever, not when his son and grandson had both long since proven their worth.

Brandon studied the scrap of paper he held in his hand and wondered if it had the answer.

Just before he'd left the office, he'd finally gotten a call from the detective he'd hired a few months back. Hiring the man had been an impulsive action, one of those spur-of-the-moment, middle-of-the-lonely-night decisions that didn't make a bit of sense in the cold light of day. Still, he'd gone ahead with it, caught up in a need to finally know, after all these years, what had happened to the one woman he'd never been able to forget. He was sure his beloved Grace would forgive him this bit of foolishness.

"Lizzy," he'd scrawled and then a phone number somewhere in Southern California. Elizabeth Forsythe Newton. It had been Elizabeth Forsythe when they'd met nearly a half century ago. Now, according to the detective, she'd been widowed five years, had two daughters and three grandchildren. She still taught school, substituting now, not full-time. She attended church on Sunday, went to an occasional movie. If there was a man in her life, the detective had made no mention of it. He'd promised to mail his complete report in the morning.

Brandon couldn't ask the detective the one question that was uppermost in his mind: did she remember those long-ago days they had shared, at all? Time blurred most things, but for him the memory of those days with Lizzy were every bit as vivid now as they had been hours or even weeks after they'd occurred. Not even a long and happy marriage had entirely erased thoughts of what might have been.

His housekeeper rapped on the door, then opened it. "Sir, your dinner is ready."

Another depressingly lonely meal, he thought and then made up his mind. "I know it's late, but can you hold it a bit, Mrs. Farnsworth? There's a phone call I need to make."

"Certainly, sir. A half hour?"

"That will be fine."

Even before she'd quietly closed the door, he reached for the phone and punched in the numbers before he could change his mind.

As the phone rang more than three thousand miles away, Brandon thought back to the summer day he'd first seen Lizzy, racing hell-bent for leather along a cliff overlooking the Atlantic. Her auburn hair caught the sun and gleamed like fire. Her white cotton dress had been hiked up daringly above her knees as she ran barefoot through the damp morning grass. He had been stunned by her beauty, but it had been the sheer joy in her expression that had captivated him.

The image lingered as the phone was picked up. "Yes, hello?" a tentative female voice said.

Brandon's breath seemed to go still, as a powerful sense of déjà vu swept through him. The sweet, musical tone still held some little hint of bubbling laughter beneath the hesitancy. His heart, which had no business doing such things at his age, lurched and took up a quickened rhythm.

"Elizabeth Forsythe? Lizzy, is that you?"

He heard the faint gasp, then the whispered shock of recognition. "Brandon?"

"Yes, Lizzy, it's me. Brandon Halloran. Do you remember? It's been so long."

"I remember," she said, her voice sounding oddly choked. "You were the only one who ever called me that. Where on earth are you?"

"In Boston."

"How did you find me?"

He thought back to how hard he'd tried all those years ago, only to have her prove elusive. This time he'd taken no chances, spared no expense. "I hired a very smart detective."

"A detective? Oh, my. Why on earth would you do that after all this time?"

Elizabeth sounded nervous, maybe even troubled. It puzzled him, but he dismissed it as nothing more than the surprise of hearing from him out of the blue like this.

"Maybe I just wanted to hear the sound of your voice. You sound exactly the same, as if someone's just told you something that made you want to laugh. I've missed you, Lizzy. How are you? Are you well?"

He knew the answer to that much at least, but he was afraid it was far too soon to ask her the questions he really wanted to ask. Most important, he needed to know why she hadn't waited for him.

As they talked, hesitantly at first and then with their old enthusiasm, the years slid away. They were simply two old friends catching up. Haunting memories came back to Brandon as he listened, then were replaced by sorrow as she described so many experiences they hadn't shared.

"You've been out there how long now?" he asked. "Since 1942."

"The year we met."

"Yes," she said softly. "The year we met."

Was there a note of wistfulness in her response? "Tell me about your life. You have children?" he asked, needing to hear her confirm every word in the detective's report.

"Yes, two daughters. They're grown now. The oldest, that's Ellen, is married and has three children herself. The youngest, that's Kate, has a real streak of independence. She claims no man will ever tie her down."

"Like her mother, if I recall correctly," he said, imagining another redhead with a fiery temper and the strength of her convictions. Brandon wondered if meeting Lizzy's daughters would be like traveling back in time.

Lizzy laughed. "She'd never believe you, if she heard you say that. She says she's not a bit like me, that I'm old-fashioned."

"That's certainly not the way I remember you."

He heard her quiet sigh and wondered at the faint hint of regret it held. "Brandon, we knew each other for such a short time. I suspect neither of us remembers those days with much accuracy."

"But you have thought of them?" he prodded, waving off Mrs. Farnsworth's second attempt to call him to dinner.

"Some, yes," Lizzy admitted. "I can't deny that."

"What do you remember?"

"That we were very young and very foolish."

"That's not the way I remember it at all," he said. "I remember that we were very much in love, that from the first instant I saw you I was enchanted."

"I think it's best if we don't talk about those days, Brandon. A lifetime has passed since then." Her voice had cooled.

Brandon released a sigh. "So you do regret it. I'm sorry, Lizzy. I don't regret one minute of that time we spent together. I can't."

"Tell me about your family," she said in a sudden rush, as if she didn't dare allow his nostalgic note to linger. "You have children?"

He thought of refusing to be turned from the past to the present, then decided there was nothing to be gained from pressing her to look back. Not yet, anyway.

"I have a son, Kevin. He's taking over Halloran Industries soon."

"You're retiring?"

"I'm thinking of it."

"Somehow I thought you'd never walk away from that company. You always loved it so, almost as much as flying. Do you still collect fabric samples the way some kids back then collected stamps?"

"I not only collect them, I improve on them."

"Okay. Of course," she said, laughing. "I'd forgotten how self-confident you are."

"I suspect conceited is what you meant," he said, laughing with her. "Oh, Lizzy, how I've missed that sharp wit of yours. You never let me get away with a thing."

"It seems to me you got away with plenty," she said tartly.

The sly innuendo had Brandon chuckling again. That was the Lizzy of old, all right. She'd never been one to dance around the truth of things.

He'd never known anyone else like her back then. Bold and sassy, she'd kept him constantly off balance, a rare occurrence for a man who even at eighteen had been pretty darned sure of himself.

"Lizzy, I want to see you again. I'll fly out tomorrow," he said, suddenly anxious to end a separation that never should have been. "We'll have ourselves a grand reunion. You can show me all the sights. Maybe we'll even go to Disneyland and pretend we're just a couple of kids again."

Silence greeted the suggestion, then, "No. Absolutely not. I'm sorry, Brandon."

"But, Lizzy, we owe it to ourselves. For old times' sake," he coaxed. "What's the harm?"

"No, Brandon," she said, her tone suddenly cold and forbidding in a way it never had been before. "It's best to leave the past where it belongs, in the past."

The phone clicked quietly, cutting him off. He called back immediately, only to get a busy signal. He tried again and again throughout the evening, but by midnight he knew she wasn't going to take his call.

"Well, I'll be damned," he muttered, staring at the phone. No little slip of a woman was going to thwart his dreams. Not a second time. Surely if Lizzy remembered him at all, she remembered that he liked nothing better than the challenge of a chase.

For what seemed like hours, Elizabeth sat staring at the phone, the receiver defiantly left off the hook. No, she corrected. It wasn't defiance. It was sheer terror. Brandon Halloran made her feel things—crazy, impossible things—she hadn't felt in years.

A day ago Elizabeth would have sworn that her life was complete. She would have laughed at the thought that a sixty-seven-year-old woman's pulse could flutter at the mere sound of a man's voice. Gracious, the last time her heart had pumped this fast, she'd been on a dance floor doing a pretty spirited tango with a man wearing a polyester suit and too much shaving cologne.

She tried to imagine Brandon Halloran in polyester and couldn't.

Cashmere or the finest linen would be more his style. She could recall, all too vividly it seemed, the way his skin had felt beneath her nervous touch. She absentmindedly picked up a magazine and fanned herself, then realized what she was doing.

"Elizabeth, you're an old fool," she lectured herself aloud. "What do you think you're doing dredging up thoughts like that? Your daughters would be shocked."

Of course, the subconscious wasn't nearly as easily controlled as she might have liked. She deliberately walked away from the off-the-hook phone, hoping she could forget all about the long-buried memories Brandon had just stirred to life, memories she had done her very best to forget.

Some, admittedly, were sweet and filled with a rare tenderness. Some were wildly wicked, which certainly explained the way her pulse was thundering. And others, the ones she needed most to remember, were filled with hurt and anger and a deep sense of betrayal.

Nearly fifty years ago Brandon Halloran had roared into her life, swept her off her feet and then vanished, leaving her to suffer the consequences of a broken heart. He had no right to think he could do the same thing again, not at this late date. Not even one word of apology had crossed his lips.

Instead, the conversation had been laced with persuasive teasing, riddled with nostalgia. She was no longer a naive seventeen-year-old. She wouldn't give in to the smooth and easy charm a second time.

Elizabeth felt the anger mount and clung to it gratefully. As long as she felt like this, she would be able to remain strong. She would be able to deny whatever pleas Brandon made. She could ignore his coaxing, as she should have done so long ago.

Still and all, she wondered just a little about how he'd changed. Was he still as handsome and dashing? Back then he'd had a smile that could charm the birds out of the trees. It had certainly worked its magic on her. He'd walked and talked with an air of bold confidence. He'd had unruly blond hair that had felt like the silk that was spun in his factory. His piercing eyes had been the color of the ocean at its deepest—blue and mysterious. When his eyes lit with laughter—or desire—she'd been sure that what they shared was rare and certainly forever.

Believing all that, Elizabeth had been tumbled back to reality with an abruptness that had shattered her. Only by the grace of God and through the love of her parents had she been able to pick up the pieces of her life and move on. David Newton had played a huge role in that as well.

Her senior by ten years, David had been a fine man, tolerant and sensitive. And he had loved her unconditionally and without restraint. She owed him her thanks for seeing to it that she finished college, that she was able to enter a profession that had been more fulfilling each year. More than that, she owed him for giving her the very best years of her life, while asking so little for himself in return. She'd been content with their bargain, happy with the life they'd shared. Maybe there had been no glorious highs, but there had never been the devastating lows she'd known with Brandon.

Unlike David, Brandon Halloran had demanded everything and had very nearly cheated her of any future at all.

The ringing of the doorbell interrupted her thoughts. Suddenly realizing that she'd been sitting here in the dark for hours, she snapped on a light on her way to the door. When she opened it, she found Kate, flanked by Ellen and the youngest of Ellen's girls, fifteen-year-old Penny.

"Goodness, what a surprise!" she said, delighted by the distraction their arrival promised.

"Surprise?" Kate repeated, sounding miffed. "Mother, your phone has been off the hook for the past three hours." She marched into the living room and hung it up. "We've been worried sick about you."

"Kate's been worried," Ellen corrected. "We just came along as moral support. She said it was us or the police."

Elizabeth managed an astonishingly casual air, hoping to forestall too many questions. "Well, as you can see, I am perfectly fine. The cat must have knocked the receiver off when she jumped on the table. It's not the first time that's happened," she said, because she was not about to tell them about Brandon's call and the way it had shaken her.

Ellen regarded her speculatively, as if she could almost read her mother's thoughts.

"Mother, are you sure you're all right?" her oldest asked quietly. "Certainly. Why wouldn't I be?"

"It's just that you look, I don't know, a little flustered. I've never seen you look quite that way before."

Her granddaughter peered at her closely. "Mom's right," Penny announced. "Are you sure you don't have some man stashed away upstairs?"

"Penny!" Ellen said sharply.

"Oh, Mom, don't act so shocked. Sex doesn't end just because you're over sixty."

"And just where did you hear that?" Elizabeth inquired, tucking an arm around her granddaughter's waist and steering her into the kitchen.

"It was in my health class. I could lend you the book, if you want."

"Penny!" Ellen exclaimed again with obvious dismay.

Elizabeth shot a grin at her daughter. "Chill out, Ellen." She turned to Penny. "That is the expression, isn't it?"

Ellen groaned. Kate looked from one to the other

of them, her hands on her hips, her expression radiating indignation. "Well, I'm delighted you all find this so amusing."

Tension seemed to simmer in the air until Ellen gave her sister a hug. "Oh, come on, Katie dearest. Chill out. As you can perfectly well see, Mother's just fine. You were worried over nothing. You should be relieved."

"Why don't I fix us all some hot chocolate?" Elizabeth suggested. "The air's a bit damp tonight, don't you think?"

"Lace mine with brandy," Kate muttered, regarding the rest of them with a sour expression.

Elizabeth looked at her too-serious younger daughter and sighed. "I'm sorry you were worried, dear. I really am."

Some of the tension in Kate's shoulders eased. Finally she grinned. "Oh, what the hell. Let's go whole hog and order in a pizza, too. It's after nine and I just left the office. I missed dinner altogether."

"Now that's the spirit," Elizabeth said, noting that despite the long day Kate looked neat as a pin, every dark hair in place. What a contrast to Ellen's careless sandy hairstyle. "A large pizza with everything. I haven't eaten, either."

"Everything except anchovies," Penny countered.

"I happen to love anchovies, young lady. You can either learn to like them or pick them off."

Ellen and Kate shared an amused, conspiratorial glance at the familiar argument.

"You might as well give in kiddo," Ellen told her daughter. "Your grandmother will not budge on this."

By the time they'd finished the pizza, it was close to midnight.

Elizabeth said good-night at the door and stood watching long after the taillights of their cars had disappeared.

She regretted worrying them earlier, but she was glad that it had brought them by, just when she needed a distraction the most. Now that they'd gone, the house felt empty and lifeless. It had never felt that way before. She'd never noticed the loneliness as she did tonight. Under the circumstances it was a dangerous state of mind.

For as long as Kate, Ellen and Penny were there, Elizabeth hadn't allowed a single thought of Brandon Halloran to creep in. Alone again, however, she knew that she had only delayed the inevitable. Brandon wasn't the type of man to be banished so easily from her thoughts.

To her dismay it seemed that that much at least hadn't changed over the past fifty years. He still had a way of capturing her attention and driving out all rational thought. She could only pray that some of that single-minded purpose with which he'd pursued her all those years ago had faded with age.

Chapter 2

Now that he'd found Lizzy, Brandon was not about to be thwarted in his campaign to arrange a reunion. What on earth could she find so threatening about a couple of old friends getting together to reminisce?

The next day he sent her two dozen pale pink roses, the day after that a huge basket of wildflowers. He followed up with rare orchids. The Beverly Hills florist was ecstatic over the lavish orders he phoned in daily. Brandon wasn't at all certain what Lizzy's reaction was likely to be. He figured it would be best not to call, to be patient and let her get used to the idea that he intended to become an important part of her life again.

It had been years since he'd courted a woman, but he knew the techniques couldn't have changed all that much. He would fill her whole damn house with flowers if he had to. Sooner or later she was bound to start chuckling at his extravagance. Then maybe she would experience a little twinge of purely feminine delight. By the time he exhausted the rare and exotic floral possibilities, he was hoping she'd cave in and track him down. Halloran Industries hadn't moved in nearly a century. She could find him anytime she wanted to.

Yet there were no calls, no letters as March gave way to April, so Brandon started sending extravagant boxes of candy. Lizzy had always had a sweet tooth. Half their dates had ended in a soda shop over hot-fudge sundaes. This time, though, a full week of chocolates produced no results. His patience started wearing thin.

Brandon was standing in front of a department store display of outrageously expensive French perfumes, totally at a loss, when Jason's wife sneaked up beside him.

"My, my, what are you up to?" Dana inquired, linking her arm through his.

He scowled at her. "How do you make heads or tails of all this?"

"Don't ask me. All those scents make me queasy."

He glanced at her swollen belly, which not even one of her boldly designed, loose-fitting sweaters could camouflage at this stage of her pregnancy. "Why aren't you and my great-grandbaby at home resting?"

"Because your great-grandbaby is coming in just a couple of months and I need to start buying things for the nursery."

"Nursery?" he said, readily dismissing the perfume as a purchase he could make later. "Let's go. I can help."

Dana stood stock-still. "Not until you tell me what you're doing surrounded by the most expensive perfumes in the store."

"Just looking."

His granddaughter-in-law rolled her eyes. "Come on, Brandon. You can't kid a kidder. Who's the woman?"

"Young lady, mind your own business," he said, trying to sound stern, rather than flustered. He'd hoped to keep all this to himself. He could swear Dana to secrecy, but that seemed slightly absurd given the lack of anything much to talk about in the first place.

She grinned at him. "Talk about the pot calling the kettle black. If you ask me in this instance, turnabout is definitely fair play. You started meddling in my life on the first day we met and you haven't stopped yet."

"I think it's time we had another one of those talks about respecting your elders. Even that rapscallion brother of yours shows me more respect."

Dana didn't look the least bit intimidated. "Save the lecture for the baby," she told him. "Maybe you'll be able to convince your new great-grandchild to worship the ground you walk on. I'm just plain nosy, especially when my single grandfather-in-law is showing all the signs of courting some mysterious woman."

"Looking at perfume does *not* constitute courting. I could be buying the perfume for my secretary."

"Oh? Is it Harriet's birthday? Is she the one you've been lavishing all those flowers on?"

Brandon glared at her. "What do you know about any flowers?"

"Just that last month's florist bill nearly put Kevin back in the hospital with another heart attack. You really should pay cash, if you intend to keep these things secret from your nearest and dearest. Kevin reads the fine print on every one of those invoices, remember?"

"I remember," he grumbled. Unfortunately he hadn't considered that when he'd placed the orders. "Are we going to look at baby things or not?"

"Sure," Dana said finally. "That'll give me that much longer to try to pry some real information out of you."

He waggled a finger under her nose. "If I weren't afraid you would go out and buy little pink sissy things for my great-grandson, I'd let you go alone."

"Your great-grand*daughter* may want little sissy things."

"There hasn't been a girl born into the Halloran family as far back as I can remember."

"Probably because nature knew what it would take to put up with the Halloran men. Now, come on. Let's look at wallpaper. I was thinking clowns. What do you think?"

"Clowns? Why not trains or boats?"

"How about little yellow ducks?"

"My great-grandson is not going to live with little yellow ducks," Brandon said indignantly. "He'll quack before he talks."

"Maybe we should look at cribs instead," Dana said. "Or diapers? Do you have firm convictions about diapers? I was thinking cloth because of the environment."

"Cloth is good," he conceded, then studied her worriedly. "Are you sure you should be doing all this running around? Maybe you should go back home and rest. Leave the shopping up to Jason and me."

"Not a chance. Now let's get moving. I have a list."

Dana dragged him through the department store at a pace only slightly slower than a marathon runner's. She found at least a half-dozen more opportunities to slip in questions about his social life. Brandon had to be quick on his feet to keep up with her and even quicker to avoid the verbal traps she so neatly set.

When they'd finally put the bundles into the trunk of Dana's car, he shot her a triumphant look. "Thought you could wheedle it out of me, didn't you?"

She turned on her most innocent expression. "You mean the fact that this woman lives in California and her name is Elizabeth?" she asked as she slammed the car door.

Brandon stared at her in astonishment, then rapped on the window until she rolled it down. "How'd you know that?"

"Those invoices reveal a whole lot more than the cost of your flowers," she said smugly. "The word is out."

"If you knew all that, why'd you ask?"

"I wanted to watch you squirm," she admitted with a grin. "You've done it to us often enough."

Brandon couldn't stop the laugh that bubbled up despite his indignation at being caught. "I suppose you're feeling mighty proud of yourself?"

"As a matter of fact, yes."

"I wouldn't go getting too smug, young lady. There's still time for me to sneak my workmen into that nursery and paper the walls with itsy-bitsy footballs and baseballs."

"You do and your great-grandchild will be in college before you see her."

"You're mighty sassy," he observed with a chuckle. He leaned down and kissed her forehead. "Come over some night and dig around in the attic. There just might be an old cradle up there you could use."

"Was it Jason's?" she asked with an immediate spark of enthusiasm in her eyes.

"His and Kevin's before him. Might even have been mine."

"Oh, I'd love to have that. I'll stop by."

"Anytime you like. In the meantime, you take care of that baby."

"Between you and Jason I don't have a choice." She backed the car out of the parking space, then called to him. "Whatever's going on with you, I hope you're having fun."

"Not yet," he admitted glumly, then brightened. "But I expect to be."

One week later Brandon packaged up a vintage recording of the song he and Lizzy had considered to be theirs—one of Glenn Miller's best to Brandon's way of thinking. He sent it overnight express. If that didn't get to her, he didn't know what would.

Sure enough, Elizabeth called that night just as he was getting ready to leave the office. "Brandon, this has to stop."

"Why?"

"I don't want all these gifts. Do you have any idea how overpowering all these flowers are in a five-room house? I feel like I'm sleeping in a garden."

"Sounds romantic to me."

"It might be, if I didn't have allergies," she grumbled, sneezing as if to prove the point.

Despite himself, Brandon chuckled. "Send the flowers to a hospital or a nursing home."

"Why are you doing this?"

"I told you. I want to see you. Why are you so reluctant?"

"I think it's wrong to try to go back."

It sounded to Brandon as if she'd wanted to say something else. The reluctance puzzled him. "We're talking dinner, maybe a little dancing. You always did like to dance, Lizzy. I remember the way you could waltz. I'll never forget the night we danced in that gazebo in the town square. I can still smell the honeysuckle. I loved holding you in my arms."

"No," she repeated, but there was less starch in her voice this time. "You're weakening, aren't you? I'll be out tomorrow. Once I'm standing on your doorstep, you won't be able to resist."

"That's what I'm afraid of," she muttered.

Brandon waited as she drew in a deep breath. Finally, after yet another silence that seemed to last an eternity, she said, "I don't want you out here. I'll come there, Brandon. It's been a long time since I've been back to the East Coast."

"Tomorrow?" he said. "I'll call my travel agent and have her book you on the first available flight."

"You always were so impatient," she said on a breathless laugh. "Not tomorrow, but soon."

"Promise?"

"I promise. But I'll buy my own ticket, Brandon… when I'm ready."

He heard the determined note in her voice and knew she wouldn't budge. "I won't argue with you over the ticket," he said reluctantly. "But if you don't show up soon, I'll come after you, Lizzy. I swear I will."

That night, like so many others in recent months,

Brandon Halloran lay awake staring into the darkness. Unlike those other nights, though, this time he was filled with excitement, rather than loneliness. He felt as if nearly fifty years of his life had vanished in the blink of an eye and he was an impetuous, daring young man again.

There was nothing that eighteen-year-old Brandon Halloran loved more than flying. From the day he'd graduated from high school he'd wanted nothing more than to join the Air Force and do his part in World War II. His parents had been appalled when he'd gone and enlisted rather than pack his bags for the Ivy League college that had accepted him. Now with his training complete and his orders for overseas in his pocket, he had ten days to say goodbye.

Unfortunately, every time he tried to say the words, his mother burst into tears and left the room. His father, who'd come to the United States as an immigrant from England, understood only that he was in some way responsible for Brandon's decision. He and his uncles had told Brandon stories about England from the day he was born. Because of those stories, Brandon felt this compelling need to fight in a war that was endangering their homeland.

Besides, he looked damned good in his uniform. Everyone knew that soldiers and fly-boys had their pick of women caught up in the drama of sending young men off to war. He didn't delude himself that what he was doing was part idealism and part ego. He liked the image of himself as a hero, liked even more the idea of flirting with danger.

"I'd rather have my son alive," his mother said when Brandon tried one last time to explain. She slammed a plate onto the kitchen counter with such force it shattered. Then came the tears and she hurried away, refusing to meet his distraught gaze.

His father came in just then. "You've upset your mother again, haven't you?"

"Dad, I don't know what else I can say to her."

"She's afraid for you."

"I'm good, Dad. I'll come out of this okay."

In a rare display of emotion, his father gripped his hand. "I hope so, boy. For all our sakes. She'll never forgive me if you don't."

"You do understand why I need to go, though, don't you?"

His father nodded. "If I were a younger man, I'd be going with you."

It had been more of a blessing than Brandon had expected. "I think I'll hitch a ride up the coast with a friend of mine for a couple of days. Maybe that'll give Mom some time to adjust."

"I think that would be best. Make the most of these days, son. Once you ship out, it's hard telling when you'll have another chance to relax."

Jack Brice picked him up a few hours later and they headed north. Jack's family had a place overlooking the ocean on the coast of Maine. Brandon had agreed to come along as much to cushion the blow when Jack told his family about his overseas orders as he had to relax.

When Jack broke the news the following day at lunch, his parents and sisters were every bit as stunned and dismayed as Brandon's family had been. After a while Brandon left them alone and went for a walk along the cliff overlooking the sea.

Even in summer there was always a stiff, chilly breeze blowing in hard from the north along there, but the sun beat down to counteract the cold.

With his hands jammed in his pockets, he walked for the better part of an hour, thinking about the war taking place directly across the ocean that was splashing against the rocky coastline below.

He thought of the way the planes responded to his touch, the power he felt sitting at the controls defying gravity. And he thought of the reality of combat which up to now held no meaning for him. His mother, his father, the Brices, they were all right to be afraid. Hell, he'd be scared to death, too, if he allowed himself to ponder all the things that could go wrong on a mission. Fortunately he'd been blessed with an abundance of optimism.

Hallorans made their own luck, and he intended to grab quite a handful.

Brandon was thinking about luck when he first saw the streak of white flashing past, a woman's bare feet kicking back, her hair streaming. The sunlight caught in the hair and turned it into fiery ribbons. He'd watched her run for no more than a heartbeat before the same compelling sense of fate that had drawn him to enlist sent him racing after her.

With his long, loping strides he could have caught up with her in no time, but he held back, enjoying the sight of her wide-flung arms, her bare legs, the way the white cotton dress clung to her curves.

He was so surprised when she suddenly whirled

around and stopped stock-still that he almost ran into her. He drew up just in time to catch the bright spark of curiosity in her eyes, the faint sound of laughter on her lips. The run had pushed color into her cheeks and had her bosom rising and falling in a way that was all too provocative despite the demure style of the dress. Brandon felt his breath go still as awareness slammed through him.

Hands on hips, an arrogant tilt to her chin, she demanded, "Who are you?"

"Brandon Halloran."

"You don't live around here."

He grinned at her certainty. "I suppose you know everyone?"

"Every handsome man, at any rate," she said boldly.

Brandon had a hunch her daring tone was one she never would have used under ordinary circumstances. She looked as if she were trying it out for the first time, a little hesitant, a little defiant.

"Who are *you*?"

"Elizabeth Forsythe, which you would have known if you lived around here," she said smugly.

"I suspect you have a reputation with all the men for being outrageous." She grinned in obvious delight at that. "Why, of course."

"How old are you, outrageous Lizzy?"

"No one calls me Lizzy."

"I do," he said matter-of-factly, enjoying the notion of standing out in her memory. "How old are you?"

"Seventeen," she said. "And a half."

"That half certainly is important," he said solemnly,

all the while thanking all the gods in heaven for making her old enough for him to court.

She regarded him intently. "You're teasing me, aren't you?"

"No more than you're teasing me."

She turned away from him then and started walking. He fell into step beside her. "Tell me all about yourself, Lizzy Forsythe."

"Why?"

"Because I have a feeling we are going to be very important to each other and I want to know everything about you."

She glanced up at him with a look that was both shy and impish. "Now who's being outrageous?"

"We'll see about that," he said softly, wishing he dared to tangle his fingers in the silken threads of her hair, wishing he could see if her skin was nearly as soft as it looked.

"How long will you be here?"

"A week," he said. "Then I'm going to England."

"To fight?" she asked with a note of excitement threading unmistakably through her voice.

"Yes. Do you think a week is long enough for me to make you fall in love with me?"

She shook her head. "Not nearly long enough."

Brandon wondered how she could say that with such certainty, when he felt as if he'd been struck by lightning. There was no sense to the way he was feeling, no logic at all, just the gut-deep conviction that he'd finally met the woman with whom he would share the rest of his life.

He saw the strength in her and sensed that Elizabeth

Forsythe could meet arrogance with confidence, passion with boldness. He knew intuitively that she was the sort of woman who could meet a man on his own terms.

Making her fall in love with him might not be easy, but that would be more than half the fun of it.

Lying awake in the middle of the night nearly a half century later, Brandon sighed as he thought back to that time so long ago. How naive he'd been. And yet nothing that had happened in all the years since had changed the emotions that had filled his heart that day.

Brandon wondered if he would still feel that same sweet certainty when he saw Lizzy again. Maybe he was an old fool for wanting to tempt fate a second time, but he could hardly wait.

Chapter 3

Brandon waited impatiently for Lizzy to make good on her promise. There was a new spring in his step. He was actually humming an old tune—that Glenn Miller classic—in the office as he began planning in earnest for the retirement that had terrified him only a few weeks before. Kevin was back at work, his marriage on solid ground at last. Brandon finally felt he could leave Halloran Industries with his mind at ease. More importantly, he had something to look forward to.

Jason and Kevin clearly didn't know what to make of the change in Brandon's mood or the flurry of activity that accompanied putting his retirement plans into action. He caught their bemused expressions, the shake of their heads, more than once. It amused the hell out of him to keep them in the dark.

They probably thought he was getting senile—unless

they'd added up the meaning of all those florist bills as cleverly as Dana had. Knowing Kevin, though, he'd probably only worried that there had been no line item in the corporate budget to justify the expense. Sooner or later he would grumble at his father for mixing his personal spending with the legitimate charges for Halloran Industries.

It was two long weeks before Lizzy's call finally came—enough time to plan, enough time to worry that she'd changed her mind, enough time to grow impatient.

When Brandon's housekeeper finally announced that a Mrs. Newton was on the phone, he was pacing the library like a caged lion, debating whether he ought to call her himself and put an end to this interminable waiting. Delighted he wouldn't have to make that decision, he grabbed the receiver before Mrs. Farnsworth had even left the room.

"Lizzy?"

"I'm here," she announced without preliminaries.

"Where?"

She named a hotel where they had once shared an intimate dinner. He wondered if she'd chosen it deliberately or merely because it was the only one she could recall when making her reservation. It pleased him to believe the former, rather than the latter, so he didn't ask.

"Alone?" he inquired with surprising hesitancy for a man who'd once been a daredevil fighter pilot and after that had commanded a large corporation and hundreds of employees for nearly fifty years.

Her sudden laughter seemed to float in the air between them. "You never did like to share, did you, Brandon?"

He knew she'd only meant to tease, but he answered the question seriously. "No, Lizzy, I never did. Not where you were concerned, anyway. You still haven't answered my question. Are you here alone?"

He feared more than he cared to admit that she would have packed up one of her daughters, maybe even the grandkids and brought them along as chaperons.

"Yes," she said, sounding satisfied that she'd taunted him into revealing a tiny hint of insecurity, "I'm alone."

"Then you'll come to the house for dinner," he said decisively. "I'll send a car at once. Can you be ready in ten minutes?"

Again she laughed, and he was transported back half a century to a time when life had been filled with possibilities and even minutes weren't to be squandered.

"Make it thirty minutes and I'll be waiting," she promised as she had then.

This time, Brandon thought, *nothing* was going to stand in their way.

Elizabeth stood in her hotel room for several minutes after hanging up the phone. It was just like Brandon to start making plans without giving her a second to think over her answer. Only just now had she realized how much she had missed that quick decisiveness, that rush of enthusiasm that spoke volumes about his feelings even when he couldn't say the words. A woman would always know where she stood with a man like Brandon.

If he'd had his way nearly fifty years ago, they'd have been married a week after they met. Truth be told, she'd wanted that as much as he had, but she'd been reared as a proper young lady and proper young ladies back then hadn't gone rushing off to get married on a whim, not when they'd barely turned seventeen and when the man was very nearly a stranger.

Brandon had coaxed. He'd wooed her with every bit of inventiveness at his command. He'd wanted to ask her father for her hand. She had believed in his love, but she was too cautious by far to give in, even to a handsome airman about to go off to war.

Even if she had been willing, her parents would have come between them. They had dreams for their only daughter and those dreams didn't include an impetuous marriage to a man heading straight into harm's way.

Nothing had stood in the way of her giving him her love, though. Right or wrong, Elizabeth had not wanted that regret weighing on her forever.

There had been time enough later to consider that single, glorious night in his arms and all its implications in an era when nice girls definitely didn't go to bed with young men before marriage.

And she had paid for that night. Oh, how she had paid, but she hadn't been able to resent him for turning her into what her staid parents had called soiled goods. How quaint and unimportant that sounded in this day and age. At the time, though, it had seemed a calamity.

As she touched a bit of blusher to her cheeks and wondered what he would think when he saw her after all these years, she recalled the way he'd looked at her when she'd turned down his marriage proposal.

"You're saying no?" he'd said, his stunned expression reflecting the bemusement of a young man already used to getting his own way in everything that mattered. He'd counted on a splashy diamond ring to persuade her, but she'd refused to allow him to slip it on her finger. She was desperately afraid of being tempted to change her mind. It was difficult enough not to give in to the lure of an impulsive elopement.

"I'm saying no...for now," she'd told him gently, but firmly. "Our time will come when you're home again. I promise I'll wear the locket you gave me, every single day, and I'll be waiting."

She had meant it with all her heart.

But their time hadn't come. Brandon had gone off to England to fly daring missions that had terrified her more with each descriptive letter he sent. Those letters had reminded her how brave he was. Though he had thought her bold, she was weaker by far than he'd imagined. It would never have worked between them. Or so she tried to tell herself as the daily letters had slowly trickled down to one a week or less.

A few months later her family had left Maine and there had been no choice for Elizabeth but to go with them. They had made that clear, just as they had their feelings about Brandon. Brandon's letters had stopped altogether then. She'd been devastated, but not terribly surprised. Her parents told her over and over that he'd never loved her at all. She'd guessed he'd found someone else overseas, someone all too willing to make a commitment to a man with his money and charm and daring. Envisioning him with a war bride from England had hurt her more than she'd ever let on to anyone.

Resigned to never seeing him again, she had finally taken off the locket and relegated it to a box with other treasures. She made a safe, secure life for herself in California. She'd married and taught school. Widowed

now, she had two beautiful daughters and three ener-
getic grandchildren, two of whom were already older
than she had been when she and Brandon had met.

Just this week it had been Ellen, her oldest daughter,
who'd found the gold locket with Brandon's picture in
it sitting in a crystal bowl on the coffee table. Elizabeth
had placed it there after looking at the picture inside
time and again, trying to make up her mind about the
folly of taking this trip.

"I've never seen this before," Ellen said as the fragile
gold chain sifted through her fingers. The heart-shaped
locket had rested in her palm.

Elizabeth reached for it, flustered and uncertain,
but she hadn't been able to prevent Ellen from looking inside.

Her daughter had studied the tiny photograph for
several minutes before looking up and saying quietly,
"He's very handsome. Who is he? It's not Father."

"No," Elizabeth admitted. "It's someone I knew long
ago, before I met your father."

Ellen studied her face for what seemed an eternity,
then said with obvious amazement, "You loved him
very much, didn't you?"

Elizabeth shrugged nonchalantly, but her pulse
scrambled. "I thought I did, but I was very young."

"What happened?"

"I'm not really sure. He went off to war and we lost
touch." It was the simplest explanation she could think
of for something that had seemed so terribly complicated at the time. She managed to keep any hint of bitterness out of her voice.

"Were you engaged?"

"Not officially, though he wanted very much to marry me before he left. I turned him down."

"But why, if you loved him?"

Elizabeth sighed. "You can't imagine how many times I asked myself that same question. In the end, though, it seems I made the right decision."

"Why do you have this out now?"

"I heard from him a few weeks ago."

Ellen's eyes lit up at once, clearly fascinated. "Really? He found you after all this time?"

"Yes," she said. Then because she was still amazed by it, she added, "He hired a detective of all things."

"Oh, Mother, that's so romantic."

Romantic. Yes, that definitely summed up Brandon. Romantic and, as it had turned out, irresponsible. Elizabeth took the locket from her daughter's hand and ran her fingers over the simple design engraved on the face of the heart. It felt warm from Ellen's touch.

"I don't know what to do," Elizabeth admitted. "He wants to see you. Is that it?"

She nodded. "And I promised I'd go to Boston, but now I'm not so sure."

"Mother, you have to go. You promised, didn't you? He doesn't sound like the kind of man who'd let you go back on your promise. Besides, what's the worst that could happen?" her dreamy, romantic Ellen said with stars in her eyes. "He's gotten fat and bald?"

Even now that she'd made it as far as Boston, Elizabeth could think of a dozen worse things than that, that could go wrong with such an impetuous trip. None of them had she dared to share with Ellen.

There was no denying, though, that she wanted to be

here, wanted to see Brandon again, if only to resolve all the old hurts that she'd so carefully banked in order to get on with her life. Maybe now, at last, she could truly put the past behind her.

It had surprised Elizabeth that Brandon had sounded almost as nostalgic about their brief romance as she felt. If the memories hadn't faded for him after all this time, why had he let her go so easily? Why had he abandoned her?

Her heart still ached when she thought about the way she'd watched the mail day after day, only to be disappointed again and again, until finally it had become too painful to watch. Now she would ask him why. She would satisfy herself that she'd gilded the memory, that Brandon Halloran wasn't the romantic hero she remembered at all.

And then she would run back to her full, satisfying life in California and live out her days in peace. One last piece of unresolved business would be finally put to rest. Until he'd called, she'd had no idea that it still mattered so much to her to know what had happened.

So here she was, back in Boston for the first time in decades, her stomach tied in knots, her fingers trembling. Even at seventeen she was certain she'd never felt this giddy sense of anticipation.

Elizabeth ran a brush through the short hair that she'd finally allowed to turn gray. Oh, how she wished it were the same rich auburn it had been way back then. Brandon had loved her hair, long and touched with fire, he used to say.

When they'd made love on that one incredible moonlit night, he'd allowed the strands to flow through his fingers like silken threads, fascinated with it. What would he think of this short cap of waves that her daughters said took ten years off her age, despite the gray?

She smoothed her pale blue suit over hips that were still slender and adjusted the flowered silk scarf at her throat. Beneath the scarf she could feel the locket pressing against her skin, its once-familiar touch oddly reassuring.

Still, she was filled with trepidation as she went with the driver Brandon had sent. Were either of them prepared for the changes? Could they possibly avoid disappointment?

When the car drove up the winding driveway of the same impressive brick Colonial family home that she recalled from one brief visit years before, for one instant she wanted to turn back. She wanted to flee before illusions were shattered—or confirmed.

She wasn't sure which she feared more, the answers he would give or the disappointed realization that things between them could never be the same. Maybe it would have been wisest, after all, to keep the past in the past, where memories could live on untarnished.

Then the door opened as if Brandon had been watching impatiently for her arrival from just inside. He stepped outside into the glow of the brass lamps on either side of the door. Elizabeth's breath snagged in her throat as she allowed herself the freedom to study him unobserved through the limousine's tinted windows.

He was older to be sure, but he was just as tall and handsome as she remembered him. Like hers, his hair had gone silver, but it only made him look more distinguished in his dark suit. Any woman would be proud to appear on his arm. She had envisioned him once exactly like this—lean, sophisticated, impressive—back in the days when she spent too many hours imagining the two of them growing old side by side.

The quick, once-familiar flutter of her pulse took her back nearly fifty years and she knew that, in this way at least, time had stood still.

Chapter 4

At the first sign of headlights turning into the driveway, Brandon felt his pulse begin to race. He had the front door open, his heart thudding with anticipation, before the limousine could brake to a stop. It took every last bit of restraint he possessed to keep from sprinting down the steps. Instead he waited impatiently for his driver to open the door, more impatiently yet for Elizabeth to emerge.

For no more than the space of a heartbeat he was taken aback by the short hairstyle, the unapologetic gray that had replaced the stunning auburn he'd remembered. Then he looked at her tanned face, the way the sassy style emphasized her unchanged, twinkling eyes and admitted that the short cut, even the gray, suited her.

He noted that her legs, as she swung them out of the car, were still slender, her figure still girlish in a sedate blue suit with a twist of something silky at her throat. By golly, she was still a looker all right.

Brandon thought back to the snapshot he'd carried off to war. It had shown off that figure. She'd worn white shorts and a skimpy top that tied behind her neck and at her waist. The provocative outfit had left her legs and back bare and gave the impression of height far taller than her actual five foot-two. She'd been glancing over her shoulder at the camera, Betty Grable pinup style.

He had pulled that picture out a dozen times a day, considering it his good luck talisman. Only after she'd stopped writing and vanished had he angrily torn it into shreds and thrown it away. The memory had lingered for far longer, along with regrets for his brash, ill-considered act.

He pushed the memories aside and went to meet her, holding out his hands. "Lizzy," he said, his gaze meeting hers, detecting the nervousness behind the brave smile. "It's wonderful to see you."

Her hands were like ice in his. She glanced at him far more shyly now than she had on the day they'd met, though her words were calmly gracious.

"Brandon. It's good to see you, too. You look well," she said.

"I'm better, now that you're here." He tucked her hand through his arm and led her inside. "I'm afraid I've rushed the housekeeper. She already has dinner on the table. Do you mind if we go straight in?"

"Of course not," she said, sounding surprisingly relieved.

He wondered if she'd feared the idle moments before the meal as he had, if she'd worried that conversation would lag, if she'd dreaded an endless evening begun in hope and ending in disappointment? How could a man who'd entertained politicians and celebrities in his time be so nervous about an evening with someone he'd once thought he knew even better than himself?

The elegant Queen Anne table in the formal dining room had been set for two with the finest Halloran china and crystal, brought over by his father from England at the beginning of the century. Candles glowed. A bottle of Brandon's best vintage wine was ready to be poured. White roses, opened just enough to scent the air, had been arranged dramatically in a crystal bowl in the center of the table. Even with such short notice, Mrs. Farnsworth had outdone herself. Although, she had told him with an indignant huff, no thanks to his agitated hovering.

Even with those exquisite touches, all Brandon noticed was the shine in Lizzy's eyes. She'd always had a twinkle in those eyes, a daring glimmer that belied her cautious nature.

Obviously, daring had overcome caution to bring her back to Boston, to bring her here tonight. He wondered why she'd been so reluctant in the first place. This wasn't some silly blind date she'd had cause to fear. But there'd been no mistaking the earlier reluctance, no ignoring the hesitation even now, a hesitation that he was certain went beyond simple nervousness.

Still he pushed curiosity aside and went through the motions of settling her in the chair next to his. He wasn't about to relegate her to the far end of a table big enough for Halloran family reunions.

Brandon's own meal cooled, untouched, while he

listened to Elizabeth fill in the gaps they hadn't covered on the phone. More than the details, he heard the humor, the love, the fulfillment, and regretted more than he could say that he hadn't been the one to share them. How he wished that he'd been there to witness the shift from youthful impetuosity to mature strength, that he'd been the one to bring her laughter and contentment.

"Tell me about your husband," he said.

"He was a wonderful man, kind, thoughtful, generous. The girls adored him, especially Kate. She came along late, when we weren't sure we'd have another child. He doted on her. I wasn't sure what would happen to her when he died. For a long time she seemed almost lost without him."

"He made you happy, then?" Brandon asked, hiding the resentment that crept over him. It was foolish to be jealous of a man he'd never met, a man who'd been dead for five years. Yet knowing that didn't stop the pangs of regret.

"Very," she said.

Brandon regarded her speculatively, trying to interpret the note of determination in her voice, the defiant gleam in her eyes. "And love, Lizzy? Did he love you?"

"Perhaps more than I deserved," she said. "What an odd way to put it."

"Don't you find that in relationships more often than not one partner cares more than the other, that one gives and the other takes? What about in your own marriage?"

Pained that she had hit upon something he had thought more than once about his relationship with Grace, he nodded. "I suppose that's so, about relationships, I mean."

"And your own?" she prodded, her gaze relentlessly searching his.

He felt it would be a betrayal of Grace to admit that she had loved more than he, yet he couldn't bring himself to lie. "I suppose we found a balance," he said finally, skirting the truth of it. There had been a balance of sorts. He didn't think his wife had ever felt cheated. He had cared deeply for her, honored their vows, and to his dying day he would be grateful for the life they had shared, the son she had borne him.

"Tell me more about your life in California," he said at last.

He sat back, then, and listened, watching the way laughter put such sparks in her eyes, the way her face became animated when she talked about her daughters and grandchildren. Then there was no mistaking the radiance of love, which proved he'd been right when he'd guessed she hadn't felt it nearly so deeply for her husband.

Finally, when she'd been talking nonstop for some time, Elizabeth lifted troubled eyes to his. "You've been awfully quiet, Brandon. It's not like you."

"I like listening to you. I've had too many quiet meals in this room over the past couple of years. It's wonderful to have some laughter in here again."

"Then why do you look so sad?"

"I suppose I was thinking about how much I missed."

She looked startled by the candid answer. "Don't try to make me believe you haven't had a good life," she chided. "You're not the sort of man to let life pass you by."

"No, I've had a wonderful life," he admitted. He told

her about his business triumphs and his family, omitting the inexplicable emptiness that had nagged despite everything. He wouldn't have her thinking him ungrateful for all the genuine blessings in his life.

"The years since Grace died have been lonely, though. These past weeks I've been thinking how much I wished I had someone to share things with again."

"You're a handsome, successful man, Brandon. I'm sure there are dozens of women who'd be pleased by your attention."

It was odd, but he'd never really thought of that before. He supposed it was true enough. There had been invitations to dinners, the symphony, the ballet, charity affairs. He'd even accepted a few, but always in the back of his mind he must have been waiting for his search for Lizzy to be successful. He hadn't seriously considered any of those other women as candidates for his affection.

Brandon gazed solemnly into Elizabeth's eyes and took her hand. "I think fate has done it again, Lizzy. I think there was a reason for my finding you after all this time. Not a woman I know could hold a candle to you."

"And I think you've had too much wine to drink," she retorted, but there was a becoming blush of pink in her cheeks and she didn't withdraw her hand.

"Don't pretend you don't know exactly what I mean. You didn't come all this way just to say hello, did you?" he countered, watching the blush deepen.

"Of course not," she said hurriedly. "It's been years since I've seen Boston."

"Are you trying to say that I'm just one of the sights

on your schedule?" he teased. "I'm old, Lizzy, but I'm not a monument."

"You still have a sizable ego, I see."

"You'd never want a man who wasn't sure of himself."

"And how would you know that?"

"No one changes that much, not even in a lifetime."

"Perhaps at my age I'm not even looking for a man," she said. "Did you consider that?"

"Then you're here for nothing more than a little talk about old times?"

"Yes," she said, but there was something wistful in her voice that touched his heart and told him the quick response wasn't quite the truth. She needed more than memories, the same way he did. Just thinking about proving that to her made his tired old blood pump a little faster.

"And maybe some answers," she added determinedly then, not quite meeting his gaze as she withdrew her hand from his. She folded her hands together as if to keep them from trembling. Her knuckles turned white and there was a sudden frost in her voice.

"Answers?" he asked warily, startled by the shift in her mood.

She looked up then, her gaze colliding with his. "What happened back then, Brandon?" she asked indignantly. "Did you meet someone else? Did you forget I was waiting? Explain it to me. I think you owe me that much."

Stunned by the sudden burst of anger over hurts a half century old, he simply stared at her. "Forget you? Never, Lizzy. Never!"

He hit the table with his fist and suddenly he was

every bit as angry as she, drawing on emotions he'd thought dead and buried long ago. He shoved his chair back and stood, towering over her. She never even flinched, though her hands clenched even more tightly.

"How could you even ask something like that?" he demanded. "Then why did the letters stop?"

"I could ask you the same thing," he shot back. "For weeks after I got your last letter, I kept on writing. Not a day passed that I didn't write some little note at least. Do you know what it's like being away from home, alone?" He held his fingers a scant inch apart. "This close to dying every single day, only to think that the woman you love more than life itself has forgotten all about you so quickly?"

"But *I* wrote," she swore just as vehemently. "It was *you*. I never got any letters, not after we moved."

Suddenly they stopped and stared at each other as the meaning of the furious words sank in. Brandon sank back into his chair as he realized that trust, as much as anything, was at stake. Either or both could have been lying.

To his regret, he saw that there was no way of proving what they said, not after all this time. There was no way of knowing for certain if the letters had simply been misdirected, lost in the chaos of war, destroyed by her parents—or never sent in the first place.

"We'll never know," she said finally, her voice filled with a sadness as deep as his own as she came to the same realization. "Will we?"

Brandon couldn't bear the uncertainty he saw in her eyes, heard in her voice. "You must believe me," he insisted. "I sent those letters. I swear I did. When I was injured and sent home, I moved heaven and earth to try to find you, but it was as if you'd vanished without a trace."

"You were injured?" she said, her eyes wide. "How seriously? What happened?"

"I'd only been there a few months when my plane went down. I got out with no more than some broken bones, but it was enough to get me sent home."

"So my letters could have gone astray?" she said slowly. "Yes, as could mine."

He hoped she could see the truth in his eyes, could read the bitter agony of loss on his face. If only he'd hired a qualified detective back then, rather than counting on unreliable acquaintances in Maine and eventually in California. Leads had dwindled, then turned cold. By the time Grace had been introduced and encouraged as a suitable match, he had only discouraging answers. Grace had been there during the recuperation, not Lizzy. They had been, at the least, compatible. With no word on Lizzy, the choice had seemed clear.

"Only then did I give up," he swore. "That's the truth, Lizzy. You must believe me."

But rather than unqualified trust, all she said was, "I want to, Brandon. I want to believe you."

"We have another chance. Let's not let it go so easily this time," he urged. "Please, Lizzy. We're too old for more regrets. Say you'll stay and give me a chance to make it all up to you. We'll do all the things we never got to do back then."

For the longest time she looked indecisive, avoiding his eyes. Finally she said simply, "A few days, Brandon. I'll stay on for a few days."

There was an implied finality to the limit she set that
nagged at him, but for the moment at least he would take
what she was willing to give. He trusted in his own per-
suasiveness to see that a few days turned into weeks,
then months and eventually a lifetime. He could explain
his determination no more clearly now, than he could
have decades ago. He only knew what he felt in his
heart. It was there again, beating with the same strong
certainty that had guided everything he did.

The phone in her hotel room was ringing when Elizabeth walked in, still shaken by the powerful emotions
that had gripped her from the first instant she had seen
Brandon again. It was after midnight, three hours earlier in California. She had no doubts at all that it was
Ellen calling to see how this first meeting had gone.

Desperately needing the sense of grounding that a
talk with her daughter would provide, Elizabeth kicked
off her shoes as she reached for the phone.

"Hey, Grandma, how was the hot date?" Penny
asked. Obviously she'd pried the information about
Brandon out of her mother and wanted details.

"We had a lovely dinner," she said primly.

"Boring," Penny pronounced. "Where'd you go?
Some real fancy restaurant?"

"His house."

"Better," the teen decreed. "Did he ask you to stay
over?"

"I'm here, aren't I?"

"That doesn't mean he didn't ask."

Elizabeth held back a chuckle as she heard a muffled
discussion on the other end, then Penny's disgusted,

"Hold on, here's Mom. Don't tell her any of the juicy details. Save 'em for me."

"There are no juicy details," Elizabeth said, wondering precisely when Penny had become so precocious. Maybe it was the result of being the youngest by nearly ten years, a delightful, much-loved surprise who, because she'd always had the company of those older than she, had grown up too fast by far.

"Okay, Mom," Ellen was saying, "let's cut to the chase. Is he bald?"

As Elizabeth settled herself on the bed, propped up by pillows, she thought of Brandon's thick silver hair. "Hardly."

"Fat?"

She recalled his trim body, which still did astonishing things for a custom-tailored suit. "Nope."

"Was that old zing still there?"

"For him or for me?"

"You're being evasive," Ellen accused. "That must mean it was there in spades."

"He is a very attractive man," Elizabeth conceded, regretting that she still felt that way about him despite everything. "Quite dashing, actually."

"And you're a gorgeous woman."

"A gorgeous *old* woman," Elizabeth corrected. "Stop talking foolishness. How's everything out there?"

"About the same as it was when you left here this morning," Ellen said dryly. "Don't try to change the subject. When are you seeing him again?"

"Tomorrow. We're going sight-seeing."

"And then?"

"And then I'm coming back to the hotel and going to bed."

"Oh, really?"

"Alone, Ellen. Alone," she said emphatically, but she couldn't help the feeling of anticipation that rushed through her as she considered the possibilities. She really was an old fool, she thought as the heat of embarrassment climbed in her cheeks.

"Sweetie, I'm awfully tired. I'll call you in a few days."

"Mom, you sound funny," Ellen said, her tone suddenly serious. "Are you sure you're okay?"

"Just tired."

"And a little nostalgic?"

"A lot nostalgic," she admitted with a rueful chuckle. "I think I'd better sleep it off."

"Mom, if there's still something special with this man after all this time, go for it. Okay? Promise?"

"Good night, Ellen," she said deliberately and slid the phone back into the cradle. She wasn't ready yet to dissect all the feelings that had crowded in after seeing Brandon for the first time.

There was no denying that the thought of him moving heaven and earth to find her at this late date appealed to her sense of romance, just as it did to Ellen's and Penny's.

Kate—practical, down-to-earth Kate—would be appalled that Elizabeth had even spoken to a man who'd betrayed her, much less flown clear across the country to see him. Kate held on to hurt, too long by Elizabeth's standards. She'd never gotten over the awful man who'd thrown her over.

Ellen was more like Elizabeth herself had been five

decades ago, willing to throw caution to the wind, especially when it came to her heart.

What Elizabeth needed now was a good strong dose of Kate's tougher nature. Something told her if she didn't cling for dear life to rational thought, Brandon Halloran was going to sweep her off her feet all over again and that was the very last thing she could allow to happen. She'd meant to put the past to rest. Instead it seemed she'd merely stirred cold ashes back to flame.

Just a few days, she promised. She would indulge herself in some old dreams, allow herself the rare thrill of feeling desirable again. She deserved one last rollicking fling. Then she would don a shroud of common sense and go back to California with enough memories to carry her through the rest of her days.

Chapter 5

Brandon knew he should have expected the commotion that followed his call to the office in the morning, but he hadn't. Within minutes of telling his secretary that he wouldn't be in, first Kevin and then Jason called.

"Are you okay, Dad?" Kevin asked. "Harriet told me you called and said you weren't coming in today."

"Maybe I just thought you ought to get used to running things without me. I am retiring, remember?"

The comment was greeted with a heavy silence. Finally Kevin said carefully, "We haven't even talked about that. Are you sure you've given the idea enough thought? It seems to me you decided that all of a sudden."

"It was hardly sudden. You and Jason have been chomping at the bit to do things your own way for the past couple of years. I'd say it's past time for me to let you."

"We're not trying to shove you out, Dad."

"Hell, you think I don't know that? I just decided it was time to develop some new interests while I have time."

"While you have time," Kevin repeated slowly. "What's that supposed to mean? Dad, are you okay?"

"I think that's how this conversation started. I'm fine. I'm taking the day off because I have things to do. I can't recall the last time I took a long weekend."

"Neither can I. That's why I'm worried."

"Well, stop making such a fuss about it. I may even take the whole danged week off next week," he said irritably.

"Dad!"

Brandon ignored the note of alarm in Kevin's voice and hung up. Five minutes later he went through essentially the same conversation with Jason. At this rate he'd never finish his first cup of coffee, much less the once-fluffy scrambled eggs that had turned cold and hard while Kevin and Jason carried on about nothing. When a man got eggs only once a week, it was infuriating to see them ruined. He would never convince Mrs. Farnsworth he ought to have them again another morning. She was as rigid with his diet as any chef at some fancy health spa.

He regarded the eggs ruefully, muttered a curse and poured himself another cup of coffee. Decaf, but at least it was still hot.

He figured Kevin and Jason weren't done with their questions yet, but he rushed through the paper in an attempt to evade whatever meddling they were likely to do.

Unfortunately he wasn't fast enough. He was on his way out the front door when Dana's sporty little car screeched to a halt in front of him, kicking up gravel.

She hauled her bulky form out. It was evident from the haphazardly chosen clothes, the lack of makeup and the mussed hair that she'd been roused from sleep and sent over here on the double to check up on him.

Hands on hips, Jason's wife looked him over from head to toe. "You don't look sick," she pronounced.

"Never said I was."

"But Jason—"

"Is an astonishing worrywart for someone his age. Maybe if he had a couple of babies to keep his mind occupied, he wouldn't carry on so about me."

Dana grinned at him and patted her belly. "I can't make this baby come a minute sooner just to keep my husband off your back," she said. "Where are you off to?"

"I'm going sight-seeing, not that it's any of your business."

"Sight-seeing? Is there any part of Boston you haven't seen a hundred times?"

"I'm taking an old friend on a trip down memory lane."

Clearly fascinated, Dana said, "I don't suppose you'd want company."

"You suppose right. Now get on about your business and tell that husband of yours next time he wants to check up on me, he should do it himself."

"And have you pitch a fit because he's away from his desk? Besides, I worry about you, too, you know."

Brandon squeezed her hand. "There's no need, girl. I'm better than I've been in a very long time."

She nodded. "I can see that. In fact, you look downright spiffy. I can't recall ever seeing you in anything but a suit on a weekday." She smoothed his blue cashmere pullover across his shoulders. "Must be a woman involved. I don't suppose that mysterious Elizabeth from California has anything to do with your dapper attire?"

"Have I mentioned that you're a nosy little thing?"

"More than once," she said. "Just giving you a taste of your own medicine."

"I'll reform," he vowed.

"And pigs will fly," she retorted as she gave him a kiss on the cheek. "Wherever you're off to, have fun."

"I intend to." He waggled a finger under her nose. "And don't you go sneaking around trying to see what I'm up to."

"I wouldn't dream of it."

Brandon eyed the sporty little convertible Jason had given her on their wedding day. Dana had adamantly refused a new car, so his grandson had given her his, then bought himself a new one. It was an interesting compromise. Brandon made note of the technique. It might come in handy with Lizzy.

"I don't suppose you'd like to trade cars for the day?" he asked. Dana's mouth dropped open. "You're kidding?"

"Nope. I think a ride in a convertible on a beautiful spring day is just what I need to impress…" He hesitated.

"Impress who?" she taunted. "Someone."

"If you want my car, you're going to have to do better than that."

"No wonder Jason thought you were one tough cookie," he grumbled. "Okay. You've got the name right. It's Elizabeth."

"I already knew that much."

"Take it or leave it."

"I get the Mercedes for the day?"

"Yes."

"I'll take it. It's getting harder and harder to squeeze

myself behind the wheel of my car." She exchanged her keys for his and sauntered over to the luxury car his driver had brought around earlier. She ran her hand lovingly over the metallic gray finish, then shot him a look that had him thinking maybe the exchange had been made too hastily.

"Drive carefully," he said, suddenly recalling the way she tended to take curves as if she were on the Indy 500 course.

"I should be saying that to you. If you put even a tiny little scratch on that car Jason gave me, you'd better trade it in on a new model on the way home. He might have put the title in my name, but he still considers that car his baby."

"As long as I don't catch sight of you in the rearview mirror, I'll be just fine," he warned.

"No problem," she promised.

"Let me see those fingers," he ordered. "You got any of them crossed?"

"Nope," she said, laughing as she held out her hands for his inspection.

"I'm as good as my word."

Brandon wasn't so sure her promise was worth spit, but she did take off and he didn't see any sign of his Mercedes as he drove into town to pick up Lizzy.

Lizzy was waiting for him in front of the hotel. She took one look at the flashy little car and a smile spread across her face. "Don't tell me this is yours?"

"I borrowed it from Jason's wife. Do you mind the top down?"

"On a day like today? Absolutely not. One of the advantages to short hair is that I don't need to worry about a little wind. Where are we going?"

"I thought a leisurely drive so you could get your bearings, then maybe lunch at Faneuil Hall Marketplace. If you haven't been back to Boston in years, you probably haven't seen what they've done to it."

Lizzy sat up just a little straighter, her eyes alight with curiosity. With the trees budding new green leaves, the sky a soft shade of clear blue and just a handful of clouds scudding overhead, it was the perfect spring morning, one of Boston's finest.

Brandon felt rejuvenated at Elizabeth's exclamations of delight over everything she saw. It was as if he were seeing his beloved city through new eyes. Because she'd taught American history, Lizzy knew as much if not more than he did about the significance of many of the sights. She imbued the telling with a richness of detail and a liveliness that suggested what a magnificent teacher she must be.

"You've got to meet Jason's young brother-in-law while you're here," he told her. "He'd be fascinated by your stories. Sammy's not much for learning from books, but the boy has a lively mind. It came tragically close to being wasted."

"So many of them do," she said sadly. "It breaks my heart to see youngsters today graduating without the skills they need to make a go of it in today's world. There's no combatting crowded classrooms, the gangs and violence in so many cities. It's a wonder some of them get out alive, much less with any education."

"You're still teaching?"

"Substituting. In many ways that's the most frustrating of all. I go into a classroom not knowing the children. I see how they struggle. Maybe, if the teacher's out a week or more, I can see some tiny sign of progress and then it's over. I never know if they build on what I've been able to teach them, or if they simply go on muddling through."

"It sounds frustrating."

"It is. But I love being in the classroom so much that I wasn't prepared to give it up entirely."

A sudden thought struck him. "Why don't you found a school, Lizzy? A special one for the youngsters with disadvantages who could learn if only they were given the proper chance."

He could see the sparks in her eyes as her imagination caught fire.

"Oh, Brandon, wouldn't that be wonderful?" she said, then sighed. "But it's impossible."

"Why?"

"Money, for one thing."

"I have more than I could ever spend," he said, thinking of what such a school might have meant for a boy like Sammy. "I think a school might be the kind of legacy a man could be proud of. Lacey's looking for projects, too. She's talked Kevin and me into a Halloran Foundation. It's a grand idea. I can't imagine why I never thought of it myself. Come on, Lizzy. What do you say? You provide the brainpower and I'll provide the cash."

She reached over and patted his hand. "You are a dear for even thinking of such a generous offer, but no. It's impossible. You're being impulsive and I'm far too old to begin such a massive endeavor."

"No," he said fiercely. "The idea may be impulsive, but it's a sound one. And don't ever say you're too old, Lizzy. Thinking like that will make you old before your time. I've found that looking forward to a new challenge each and every day keeps a man alive. Promise me you'll think about it."

She hesitated, then said, "I suppose I could promise that much, at least."

He nodded in satisfaction as he found a parking space near the marketplace. "That's good. Now let's find some good old-fashioned junk food and indulge ourselves without a thought for cholesterol or fiber."

That lively spark was back in her eyes when she met his gaze. "Hot dogs with mustard and relish, French fries—"

"And a hot-fudge sundae for dessert," he said, completing the menu they'd shared more than once in those long-ago days. He'd wanted to eat his fill of those American favorites before being relegated to the dismal rations of wartime England. "Do you have any idea how I missed those things while I was gone?"

"I don't see how you could. It's a wonder you didn't make yourself sick, you ate so many hot dogs."

Brandon couldn't help chuckling at the memory. Lizzy was laughing right along with him, her lips parted, her eyes alight with shared amusement. Suddenly he couldn't resist leaning toward her and touching his lips to hers, catching the sound of her laughter. The kiss lasted no longer than the melting touch of a snowflake, but it stirred the embers of a fire that had once burned more brightly than anything either of them had ever known.

Shaken to discover that those old feelings could be rekindled so easily and with such a sense of inevitability, Brandon drew back slowly.

"Ah, Lizzy," he said softly. "You'll never know how happy I am that you decided to come to Boston."

Her voice just as quiet and serious as his, she said, "I

think maybe I do." The silence that fell then was alive with a new, exciting tension.

Brandon wondered how he'd gone so long without such feelings. Had he simply forgotten what it was like to experience this edge-of-a-precipice sensation? Now that he'd rediscovered it, would he ever be able to go back to the dull loneliness he'd almost fooled himself into thinking was bearable?

Since such questions couldn't be answered in the blink of an eye, he finally broke the tension by catching Lizzy's hand in his. "Come on, gal. Let's go see how much trouble we can get ourselves into."

Aside from their culinary indulgences, though, they left the marketplace by mid-afternoon with no more than a handful of souvenirs for Elizabeth to take back to her family in California. There'd been a dozen things he'd been tempted to buy for her, but she'd firmly declined each and every one.

"It's far too soon to call it quits for the day," Brandon said when they got back to the car. "How do you feel about visiting the public gardens? If I remember correctly, the swan boats are back in the water."

"Oh, what fun!" she said.

The ride aboard the paddleboats was over far too quickly for either of them, so they took a second ride and then a third until the boat's captain began regarding them with amusement.

When they finally left the boat, he winked at Brandon. "Now you folks have a nice afternoon."

"We already have," Lizzy told him. "This has been a wonderful chance to put our feet up."

"And I thought it was holding my hand you enjoyed most," Brandon said, bringing a blush into Lizzy's cheeks.

As they walked away, she said to Brandon, "What must that man think of us?"

"That we're very lucky," he told her as they walked lazily along the paths. "And we are lucky, Lizzy. We're more fortunate than most people. We've found each other, not once, but twice. Now how shall we spend our evening?"

"I intend to spend mine with my feet propped up and a cup of tea from room service. I haven't walked so much in ages."

"What a waste of time that would be. I know a wonderful neighborhood Italian restaurant with red-checked tablecloths and candles stuck in old Chianti bottles. The owner makes an absolutely decadent lasagna."

"Another time," she said firmly.

He could see that there would be no swaying her on this. He hid his disappointment and said only, "If you promise that you'll give me time enough to show you all my favorite places, I won't press about tonight." He grinned. "You know how persuasive I can be when I set my mind to it."

"Oh, yes," she said. "I do know that."

"Then you promise?"

"I promise to think about it," she agreed.

Content that that was the best he could manage, he drove back to her hotel and helped her inside with all of her packages.

"It was a splendid day," Elizabeth said, squeezing Brandon's hands as they stood in the lobby. "I really can't remember when I've had such fun."

"Are you sure you don't want a cocktail at least?"

"Absolutely. You've worn me out. I'm just going to

pick up my messages and go upstairs and get out of these shoes."

"You should have let me buy you those high-top sneakers we saw," he teased.

"If I went home with high-top, hot-pink sneakers, my daughters would have me committed."

"Wouldn't hurt to shake them up once in a while. That's what I've found with Kevin and my grandson. Whenever they get to thinking I'm stodgy, I do something outrageous. I want you to meet them while you're here."

"Am I the outrageousness you mean to stir them up with this time?"

"I suppose they might see it that way. Seriously, Lizzy, shall I plan a family dinner?"

Elizabeth tried to imagine such a scene. One part of her wanted desperately to meet his son and the lovely daughter-in-law Brandon had described so clearly. She felt an inexplicable bond with his zany granddaughter-in-law. And she suspected Jason would be a heartbreaking reminder of the way Brandon had looked when they had met. Could she possibly meet them all and not regret the past that had made them another woman's family, instead of her own?

"I think not," she said a little sadly.

Brandon's gaze narrowed as he studied her. "Why? What's wrong, Lizzy?"

"Nothing's wrong, Brandon. I just don't see any point to it."

"Does there have to be a point to having dinner with an old friend's family?"

"Are you saying this would be no more than a casual get-together?"

"Did you want it to be more?"

With his gaze burning into her, she shook her head and put a decisive note into her voice. "No. I made my intentions clear, Brandon. There's no going back for us."

Finally he shrugged. "Whatever you like. We'll discuss it again tomorrow. What time shall I pick you up? Or would you rather come to the house for breakfast? I could send the car."

The idea of sitting across a breakfast table from Brandon held a provocative appeal she couldn't resist. "I would love to come for breakfast."

"Wonderful. I'll have Mrs. Farnsworth make her famous apple pancakes."

"A bowl of cereal and some fruit would do. She needn't go to any trouble for me."

"Apple pancakes are her specialty. She would be disappointed if you didn't try them. Besides, she never makes them just for me and I love them."

"Then, by all means, the apple pancakes. About eight-thirty?"

"I'll send the car at eight," he said.

Secretly delighted by his impatience, she repeated firmly, "Eight-thirty. You have to remember I'm still on California time. That's practically the middle of the night for me."

"I seem to recall nights when we sat up until dawn."

"And I seem to recall that at that age we never required eight hours of sleep. We could run on pure adrenaline."

"Don't you go trying to make yourself sound old. I saw the way your foot tapped when we heard that music earlier at the marketplace. I'm taking you dancing one of these nights."

She chuckled at the feigned ferocity in his expression. "Is that an invitation or a threat, Brandon Halloran?"

"Whichever works," he said, reaching out with surprisingly unsteady fingers to trace the curve of her cheek. He brushed gently at the wisps of hair that feathered around her face. "I can't get over the way you look with your hair like this. I couldn't imagine you ever being more beautiful than you were when we met, but you are, Lizzy. Like a rare wine, you've aged with dignity."

"And you're a sentimental old fool," she said gently, but she couldn't deny the sweet rush of pleasure that sped through her. She placed her hand over his and before she could think about it, brought his hand to her lips and pressed a kiss to his knuckles. "Good night, Brandon."

He leaned forward and touched his lips to her forehead. "Night, Lizzy. I can't wait till morning."

He turned then and strolled away, his step jaunty, his shoulders squared. She couldn't be sure, but it sounded as if he might be whistling the chorus of that old Glenn Miller song they'd called their own.

Chapter 6

When he'd encouraged Elizabeth to come for breakfast, Brandon hadn't stopped to consider that the next day was Saturday. On Saturdays he could never count on not having the morning interrupted. More often than not, Jason and Dana dropped by with Sammy in tow. Occasionally even Kevin and Lacey turned up, lured by Mrs. Farnsworth's delectable apple pancakes.

Perhaps, subliminally, he had hoped the whole clan would drop in, taking matters out of his hands. It would give him a chance to introduce Elizabeth despite her uncertainty about the wisdom of such a meeting. He might have mixed feelings about subjecting her to their scrutiny, but his desire to hasten a relationship between them far outweighed any reservations he might have.

Sure enough, no sooner had he seated Lizzy at the dining room table and served her a cup of coffee than the front door banged open and Dana's brother came barreling in.

"Hey, Grandpa Brandon, are you up yet?" Sammy yelled loudly enough to wake the dead.

"If I weren't, I would be now," he observed mildly as Sammy rounded the corner into the dining room.

Looking nonplussed, the teenager screeched to a halt at the sight of Brandon's company.

Elizabeth looked equally startled by the sight of the lanky young man with his hair moussed into spikes, his jeans frayed and a T-shirt that was emblazoned with the perfectly horrid bloodred design of some new music group. Actually it was one of his more reserved outfits.

"Sorry," Sammy said, his gaze shifting from Elizabeth to Brandon and back again. A knowing grin spread across his face. "I guess we should have called, huh?"

"It wouldn't hurt to observe the amenities," Brandon confirmed. Sammy regarded him blankly. "The what?"

"You should have called. How'd you get here?" he asked suspiciously, expecting the worst.

His answer came in the form of the front door opening again. "Hey, Granddad," Jason called from the foyer. "We just came by to drop off your car and see how you're...." His voice trailed off as he reached the dining room and spotted Brandon's guest. "I guess you're doing fine."

"I was," Brandon said with an air of resignation. Suddenly he wished he'd relied more on caution, than impatience. "Lizzy, my grandson Jason. And our first intruder with the lousy manners is his young brother-in-law, Sammy Roberts. This is Elizabeth Newton."

"Hey," Sammy said, already seated at the table.

"Jason, you were right. Mrs. Farnsworth is making those funny pancakes."

Brandon glanced at Lizzy's frozen expression and sighed. "I don't suppose you're in a hurry?" he inquired of the interlopers. The broad hint fell on deaf ears.

"Nope," Jason confirmed entirely too cheerfully. "We have all morning. Right, Sammy?"

"Yep. All morning."

"How lovely," Brandon said dryly. "Before you sit down, stick your head into the kitchen and tell Mrs. Farnsworth there will be four of us for breakfast, unless of course Dana is planning to wander in at any moment, as well."

"Nope. I think you can safely count her out. She's home practicing her breathing," Jason said.

"I thought you were supposed to help with that."

"She says I make her nervous."

"Probably because you hyperventilate," Brandon said critically. "I told you I'd be happy to assist. I have much more experience at remaining calm under trying circumstances." He purposely neglected to add that this morning was rapidly turning into a perfect example.

"Granddad, as much as I adore you, you are not going to take my place in the delivery room," Jason said patiently.

"You and me can pace the halls together," Sammy offered as a consolation. "You gotta bring the cigars, though. Dana says if she catches me with one, she'll tan my hide."

Brandon glanced over to see if Elizabeth was beginning to take all this with the sort of aplomb she'd been capable of years ago. Given her protest the day before when he'd suggested a family dinner, he thought she was doing rather well. He couldn't quite identify her expression, though.

Astonishment and dismay seemed to have given way to fascination. In fact her gaze was fastened on Jason as if just looking at him carried her back in time.

"Lizzy?" Brandon said softly.

She blinked and turned to him. "The resemblance is remarkable," she murmured. Then as if she thought she'd said too much, she added quickly, "Do you really want to be in the delivery room?"

Jason, apparently oblivious to the meaning of her first remark, seized the second and grinned at her astonishment. "He's afraid the rest of us will botch it."

Brandon considered offering a rebuttal, but decided that Jason was pretty close to the truth. He wanted nothing to go wrong with the birth of his first great-grandchild. He hated trusting anything so critical to other people.

Of course, he hadn't been anywhere near the delivery room when Kevin was born. Even if the hospital had allowed it back then, Grace would never have permitted it. She would have thought it unseemly for him to witness her in the throes of labor. He was downright envious of all these young husbands today who got to share in one of God's own miracles.

"So, how do you and Granddad know each other?" Jason asked Elizabeth.

Jason's tone might be all innocent curiosity, Brandon thought worriedly, but that gleam in his eye was pure mischief. He had a hunch Dana had encouraged this visit by providing a few details about their encounter the previous morning. Elizabeth must not have caught that spark of devilment or she'd have been more cautious with her answer.

"We're old friends," she said, opening the door to a Pandora's box of speculation.

"You live here in Boston?"

"No, California."

"Ah, I see," Jason murmured, looking infinitely pleased. "What are you grinning at?" Brandon grumbled.

"The flowers," Jason said. "What flowers?" Sammy asked.

"Grandpa Brandon has been sending a lot of flowers to California lately."

"Why?" Sammy glanced at Elizabeth. "Oh, yeah, I get it. I guess that's why there are roses on the table, too, huh? There never have been before."

Sammy looked as if he were on the verge of making some even more outlandish remark. Brandon grasped at the first conversational gambit he could think of to deter him. "Sammy, if you're finished with breakfast, perhaps you'd like to go play some of those infernal video games you insisted I buy."

"Nah, I think I'll stick around for another pancake. Besides, it sounds like this could get interesting."

"I assure you it will not get to be anything close to interesting by your standards," Brandon commented. "Go play video games. Mrs. Farnsworth will be happy to bring your pancake to you in the library."

Sammy had no sooner shoved his chair back and departed than Jason said cheerfully, "So, Mrs. Newton, what exactly brings you to Boston?"

Color suddenly flooded Lizzy's cheeks as she realized how neatly Jason was backing her into the proverbial corner. Brandon tried to rescue her. "She's just here to do a little sight-seeing."

"That's right," she confirmed hurriedly. "It's been ages since I've seen all the sights in Boston."

"And how long has it been since you two last saw each other?"

She glanced desperately toward Brandon, then said, "Nearly fifty years."

"My goodness," Jason said, looking a little taken aback himself. "You've kept in touch, though, right?"

"No."

"Jason!" Brandon said with a soft warning note in his voice. "You're being impertinent."

His grandson ignored him. A grin slowly broke across his face. "This gets better and better, like one of those newspaper features you see on Valentine's day. Are you saying you'd lost touch? How'd you find each other again?"

Brandon watched as Elizabeth grew increasingly flustered. Finally he snapped, "Jason! This is none of your business."

His blasted grandson laughed at that. "I know," he said delightedly.

"Jason Halloran, I am warning you," Brandon blustered. "If you don't behave, I'll…." Words failed him.

"You'll what, Granddad? Cut me out of the will?" He turned to Elizabeth. "I apologize if I've made you uncomfortable, but Granddad has this habit of meddling in our lives. He thinks it's his God-given right."

Apparently no longer caught off guard, the take-any-dare Lizzy of old suddenly emerged and seized the opportunity Jason had just handed her. She grinned, a genuine spark of devilment flaring in her eyes. Brandon didn't trust that spark one little bit.

"I can see how that would be taxing," she said. "Perhaps it would help if I offered a little ammunition. I gather he hasn't mentioned how he tracked me down?"

Brandon regarded her indignantly. "Et tu, Brute?"

She smiled and delivered the knockout punch without so much as an instant's caution. "He hired a detective. Isn't that like something right out of a movie?"

"Oh, Lord," Brandon moaned. "I will never, ever hear the end of this."

"No," Jason said, "you won't. I'm just sorry I didn't know about Mrs. Newton sooner. I might have hired that detective myself and brought her here to surprise you. I do love surprises, don't you, Mrs. Newton?"

"Absolutely," she said.

"If the two of you are going to be in cahoots," Brandon grumbled, "I might as well go play those video games with Sammy."

"Go ahead, Granddad. I'm sure Mrs. Newton and I could find plenty to talk about."

"Yes," she agreed. "I suspect we could. You'd probably find a talk about old times fascinating. My youngest granddaughter surely does."

Brandon regarded the two of them irritably. "On second thought, I guess I'll sit right here and watch out for my interests. I might remind you, though, Jason, that if it weren't for my meddling, you and Dana would probably not be married."

Jason instantly sobered. "You're right. I do owe you one for that."

"I should say so," Brandon said.

"Perhaps now would be the time to return the favor," Jason said slyly.

Brandon's gaze narrowed. "You could find yourself peddling pencils on street corners, if you're not careful," he warned grimly. "Now could we please talk about something else? Or perhaps you and Sammy would like to run along so Lizzy and I can get started on another day of sight-seeing."

"Where did you go yesterday?" Jason asked.

"The public gardens," Elizabeth said. "Rode in one of the swan boats, I suppose?"

"Of course," she said, giving Jason a conspiratorial wink. "Three times. Your grandfather's quite the romantic, especially on these summer-like days. That's when we met, you know. The summer of 1942. He was about to ship out for England. He swept me off my feet."

"Oh, really," Jason said, shooting his grandfather a speculative look.

Brandon glared at both of them. "Lizzy, if I'd known what trouble you were going to give me, I would have insisted on coming to California. You just wait. I'll get even when I meet up with those daughters of yours. You won't know a moment's peace when I'm through."

Instantly her amusement vanished. The change was so subtle that at first Brandon thought maybe he'd imagined it, but when she remained too silent for too long, he shot her a look of genuine concern.

"Lizzy?" he said softly. "You okay?"

"Fine, Brandon."

She'd said the words, but there was no spunk behind them. Even Jason seemed puzzled by the change that had come over her.

"I'd better get Sammy and go," he said. "Dana will be wondering what happened to us. We told her we were going out for juice."

"And then you sneaked over here to spy on me," Brandon said. "Now that's one I can hold over you."

"Don't get your hopes up, Granddad. I suspect Sammy will spill the beans before you ever get a chance to." He turned to Elizabeth and clasped her hand in his. "It was nice meeting you, Mrs. Newton. I hope you'll be around for a while."

Lizzy's smile was genuine. "Meeting you and Sammy was my pleasure."

Jason leaned close and whispered something that made her laugh. Only after his grandson had gone did Brandon ask, "What was that he said to you?"

"He suggested I give you a run for your money."

"I like the sound of that," he said. "Lizzy, why did you go so quiet a few minutes ago? When I mentioned California, you clammed right up. You did the same thing the first time we talked on the phone."

He could tell how flustered she was by the way she was twisting her napkin and by the way her gaze evaded his. He'd never known the Lizzy of old to be at a loss for words. One of these days he'd have to accept that there were bound to be some changes over all this time, but at the moment he found this change particularly puzzling.

"I just can't see you being comfortable in my world," she said finally in a desperate tone that had him guessing that she was improvising.

"I never heard such a crazy idea," he protested, startled that she could even think such a thing. "You and I were comfortable from the first minute we met. Nothing's changed, Lizzy. Nothing. Why, when you stepped out of my car night before last, I felt all those years just slip away. I could be comfortable anywhere with you."

"You're wrong if you think there haven't been changes," she said adamantly. "A lot of time's gone by since then. We aren't the same people."

"We are in all the ways that count," he insisted just as stubbornly. "Don't press, Brandon. Not on this."

Troubled by the expression of genuine dismay on her face, he reluctantly nodded his agreement. Then he spent the rest of the day wondering if he'd made a terrible mistake not forcing her to explain why she was more skittish around him now than when she'd been an innocent young virgin.

Elizabeth couldn't get to sleep, despite another long day of visiting Brandon's favorite haunts all over Boston. She was still deeply troubled by the conversation they'd had that morning.

Brandon had seen right through her. He'd guessed that she didn't want him in California, which was why she had to go back before he could get any notions about coming with her. Unfortunately he already seemed to have some pretty strong ideas about the future—crazy ideas that a man his age shouldn't be thinking. Even if she could entirely forget old hurts, too many things stood in their way. Things she could never explain. She had to put his crazy ideas out of his mind.

Because she didn't want to get caught up in the same fantasy, Elizabeth tried reading a paperback she'd picked up at the airport, but it was no better now than it had been when she'd tried to read it on the plane. She used the remote to switch on the television, skipped through the channels and couldn't find even an old movie to hold her interest.

"Face it, Elizabeth," she muttered under her breath, "you're not going to sleep until you deal with what's going on between you and Brandon."

He seemed to have this ridiculous notion that they could pick up right where they'd left off, as if they were a couple of kids. Why couldn't he see that the years had shaped them into very different people?

He was a business tycoon, for heaven's sake. She was a semiretired school teacher. He had traveled all over the world. Since moving to California, she'd rarely left—except for one incredible trip to Hawaii that the kids had given to her and David for their anniversary the year before he'd died. Brandon had a custom-tailored wardrobe, a six-bedroom mansion, a housekeeper and a chauffeur. Her clothes were off the rack, she owned a five-room house and did all of her own cooking, cleaning and driving. Years ago maybe none of that would have mattered. Today it seemed insurmountable.

It wasn't that she was insecure. Far from it, in fact. She knew her own worth, but she could take a realistic measure of that and see that it didn't stack up to be the right woman for a confident, sophisticated man like Brandon Halloran.

Of course, those were only excuses, she admitted reluctantly. There were far more pressing reasons why they couldn't have a future together, but she couldn't even bring herself to think about those.

Elizabeth was questioning whether it was even wise to remain in Boston for the duration of her promised visit, when the phone rang. It was nearly 1:00 a.m., but just before 10:00 p.m. in California.

Almost glad of the late-hour interruption, she grabbed the phone on the second ring, only to be greeted by Kate's exasperated "Mother!"

"Hello, darling. I see you've tracked me down."

"I wouldn't have had to do any tracking, if you'd seen fit to tell me you were going away," she declared, clearly annoyed.

"Sweetheart, you've been away on business for the past two weeks. How was I supposed to tell you?"

"The office would have told you how to find me."

"And if it had been an emergency, I might have called," she said reasonably. "I saw no reason to do so just because I was flying to Boston for a few days."

"Why on earth would you go to Boston after all this time? You haven't been back there in years."

"Decades, actually."

"So, why did you decide to go on the spur of the moment?"

Since Ellen had obviously reported the trip to Kate, Elizabeth wished her older daughter had also given Kate all the explanations. Maybe then Elizabeth would be feeling less defensive.

"An old friend called and invited me."

Kate paused at that. "I didn't know you kept in touch with anyone back there."

"Dear, you haven't exactly kept tabs on my correspondence, have you? Nor do you tell me about all of your trips and contracts," she pointed out.

"Then you have been in touch with this person?"

"Kate, darling, I really think you're making much

too much of this. I'll be home in a few days and I'll tell you all about it. In the meantime, why don't you tell me how your business trip went? Did you win that divorce case for your client in Palm Springs?"

Momentarily distracted just as Elizabeth had hoped she would be, Kate said, "We're still haggling over the settlement. The man has become a multimillionaire, thanks to his wife's investment savvy. He wants to hold her to a prenuptial agreement written in the dark ages."

"I really do wish you'd gotten into some other aspect of law," Elizabeth told her. "I think you've developed a very jaded view of marriage by handling all these high-profile, nasty divorce cases."

"Mother, I do not care to discuss my views on marriage and romance. We both know that I think they're highly overrated."

Elizabeth sighed wearily. "I can't imagine how you could come to that view after growing up around your father and me."

"Believe me, you were the exceptions, not the rule. Don't blame yourself. You set a wonderful example. I've just seen too many of my friends and my clients get royally screwed once the romance dies."

"I think you'd change your mind, if you ever met the right young man," Elizabeth countered. "How is that attractive new partner in your firm? Lance Hopkins, wasn't it? I believe you mentioned he's single."

"You and Ellen," Kate grumbled. "You're both far too romantic for your own good. I never mentioned that Lance Hopkins is single and you know it. Ellen concocted some excuse to pry the information out of my secretary. Now stop trying to change the subject. I want to know whom you're visiting and when you expect to be back home."

"I'll be back in a few days. We'll talk about it then," she replied firmly. "Mother, are you there with some man?" Kate asked suspiciously.

"If I were, it would be none of your business. You worry about your social life, young lady, and let me take care of my own."

"Mother," Kate protested, but Elizabeth was already lowering the phone back into its cradle.

Okay, maybe hanging up was the cowardly way out. But it was one thing to sit in this hotel room so far from home wondering if she was crazy for coming to Boston, crazier yet for not running away as fast as she could. It would be quite another to have her levelheaded daughter confirm it.

Chapter 7

Brandon was up at the crack of dawn, anxious to get the day under way, more optimistic than he had been in years. Since Mrs. Farnsworth was off on Sundays, he made his own coffee, then glanced through the first section of the paper. Not one paragraph, not even one headline he read registered. He turned the pages mechanically, thinking only of how light his heart had become since Lizzy had come back into his life.

Unfortunately the cursory study of the newspaper didn't waste nearly enough time. It was barely seven. He read the business section, then the sports section, and killed another half hour. He glanced at his watch impatiently, muttered a curse and picked up the phone.

Elizabeth's sleepy greeting set his blood to racing. How many times had he dreamed of waking beside her and hearing just such an innocently seductive purr in her voice? A half-dozen times in the past few weeks alone. Multiply that by years, when the memory of her crept in when he least expected it.

"Good morning," he said briskly. "I'm sorry if I woke you."

"You don't sound sorry," she said, laughter lacing through her voice. "What are you doing calling so early?"

"I didn't want to waste a minute of this beautiful day. How about coming to church with me, then going for a drive to see all the spring flowers in bloom? I know a wonderful old inn that would be the perfect place for lunch. If I play my cards right, I might even be able to borrow Dana's car again."

"It sounds lovely."

"Can you be ready in an hour? The service I had in mind is at nine."

"I'll be ready," she promised.

Brandon tried not to feel guilty as he rushed through his shower and dressed in a dark blue suit, a pale blue shirt and a silk tie—all made of Halloran fabrics. Maybe he should have mentioned that Lacey and Kevin were likely to be at the services.

Then again, he consoled himself, he wasn't absolutely certain they would be. They might even be out on Cape Cod, where they were spending more and more time since Kevin's last heart attack. No need getting Elizabeth all worked up over nothing. She'd handled the impromptu meeting with Jason and Sammy blithely enough. In the long run maybe it was better to spring things on her, so she didn't have time to fret and find a dozen excuses for saying no.

An hour later, with Lizzy by his side, he was pulling into the church parking lot.

"What a beautiful old church," Elizabeth said of the plain white structure with its intricately designed stained glass windows and towering steeple.

"Wait until you see it inside," he told her, imagining it through her eyes. "The light filters through all that glass and creates a rainbow of colors."

Just then the bell began to chime, its resonance pure and strong as it filled the air.

"Let's get inside before the processional starts," he said.

He led the way to a pew halfway up the wide, carpeted aisle just as the first hymn began. He found the song in the hymnal and offered it to Elizabeth, but she was already singing in her clear soprano. Even so, in a gesture he remembered vividly from another long-ago Sunday, she placed her hand next to his so they could share.

As he stood next to her, fingers barely touching, and listened to the verses of the hymn, he realized that he had never felt so blessed or so joyous. Unexpected contentment stole through him. Finding his precious Elizabeth again must have been God's work.

She glanced up then and smiled, her face radiant. "You're not singing," she whispered.

He looked down, reminding himself of the familiar words, and then he too sang along with the congregation, his bass joining her sweet voice to soar above all the rest.

Brandon was oblivious to the rest of the service. Though he normally found the minister's sermons to be lively and meaningful, today he was far too conscious of the woman seated next to him. He couldn't stop himself from thinking that if all had gone the way he'd wanted years ago, she would have walked down this very aisle to become his bride.

As the service ended, he took Elizabeth's elbow and steered her through the crowd, murmuring greetings to friends, many of whom he'd known his whole life. He liked the continuity of that, just as he liked thinking that a relationship he'd once cherished was just as strong decades later.

But only for him, he conceded reluctantly. He knew deep down he had yet to win Lizzy over to that way of thinking.

Outside they lingered to chat with the minister. Elizabeth praised the sermon, but Brandon was forced to mutter some innocuous statement because he couldn't recall the topic, much less anything his old friend had said.

He was just about to beat a hasty retreat, when he heard Kevin's voice behind him.

"Dad, I didn't see you earlier. You must have been late."

"We got here just before the processional," he said, turning to face his son and Lacey. He kissed his daughter-in-law. "Good morning, you two. I thought maybe you'd be out at the Cape this weekend."

"Thought or hoped?" Lacey asked, with a pointed glance at Elizabeth. "I understand you have company. Hello, I'm Lacey Halloran and this is Kevin."

"This is Elizabeth Newton," Brandon said, watching Lizzy's face for some indication of her reaction to this chance meeting with his son and daughter-in-law. Judging from the glance she shot his way, he was going to hear about this encounter later. She might forgive one meeting as chance, but two in a row were bound to look suspicious in her eyes.

"It's a pleasure to meet you both," she said graciously. "Brandon has told me quite a lot about you."

Kevin scowled. "Funny, he hasn't told us a thing about you. Have you been keeping secrets, Dad?"

His tone was teasing, but there was an underlying thread of dismay that Brandon caught even if no one else did. Fortunately Lacey had a knack for putting people at ease and she was already chatting a mile a minute with Lizzy, asking about California, her family, her teaching.

"That reminds me," Brandon said. "Lizzy and I were talking about the need for a school that could cater to youngsters like Sammy, children who are bright enough, but need an extra boost if they're to succeed. You two should talk about it."

"What a wonderful idea!" Lacey exclaimed and began asking Lizzy questions in a voice filled with enthusiasm.

Brandon listened to them in satisfaction. Two of a kind, he thought complacently, just as Kevin pulled him aside.

"Who is this woman?" his son demanded.

Brandon stared at him, startled by his thoroughly disgruntled tone. "You say that as if she's got a big scarlet A pinned to her dress. What on earth's the matter with you?"

"I don't like it, Dad. You're quite a catch for any woman. I don't want to see you taken advantage of.

Jason mentioned you hadn't seen this woman for almost fifty years. Out of the blue, she turns up again, now that Mother's dead. Quite a coincidence, wouldn't you say?"

Brandon felt his temper starting to boil. "Son, that is enough! Elizabeth is a fine woman. If you'd done a little checking instead of flinging around slanderous opinions, you would have known that I went after her, not the other way around."

The visible tension in Kevin's shoulders eased some at that explanation. "Okay, maybe I misunderstood, but a man in your position needs to be careful, Dad. You're vulnerable with Mother gone. It would be easy enough for some gold digger to come along and take advantage of you. There are a dozen women right here in town, women you've known forever, who would be happy to share your life with you, if you feel the need for companionship."

"You make it sound about as simple as choosing a puppy and training it to fetch my slippers," Brandon grumbled. "I suppose I should have expected this. It's more retaliation for all my meddling over the years.

Kevin, don't you think I have sense enough to spot a devious, conniving woman?"

"Frankly, no. You always did have a romantic streak. You'd imagine you were in love, no matter what the circumstances were."

"You let me worry about my imagination. Unfortunately, I suspect what you're really worried about is your inheritance," he said with an undeniable edge of sarcasm.

Kevin couldn't have looked more shocked if Brandon had accused him of embezzling. "Dad, you know that's not true."

Brandon sighed heavily. "I'm sorry. You're right. I know you're just thinking of me, but believe me, son, I know what I'm doing."

"Is this relationship serious?"

"At the moment, let's just say it's a serious flirtation. I don't think Lizzy would stand for anything more." He glanced at her and his expression softened. "I do believe, though, that I will do anything in my power to change that."

"Just go slowly, Dad. Promise me that."

"Son, at my age, there's not time enough left to go slow. I plan to grab whatever happiness I can. Don't begrudge me that." He moved back to Lizzy's side. "You ready for that drive in the country?"

"Indeed, I am," she said, smiling up at him. "Have a good time, you two," Lacey said.

"We intend to," Brandon replied, hoping that Lizzy hadn't noticed Kevin's failure to join in Lacey's best wishes.

When they were alone in the car, though, she turned a troubled gaze toward him. "Kevin's unhappy about my being here, isn't he?"

"I wouldn't say unhappy."

"What would you say?"

"Concerned."

She sighed. "Isn't it amazing that we can live an entire lifetime, raise families, hold jobs, suffer devastating losses, and our kids still think we haven't got the brains the good Lord gave a duck?"

He chuckled. "You've been getting the third degree, too?"

"Only from my youngest. She called last night to fuss at me for not notifying her that I planned this trip. I tried to point out that she almost never tells me when or where she's going on a business trip, but she didn't quite get the similarity."

"Are you sure it's the same thing?" he asked. "Or did you make a point of *not* telling her, because you knew she wouldn't approve?"

"I could ask you the same thing. Seems to me like I was a big surprise to everyone in your family."

"Touché," he said. He glanced over at her. "Let's make a pact that we will not allow family interference to get in the way of you and me having the time of our lives."

"If we had a little champagne, I'd drink a toast to that," she agreed, reaching for his hand. "Sometimes it seems you know exactly what's on my mind."

"Because we're more alike than you want to admit. Now let's forget all our cares and take in this beautiful scenery. I'm sorry Dana wasn't at church so we could borrow her car, but spring's putting on a show for us just the same. And I, for one, don't want to miss it."

Elizabeth released his hand and looked out the window at the budding trees about to burst forth with dogwood blossoms. Bright yellow forsythia spilled over split-rail fences. Purple and white lilac scented the air.

"I'd forgotten how beautiful it is here in the spring. We have a change of seasons in California, but it's not nearly as dramatic. Everything is bright and bold there, almost the whole year around. Here you go from dreary grays and stark browns to pastels. I guess it's sort of like comparing the soft colors chosen by Monet to the brilliant palette of Van Gogh or Gauguin."

"With that kind of poetry in your soul, you'll love the place we're going for lunch."

"Tell me," she urged, her voice laced with curiosity. She'd always wished for the time to discover romantic hideaways. David had been content with bland, ordinary restaurants and hotel chains.

"I'm not spoiling the surprise. You'll have to see what I mean when we get there."

They reached the inn a half hour later, a huge old clapboard house painted white and trimmed with black shutters. A weather vane on the roof twirled in the breeze. Though it was lovely, it wasn't until they were inside that Elizabeth could see what Brandon had meant.

The entire back of the house had been redone with French doors that were glass from floor to ceiling. Beyond the doors was a patio that had not yet been opened. It was edged with honeysuckle tumbling over a white picket fence. The scent was sweeter than any air she'd breathed in years.

Beyond the inn's yard, the hillside spilled into a valley that was brilliant with thousands of tulips, daffodils and the bright green of new grass. If they'd taken a patch of the Netherlands in springtime and transported it to this site, it could not have been more beautiful.

Elizabeth drew in a deep breath of the air coming through the open doors and smiled in delight. She looked over and caught Brandon's gaze pinned on her.

"You like it?" he asked anxiously.

"I've never been anywhere like it. Thank you for bringing me."

"I didn't bring you just because of the picturesque view. The food is marvelous here, too."

Everyone seemed to know Brandon well, from the hostess to the waitress to the owner, who stopped by to ensure that everything was to their liking.

"You must come here often," she said, realizing as she said it that she sounded oddly miffed.

"Once or twice a year," he said.

"Then you must tip very generously to warrant all the attention." He grinned so broadly that she felt color flooding into her cheeks. "Jealous, Lizzy?"

"No, I am not jealous," she snapped. Then because her tone made it sound more like a confirmation than a denial, she added, "It's certainly none of my business what you've done."

"That doesn't keep you from being a mite curious. Am I right?"

"Absolutely not!" she said with as much conviction as she could muster. "I should let you go on trying to squirm off the hook, but I'll have mercy on you," he teased. "The owner is a client. Halloran provides all the custom fabrics for the place—from the draperies to the tablecloths to the seat cushions. Notice how they pick up the colors from outdoors and bring them inside."

"Oh, my," she said with delight as she caught the similarity. "Brandon, you amaze me. I should have guessed it was something like that."

"Instead of the wild, clandestine rendezvous you were imagining? Made me feel young again, just to know you thought me capable of such carrying on."

She gazed boldly into his eyes. "I don't know why I let you agitate me so. You always did love to tease me."

"Do you know why?"

Her breath seemed to go still. "Why?"

"Because you blushed so prettily. You still do, Lizzy."

He reached across the table and took her hand in his. She told herself she ought to draw away, but she couldn't bring herself to do it. His hand was warm and strong, a hand that could comfort or excite. She recalled that all too vividly despite the time that had passed. Foolish notions, she chided herself.

"Lizzy, do you know that not once in all the times I've been here did I bring another woman with me. Not even Grace."

"Why?"

"Because from the first time I saw it, it made me think of you." Emotions crowded into her throat and tears stung her eyes. "Oh, Brandon, even if they're lies, you do say the most romantic things."

"It's not a lie," he said softly.

Whether it was or it wasn't, Elizabeth knew she didn't dare allow herself to fall for the tender web he was trying to spin around her heart.

It worried Brandon that Lizzy didn't trust him, especially when he knew he had only a short time to convince her of his sincerity. He wined and dined her. He wooed her with flowers. They shared quiet evenings at home and passionate arguments after movies. He tried to convince her to move into one of his guest rooms, but she was adamant about staying on at the hotel. He guessed that had as much to do with caution as it did with her sense of propriety.

In between, there were frantic calls from Kevin, who'd managed to dream up more questions about the running of Halloran Industries than he'd asked during the entire decade they'd worked together.

"Dad, can't you come in tomorrow? I think we should meet on the new contracts."

"You've been negotiating those contracts on your own for the past five years. You know I don't like to mess with that sort of detail. I was delighted to have you take it off my hands. Why should I want to change that now? Besides, Lizzy and I have plans."

"What plans?"

"None of your business," he said, because he was thinking of taking her to Maine for a nostalgic visit to the place they'd met. He intended to ask her tonight. "Kevin, I trust you to run Halloran Industries. I really do."

Kevin merely sighed in defeat and hung up.

That night Brandon took Lizzy dancing, though he stopped short of trying some of those fancy new steps that looked more suited to a bedroom than a public dance floor. In his day a man could have gotten his face slapped for some of those maneuvers. Damn, but they looked like fun, though.

Back at his place, he turned on the stereo and shot a glance at Lizzy, who'd ended the evening with her hair mussed and her cheeks flushed. He held out his arms.

"What do you say? Want to try one of those new-fangled dances we saw tonight?"

"Get out of here, Brandon Halloran. We're too old."

Despite the protest, he saw the hint of curiosity in

her eyes. "Not me. I'm feeling chipper as the day we met. Come on, Lizzy."

Breathless and laughing, they tried to imitate the intricate steps they'd seen earlier. As their bodies fit together intimately, the laughter suddenly died. Lizzy's startled gaze met his and years fell away.

Brandon touched his lips to hers with surprising caution, almost as if he feared a ladylike slap in response to a daring kiss. There was tenderness and longing in the tentative, velvet-soft kiss and the first breath of a passion that both had thought long over.

The flowery scent of Lizzy's perfume took Brandon back to the first time he'd dared to steal a kiss.

They had been in the garden behind the Halloran mansion, surrounded by the scent of spring and the gentle whisper of a breeze. He'd wanted Lizzy to meet his family, to see his home back then, too, but she'd been afraid. A little awestruck by the size of the house, she had come no farther than the garden before being overcome by second thoughts.

"They'll love you," he'd vowed, ignoring his own uncertainty to quiet hers.

"You can't just spring me on them days before you leave. They'll be certain you've taken leave of your senses."

"Do you love me?" he'd asked her quietly.

"Oh, yes." Her blue eyes sparkled like sapphires when she said it. "Then that's all that matters." His mouth had covered hers, stilling her trembling lips.

There had been so much hope, so much sweet temptation in that kiss, he thought now. Was it any wonder she'd remained in his heart?

Brandon felt the stir of those same fragile emotions now, an echo that reverberated through him. They gave him the courage to speak his mind.

"Marry me, Lizzy," he said impulsively. "Don't let's make the same mistake twice."

Before the words were out of his mouth, he knew he should have waited, knew he should have settled for asking her to go back to Maine with him. There was no mistaking the flare of panic in her eyes, the way she trembled in his arms.

It was the sort of careless error that a man new to making deals might make, misjudging the opposition. Brandon cursed the arrogance that had misled him into thinking her misgivings were of no importance. Only a man totally blinded by love would not have seen that Lizzy wasn't ready to consider marriage.

Even so, he couldn't bring himself to withdraw the proposal, because more than anything he wanted her to say yes to it. But once the words were spoken, he could see that he'd made a terrible mistake. He'd underestimated her fears and exaggerated his claim on her heart.

Brandon's breath caught in his throat as he waited to see how much damage his impetuous proposal had done.

Chapter 8

Elizabeth was caught off guard by Brandon's proposal now, just as she had been all those years back. For one crazy split second, she imagined saying yes. The word was on her lips as she thought how wonderful it would be to know that this strong, exciting man would spend the rest of his life at her side. She indulged herself in the fantasy that they would have a second chance at all the happiness they had lost.

As she struggled against her powerful desires, she was vibrantly aware of the ticking of an old grandfather clock, the whisper of branches against the library's glass doors. Everything seemed sharper and somehow dangerous as she flirted with Brandon's tempting offer.

There was no denying that it was romantic notions like that that had pulled her back to Boston in the first place. Yearnings, aroused by this compelling man, had kept her here beyond the scheduled end of the trip, but marriage? She had never really considered that an option because she knew it could never be. Never. Far too much was at risk. Once again she realized she would have to disappoint him—and, perhaps even more, herself.

She touched her fingers to his cheek. His skin was tanned and smooth with fine lines fanning out from the corners of his clear blue eyes. She recalled as vividly as if it had been only yesterday the first time she had dared to touch him intimately, the first time she had felt the sandpaper rasp of his unshaven face after they had lain in each other's arms for nearly an entire night of daring, blissful pleasure before parting discreetly before dawn. Then, as now, there had been as much sorrow as joy in her heart, knowing that their time together was drawing to a close.

"Oh, Brandon," she whispered now with a sigh as she tried to find the right words to make her refusal less painful for both of them. "You are such a dear, sweet man to ask. You almost sound as if you mean it."

"I *do* mean it," he said, radiating indignation. "I've never meant anything more. We're still good together, Lizzy. You can't deny that."

She tried to counter passionate impulsiveness with clear, cool reason. "No, I can't deny it. But you have your life here, and I have mine in California. This has been a wonderful time for us, but we can't go shaking things up so drastically. Not overnight like this. What would our families think?"

"That we've waited entirely too long," he said flatly. How could he not see, she wondered, that what he said was only partly true? "Jason, perhaps. He's young and newly in love himself. Kevin is another story. Even you must recognize that. He sees me as an intruder, I'm sure."

"He'd see any woman who stepped into his mama's place that way. He'll come to terms with it. Besides, what does it matter what he thinks? If his attitude upsets you, I'll have another talk with him, explain the way it is with us. I won't allow him to make you feel uncomfortable."

Elizabeth laughed at his conviction that he could mold people's thoughts and deeds so easily. "Brandon, you might be able to force him into polite acceptance, but you can't very well change the way he feels. And isn't that what really counts?"

For an instant Brandon looked defeated, then his expression brightened. "I'll just remind him of how foolishly I behaved when I refused to recognize how important Lacey was to him. That'll make him see things more clearly."

"And what should I tell Kate? She'd be no happier to learn of our relationship than Kevin."

"Tell her that you love me," he said simply.

"I'm afraid she thinks that love is an illusion. At our age, she'd probably consider it insanity."

"Then we'll just have to show her otherwise. Lizzy, we can't let our children dictate our lives, any more than they allow us to interfere in theirs."

Elizabeth couldn't deny she was tempted, but she knew that part of the temptation for her—and for Brandon, whether he wanted to admit it or not—was based on memories that had managed to intertwine with the present. Those memories had given each moment of the past few days a bittersweet poignancy, had heightened every thrilling sensation. The tenderness, the laughter, the joy, how could they possibly be sure any of that was real?

Besides, she had meant what she'd said about their having separate lives. It was hard to get much farther apart than Boston and California. She couldn't bear the thought of not seeing her grandchildren.

And for all his stubborn denial, Brandon wouldn't like being separated from his family, either. Not that that was even a possibility. She would never have him in Los Angeles. The strain of it would kill her, though she couldn't tell him that. He'd guess in a minute the secret she was determined to keep to her death, no matter the cost to her personal happiness.

"What's the real reason, Lizzy?" he said as if he could see that she was dissembling. "You afraid to take a chance on a man my age?"

She scoffed at the ridiculous notion. "Brandon, you have more energy than men half your age. You'd still be running me ragged when we both turn eighty."

"I know that," he said with a twinkle in his eyes. "I just wondered if you did."

She raised her concerns about life-style and distance. But he shot each down promising to charter a jet if he had to to take her back and forth to California.

"So, you've assumed we'll settle here," she countered. "There you go again, making plans without a thought to what I might want."

"No, indeed. The only thing I care about is what you want. I'm just not sure you recognize what that is."

"Brandon, I do believe I know my own mind."

"Then say something that makes sense," he snapped impatiently.

His tone set her teeth on edge. "Just because you don't want to hear what I'm saying doesn't mean it doesn't make sense. Don't you think deciding where to live is critical for a couple our age?"

"I don't aim on settling anywhere. I'm thinking of seeing the world, getting myself out of Jason and Kevin's hair. Think about it, Lizzy. Have you been to Rome? Paris? Tahiti?"

Naturally Brandon would hit on an almost irresistible lure, she thought irritably. Just the sound of all those fascinating places thrilled her. They were rich with culture she'd only read about in books. She'd promised herself that one day she would see them all. Time was running out, but this wasn't the answer. They couldn't roam the world as if they were rootless, when the very opposite was true.

"Tahiti?" she inquired quizzically. "Isn't that a little exotic for the likes of us?"

"Why? I'll bet you still cut a fine figure in a bathing suit." His mood obviously improved, he winked when he said it, then sobered and added more seriously, "Besides, there are a lot of books I've been wanting to read. A month or two on the beach would help me to catch up." The twinkle came back. "Unless you'd prefer to lure me off to our room and have your way with me."

"Brandon!" Despite the stern disapproval in her tone, she couldn't banish the devilish quickening of her pulse. Brandon did have a way of saying the most outrageous things to shock her. Was she going to let silly fears and practicality stand in the way of happiness again? Perhaps a compromise was possible, a way to snag a few weeks or even months of pleasure.

"I've always wanted to run away to a tropical isle with a handsome stranger," she admitted, not even trying to hide the wistfulness.

Brandon's big, gentle hands cupped her cheeks. "We're hardly strangers, Lizzy. We've known each other our whole lives."

"But we've only been together less than a month, counting these past few days. Isn't that part of the appeal? We've never had time to recognize all the little idiosyncrasies that might drive us crazy."

"Is there anything important about me you don't know?"

"No," she had to admit. But there were things he didn't know about her, could never know. She could have a few more weeks, though. Just a few weeks of stolen happiness. They deserved that much.

"Let's just run away, Brandon," she coaxed. "There's no need for a ceremony. We needn't worry about shocking anyone in this day and age."

His hands fell away from her face. His eyes turned serious. "Do you think our children would be happier to see us having an affair than they would be seeing us married? I doubt it. Besides, I can't bear the thought of waking up some morning to discover you've vanished during the night. I want a real commitment this time, Lizzy. I won't settle for less."

"I can't give you that. I was never as brave or as strong as you, Brandon. I don't take risks."

"But there's no risk involved. Can't you see that?

After all these years our feelings haven't changed. That should tell you how right they are.

We've cherished them in our hearts. Not that either of us shortchanged the people we married." He tapped his chest. "But here, where it counts, we've never forgotten."

"Our feelings aren't the only ones that count anymore. We have families to consider."

"Dammit, Lizzy, you're thinking up excuses, not reasons."

"No," she said gently. "Your family is every bit as important to you as mine is to me. Neither of us could ever knowingly do something that would bring them unhappiness or pain."

"Lizzy, you're not making sense. How could our happiness cause them pain?"

She couldn't explain, no matter how badly she wanted to erase the confusion and hurt in his eyes.

"I'm sorry, Brandon," she whispered, fighting to hide the tears that threatened as she finalized the decision she should have made days earlier. "I'm going home in the morning. Alone."

He backed away from her then, and his expression turned colder than she'd ever seen it before. "I won't chase after you again, Lizzy."

She felt his anguish as deeply as her own. "I know," she said in a voice filled with regret. "Perhaps you should call a taxi to take me back to the hotel. We'll say our goodbyes here, just as we did the first time."

"No. I brought you here. I'll take you back," he said with stiff politeness.

"Really, it's not necessary."

"Yes," he said firmly. "It is."

The drive to the hotel was made in silence. It was colder by far in the car than it was outdoors. Elizabeth felt as if her heart had frozen inside her. She was certain she would never feel anything as magnificent as Brandon's caring again. She was trading love for peace of mind, and at the moment it seemed to be a lopsided exchange all the way around.

Brandon wondered how the devil things had gone so wrong again. Day after day, he'd seen the way Lizzy looked at him. He'd felt her pulse quicken at his touch, felt her flesh warm. Whatever the real explanation for her withdrawal, he knew he hadn't heard it yet. Not that she was lying. But she definitely wasn't telling him the whole truth.

He was a proud man, though. He wouldn't chase after her like some lovesick adolescent. If she couldn't be honest, if she couldn't trust him with the truth, then perhaps he'd been wrong all along about the depth of her feelings.

Perhaps it was just as well to discover now that there was no trust between them. They'd lost it over those damned letters decades back and nothing that had happened in the past few days had helped them to recapture it.

Maybe he'd fooled himself that what they'd once shared had been deeper and more meaningful than anything he'd experienced before or since. Maybe he'd simply been making a desperate, last grab for what had turned out to be no more than an illusion. Maybe love and marriage weren't even possible at his age. Perhaps he should be willing to settle for the fleeting companionship Lizzy offered. There were so damn many maybes, and so few solid answers.

Despite Lizzy's objections, Brandon turned the car over to the valet at the hotel and followed her inside. In front of the elevator he studied her and tried to convince himself that he'd been wrong about everything, but his heart ached with a real sense of loss. He might have tracked her down on impulse, but he'd kept her in Boston because she'd engaged his heart as no other woman ever had. He couldn't explain it, it just *was*—like the rising of the sun or the pull of the tides.

He brushed a wisp of hair back from her cheek and felt her tremble. His gaze caught hers and held them spellbound. Her lips parted on a soft sigh that could have been either pleasure or regret.

"I've spent the whole drive over here trying to convince myself that I'm wrong about us," he said finally, his knuckles grazing her soft cheek. "But I'd be a liar if I told you I believed it. There's a bond between us, Lizzy, one I can't deny. Can you?"

Her hand reached up and covered his. "No," she said. "I can't deny that."

"Then why won't you marry me?"

"I can't," she said with stubborn finality, slipping away from his touch. "I won't make it easy for you to walk away," he warned, just before he pulled her into his arms and brought his mouth down to cover hers.

Oblivious to everything except the woman melting in his embrace, Brandon plundered. It wasn't a kiss meant just to remind. It was meant to brand. It was a hot, hungry claiming of a kind he'd nearly forgotten until Lizzy had come back into his life.

Her scent, like that of spring rain and sweetest flowers, surrounded them. Her skin was petal soft, her lips moist and inviting after that first shocked instant when his tongue had invaded.

Despite its urgency, the kiss should have been the end of it, but it brought too many provocative memories, too many seductive images of another time, another place. His pulse bucked like a young man's, as it had on that single splendid night he and Lizzy had shared.

"Let me come to your room," he whispered in a voice husky with desire. "If nothing else, let me hold you through this one last night." The words were an echo of a long-ago plea and he waited just as anxiously for her response. "Don't deny us that," he coaxed.

"Sometimes I wonder how I ever denied you anything," she said ruefully. She slid her hand into his. "One night, Brandon. I suppose there's no harm in grabbing that much happiness."

The elevator ride was the longest he'd ever taken. He couldn't stop looking at Lizzy, with her cheeks flushed with color and her eyes bright with anticipation. She looked every bit as beautiful tonight as she had as a girl, and he wanted her in his arms with the same aching urgency. Since Grace had died, he'd thought he would never again experience this fire in his blood, but it pulsed now with a demanding roar.

In Lizzy's room, the maid had turned down the expensive covers on the queen-size bed. A foil-wrapped candy was on each pillow. Light from the hall spilled in, until Brandon slowly shut the door behind them, leaving them in shadows.

He reached for the light, but Lizzy stayed his hand. "No," she whispered. "I want you to remember me the way I was, not the way I am now."

He touched her cheek in a gesture meant to reassure. "You will always be beautiful in my eyes. Time could never change that."

"Spoken like a true romantic," she said with a nervous laugh. "But I'd rather not take any chances."

"We don't have to go through with this," he said, cursing the sense of honor that demanded he offer to stop right now.

He heard her intake of breath and felt his own go still as he waited for her decision.

"I want you to hold me again," she said finally and his breath eased out in a soft sigh of relief.

A lifetime of marriage hadn't taught him enough patience to go as slowly as he knew he needed to tonight. He sensed that any moment Lizzy would panic and change her mind, unless he claimed her with only the tenderest of touches, the gentlest of words.

In the shadowy darkness Brandon pulled Lizzy into his arms and touched his lips to hers again. This time he allowed himself the delight of savoring, the slow exploration of tastes and textures. His senses exploded with a clash of sweet, poignant memory and glorious reality. As slowly and inevitably as the passage of time, he felt her hesitancy become bold desire.

And still he moved cautiously, allowing the weight of her breast to fill his hand, allowing his fingers to skim lightly over the sensitive nipple that had peaked despite layers of fabric. She moaned at the teasing, eyes closed as she gave herself up to his caresses.

"You're so responsive," he murmured. "Sometimes I ached to experience that again and I envied the man who'd replaced me in your life."

"I never expected to feel like this again," she admitted, meeting his gaze. "Thank you for that."

"No," he whispered. "Don't thank me. Just love me as you did that night."

Each touch after that became an echo of one that had gone before. Their bodies responded in harmony, as if they'd been made to fit together.

Brandon didn't feel old in Lizzy's embrace. He felt rejuvenated, more passionate than ever before, more determined than ever not to sacrifice what they had found.

He did everything he could to see that she felt the same. The woman who came apart in his arms, the woman whose tears spilled onto his burning flesh was as spirited and as passionate as the one he'd held decades earlier.

Experience and time had taught them to be bolder, more demanding lovers. Love had taught them to give as much as they received.

As they lay in each other's arms, exhausted, sated, Brandon thought he had never known such joy or peace of mind. His fingers skimmed across her flesh, then halted at the locket that lay between her breasts. He heard her breath catch as he traced the shape and realized then that she was wearing the one piece of jewelry she had accepted from him years before.

"Why would you still have this, if you didn't care?" he murmured. "I never said I didn't care."

"Have you always worn it?"

"No."

"But you did save it," he said in what sounded like an accusation. "Is my picture still inside?"

"Yes."

"Doesn't that tell you something, Lizzy? You can't mean to walk away from this," he said finally. "You can't."

He felt another hot tear spill onto his chest, and he propped himself up on one elbow to gaze down at the woman in his arms. "Why are you crying?" he asked, wiping away the tears.

"Because you're wrong," she whispered in a voice that broke. "I must walk away."

Though she seemed to choking back a sob, there was no mistaking the stubborn finality in her eyes. Brandon felt his heart grow cold. "You mean that, don't you?"

She nodded, not looking at him. Then she lifted her gaze to his and said, "But it will break my heart."

Chapter 9

There were times over the next few days when Brandon wondered how he'd ever gotten home from Lizzy's hotel that night. He'd risked everything on the hope that once they had made love again she would never walk away.

He should have known better. If she hadn't consented to marry him when they'd been wildly in love in their teens and she'd been an innocent virgin, she would never give in so easily now.

She had always been far stronger than he'd realized, perhaps even than she herself realized. Whatever was driving her back to California was not something he knew how to combat. She'd allowed him a peek inside her heart, but he knew nothing of her soul. She'd kept that part of herself private—a secret she wouldn't share, even with him. He'd left her room feeling a depth of sorrow and regret that matched the grieving he'd done for Grace and had hoped never to experience again.

Despite that, he called in the morning, intending one last-ditch attempt to persuade her to stay or, at the very least, to wrench a truthful explanation from her. But she had left already, without a note, without a goodbye.

Brandon thought back to another time when Lizzy had refused him in much the same way. Perhaps he'd been naive to expect a seventeen-year-old girl to make a lifetime commitment to a man she'd known only days. Yet he'd known in a matter of minutes that she had brought an inexplicable, heart-stopping excitement into his life.

Because he hadn't considered himself a man prone to sentiment at that time, he'd been stunned to learn that he was capable of such deep emotions. The discovery was especially unsettling since only moments before, he'd been anticipating the hero's welcome that would await him after the war and wondering how many women it might allow him to charm into his bed. In the blink of an eye an encounter with a dazzling, barefooted girl had changed all that. He'd been able to imagine no one in his life except Lizzy.

Up until the moment when she'd turned down his proposal on the eve of his departure for England, he'd been convinced she'd felt the same rare magic. Nothing she'd said back then had made a bit of sense, either. That's when he'd first realized that Lizzy had a stubbornness that matched his own. It had made her all the more appealing.

But that was then and this was now. All he felt now was anger and betrayal. Brandon swore he would never give her the chance to hurt him again. There would be no flood of flowers, no Belgian chocolates, no pleas, no coaxing. She had made her choice, for whatever reason, and he would honor it. He'd grown far too weary of challenges.

Instead Brandon ranted and raved at everyone else, making their lives a living hell. He dropped his plans to retire, offering no explanation. He filled up the lonely hours of each and every evening with work, littering Kevin's desk and Jason's with the memos he spent the night writing. When Sammy came around, eager to learn more about Halloran textiles, Brandon even chased him off with his foul temper.

The next day at the plant he overheard Sammy telling Dana about the encounter.

"Something's wrong with Grandpa Brandon," Sammy said, clearly worried. "He wouldn't even talk about that new silk stuff when I asked him. You think maybe he's sick?"

Just out of sight, Brandon listened in dismay, knowing he owed the boy an apology. Aside from Dana, Sammy hadn't had a lot of people in his life he could count on. Brandon considered himself lucky to be one of them.

Now, because of his own bleak outlook, he was letting Sammy down, and Dana was put in the awkward position of trying to make excuses for him.

"I'm sure he didn't mean to cut you off," she said. "I have a pretty good idea what's troubling him, and it doesn't have anything to do with you. This moping around has gone on long enough, though. I intend to talk to him."

Guilty over having eavesdropped, and guiltier yet over the way he'd yelled at Sammy to leave him be, Brandon went back to his office and tried to figure out how the devil he was going to get his life in order before everyone around him formed a lynch mob.

He was prowling around his office when Dana sashayed in. She looked as if she were just itching for a fight. She ignored his forbidding scowl and settled into the chair opposite his desk. It was obvious she had no intention of being scared off, but that didn't stop him from trying.

"What do you want?" he grumbled in a tone meant to intimidate. He stood towering over her as he asked.

"The truth," she said without blanching the way he'd have liked. "About what?"

"Whatever's bugging you."

"Who says anything is bugging me?"

"Are you suggesting old age has suddenly made you crotchety?"

"Could be," he said, though he was suddenly fighting an unexpected grin. She was a tough one, all right. Just like Lizzy, he thought before he could stop himself. He moved to the window and stared out at the dreary April day that mirrored his mood.

"You weren't acting old when I saw you dancing a couple of weeks back," she commented idly. "I believe that was the lambada you and Elizabeth were trying."

Surprise and dismay left Brandon openmouthed. He turned to glower at her. "You were spying on me?"

"I was not," she retorted emphatically. "I stopped over to pick up that baby cradle you told me was in the attic. Mrs. Farnsworth let me in and said you'd gone out for the evening. I didn't even know you'd come home until I was on my way out. I started to say hello and then I realized you weren't alone."

"So you spied," he repeated.

She grinned. "Call it whatever you want. It was pretty interesting stuff. I didn't stick around for the finale, though. I left when things started heating up."

"Thank goodness for small favors."

"You still haven't said—is she the reason you've been in this funk? Has Elizabeth gone back to California?"

He considered lying to protect his privacy, then didn't see the use of it.

Dana was too smart to buy a small fib, and he had too much integrity to offer a blatant lie. She'd obviously figured it out, anyway.

"Yes," he muttered finally. "When do you plan to visit her?"

"I don't."

"Why on earth not?"

"She won't have it."

"Why?" she asked, sounding every bit as astonished and confused as he felt.

Relieved to have someone to talk to, someone who wasn't likely to laugh in his face or to make judgments, he cleared a spot on the sofa, tumbling bolts of fabric onto the floor, and sat down. Then he told Dana the whole sad story—at least as much as he understood of it.

"She said no," he concluded. "Again."

"And you're just giving up," she retorted in a tone that was part disbelief, part accusation. "Again."

"No," he said, but further denial died on his lips. "I can't go chasing all over the countryside for her."

"I don't see why not. You were planning to chase all over the world with her. Why not start in California?"

"I won't settle for less than marriage this time and she won't hear of that."

"Then I guess you'll just have to be more persuasive. Lord knows, you didn't give up on Jason and me or on Lacey and Kevin," she said. "You know what your trouble is? You're too used to getting your own way without a fight. Maybe this Lizzy of yours is smarter than you think. Maybe she sees that it'll do you good to have to work for something for a change. Maybe she needs to know she's worth fighting for this time."

Recognizing the wisdom and clinging to the tiny shred of hope in what she'd said, Brandon stood and scooped his granddaughter-in-law up in a bear hug.

"Damn, I did right by Jason when I picked you," he said with satisfaction. "My grandson is one very lucky man. I hope he knows that."

"I remind him all the time."

"I think I'll just stop by his office and tell him myself. At the same time I'll tell Kevin that I'm leaving the two of them in charge. I'm officially retiring as of today. Tonight I'll pack my bags, and in the morning I'll take the first flight to California. Don't you dare have that baby while I'm gone," he warned.

"I wouldn't dream of it. I promise," she said.

The next morning Brandon dug the detective's report out of his desk at home and made note of all the pertinent addresses and phone numbers—Lizzy's and those of her daughters. Then, his step lighter than it had been in days, he left for the airport. He refused to even consider the possibility that Lizzy wouldn't see him when he got there.

"Mother, what are you doing here?" Ellen asked when she walked into her own kitchen and found Elizabeth sitting there, staring out the window at the rain, a pile of socks on the table in front of her.

Elizabeth avoided her daughter's gaze.

"Not that I'm not glad to see you," Ellen added hurriedly as she plunked her bag of groceries onto the counter and dropped a kiss on her mother's cheek. She shrugged out of her raincoat, then ran her fingers through her short sandy hair. The damp strands fell back into enviable waves.

Finally she sat down across from Elizabeth, her expression worried. "Are you okay?"

"Of course I'm okay. I'm just darning Jake's socks," Elizabeth said defensively, picking up another pair of her son-in-law's heavy athletic socks from the stack of laundry. She reached for needle and thread.

"Why on earth would you be doing that?"

"It needs to be done."

Ellen plucked the socks from Elizabeth's hands and tossed them into the garbage. "It does not need to be done. You're bored, Mother. You've been restless ever since you got back from Boston and you haven't said a word about Brandon Halloran. I haven't wanted to press before, but enough is enough. Did something go wrong between you two? I thought you stayed on because you were having such a wonderful time."

"It was okay," she said, feeling heat climb into her cheeks at the memory of that last night. That was the second time in her life she'd made a dreadful mistake with Brandon. It had taken her decades to get over the first time. She didn't have decades left this time.

"Just okay?" Ellen asked, reaching for the teapot

Elizabeth had filled and set in the middle of the table. She poured them both a cup of tea.

Elizabeth met her daughter's intense gaze and sighed heavily. "No," she admitted reluctantly. "It was more than okay."

"And?"

"And what?" she snapped, sitting her cup down so hard that tea sloshed onto the table. She ignored the mess and reached for another sock. "Why are you so interested, anyway?"

"Because when you left for Boston, there was a sparkle in your eyes and a spring in your step. When we talked on the phone, you sounded excited, alive. Now you look as though you've lost your best friend, and you sound perfectly miserable. To top it off, you're darning socks, something no one in this family has done since I was a child. Even then you only did it when you were angry or distraught," Ellen said bluntly. "Now if that man did something to upset you, I want to know about it."

Elizabeth hesitated, then finally blurted, "He asked me to marry him."

She dared a glance at her daughter. Ellen's mouth dropped open. The next instant she was on her feet, enveloping her mother in a hug. Elizabeth endured the embrace stiffly.

"He asked you to marry him?" Ellen said, barely containing her exuberance. Her blue-green eyes sparkled. "Mother, why didn't you say something sooner? That's wonderful. When's the wedding? Does Kate know? Penny will go nuts. She said you were probably...well, never mind what Penny said. I should have washed her mouth out with soap."

"Penny is entirely too precocious. Besides, I turned him down."

Looking stunned, Ellen sat back down and simply stared at her. "Why would you do that? Weren't the sparks still there, after all? They must have been for him if he wants to get married. I could have sworn they were there for you, as well."

"Oh, yes," she admitted reluctantly. "The sparks were there."

"Then what happened? Why did you say no?"

"It was a little frightening," she explained. "Brandon can be a bit overpowering when he sets his mind to something."

"Which is what you always said you wanted. Dad let you run the show."

"Don't criticize you father, Ellen," she said sharply. "He was a good man."

"Oh, for heaven's sake Mother, I never said he wasn't. But you know what I said is true. He gave in to you on everything. I always thought you would have been better off with a man who would stand up to you. Now what's the real reason you said no to Brandon Halloran? You weren't worried about our reaction, were you?"

Elizabeth picked up her cup of tea, then set it back down. She wished more than anything that she could have this same conversation with Kate, so she could say everything that was on her mind. But, ironically, Kate was the one who wouldn't understand and the only one she could tell.

"Not exactly, but I couldn't go off and leave all of you," she said eventually, giving the truth a wide berth.

Ellen moved her chair closer to Elizabeth and took her hand. "Mom, are you sure that's not just an excuse? How often do you see us, anyway? I know we're all in the same city, but the only times we get together as a whole family are holidays. We could still manage that."

"But now I know you're just a phone call away."

Ellen grinned at her. "There are airplanes. We still would be a phone call away."

"I couldn't just drop in like this."

"Which you haven't done in months. You're usually too busy. You've spent more time here moping around since you got back, than you did in the entire six months before you left."

"I guess that's true."

Ellen's expression grew puzzled. "Mother, don't you want to marry him?"

Elizabeth took a deep breath, then met her daughter's gaze evenly. "More than anything," she said before she could stop herself.

"Then I say go for it."

"But there are things you don't know," she began, her voice trailing off helplessly. Things she could never tell her.

"What things?"

She shook her head, knowing she'd already said far too much. "Never mind. I'm just prattling on. I made my decision. I'll just have to learn to accept it."

"Mother, you're not making a bit of sense."

"Nobody ever said love made sense," she observed.

They both jumped at the sudden pounding on the

front door. It was interspersed with the impatient ringing of the doorbell.

"What on earth?" Ellen muttered as she went to get
it. "I suppose Penny must have forgotten her key."

But it wasn't Penny. Even from the kitchen Elizabeth could hear enough to send panic racing through
her. There was no mistaking the gruff timbre of Brandon's voice.

"Oh my Lord," she whispered, wishing she could
flee out the back door.

He'd come. He'd actually come all the way to California for her, even though he'd sworn he wouldn't.

And he'd met Ellen, she realized with sudden, heart-
stopping fear. My God, he'd met her daughter. She could
practically feel the color drain from her cheeks as she
stood up, uncertain whether to run to him or hide. "Elizabeth," he said softly from the doorway, his voice a low
command.

Just hearing him did astonishing things to her insides. Drawing on all her reserves of strength, she faced
him sternly, wanting him gone, out of the house before
he ruined everything. Even so, she couldn't help noting his haggard face, the glint of determination in his
eyes—both were equally worrisome.

"Why have you come? You know I don't want you
here," she said, her voice trembling with anger and frustration.

"I don't believe you. For just an instant, before you
caught yourself, I could see the expression in your eyes.
It wasn't dismay, Lizzy. It was longing."

"That's ego and imagination talking," she said, dismissing them. "Please, Brandon. Leave now. I meant what I said in Boston. It would never work between us."

"I'm not leaving without you," he said stubbornly. "I've made up my mind. You just might as well accept it."

She was as certain that he meant that as she was of the next sunset.

Knowing that and desperate to have him out of Ellen's house, she snatched up her bag.

"Have it your way, then," she said grudgingly and marched through the house. "Dear, we'll be going now," she told her daughter.

"It was a pleasure meeting you, Mr. Halloran," Ellen said at the door. "I hope we'll see more of you while you're in town."

"Believe me, I would love to get to know you, as well," he said. "I've heard a lot about you from your mother."

Elizabeth brushed past the two of them and hurried down the sidewalk to her car. Brandon's fancy rental car was parked right behind the small economy car she'd owned for five years. She turned back just once and saw that Ellen was watching them go with an expression of satisfaction on her face.

If only she knew, Elizabeth thought. If only they both knew.

But they couldn't and that was that, she thought with a sigh of resignation. She would not destroy her daughter's life, not even for a few years of happiness for herself. The secret she'd kept all these years was so explosive it might destroy that prospect for happiness, as well.

Without another word, Brandon climbed into his own car and followed Elizabeth home. For one wild instant she wished she had the evasive skills of some TV criminal, who could skid around corners and lose the police car following. The effort would be wasted, anyway. If Brandon had tracked her to Ellen's house, then surely he could find her own.

As she drove up in front of the small stucco house with its red-tiled roof and pink bougainvillea climbing up the sides, she tried visualizing it through Brandon's eyes. It came up wanting, especially when stacked against that lovely, roomy old mansion he owned in Boston.

Once inside, he stalked through her house so possessively, she wondered if she'd ever be able to forget his presence here. He paused in front of a credenza on which there were pictures of both her daughters and all the grandchildren. The photo he lingered over, though, was the one of her on her wedding day.

"I always imagined you just this way," he said regretfully. His gaze met hers. "You were a beautiful bride, Lizzy. David Newton was a lucky man."

"I was the lucky one," she said staunchly.

He went back to studying the pictures one by one, picking them up and gazing at them, his expression sad. He put the one of Ellen back last and turned to face her.

"I've made up my mind to something, Lizzy. You might as well know it up front."

"What?" she said nervously.

"I won't leave California without you," he said. "I suppose I owe this visit to that detective, too."

"He did supply the addresses, if that's what you mean."

For the first time, she viewed the detective's invasion of her privacy as something less than romantic. "What else did he tell you?" she asked, a note of alarm in her voice.

"That was the gist of it," Brandon said, regarding her with an expression of puzzlement. "Why?"

To cover her anxiety she injected an edge of sarcasm into her tone. "I just wondered if he'd bothered to include the color of my wallpaper and made a note of the salon where I get my hair done."

"No, Lizzy," Brandon said impatiently. "Now stop trying to change the subject. Are you going with me or am I staying here?"

Her heart thumped harder with a beat that was surely as much anticipation as panic. She couldn't afford the eagerness. "You have to leave, Brandon. Alone. This is pure craziness. I can't just pick up and go traveling at the drop of a hat." She ignored the implied marriage proposal entirely.

"I don't see why not."

"Because I have responsibilities, a family."

"You're making up excuses, Lizzy. I wonder why? What are you so afraid of? Are you worried you will fall in love with me again, and then I'll disappear like before? I can promise you that won't happen. What I want for us means taking a risk, I know, but isn't that better than leading a lonely, solitary existence? Surely you feel something for me, enough to make a commitment, enough to build on."

Of course she did, she thought miserably. But that changed nothing for her. She had to deny her heart in favor of cool logic. "Brandon, what makes you so sure you know what I feel? No matter what you want to believe, I'm not the same silly girl you once knew."

He regarded her with an intensity that made her blood race. "Maybe not," he conceded. "But that daughter of yours didn't throw me out. In fact, she acted downright glad to see me. That must mean you've spoken of me favorably. I'll take that as a promising start."

The man had always had the perceptiveness of a clairvoyant, she thought dully. How could she convince him to go, when he read her so easily?

She weighed her options, then drew in a deep breath. "I told you before, Brandon. I'm willing to compromise. I'll travel with you, if you wish. I'll visit you in Boston as often as you like. But I won't marry you and I don't want you here." She recited the conditions as if they'd been etched in her mind, then waited for the explosion of impatience.

Instead he nodded slowly. "Okay," he said, his agreement coming far too readily. "I can see we're going to have to do this your way. We'll go to New Mexico to start with. There's a place there I've been wanting to visit. Pack your bags, woman. I'll call the airlines."

Despite herself, Elizabeth felt the dull pain in her chest begin to ease. A few days, she thought all too eagerly. She would have a few more days with Brandon before she did what had to be done and let him go.

Chapter 10

Brandon hadn't expected to win quite so easily. On the flight from Boston to Los Angeles, he'd come up with an entire arsenal of arguments to convince Lizzy to marry him or at the least to take off on an adventure with him. That she herself had again suggested they go away together delighted him. It didn't, however, erase his confusion over what the devil made her tick.

Now, more than ever before, he was puzzled by her almost panicky determination to keep him away from California. He had the sense she would have agreed to follow him to Timbuktu, if it had meant catching an earlier flight away from her home.

Brandon waited until they'd reached Albuquerque, settled into very proper, separate rooms in a hotel and found a lovely restaurant that served fiery Mexican food before he dared to broach the subject. Even then he took a circuitous route.

As he sipped a glass of fruity sangria, he studied the woman seated across from him, her blue eyes luminous in the candlelight, her gray hair softly feathering around her face.

"Having fun so far?" he asked.

Elizabeth smiled at him, clearly amused by his obvious impatience and his need for reassurance. "Brandon, we've only been gone a few hours. What do you expect me to say? The flight was smooth. The hotel seems quiet and clean. This salsa is the best I've ever eaten. Unless you want me to praise your tipping technique, I don't know what more I can say about the trip so far."

He chuckled. "Okay, make fun of me, but I'm damned proud of my tipping technique," he said. "I can calculate the proper percentage in no time. I can manage it in at least a half dozen foreign currencies as well."

"Then I assure you I'll praise your technique lavishly the next time the matter comes up, along with any of the other experiences we share."

He reached across the wooden table and rested his hand on top of hers.

Gazing deep into her eyes, he tried to read her thoughts. He couldn't.

"Seriously, Lizzy," he said then, "are you looking forward to all of this or have I simply pressured you into it by turning up on your doorstep?"

"You've done your share of pressuring and you know it, so don't look for absolution from me," she accused.

To his relief she didn't really sound angry about it. If anything, there was a teasing note in her voice.

"Even so," she admitted, "It's a heady thing at my

age to have a man sweep into town and carry me off to a place I've never seen before. It's the stuff romance novels are made of."

"And do you frequently indulge in romance novels?"

"They do remind me of a certain time in my life," she said with that now familiar wistful note in her voice.

"Dare I ask if that was the time you and I first spent together?"

"I suspect you'd dare just about anything. Don't fish for compliments, Brandon. You know remember those days just as vividly as you do." A nostalgic note crept into her voice. "There is nothing in a woman's life quite like falling in love for the first time. If you'd asked me a few months ago if I would ever have the chance to recapture those feelings, even in some small measure, I'd have told you no."

"Do you regret my finding you, Lizzy? Has it been…" He searched for the right word, the one that captured the impression he had of her nervousness. "Has it been difficult for you?"

Her gaze rose and collided with his. "Why would you ask that?"

More than the question itself, the tone of her response bordered on panic, it seemed to him, confirming what he'd guessed. "I asked because it's been obvious from the start that you don't want me around your family. Is that because you never told them about me?"

At first she looked at a loss for an answer. Finally she said, "It's not easy admitting to your children that you might have feet of clay."

"Then you think of that time in your life as a mistake?" he prodded. "Not a mistake exactly, but it was certainly an indiscretion. Neither of us were thinking clearly. We didn't have a bit of regard for the consequences."

"No. We were thinking more of life and death, more of love, than we were of the repercussions. I can't deny that. We might have been too impetuous, but our actions were rooted in love, Lizzy. Nothing less." He paused. "At least for me."

She sighed. "You're so sure of that, Brandon. Have you never doubted what we felt? Have you never once thought that maybe we were just caught up in all the drama of your leaving to fight overseas? We wouldn't have been the only couple to rush headlong into romance, thinking that there might be no tomorrow. Maybe it was nothing more than infatuation."

"No," he said with absolute certainty. "I think the fact that we are here together now proves the point. We have always held a place for each other in our hearts, even when we thought our paths might never cross again." He regarded her intently. "Or am I presuming too much?"

"No," she said softly and with a trace of reluctance. "I suppose I could deny it, but what would be the point? You may take far too many things for granted, but that's not one of them."

"You aren't feeling guilty because of that, are you?"

"Guilty? What on earth would I have to feel guilty about?" Elizabeth asked.

The denial was adamant, her tone clipped. Even more telling was the fact that her gaze slid away from his in a way that confirmed the very point he was making, despite her contradictory words.

Brandon deliberately shrugged with casual indifference, though he was filled with questions. "From my point of view, you've done nothing to feel guilty about. I'm not so sure, though, that you don't feel that you shortchanged David Newton in some essential way."

Again the response was lightning quick—too quick to Brandon's way of thinking.

"He never felt that way," she said.

He scooped up her hand and held it tight. Again, as they always were when she was most nervous, her fingers were like ice as they laced through his. Still he pressed her, ignoring the increasingly anxious expression in her eyes. He had this feeling that they were finally getting close to the truth. He sensed if he could just find the right question, he would unlock this mysterious attitude of hers that taunted him.

"I'm not talking about how David Newton felt, Lizzy. How did you feel? Are you feeling the weight of his blame even now for being here with me? Who are you cheating by being here tonight, sharing a full moon and a glass of sangria on this terrace, rather than being home alone?"

"No one," she said emphatically, but she withdrew her hand and covered the nervous gesture by quickly picking up her glass. "It's not as though we're doing anything immoral, for goodness' sake. I never thought of it that way even back then. It felt right to be with you from the very beginning."

"And now?"

"I'm not so sure I can describe the way it feels now."

"But not quite so right?" he said a little sadly. "Why not, Lizzy? What's changed? Now we have all the time in the world to get to know each other, to share adventures. No one will begrudge us that. Our children are grown. They don't need us anymore, despite what we may tell ourselves to feel useful. We've had full, satisfying careers. These are our precious golden years. It's time to live every minute to the fullest. Why can't you just relax at last and enjoy every experience?"

"I can't explain it," she evaded again, her gaze skittering away from his. "Can't or won't," he pressed. "Is there something you're hiding from me, Lizzy? Something you fear I'll discover if we spend too much time together?"

"No, of course not," she said in a rush of words that came out sounding far more nervous than convincing. She snatched up her purse and scooted from the booth as if she couldn't wait to escape. "I believe I'll visit the powder room before they bring our dinner. Will you excuse me, Brandon?"

He wanted to tell her no. He wanted to force Lizzy to sit right where she was and tell him what had her so worried. But the genuine panic in her eyes wouldn't allow it.

"Of course," he said, standing while she hurried away from the table. Away from answers.

Away from him.

While she was gone, he reluctantly resolved to probe no more that night. Whatever she was worried about would come out in due time, if he was patient. He sighed heavily. Lizzy always had asked things of him that taxed him. Patience was just one more thing to add to the list. Holding back alone ought to prove to her just how much he cared.

When she returned to the table, Brandon determinedly changed the subject and saw relief wash across her face. Her eyes brightened, and in no time at all they were laughing together as they once had, laughing as if they had not a care in the world. Whatever dark undercurrents he'd felt earlier seemed no more than a distant memory.

They walked back to the hotel, hand in hand like a couple of kids. The sky was filled with stars, diamonds on black velvet with a showy full moon. The temperature had fallen, bringing a chill to the air. Even with a delicate, lacy shawl of pale pink wool tossed around her shoulders, Lizzy shivered.

Brandon shrugged out of his jacket and draped it over her shoulders, allowing his arm to linger in a casual embrace once he was done.

"Have you ever seen such a sky, Lizzy?" he asked, looking up at the cover of brilliant stars.

"Certainly not in Los Angeles," she said dryly. "With our smog, I'm lucky to get a decent view of the moon."

"Then I'm going to make a proposal."

"Oh?" she said, sounding cautious.

He smiled at her. "Come on, Lizzy. What I'm proposing is not indecent."

"That remains to be seen."

"Quiet, woman. Let me get it out. I propose that you and I spend the next few weeks auditioning the skies in all the corners of the globe until we find one that's perfect. What do you say?"

"It sounds romantic," she said with an undeniable eagerness, which gave way at once to sober reflection. "And impractical."

"Forget impractical. We can do anything we want, remember?" he asked, turning her until she faced him. He could read the wistfulness in her eyes, then the hesitation. "Come on, Lizzy. Say yes."

Seconds turned into minutes as their gazes clashed. "Lizzy?"

"Okay, yes," she said, a trifle breathlessly. She drew in a deep breath, squared her shoulders and met his gaze evenly, adding more firmly, "Yes, Brandon. I think we should."

"That's a verbal contract now," he teased. "I'll hold you to it."

"Brandon, tell me something," she teased right back. "Do you always get your own way?"

"Almost always, at least until I met you."

"Then perhaps it's good that I say no once in a while."

"It probably is," he agreed. "Just don't make a practice of it, Lizzy. I might get discouraged."

"Something tells me a challenge never discourages you. It only draws out your competitive spirit. Just look at the way you turned up in L.A., after vowing never to chase after me."

Brandon touched a finger to her chin and tilted her head up so he could look directly into her eyes. "Don't you try telling me that was a test, Elizabeth Newton. I won't believe it."

"Whether it was or it wasn't, the result's the same. We're here together now. What puzzles me is why I can't seem to resist you, no matter how hard I try. My daughters would tell you that I'm stubborn as a mule, unshakable in my convictions and a stick-in-the-mud of the first order."

"Funny," he observed. "I hadn't noticed your inability to resist me. Does that mean if I were to try to kiss you now, you wouldn't slap me?"

Rather than waiting for her response, he lowered his head until his lips were no more than a hairbreadth from hers. He could feel the soft whisper of her breath on his face as he heard it quicken.

"Ah, Lizzy," he said with a sigh, right before he slanted his mouth over hers, capturing either protest or acquiescence.

Elizabeth felt as if the world had suddenly tilted and the ground had fallen away. Brandon's kiss stole her breath and left her dizzy. If she'd experienced the same symptoms anywhere other than in his embrace, she thought wryly, she'd have taken herself straight off to a doctor. It had been a long time since she'd known the head-spinning whirl of a man's passionate kiss. Since being reunited with Brandon, it was becoming a habit.

A wonderful, frightening, exciting, dangerous habit! How was she supposed to resist a man who considered it his duty to turn her world topsy-turvy? What possible defenses could she mount against a man who thought nothing of whisking her off to the far corners of the earth just to compare the brightness of the stars? There was clearly nothing tentative or halfway about the way Brandon intended to pursue her. She would have to struggle to keep her wits about her. She'd done that once and lost to his more persuasive determination.

She would fight harder this time, she thought, just as soon as she knew every nuance of this kiss. When she tired of the way his lips coaxed, when she grew bored with the way his tongue invaded, when she no longer felt this dark, delicious swirl of temptation, then she would fend off his advances. However at the moment, with her pulse scrambling and her insides melting, that seemed eons away.

Elizabeth was shaky when Brandon finally released her, as shaky as she had been the very first time he stole a kiss. Back then, though she'd acted bold, she'd been new to a woman's lures, newer yet to a man's commanding, overpowering sensuality. From that first instant she had known that she belonged with Brandon in an inevitable way she had never belonged with another man. She felt complete in his embrace, radiant beneath his gaze, sensual beneath his touch.

Once he'd vanished from her life, she had convinced herself that what she'd felt was no more than the product of a child's romantic fantasies.

She'd given up any expectation of feeling that way again. She had settled for what she knew now had been second best. That didn't make her marriage to David Newton a bad bargain. Perhaps just a misguided one. She hoped he'd never, ever known that.

Discovering, back in Boston, that she could recapture these incredible, spilling-through-the-sky feelings had both delighted and dismayed her.

While it proved, as Penny's health book contested, that age was no barrier to sexuality, it also indicated that Brandon was the one partner who was expert at stirring her senses.

Perhaps she had fled California to protect a lifetime of secrets, but the action very definitely had a positive side. For as long as it lasted, she would know the wonder of Brandon's love again. As long as he didn't press her for any more than this, she would be content, ecstatic in fact.

She was still under the spell of his kiss when they reached the hotel.

Outside her room, he took her key and opened the door in a charmingly old-fashioned gesture of gallantry, then stepped carefully aside to let her enter.

Her blood raced with anticipation as she met his gaze and saw that familiar spark of desire in his eyes. She had newer, far more recent memories of all the promises that look implied.

He held out his hand and after an instant she took it, then started at the press of cold metal against her palm.

"Your key," he said, grinning smugly at her astonishment. "Good night, Lizzy."

Before she could recover from the shock, before the stir of disappointment could begin, he had strolled away, whistling under his breath. When Brandon had been a jaunty, self-confident young airman, that whistling had pleased her. Now it began to grate on her nerves.

She was tempted to march down the hall after him, then tried to envision herself demanding to know why the man had no intention of sleeping with her. Worse yet, she tried to imagine someone overhearing. It was too ludicrous and humiliating to contemplate.

Wide-awake and all stirred up, she slammed the door to her room with a moderately satisfying thud. Her only regret was that she hadn't caught some part of that sneaky man's anatomy between the door and the jamb.

She turned the television on full blast, soaked herself in a hot tub filled with the fragrant bath salts supplied by the hotel, then ordered a brandy sent up from the bar. She was still muttering about Brandon's low-down tactics and getting pleasantly drowsy, when the phone rang.

"Yes," she snapped, knowing instinctively it was him. "Having trouble sleeping?" Brandon inquired lightly. "What makes you ask a thing like that?"

"I was having a nightcap in the bar when I heard your order come in. Then I heard the TV when I passed by on my way back to my room. I can't be sure, but it also sounded as if you might be cussing a blue streak in there."

"Listen to me, you cantankerous old man," she began, then caught herself. Two could play at his game. Her tone was sweet as honey, when she added, "I've just spent a relaxing hour in a bubble bath. Didn't you mention that honeysuckle is one of your favorite scents?"

He cleared his throat suspiciously. "Okay, Lizzy, what are you up to?"

"Me?" she inquired innocently. "I'm just enjoying the luxury of this big queen-size bed. The sheets are so nice and cool against my skin."

She couldn't be absolutely certain, but it sounded as if he'd groaned. "I feel absolutely decadent, lying here naked," she added for good measure. "Good night, Brandon."

This time she was certain that he groaned as she quietly hung the phone up. There were a few benefits to getting old, she decided. At the top of the list was the ability to give as good as you got. She switched off the light and snuggled beneath the covers. Minutes later she was sound asleep.

And minutes after that, her dreams turned downright steamy.

Chapter 11

When the phone in his room rang, Brandon was shaving and thinking of the sly way Lizzy had gotten even with him the night before. Anticipating her on the phone, he was unprepared for Kevin's voice.

"Dad, what the devil are you doing in New Mexico?" he asked, sounding thoroughly miffed. "I heard you went to California. Even that I got secondhand."

"Good morning to you, too, son," Brandon said, keeping a tight rein on his own temper. He didn't want to get in some shouting match with a man who'd been warned to avoid stress. He especially didn't want to risk alienating the son from whom he'd already been estranged once. His tone mild, he added, "You'd have got it from the horse's mouth if you'd been in your office when I looked for you on the day I left."

"So it's my fault that I have to find out from my

son that my father is chasing around the country after some woman?"

"I'm on vacation," Brandon corrected. "Besides, what does it matter to you which state I'm in? I'm retired. You and Jason are in charge."

"Pardon me if I don't take your name off the letterhead just yet. You have a way of changing your mind."

"I'm entitled," he grumbled. "Now was there a reason for this call? I have places to go."

"What places?"

"I'm in Albuquerque. Get a guidebook and figure it out."

"Dad, you are straining my patience."

"I know the feeling."

"Is that woman with you?"

"*That woman* has a name."

He heard Kevin suck in his breath before he finally said more calmly, "Is Mrs. Newton with you?"

"As a matter of fact, yes."

Kevin groaned. "I knew it. I just knew it. Dad, she's trying to get her hooks into you."

"You've got that backward and we've already had this discussion once. I don't expect to have it again," he snapped, then reminded himself that Kevin's concern quite likely stemmed from having his mother replaced in Brandon's affections.

"Son, my being here with Lizzy isn't some sort of slap at your mother," he said more calmly. "I cared very deeply for your mother, but she's gone now. Nobody's sorrier about that than I am, but I don't want to spend the rest of my days all alone. Your mother wouldn't want that for me, either. If you'd give Lizzy a chance, I'm sure you'd come to love her."

"Love her?" Kevin echoed dully. "Does that mean you're planning on her becoming an important part of your life?"

"For a man who deals in bottom lines, you sure have a way of dancing around the real question on your mind. I would be very proud to have her marry me. So far, though, she's not so inclined. Now, if you don't mind, I'm going to hang up. This conversation is making me cranky."

"Me, too," Kevin said as he thumped the receiver back on the hook.

Brandon wondered idly if it was possible to disown his son at this late date. He glanced in the mirror and caught the scowl on his face and forced a smile. "Just getting a taste of your own medicine," he said ruefully to his reflection. It seemed all the Halloran men were genetically inclined to meddle.

In the long run, Kevin would come around, he decided. Lacey and Jason were far more understanding. Dana was downright tickled to be a coconspirator. They all could probably make Kevin see reason eventually.

And if he didn't, so be it. Brandon figured he had enough on his mind trying to win Lizzy over without worrying about his son, too.

The thought of Lizzy had him rushing to get ready. He hadn't been this anxious to start a day since she'd left Boston weeks earlier.

Unfortunately before he left the room he made the mistake of answering the phone again.

"Dad?"

Lord, give me patience, he thought. "What is it now, Kevin?"

"I know you said you didn't want to discuss this again, but I have to ask you one thing. You hired a detective to find this Mrs. Newton for you, didn't you?"

"Yes. What's your point?"

"Did you have him look into the sort of life she's been leading since you last saw her?"

"What the devil kind of question is that to be asking? Are you implying that there's something shady about Lizzy? If you are, you couldn't be more off base. She's a fine woman. Now, I've had about all I can take of your innuendos and slurs. Maybe it's just my comeuppance for putting in my two cents worth about Lacey, but I was wrong then and *you* are wrong now. Am I making myself clear?" he said, angrier than he'd ever been with his son.

Apparently Kevin sensed his wrath. He sighed heavily. "I'm sorry, Dad.

You're right. It's none of my business."

"Thank you."

"You will stay in touch, though?"

"I'm in New Mexico, not some primitive backwoods in the Amazon. They've got phones here. I'll use 'em. Now stop worrying before Lacey comes after me for ruining your recuperation. Goodbye."

"Goodbye, Dad." There was a hesitation, then, "I do love you, you know."

Brandon felt the sting of unexpected tears. "I love you, too, Kevin. Give my love to Lacey and Jason. And tell Dana she is not to have that baby until I get back."

"She says you already warned her. She also says if you want her to delay things one second longer than nine months, then you can come back here and lumber around in her place."

Brandon was chuckling when he hung up. "I guess I'd better hurry Lizzy along, if I want to be back in Boston for the birth of that great-grandbaby," he said as he closed the door to his room behind him.

In many ways, she and Brandon were perfectly suited traveling companions, Elizabeth thought as they took a midday break for lunch several days into the trip. In fact, she could already see that traveling with Brandon would be more torment than fulfillment, precisely because she was starting to recognize just how much she was destined to give up.

How would she explain walking away when it was obvious to anyone how compatible they were? She had a natural curiosity about everything, and Brandon seemed to have an unlimited store of knowledge and the patience to share it.

Even more important, they had similar views about the pace of their days. They lingered and explored. They enjoyed a stop for a glass of wine and idle conversation every bit as much as they did a visit to some must-see historical sight. Maybe they'd go home having missed a few places, but they'd have pleasurable impressions of everywhere they had been.

Impressions and snapshots, she corrected with a trace of amusement.

She'd never seen a man so taken with a camera. He'd shot a dozen rolls of film already, most of it of her.

"What will you do with all those pictures?" she'd asked, laughing as he urged her to pose yet again.

"Carry 'em in my wallet. Now just climb up on that boulder," he'd insisted, pointing out a rocky ledge. "A little higher. Yes, that's perfect," he said as she teetered on the edge with a straight drop into a dried-up creek bed behind her. "This one will be a dandy."

He'd been so positive of that, he had rushed the entire roll of film to a same-day photo shop and waited impatiently while they'd been developed. When the pictures were finally spread on the counter for his inspection, he zeroed in on his favorite, a long-distance shot with wildflowers spread at her feet. He nodded in satisfaction.

"That one," he told the clerk. "Make me an eleven-by-fourteen print. In fact, make me four of them."

Lizzy stared at him. "What on earth for?"

"One each for your daughters, one for my den and one for my bedside until the day I can talk you into marrying me."

She was stunned into silence by the sweet gesture. "What are you thinking?" he demanded.

"I thought you always knew."

"Not always. Spill it. What put that look on your face?"

"I was just thinking what a remarkable man you are."

He nodded in satisfaction. "Good, then. We're making progress." Some days he marked the advancement of their relationship in tiny, intangible measures. On other occasions, he anticipated giant leaps. Elizabeth liked the quiet, leisurely, undemanding days the best. They'd courted once under terrible time constraints. There was something tantalizing about setting an undemanding pace, especially with a man used to grabbing what he wanted without a second's thought or effort.

"I'm surprised with the kind of life you lead, that

you don't want to rush through everything," she told him as they lingered over a ridiculously large lunch that began with a spicy corn chowder and ended with light-as-air sopaipillas dusted with cinnamon and drizzled with honey.

"I've spent my whole life rushing. I deserve to slow down and savor things," he said, his glance fixed on her mouth in a way that left no doubts at all about just what he'd like to be savoring. She caught herself licking her lips self-consciously as he added, "I'd rather see one thing in a day and enjoy it, than visit a dozen places and wind up remembering none of them."

"Have you been to New Mexico before?"

"No, but it was at the top of my list. I read an article sometime back about a small town called Chimayo between Santa Fe and Taos. We'll go there one of these days."

"Is one of the Indian pueblos there?"

"No, but there's a family of weavers there that goes back seven generations to the early 1800s. I can't wait to see how they work. A friend discovered them and sent me one of their small rugs."

She regarded him with amusement. "Somehow I don't think you're nearly as committed to this idea of retirement as you say you are."

"Kevin said much the same thing the other day." She regarded him curiously. "He called? When?"

"Tuesday. Wednesday. I'm not sure."

"Why didn't you mention it earlier?"

"I suppose because I didn't want to get into the reason for his call."

"Us," she said bluntly. "He doesn't approve of us traveling together."

"Something like that."

He reached across the table and brushed a strand of hair back from her face with a gentleness that had her heart constricting in her chest. There was so much affection in his touch, so much yearning in his eyes.

"I'm sorry his call upset you," Lizzy said quietly.

"It didn't upset me," he said, though to her ears it didn't sound as if there was much conviction behind the denial.

"Then why do you look so sad?"

Brandon smiled at her then. "I didn't realize I did. Especially since being with you makes me very happy."

"How long can that go on, though, if your son doesn't approve?"

"Dammit, Lizzy, he'll come around. Besides, we're not a couple of teenagers who need permission to get married, much less to see each other." Though there was a glint of determination in his eyes and an unyielding strength behind his tough words, Lizzy couldn't help but think Brandon was deluding himself. Kevin's opinion mattered to him, just as Kate's and Ellen's mattered to her. She and Brandon were the kind of people who had always centered their lives around family. They couldn't very well start denying the strength of the ties at this late date.

In the long run, though, what did it really matter? she thought with an air of resignation. She had no intention of ever marrying Brandon, so his relationship with his son would never be tested. It might get bruised a little perhaps, but it would never be irrevocably broken.

Determined to banish all dark thoughts for the remainder of whatever time they did have together, Elizabeth deliberately changed the subject. "Where are we going next?"

"I thought an art gallery," he said eagerly. "Perfect."

At the gallery, though, she noted he seemed far more interested in a close inspection of the attire worn by the Indians in the spectacular Western paintings, than he did in each artist's skill with a brush.

That, added to the comments he'd made earlier about the town they would visit in a few days, gave her the leverage she knew she would need when the time came to send him back to Boston and for her to return to California alone.

Elizabeth thought of her argument often over the next few days, turning the precise words over and over in her head, preparing herself for the separation she knew was inevitable. In so doing, she knew she was robbing herself of the precious time they did have. The internal torment cast a pall over everything they did.

Instead of being grateful that Brandon continued to insist on being a perfect gentleman, retreating nightly to his own room, Elizabeth grew increasingly frustrated. She didn't want her last memories of him to be of their increasingly strained conversations, their fleeting, innocuous touches. She tried her darnedest to recall the precise techniques of seduction practiced by some of the more skilled heroines in the books she read. Then she moaned aloud at the absurdity of her imitating them.

"The next thing you know, you'll be calling up your granddaughter and asking to borrow her health class textbook," she grumbled to herself as she tossed and turned through another night. "Silly, old woman," she added for good measure, but she didn't feel silly and she didn't feel old. She felt like a woman who was falling in love all over again and the roller-coaster thrill of it was nearly irresistible.

The curtains in her room billowed as the dry, desert air stirred and sent its chill across the room and through her heart. Bleak thoughts of long, empty days tormented her.

"Lizzy, is something wrong?" Brandon inquired the next morning over his spartan breakfast of black coffee and the half grapefruit she'd insisted he add to his menu. "You have shadows under your eyes. Haven't you been sleeping well?"

There was genuine concern in his voice, and for once his expression wasn't smug.

Elizabeth toyed with her own grapefruit sections. "I'm fine," she said without much spunk.

"We aren't moving around too fast, are we? We could settle in one place for a few weeks, if you'd rather. Maybe Taos. We could be there this afternoon."

"Are you sure you've seen everything you wanted to see in Santa Fe?"

"I've seen enough," he said, which wasn't really an answer to her question. "Now let me tell you more about Chimayo. We'll stop there on the way to Taos."

As they veered off the highway between Sante Fe and Taos, he began describing the small town, which was no more than a dot on the map, with an intimacy that suggested he'd been there often.

"Brandon, how many guidebooks did you read before you came to California?" she teased. "Is that all you did with your days after I left Boston?"

"No. I had no way of knowing we'd end up in New Mexico. This was just a spur-of-the-moment decision when I realized my being in California made you uncomfortable. I figured it was as good a place to run to as any."

"Then how do you know so much about Chimayo?"

"Like I told you the other day, when you love textiles as much as I do, you stumble across other people who feel the same way. The Ortegas in Chimayo are like that from all I've read about them."

She smiled faintly at his exuberance. "So this is a busman's holiday, after all, despite those staunch denials you made the other day. I suppose you'll want to adapt what you see and work it into the Halloran line for next year."

"Maybe so. I admit to having an insatiable curiosity when it comes to this kind of thing. I think southwestern style is very popular these days. Wouldn't hurt to tap into that market."

In the showrooms, Brandon headed straight for the bright room to one side where a young man worked at his craft on a hand loom that was primitive by comparison to the modern machinery in Brandon's Boston plant. Threads of darkest brown and indigo slowly formed a pattern in the beige rug he was creating.

Elizabeth found herself grinning as Brandon edged closer and closer to study the weaver's technique. He asked one question, nodded at the response and fingered the yarns being used. That one question opened the floodgate to more.

Sensing that Brandon would be engaged for hours, Elizabeth explored the attached showroom and a second one next door. She picked up souvenirs for Ellen and

Kate, books about the Southwest for her grandchildren and a small rug that would fit perfectly in her foyer for herself. Satisfied with her purchases, she lingered outdoors, taking in the unspoiled scenery.

When she finally went back inside, Brandon was still engrossed, this time with the woven jackets and vests on display. Elizabeth seized the evidence of his absorption and determined that the time was rapidly coming when she would have to use it as her only weapon to cut the ties between them.

Hours later, alone in a new hotel room, she stared silently out the window and prayed for the strength to do what had to be done, before she lost the will to do it at all.

The phone rang and she grabbed it, hoping that just this once Brandon's iron will had weakened and he would come share the night with her. To her disappointment, it was Ellen's voice that greeted her.

"Hi, Mom. I got your message, but I must say I'm surprised to catch you in this early."

"Brandon and I are both morning people. We usually get started at dawn."

"I hope I'm not interrupting anything," Ellen said, her voice thick with teasing innuendo.

"No, my darling daughter. Now, tell me, what's happening in Los Angeles."

"Nothing new here. I must say, though, that I've been wondering how things are going out there. You slipped out of town practically in the dead of night. Were you afraid Kate and I would talk you out of going?"

"Not you. You're the sort who'd hold the ladder if someone wanted to climb up and carry me off to elope."

"Kate, then?"

"Ellen, we both know how Kate reacts to anything she considers a betrayal of your father. Add that to her general view of romance and she's probably not very happy with me now."

"No, she isn't," Ellen admitted. "That's why I'm calling. I barely prevented her from getting on a plane and flying off to rescue you."

"It will probably make her feel better to know that I expect to be back in Los Angeles in a day or two."

"Is Mr. Halloran coming with you?"

"No, dear. I think not."

"But why?" she asked, her disappointment evident. "I just think it's best that way."

"Okay, Mother, what's going on? Did you two have a spat?"

"No. I just think it's wiser if we don't turn our lives upside down at this late date."

"What on earth is that supposed to mean? Surely you don't think you're too old to fall in love, especially with a man who's obviously head over heels for you? As for getting married at your age, why not? I know some couples don't because it affects their Social Security payments or something, but somehow I doubt that's an issue with a man like Brandon Halloran. He looks as if he has buckets of money."

"More likely barrels," she said dryly. "I'm not saying we'll lose touch entirely again, just that there's no reason to commit to anything drastic."

"Since when did you think of marriage as a drastic measure? That sounds like Kate talking, not you."

"Dear, your sister may be foolish with regard to her

own social life, but she does occasionally have a valid point."

"Not about this," Ellen argued. "Mother, if you're having fun, don't run away from it. Surely you don't think you could be happy with one of those old geezers in polyester at the community center?"

"No. Maybe not," she said wearily. "Darling, I'm very tired. It's been a long day. We'll discuss this more when I get home. Right now I'd like to get some sleep."

"Okay," Ellen agreed with obvious reluctance. "I love you."

"I love you, too." She just hoped that Ellen never discovered the lengths to which she was going to prove that.

Brandon was wakened from a sound sleep by the ringing of the phone.

He fumbled for it, then said hello in a voice husky with sleep. "Mr. Halloran?"

"Yes," he said, his heart suddenly hammering at the unfamiliar voice.

Kevin? Jason? Had something happened to one of them? "This is Ellen Hayden, Elizabeth Newton's daughter."

What on earth? He struggled upright in the bed and clutched the receiver even tighter. "Yes, Ellen. What can I do for you?"

"I thought there was something you ought to know," she said after a slight hesitation.

He heard a soft moan, then a mumbled comment that sounded something like, "Mother is going to kill me for this."

He had a feeling she hadn't meant him to hear the

last remark. He swallowed a chuckle. "What do you think I should know?"

"Mother seems to have some crazy idea about packing up and coming home."

Brandon felt as if the wind had been knocked out of him. "What? How do you know that? She hasn't said anything like that to me. We've just begun to see all the places we've talked about going to."

"That may be, but I just got off the phone with her and she told me she'd be back here in a day or so. When I asked why, she said some things that made absolutely no sense. I thought you ought to be prepared."

His heart thudded dully. "Prepared how? I can't very well hog-tie her and make her stay here with me, if she doesn't want to."

"But that's exactly what I think you should do," Ellen said with conviction. "I don't mean hog-tie her exactly. Oh, you know what I mean. Just don't take her words at face value. I'm convinced she's in love with you, but she's finding all kinds of excuses not to be. You do love her, don't you? I probably should have asked that straight off."

"I love her," he said, his voice tight. "And thank you for the warning. Elizabeth won't slip away from me, not without the fight of her life."

"I'm glad," Ellen said. "Good night, Mr. Halloran."

"Good night," he said softly. He had a hunch that Ellen was very much her mother's daughter and that they both spent a lot of time with stars in their eyes. All he had to do was figure out why his precious Lizzy was so damned determined to deny that.

Chapter 12

Brandon woke up at dawn with an oppressive sense of foreboding. It took him less than a minute to recall why. Ellen's late-night warning, he thought with dismay. He was grateful that she'd told him, but now that he knew, what was he supposed to do about it?

How the devil was he supposed to talk Lizzy out of going home? If he hadn't convinced her by now of the strength and endurance of their love, how could he expect to do it in the space of a single conversation or even a single act of passion? That one tender, memorable night they'd shared in Boston weeks ago certainly hadn't gotten through to her. She'd dashed off first thing the next morning as if all the hounds of hell were after her.

Tricks were out. So was hog-tying, despite its appeal to his take-charge nature. Persuasive words hadn't worked. What the dickens was left? Hell, he'd inundated her with flowers once, only to have her grumble about her allergies. He'd tried candy. He'd tried sentiment. He'd dusted off just about every last thing in his court- ship repertoire. He was getting too damned old for all this mincing around. Maybe he ought to fly her to Las Vegas, stand her in front of a minister and dare her to say anything short of "I do."

Before he could come up with a plan, his phone rang. "Mr. Halloran?"

"Yes?"

"This is John Vecchio."

His heart seemed to constrict at the unexpected sound of the detective's voice. "How did you track me down?" he inquired testily.

"Finding people is what I'm best at," the man reminded him. "But why would you even be looking for me?"

"Actually I was doing a job for someone else and something came up I thought you had a right to know about since it fits in with the investigation I was doing for you."

"Who hired you?" Brandon asked with deadly calm. He suspected he already knew the answer, and if he was right, there was going to be hell to pay back in Boston.

"That's confidential," the detective replied glibly.

"If the person who hired you is confidential, then it seems to me whatever you learned ought to be, too. Am I right?"

The man had the grace to sputter a bit at that. "Well, yes, I suppose. Although in this instance, it was made quite clear that you were to get the report."

Brandon lost it at that. Whatever curiosity he might normally have felt was overshadowed by fury. "Well, you tell your client, whoever the hell he might be, that he can take his damned report and… Well, never mind. He'll get the picture."

"But, sir, I think he's right. You'd definitely want to know this."

"No," Brandon said adamantly, "I wouldn't."

He slammed the phone back into its cradle and stood staring at it as if it were a nasty rattler about to strike. Before he could think twice, he snatched it back up and punched in Kevin's office number. When his secretary, Harriet answered, he demanded to speak to his son.

"He's on another line," she said. She served all three Halloran men but she'd been with Brandon the longest and knew all of his moods. She tried to buy Kevin some time. "Shall I have him call you back?"

"No, you'll get him off whatever damned call he's on and put me through. If he knows what's good for him, he'll get on this line before I completely lose my patience."

"Yes, sir," Harriet said. "Is everything all right, Mr. Halloran?"

"Do I sound as if everything's all right?"

"No, not really."

"That's very perceptive of you, Harriet. Now get Kevin."

"Yes, of course. I'm sorry, sir."

If he could have paced the room with the phone in his hand, he'd have done it. Instead, the short cord kept him in place, which added to his foul temper.

"Dad?" Kevin said finally. "What's wrong?"

"You know damned good and well what's wrong. You hired that detective, didn't you? How did you know which one to go to? Did you have Mrs. Farnsworth go digging around in my desk for you?"

Kevin sighed. "No, actually the bill happened to come in yesterday. I know you're probably upset, Dad. But it's better that you know this now, before you get in any deeper."

"Kevin, I know everything I need to know about Elizabeth. I told you that before and I meant it. I refused to listen to a word that detective had to say. The only reason I'm calling you is to tell you once and for all that I have had enough of your ridiculous suspicions and your meddling. If you ever expect to see me again, if you ever expect to have a civil conversation with me, you will drop this now!"

"But, Dad—"

"Goodbye," Brandon said. He hung up and then called the hotel operator. "I want no more calls put through to this room. None."

Whatever the hell his son had found out or thought he'd discovered didn't matter. He took a deep, calming breath and shoved his hand through his hair. He couldn't be at his persuasive best with Lizzy if he was all worked up like this. He deliberately forced himself to empty his mind, to dismiss the past fifteen minutes as if they'd never happened.

He could hardly wait to leave the entire incident behind. As a result, when he stepped out of his room and walked over to Elizabeth's, he still didn't have a detailed plan in mind. He rapped on the door. She took so long coming, he wondered if she'd fled during the night, and he found that more worrisome by far than any slander Kevin had intended to spread.

The door opened and Brandon's gaze took in the cool linen slacks, the rose-colored blouse, the careful makeup that made her eyes seem brighter and more compelling than ever, but didn't hide the shadows beneath. His heart ached at the prospect of losing her, especially without ever understanding why.

"Morning, Lizzy," he said and before he even realized what he intended, he hauled her into his arms for a bruising kiss that left them both gasping for breath.

"What on earth?" she murmured, her expression bemused. Her hands clung to his shoulders. "Brandon, have you taken leave of your senses?"

"No, Lizzy. I don't believe so. I believe I've just come to my senses."

"What is that supposed to mean?"

"It's just fair warning, woman. You and I have some serious things to talk about today. I figure on having a hearty breakfast and some straight answers." He scowled when he said it, so she'd know he meant business.

"About what?" she asked warily.

"Whatever you're up to," he said, figuring the enigmatic answer could take whatever meaning she wanted it to.

She immediately looked guilty, and he knew then that Ellen's fears weren't unfounded. Lizzy intended to run from him.

And, despite the way his son felt about it, Brandon intended to do everything he could to prevent her going.

Brandon certainly was in an odd mood this morning, Elizabeth thought edgily as she tried to recover from that breath-stealing kiss and the knockout punch of his warning. It was a mood that told her she'd been right to pick now as the time to flee. She couldn't withstand many more kisses like that one, not if she wanted to keep a clear head. As for answers, she had plenty. Yet none of them were likely to be the ones he wanted.

They settled at a table on an outdoor terrace, surrounded by flowering cactus. Brandon was as good as his word. He ordered bacon, eggs, hash browns and blueberry muffins. Without sparing her a glance, he ordered the same for her. Apparently he figured on needing stamina for the conversation he intended to have.

Elizabeth looked at all that food, considered the implications and felt her stomach churn. She tried to will herself to say the words she'd rehearsed again and again during the night.

A simple goodbye should have come easily, especially since she knew all the reasons why it had to be said. After all, they had parted twice before. If nothing else, practice should have made the phrasing perfect. But this one made her heart ache because she knew it was irrevocable. Brandon had put pride, love and commitment on the line by chasing after her. He wouldn't take yet another rejection.

Elizabeth surreptitiously studied him and dreaded ruining the morning.

Maybe she could wait until after breakfast, she decided, furious at the weakness that that implied, but grateful for the reprieve.

What was so terrible? she argued with herself. She was putting it off a half hour, an hour at most. Sitting across the breakfast table from Brandon had become one of the highlights of her day. There was an intimacy to sharing the first part of the day with him that she knew she'd never forget.

A sigh trembled on her lips. How she would miss the easy, companionable talks about the news, the thrill of studying his face as his expressions shifted from amusement to sorrow, from troubled to angry as he studied the headlines. Even more, she would miss the lazy planning of their day.

Capturing every last memory she could, she delayed telling him as long as possible. They were through breakfast and Brandon was on his second cup of coffee by the time she found the courage.

"Brandon, I've come to a decision," Lizzy blurted finally, seizing the initiative he had threatened to steal. She desperately needed whatever edge might be gained by saying her piece first.

"About what?" he inquired, lowering the newspaper he'd been reading for the past ten minutes. His gaze locked with hers. His brow furrowed in a show of concern. "What is it, Lizzy? You sound so serious."

"I am serious. I'm going home."

The paper slid from his grasp as an expression she judged to be incredulous spread across his face. Or was it astonishment, after all? she wondered after a moment's study. Her own gaze narrowed. Brandon looked as if he'd actually anticipated the announcement, but how could that be?

"Why?" he inquired with no evidence of the fury she'd expected.

Instead, he was all solicitous concern. "Aren't you feeling well?"

"I feel just fine," she mumbled, trying to figure out

where she'd missed the mark with her strategy. Not that she'd wanted him to fight her decision, but this absolute calm was definitely disconcerting.

"Are you homesick already? Do you miss your family? I must say I'm rather glad mine's out from underfoot."

"It's not that," she said, increasingly uncomfortable under his penetrating eyes. This was the part she'd hoped to avoid, this intense scrutiny of her motives. She didn't want to have to sugarcoat the truth. She was no good at it.

"What is it then?" he asked.

She could explain part of it, but certainly not all. She drew in a deep breath and tried to tell him what was in her heart. "I went against everything that was right and proper more than forty years ago. I can't do it again."

Lizzy wasn't surprised that Brandon regarded her as if she'd lost her marbles. The sudden surge of propriety was rather belated.

"What the devil are you talking about?" he asked.

"This," she said with a gesture that encompassed the terrace, the inn, maybe even all of New Mexico. "We're sneaking around like a couple of adolescents."

"There's one surefire way to fix that," he countered without missing a beat. "Marry me."

She was just as quick to respond. "No," she said in a rush before she dared to consider the offer. The rest came more slowly, because she had to make it up as she went along, watching his reactions, altering the excuse as necessary. "I can't leave my family and you can't leave your work. I saw that yesterday."

"Saw what, for goodness' sake?" he asked, his expression thoroughly puzzled.

He still wasn't angry, though. She found his lack of outrage just a little insulting. "You," she said grumpily. "At that weaving place. You'll never truly retire, Brandon. You love it too much. You belong back in Boston with your business, your friends, your family."

Once again he looked only slightly surprised. "Just because I looked at some old rugs, you're ready to throw away everything?"

"I won't take you away from that." If she'd meant it to sound noble, she failed miserably. Even to her own ears, she sounded like a woman grasping at straws.

"You're not taking me away from a damn thing, woman. You're giving me a future." His gaze narrowed. "Lizzy, what's really going on with you? I've never heard such a trumped-up batch of excuses from a woman in all my days. Even forty-nine years ago you were more inventive."

"Think what you will," she said stubbornly. "That's the way it has to be. You're not ready for retirement."

Despite her best intentions, tears sprang to her eyes as she confronted the actuality of losing him. He was on his feet in a heartbeat then, gathering her into his arms. Suddenly all she wanted to do was weep and have him promise that everything was going to work out just fine. When a man like Brandon said such a thing, he had a way of making it happen. She wondered, though, if even he could perform miracles.

"Oh, Lizzy," he soothed. "I'll never set foot in that company of mine again, if that's what you're worried about. It's time for Jason and Kevin to have their turn, anyway. Now tell me what's really behind all this. No man could love a woman more than I love you, more than I have loved you all these years. Surely you know that."

"But why?" she said miserably. "Why do you love me?"

"That's like asking why the sky is blue, Lizzy. It just is. From the moment I saw you running barefoot through the grass all those years ago in Maine, something within me turned inside out. There was a look about you, such a joyous zest for living. I felt as if being around you would be like basking in sunshine my whole life."

"That was so long ago, though. You were about to go off to war. You knew you could be killed. It was natural to want to grab hold of life. But what about now?"

"Nothing's changed," he said gently. "I still see endless possibilities when I look into your eyes. I still hear bells ringing when I hear your voice. I still feel sunshine when I touch you."

The beautiful, tender words spilled over Lizzy like a cozy comforter, wrapping her in warmth. The only problem was they were based on a dreadful misperception.

Those words he'd suffused with so much love brought on a fresh bout of tears and decades worth of self-recriminations. How could he possibly love her, when she knew for a fact she was a liar and a cheat?

"You don't know me, Brandon. I've done terrible things," she blurted out, then almost died from the regret that ripped through her. She'd done it now. She had really done it. He would poke and prod until the truth came out. All of it.

"Shh, Lizzy. Hush that kind of talk," he whispered, rubbing her back. Brandon scooped her up, then sat back down and settled her on his lap, oblivious to everything and everyone around them. She wanted with all her heart to rest her head on his shoulder and pretend that there were no problems, no reasons why they could never be married. She wanted to cling to the memory of the way the sun felt on her shoulders, the way his arms felt around her at this precise instant. Those were the memories she'd cherish for the rest of her life.

"What do you mean terrible?" he chastised. "You couldn't do a terrible thing if you tried."

She had to prove he was wrong about that and about her. There was only one way to do it, one way to put an end to this charade of a love affair once and for all.

"I've lied," she told him, slowly daring to lift her gaze to meet his. Tears streamed unchecked down her cheeks. There was no need to wipe them away, when more were certain to follow. "For nearly fifty years, I've lied."

"About what? What on earth would you need to lie about?" he said, and now there truly was astonishment on his face. "And even if you did, so what? Nothing could be as bad as you're making it out to be."

"You wouldn't say that if you knew," she said, finally taking the handkerchief he offered and blotting up the tears, only to have more spill down her cheeks.

"Then tell me," he said matter-of-factly in a tone that promised understanding and forgiveness that she doubted he would offer if he knew everything. "Whatever it is, we'll handle it together," he vowed.

Elizabeth supposed she must have known from the moment the conversation started—no, even before that, when they'd met again—that Brandon would have to know the truth eventually. It was not the sort of thing she could hide forever from the man she loved, even though she'd hidden it for decades from the daughter she adored.

Now that she'd admitted to keeping some deep, dark secret, it seemed there was no way to prevent revealing it at long last. Even if she tried, Brandon would hound her forever for an adequate explanation.

"It's Ellen," she began slowly. "I've lied to my daughter." She looked into his eyes, then away. "And to you," she said in no more than a whisper, filled with regret.

She couldn't be sure, but it seemed for an instant he might have already guessed. But he waited for her to go on. She clung to his hand, trying to draw on his strength, desperate for the forgiveness he'd promised.

"Finish," he said quietly, his gaze riveted to hers. In his eyes there was no mistaking the storm already brewing. It was as if he anticipated the rest even before she found enough courage to say it.

She knew now there was no turning back. She kept her chin up. It was a matter of pride that she also kept her voice steady. "Ellen is our daughter, Brandon. Yours and mine."

Chapter 13

The tension on the bricked patio of Kevin and Lacey's Beacon Hill house was suddenly so thick it was difficult to breathe the lilac-scented air. Kevin had invited Jason, Dana and Sammy over for one last luncheon before he and Lacey officially moved their residence to Cape Cod. After the closing on the sale of this house in the morning, they would keep an apartment in the city for use during the week.

Some of the rooms were already empty. Walking through the nearly barren house hadn't affected Kevin nearly as much as he'd expected it to. He was looking forward to building a new life with his wife.

Lacey had never liked this house and Jason had lived in it only briefly. Kevin's son had always preferred the smaller house he'd grown up in, more than this one that Lacey referred to as a mausoleum. They'd kept the other house, renting it out, and several years ago Jason had bought it from them and was about to start filling up its rooms with his own family.

As a result, this day, which was winding down now with coffee and dessert on the patio, seemed more of a celebration than a bittersweet farewell. At least it had until Kevin shattered the festive mood with his bombshell.

"You did what!" three members of the Halloran family exclaimed in unison when he told them about hiring his father's detective to do a further check on Elizabeth Newton.

"Well, you don't have to act so horrified," he shot back defensively. "Dad's obviously not thinking straight or he never would have done something this foolish. Somebody had to look out for his interests."

"Darling, what is so foolish about your father wanting some companionship in his life?" Lacey asked.

"Lacey's right," Dana chimed in. "I think the whole story of how he and Elizabeth were separated and how he found her again is rather sweet.

Downright romantic in fact."

"There are plenty of women right here in Boston. Women we know," Kevin argued, though he could see now that it was a useless protest.

Obviously no one saw this the way he did. In fact, none of them knew what he'd discovered about Elizabeth Forsythe Newton. He was only just now beginning to absorb the implications himself. She had an illegitimate daughter, a daughter only slightly older than himself. Given everything else he knew about his father's obsession with this woman, it was possible this daughter was his half sister.

"In other words, you figured you had the right to choose for him, just as he tried to choose for you before we got married," Lacey countered with quiet calm and a deadly accuracy that had Kevin wincing. "Darling," she said, "don't you see what you're doing?"

"I am trying to protect my father from a woman he obviously knows nothing about." Was it possible though, that his father did know, that he had kept such a secret from all of them?

"He knows he loves her," Jason said quietly. "Dad, I really think we have to trust him. If he's happy, isn't that all that matters?"

Kevin tried one last time to make them see his point. "But if he knew everything—"

"Maybe he does," Lacey said. "And maybe it doesn't matter to him."

"It *would* matter," Kevin said darkly. "I think I know Dad better than any of you, and I'm telling you that it would matter."

He picked up the detective's report that had thoroughly shaken him and offered it to them. "Read it for yourselves. You'll see what I mean."

But after exchanging glances, not one of them took him up on the offer. It appeared they were all as stubborn as his father. They'd rather avoid the truth than deal with it.

"You called Granddad about it, didn't you?" Jason asked mildly. "Yes."

"Would he listen?"

"No," Kevin admitted in frustration. "He hung up on me."

"Darling, if Brandon didn't want to hear the report, then I think we should respect that," Lacey said. "Frankly, if I were you, I'd burn the damn thing and try to forget you ever read it yourself."

"How the devil am I supposed to do that?" he demanded, then sighed deeply. "Okay, fine then. But I just hope it isn't too late when Dad finds this out. You think my telling him is a mistake, but when the information comes out eventually, I'm convinced he'll never recover from it."

"Maybe not," Lacey said gently, "but it's not up to you to deliver the blow. If your father finds out whatever it is some other way and is truly distressed by it, then it will be up to all of us to support him the same way he's been there for us anytime we've been in trouble."

"I suppose you're right," Kevin conceded reluctantly. But God help them all when the information finally was revealed. With the sort of moral code his father had always adhered to, with his absolute belief in honesty, Kevin was convinced that his father would be inconsolable when he learned the truth about Elizabeth Forsythe Newton and her illegitimate daughter.

Nothing in his life had prepared Brandon for the emotions that thundered through him at Lizzy's announcement. Shock was chased by rage, only to be replaced by a terrible, terrible sense of loss.

Brandon thought of the beautiful, gracious woman who'd greeted him back in California with a delighted twinkle in her blue eyes. Those eyes were alive like Lizzy's and the same color as his own. She had hair that caught the light in its burnished gold strands. Knowing what he knew now, he could see the Halloran genes at play.

He thought of the generous, caring woman who'd risked her mother's wrath last night in an attempt to keep Lizzy from making a mistake she would regret the rest of her life. That action bore Lizzy's sense of daring and his own determination.

That lovely, strong woman was his daughter, the daughter he'd never known, never even dreamed existed.

At least he finally understood why Lizzy had been jumpy as a june bug whenever he mentioned going to California, why she'd been so determined to keep him away, why she'd turned so pale when he'd shown up at Ellen's. Lizzy had been right to be afraid. The aftershocks from this would keep their worlds trembling for a long time to come. If this was what Kevin had discovered, what must he think? No wonder he'd been so distraught.

Brandon needed to be alone for a minute. He needed to gather his thoughts. He didn't want to say something to Elizabeth in anger. He didn't want to hurl terrible accusations at this woman he'd loved so deeply for so long. He wanted to go someplace and search his soul for the right way out of this.

There was no denying the depth of hurt he felt at Lizzy's betrayal. My God, he had a daughter and grandchildren he could claim. A daughter he'd met only fleetingly. Grandchildren he'd never even seen.

"Does she know?" he asked finally, his voice toneless, wondering if that explained the reason for last night's call. Had Ellen spent a lifetime yearning for a father she thought had abandoned her? Had she worried that this chance to have her parents reunited was slipping away? Starry-eyed and sentimental, had she envisioned a future as a family?

"No," Lizzy said, robbing him of the fantasy. Then at his look of dismay, she added in a rush, "She can never know, Brandon. Never."

"Why the hell not?" he shot back.

Her eyes flashed at his tone, but her voice was even. "Because David Newton adopted Ellen when we got married. She was just a baby. I owed him for being willing to take on another man's child. I vowed to him that she would never know. He was the only father she ever knew, and he couldn't have loved her more if she'd been his own. He gave her stability. You can't want me to rob her of that."

Lizzy couldn't have hurt Brandon more if she'd taken a knife and cut out his heart. Another man had known his daughter's love. Another man had been there to care for her, to nurture her. He'd been robbed of all that. And even now Lizzy expected him to keep the secret, to protect her lie.

"What about the truth, Lizzy?" he said, as a bone-deep weariness stole through him. For the first time since Grace's death he felt every one of his sixty-eight years. "Didn't you think you owed her the truth? And what about me? All these years, all this time I've thought there was nothing left to connect us, but you knew differently." He regarded her angrily. "Just how hard did you try to find me back then? Or was it easier to find some poor, unselfish bastard and let him take my place?"

She looked as if he'd slapped her. For an instant he was filled with regret and then the rage began to build again until he was almost blinded by it.

"I don't deserve that," she said just as angrily. "I did the best I could. I was seventeen when you left, eighteen when Ellen was born. For all I knew you were dead."

He studied Elizabeth as if he'd never seen her before. The woman he'd fallen in love with would have been incapable of such lies, such deceit. The fact that she expected him to perpetuate it simply proved that she didn't know him at all, either. He felt as if all his dreams and illusions had been shattered with a single blow. Maybe that's what came of trying to recapture the past. It would never live up to the memory.

"I have to get away," he said. He dragged himself to his feet as if he had no energy left for anything.

"Brandon, please," she whispered, her face pale and panic in her eyes. "I'm sorry. Whatever else you think, you must believe that I never meant to hurt you. Maybe it wasn't your fault, but you simply weren't there. I had to do something. Stay. Let's talk about it."

"Not now, Lizzy," he said, unable to even meet her gaze. "Dammit, not now."

Elizabeth trembled as Brandon vanished from sight, leaving her at a table cluttered with dishes. There went her life, she thought with a cry of dismay, even as she also thought, how dare he make judgments? Though she had to let him go, had no choice really, she resented his accusations while accepting the blame for his despair. For the first time in her life, she felt defeated.

Her shoulders shook with silent sobs, which she barely managed to contain until she got back to her room. Then she flung herself onto the bed and cried for what seemed like hours, cried in a way she hadn't since she'd sent Brandon off to war. It was much, much later when she finally fell into an exhausted sleep, only to have troubled dreams that gave no peace.

It was hours before she woke to the sound of knocking on the door. She opened it to find Brandon looking haggard and defeated. She would have given anything to have the right to console him, but this morning had taken away all of her rights where he was concerned.

"Are you okay?" she asked, thinking that in her worst nightmares he had never taken the news like this. He'd been rocked, but never destroyed. What had she done to him? What had she done to all of them?

"I'm just shell-shocked, I think," he said. "May I come in?"

"Of course," she said, stepping aside.

When he was in the room, he finally met her gaze, then took in the reddened eyes, the rumpled clothes. "What about you? Are you okay?"

"I'm sad more than anything. Sad over what you've been deprived of. Sadder still that Ellen hasn't had the same chance to know you that I have."

He sat on the edge of the bed, his hands folded together, his shoulders slumped. "I need answers, Lizzy."

Her own hands clenched, she sat in the chair opposite him. "I'll tell you whatever I can."

"Will you tell me what she was like as a baby? Can you describe her first words, her first steps?" he demanded heatedly. "Was she a good student? Did she go to college? Is her marriage strong? What about my grandchildren? How can you possibly expect to tell me everything I want to know?"

She drew in a deep breath and decided she would dare one more risk. "If you come back to California with me for a few days, I'll show you her baby book. I'll bring out all the photo albums, the old movies. If it will help you, I will tell you every single thing I can remember."

"A lifetime of memories in how long, Lizzy? A single afternoon? An evening?"

"In however long it takes."

"But you won't let me spend time with her. You won't let me claim her.

You'll expect me to get on a plane and go back to Boston and forget all about her. Is that it?"

Though his wistful expression came close to breaking her heart, she whispered, "Yes. That's how it has to be."

As if he were unable to bear her sad expression, he got up and crossed the room. Brandon stood at the window, gazing out at the last flames of an orange sunset. Elizabeth found she couldn't even appreciate the beauty of the splashy display. She doubted he could, either.

"Will you tell me one more thing?" he asked finally. "Why did you do it, Lizzy? Why did you keep on lying to me?" He turned to face her, his expression bleak. "When you came to Boston, why in God's name didn't you tell me everything then?"

"Brandon, I've had years to go over and over the decision I made when I married David Newton. No matter how I look at it, even now knowing that you're alive, that you still love me, I think what I did was what I had to do for Ellen's sake."

"I can't argue with you about what you decided then," he conceded reluctantly. "As much as I'd like to think I have a right to criticize your choice, I know that you did what you did out of love for your daughter. But what about now?"

He met her gaze steadily then, holding it until she trembled inside.

"What about now, Lizzy?" he demanded again. "David Newton wouldn't hold you to that promise now. If he was as fine a man as you've told me, he wouldn't deny a daughter the chance to know her natural father."

"You make it sound so simple," she said. "It is."

"No!" she argued as if her life depended on it. "Don't you see? If the truth comes out now, she'll hate me. She'll never forgive me for lying to her all this time. I know you'll think it's selfish, but I don't think I could bear losing her. And I'm not so sure she could stand it, either. Kate was always her father's daughter, but Ellen, she was mine. Just as Kate mourned her father's death, I think Ellen would mourn the loss of her trust in me."

As she said it, she knew she was leaving the fate of her relationship with her daughter in Brandon's hands. If he chose to ignore her wishes, there was nothing she could do about it. She simply had to trust him to reach a conclusion they all could live with.

Funny, she thought, almost unable to bear the irony, it all came down to trust again. Years ago she hadn't trusted Brandon's love enough to wait for him despite the lack of letters. Now she had no choice but to place her trust in a man whom she'd betrayed in a way he might never be able to forgive.

"There's no point in talking about this anymore tonight. I think it's best if we sleep on it," Brandon told her finally.

Right now he wanted to argue with her, wanted to tell her that Ellen would understand, but how could he make that sort of promise when his own world was shaken as it had never been before? If he was having trouble with the truth, if he felt this horrible, aching sense of loss, what would Lizzy's Ellen feel? Did he dare to turn her world upside down?

"I don't know how long I'll be able to stand the uncertainty," Lizzy said, her expression imploring him to reach a final decision now.

"I'm sorry. I don't think we'll find any answers tonight. All I can promise is that I won't do anything rash. We'll take our time and decide together what's best."

If his promise wasn't enough to reassure her, that was unfortunate. It was the best he could do. He gathered from her miserable expression that it wasn't enough.

"Don't try running out on me, Lizzy," he warned. "That won't solve anything."

"Brandon, please. I think it's best if I go back to California first thing in the morning. There's no future for us. I owe that much to my daughter and, for that matter, to you. It would kill you to keep silent around her day in and day out knowing what you know."

"She is *our* daughter," he reminded her angrily, forgetting all about the resolve to let things be until morning when he'd be calmer, more rational. "Remember, I do know the truth now. Maybe it wouldn't be right to claim her, but I do intend to get to know her with or without your blessing. When you go back to California, I intend to be right by your side. You owe me that."

Her eyes widened in dismay. "You can't," she breathed. "Oh, Brandon, no. Please don't be that cruel."

"To whom, Lizzy? You or Ellen?"

"Both of us. How would I ever explain what you're doing there?"

"That's your problem," he said coldly. "I've told you that I will do nothing to hurt Ellen. That's the last thing I want. But I believe it's always better to know the truth than to try to protect lies."

Brandon left her then, because he was afraid to stay. He was afraid that the terrible pain he saw in her eyes would begin to touch him. He was terrified that the love he'd treasured for so long would force him to try to understand, to forgive—not the past, but the lies of the last few weeks.

He couldn't allow that to happen. Right now, his anger was the only thing sustaining him. Without it he wasn't sure how he'd survive the hurt.

Chapter 14

Brandon's harsh words, which carried the weight of a threat, were still ringing in Elizabeth's ears as she returned alone to California first thing the next morning. Despite his warning, she hadn't been able to bear a single second more of the condemnation in Brandon's eyes.

Nor had she wanted to put him to the test. If he came with her, surely there would be hell to pay. The truth would be out and there would be nothing she could do to stop it. She might not be able to prevent him from following her, but she would not willingly set things up for him to destroy her daughter's life.

Not that having Brandon for a father would be so terrible. He was a wonderful, loving man. But he was not the father Ellen had known and loved. He was not the one who had taught her that honesty was a trait to be treasured and deceit something to be scorned. Ellen wouldn't blame Brandon for the lies, but she would blame Elizabeth.

Back home alone, though, she discovered no peace. Elizabeth wasn't sure how long she could weather the terrible strain of waiting for Brandon to make good on his threat. When he didn't come on the next flight to Los Angeles, she took heart. When he didn't appear the next day, she began to believe that he might not come at all. That didn't stop her from worrying.

With each hour that passed, each day, she anticipated the worst. Every time the phone rang she flinched. When Ellen's car turned into the driveway, she panicked, certain that her daughter was coming to denounce her for a lifetime of lies.

"Okay, Mother, I've had it. What's wrong?" Ellen asked when she arrived unexpectedly on a Saturday morning in early May.

Elizabeth had been home for nearly a week and was still as jumpy as she had been on her first day back in Los Angeles. "What do you mean?" she asked quietly, trying to calm her nerves.

"You haven't been the same since you went on that trip with Brandon Halloran. You look exhausted. You haven't been out of the house, even to visit us. You don't call. Kate's worried that you're ill."

She was ill, heartsick in fact, but not in any way she could explain to them.

"I'm fine," she said.

"You look as if you haven't been sleeping."

"Just a touch of insomnia. I'm sure it will pass. In fact, I'm feeling rather sleepy right now. If you don't mind, dear, I think as soon as you leave, I'll go upstairs and have a little nap."

Ellen regarded her intently, looked as if she wanted to ask something more, then sighed. "Go ahead, if you're tired," she said finally. "I can let myself out."

Elizabeth slowly climbed the stairs, leaving Ellen to stare after her, her brow furrowed.

Upstairs, Elizabeth stretched out on top of the bedspread, stared up at the ceiling and waited for the sound of the front door closing. Instead she heard Ellen's low murmurings, followed a short time later by the sound of a car arriving, not departing. It didn't require razor-sharp intelligence to guess that Kate had joined Ellen downstairs.

Obviously her daughters intended to gang up on her to get some answers. Given a choice Elizabeth would have pulled the covers over her head and hidden out until they both found pressing business elsewhere.

Knowing that levelheaded Kate was stubborn enough to outwait her, she got up, applied a dash of blusher to her cheeks and went down to face the music.

"Hello, darling," she greeted Kate pleasantly, as if she'd expected to find her camped out on the living room sofa looking through old issues of a news magazine. "I thought you'd be on a tennis court on such a beautiful afternoon."

"That's exactly where I will be, if you own up to what's bugging you in the next ten minutes."

"Dear, there's no reason to miss your game on my account. Are you playing with that nice young man from the law firm?"

Kate rolled her eyes. "You'll never give up, will you? No, Mother, I am playing doubles with a married couple and one of their friends who is visiting from Boston."

Elizabeth felt a dull ache in her chest. "Boston?"

Ellen regarded her speculatively. "Mother, look at yourself. The mere mention of the city practically turns you green. What on earth happened between you and Brandon Halloran?"

Elizabeth forced a smile. "Certainly nothing you need to worry yourselves about. Kate, tell me about this blind date."

"It is *not* a blind date. Their friend is a woman. I think she's in the fashion business somehow."

Fashions? Textiles? Was it possible she knew Brandon? Elizabeth wondered, then dismissed the possibility with a sigh. "Well, I don't suppose it matters whom you're playing tennis with. You shouldn't stand them up. Just run along, darling. You really needn't worry about me. I'm feeling much better since my nap."

"What nap? You haven't been upstairs more than a half hour. I'm not going anywhere without a few answers," Kate said firmly. "Sit down, Mother. Stop fluttering around as if you can't wait to get away from me. Ellen, you go make a pot of tea."

Ellen took the order more cheerfully than usual. "Has anybody mentioned how bossy you are?" she inquired as she exited.

"That's how I got to be a lawyer," Kate called after her. "I absolutely love all that undivided attention I get in a courtroom. Hurry up with that tea. I want raspberry if there is any."

"You know I always keep raspberry for you," Elizabeth said. "I'll go fix it. Ellen will never find it."

"Ellen is the best scavenger I know," Kate corrected. "Sit, Mother. You're not sneaking off on me."

"I can't imagine what you're so worked up over."

"Then your imagination is getting senile, which I seriously doubt. What the devil happened on that trip to New Mexico? Ever since you got back I've had a hard time telling if you're in mourning or terrified."

She'd never judged Kate as being that perceptive, Elizabeth thought dully. What a terrible time to discover she'd been mistaken. "Kate, you're exaggerating," she said with feigned cheer. "Naturally seeing Brandon again stirred up some old memories. Nothing more."

Kate rolled her eyes. "*Nothing more?* Mother, you are not the kind of woman who engages in some casual fling."

"Who said it was casual?"

"Well, you just dismissed that entire trip as if it were of no more importance than a visit to the dentist."

"Which reminds me, dear. Have you made that appointment to have your teeth cleaned?"

"Mother!"

"Kate, when exactly did you get to be older than I am?"

Her daughter started to interrupt, but Elizabeth held up her hand. She had to stop this now. She could maintain this cheery facade for just so long.

"Let me finish," she insisted. "I appreciate all the love and concern you and your sister are showing, but when I want your advice or your interference, I'll ask for it."

Ellen came in just in time to hear her little speech and almost dropped the tray of hot tea. Kate was regarding Elizabeth indignantly.

"If you don't want our help—"

"I don't."

"But—"

"There are no buts about it. Ellen, set the tray over here. I'll pour the tea." She might not be able to do much about some aspects of her life at the moment, but by golly, she was not going to relinquish control of the rest of it. She beamed at her two precious and meddle-some worrywarts. "You will stay for tea, won't you?"

Ellen and Kate exchanged a rueful look. Kate finally sighed. "Of course."

"I wouldn't want you to be late for your tennis game, though," Elizabeth said.

"You wouldn't be trying to rush us out of here, would you Mother?" Ellen inquired.

Elizabeth adopted her most innocent expression. "Never, darling. You know how I love to have you drop by."

For once, though, she would be very, very glad to see them go.

Brandon couldn't get the image of Ellen Hayden out of his mind. He was enchanted with the thought of hav-ing a daughter. He wanted to know what she thought, how she spent her days, what the man she'd married was like, whether she was happy.

And with every day that went by, he was more and more inclined to push his way into her life and damn the consequences.

Lizzy's departure from New Mexico by dawn's early light had infuriated him. He'd raced to the airport, in-tent on following her, but at the last second he'd recon-sidered. There was no purpose in going to California until he'd taken the time to think this situation through rationally. He'd caught a flight to Boston instead.

He'd been back in Boston for nearly two weeks be-fore anyone in the family found out about his return. He'd sent Mrs. Farnsworth on an extended holiday before leaving for California, so he'd had the house to himself all that time. Unable to bear the thought of seeing a soul, he'd been a virtual hermit from the moment he'd arrived.

This morning, though, he was drinking some of the lousiest coffee he'd ever tasted, when he heard a key turn in the front door. He peeked between the drawn drapes and saw Dana's car in the driveway. Walking toward the foyer, he saw her step inside. He waited until she'd turned around and spotted him before saying anything.

"You sneaking in here to steal the silver?" he inquired dryly.

She scowled at him, but he had to admit she didn't seem all that surprised to see him.

"Actually, I'm on a mission," she confessed readily. "Oh?"

"Word has it around the office that you've vanished without a trace."

"If I'm missing, why are you here?"

"It seems to me that a man who's hurting might sneak home to lick his wounds."

He shot her a dark look. "Who says I'm hurting?"

"Your son the mathematician, who apparently adds two and two better than the rest of us."

"What the devil does that mean?"

"It means that Kevin has been trying to track you down for the past two weeks. When he couldn't find you in New Mexico or in California, he guessed what had happened."

"So why isn't he here? I would have thought he'd want to gloat."

"Actually, quite the contrary. He had the distinct impression you might not want to talk to him about this. So I was elected. Unfortunately I have no idea what *this* is. Care to clue me in?" she asked. "And do you mind if we sit down? It's getting harder and harder to stay on my feet. This great-grandbaby of yours weighs a ton."

"You ought to stop feeding it all those salty pickles and fattening brownies," he said as he led the way back into the dining room. "Lord knows what kind of eating disorders that poor child will have." He pulled out a chair for her. "You want some coffee? It's pretty terrible. I made it."

"Based on that recommendation, I think I'll pass. Could you dredge up any milk?"

"Absolutely," he said, glad of the chance to escape for a minute and decide just how much he was willing to reveal to Dana. The girl was compassionate, but he had no business burdening her with his problems, especially not a doozy like this one.

By the time he'd poured the milk and returned to the dining room, Dana had pulled the drapes aside and opened the French doors to let a breeze in.

"I hope you don't mind. It was pretty dreary in here," she said. "No wonder you're depressed. You're not getting any oxygen."

"My state doesn't have a thing to do with the lack of air circulating in this house."

"Then what is the problem? You look like hell, by the way. I never knew you even owned a pair of blue jeans, much less a shirt quite that color. What happened? Did you wash the whites and colors together?"

He scowled at her. "Thanks. It's so nice to have someone drop by to cheer me up."

"I can't cheer you up until you give me something

to work with. What went wrong between you and Elizabeth?"

"Now you're going straight for the jugular."

"Did you want me to waltz around it instead?"

"Maybe just a quiet fox-trot around the edges would have done."

"Hey, I'm easy. We could discuss the weather, but we'll get back to this eventually, anyway."

Brandon sighed heavily and shoved his hand through his hair. "I suppose you're going to push and nag until I spill it, aren't you?"

She nodded cheerfully. "That's the plan."

"How much do you know?"

"Not a thing, except that you're upset and, if anything, Kevin's in a worse state."

"He didn't tell you why?"

"Only that he hired that detective and got a report that shook him up. He was convinced you'd be devastated by it."

"He's got that right."

Dana's expression immediately turned sympathetic and the teasing note vanished from her voice. "Did Elizabeth tell you whatever it is herself, or did you find out some other way?"

"No. She told me. She hadn't meant to, but I was pressing her to get married and telling her what a wonderful woman she was and suddenly it all came pouring out, like a dam had burst. I guess I'm the only one outside of her parents who knows the whole story. They're not alive to tell."

"The whole story is?" Dana prodded.

When he remained silent and indecisive, she picked up his hand and held it. "You know how much I owe you. If it weren't for you, Jason and I might not be together. I owe you, Brandon. More than that, I love you every bit as much as if you were my own grandfather. If I can help you in any way, I want to."

He felt the sting of tears in his eyes and turned away. He didn't want her seeing how emotional he was these days, how much it pleased him that she considered him family. Then he thought of all those other grandchildren he'd never even met and his heart began to ache all over again.

As much as he wanted someone to confide in, though, as much as he knew Dana wanted to help, he realized that he couldn't share this with her. He might be angry with Lizzy at the moment, he might even be tossing around the notion of going to California to claim his daughter, but until he'd resolved once and for all the best course of action, he couldn't involve other people. He was grateful that discretion had kept Kevin from doing otherwise, as well. One day soon he and his son would have to have a long talk. He could only pray Kevin would forgive him for the delay.

There was no doubt in his mind that the report Kevin had gotten contained the truth—or a goodly portion of it, quite enough to raise a ruckus. A good detective, one smart enough to have traced Lizzy in the first place, would surely have been able to discover the rest, even if it had been no more than the information that she'd had a child out of wedlock.

Brandon might be the only one, other than Lizzy herself, who'd been able to fill in the remaining details.

He hoped Kevin hadn't guessed anymore than that. If he had, he was likely to be every bit as tormented by the discovery he had a half sister as Brandon was to learn he had a daughter.

None of this was going to be resolved by him staying shut up in this house, though. The only way to deal with this was the same way he would deal with a business crisis, straight on.

And that meant going to California.

"Dana, why don't you get on the phone and call the travel agent, while I pack my bags?"

Her expression brightened. "You're going to California?"

"On the first available flight."

"Will you and Elizabeth try to work things out?"

"I'm not sure that's possible, child. But I do know that sitting around here struggling with things on my own hasn't accomplished a blessed thing."

Dana drove him to the airport and insisted on going inside to see him off. When his flight was called, she hugged him as tightly as she could, given the swollen state of her tummy.

"Do whatever it takes to be happy," she murmured. "Promise me that."

"I promise."

"Even if it means eating a little crow?"

Just the thought of trying to put all this behind him and mending fences with Lizzy seemed impossible at the moment, but Brandon looked at Dana's hopeful expression and knew he couldn't tell her that.

"We'll see," he said. It was the best he could do.

Chapter 15

Despite what he'd implied to Dana, Brandon had absolutely no idea where he planned to go when he arrived in Los Angeles. He had an entire flight to think about it.

He decided finally—sometime between the awful meal and the even worse movie—that he had no choice but to see Lizzy first. There were things to be resolved between the two of them before he could begin to consider what to do about Ellen.

He realized something else on that long flight. This situation he and Lizzy found themselves in was just one more test. He'd faced an abundance of them throughout his life, and more than once he'd come up wanting.

Most had been relatively insignificant, until the one with Kevin had come along many years ago. When his son had refused to join Halloran Industries, when he'd chosen Lacey despite Brandon's objections, Brandon hadn't taken it well. He'd held himself aloof, unable to forgive what he saw as rejection, impatient with himself for his inability to sway his son's decisions.

It had taken him a long time to see that patience and forgiveness were more important than pride, that a relationship with his son at any cost was worth more than the satisfaction of seeing Kevin working at a job of his father's choosing or marrying a bride who was his father's choice.

Now, half a lifetime later, he was faced with another dilemma involving forgiveness. If he'd learned nothing else over these past lonely weeks locked away in his house, it was that he missed Lizzy desperately. Until the end in Taos, he'd experienced a rare contentment in his life again, and there was no question that she was responsible. More than passion, more than memories, she'd given him back his zest for living. The old magic had mellowed into vintage fulfillment.

And she had given him a daughter. She might have made mistakes in the delay in telling him the truth, but she'd made them out of love for her daughter, not out of any intent to hurt him.

He had a choice now. He could forgive her and struggle to grab whatever years of joy they might share. Or he could allow foolish pride and misguided anger to force him into a life of loneliness and regrets. Pride and anger wouldn't keep his bed warm at night. They surely wouldn't provide much companionship.

Brandon thought of the sadness in Lizzy's eyes the last time he'd seen her and regretted, more than he could say, his responsibility for it being there. Forgiveness might not come easily, but it was the only choice he had. He could only pray that she was as ready to for-give him for his hasty condemnation of her.

Almost as soon as the decision was made, he felt his heart lighten. The dull ache in his chest eased as if his choice had received some sort of divine benediction.

At the airport he considered calling, then worried that the warning would only make Lizzy panic. Instead he rented a car and drove on the crowded highway as if he were in an Indy 500 time trial.

Parked at last along the curb in front of her house, he drew in a deep breath, praying for the courage it would take to make all of this come out right. He saw the cur-tains separate, then fall back into place and envisioned her reaction to seeing him outside.

He walked slowly up the flagstone walk, then rang the bell. When Lizzy finally opened her front door, he felt his heart climb into his throat. She looked miserable and frightened. Her hand gripped the door as if she felt the need for something to steady her. And yet there was that familiar spark in her eyes, that hint of mother-hen protectiveness and daring.

"Brandon," she said after an endless hesitation. Then as if she couldn't manage any more, she fell silent, her gaze locked with his. Time ticked slowly past as each of them measured their reactions.

"Hello, Lizzy. We have to talk."

She nodded and let him in, closing the door softly behind him. "Would you like something? Coffee? Tea?"

"No. Nothing."

She gestured toward a chair, then stood framed by the archway into the dining room as if she wanted to be in a position to flee. Suddenly Brandon saw himself as an ogre and regretted more than he could say that it had come to this between them.

"Sit down, Lizzy. I'm not planning to take your head off."

"Why are you here?" she asked warily.

"I'm not sure entirely. I just knew that all the answers I needed were here, not in Boston. I had to come."

He finally dared to meet her gaze. "I missed you, Lizzy. It's odd, but the more I thought about this, the more I wanted someone to talk to. Not until today did I realize that that someone had to be you."

Her shoulders eased some, then, and she finally sat down. "Brandon, I never meant to hurt you like this. Never."

"I know. You said it before, but I don't think I really believed it until I did some soul-searching on the flight out here. I've never been much good at forgiveness, Lizzy. Maybe when you've grown up with power and self-confidence, you start thinking that things will always go your way, that you never need to bend. I learned differently with Kevin, when we were estranged for all those years, but apparently I forgot the lesson again until you came along to test me." He regarded her evenly. "Do you understand what I'm trying to say?"

"I'm not sure, Brandon."

"I think maybe you do but you want me to spell it out. I suppose that's only fair, since I suspect my actions have put you through hell these past couple of weeks." He drew in a deep breath. "I want you to know that I forgive you for keeping the truth from me. It wasn't my place to criticize choices you made to protect your daughter and I apologize for that. And I'd like to ask your forgiveness for the way I bungled things when you told me."

Lizzy's eyes filled with tears. "Oh, Brandon, thank you. Does that mean you've changed your mind about keeping the secret? Will you go back to Boston and forget all about us?"

He shook his head. "I'm afraid that's the one thing I can't do," he said. "I can't force myself a second time to try to forget you. And the only way you and I can possibly have the future we deserve is to tell Ellen the truth." As soon as he said the words, he realized that it was what he'd known in his heart from the first.

"No," she said, her expression crumbling. "Oh, Brandon, how can you say you love me and ask me to do that?"

"Because now that you know I'm alive, now that you know that I never stopped caring for you, you will never know a moment's peace if you try to go on living with the lie. That's not the kind of woman you are, Lizzy, anymore than it's the kind of man I am. The only thing left to resolve is whether you'll tell your daughter everything alone or whether I will be there with you."

"You make it sound so easy, but then what, Brandon?" she demanded angrily. "Who will pick up the pieces?"

"We'll do that together."

"And what if I can't forgive you?"

"You will," he said confidently. "In time."

She closed her eyes, as if that would block out the pain, but he could tell from the tears tracking down her cheeks that she was still desperately afraid.

"Lizzy, I will be with you in this," he reassured her. "Together don't you think we have the strength to weather just about anything?"

"There's no way I can make you change your mind, is there?" she asked slowly, her tone resigned.

"No."

"Then I will tell her, Brandon. Alone."

He nodded. "If that's the way you want it. Shall I wait for you here?"

"No. I think I'll ask her to come here so we can be sure of some privacy."

"Then I'll go for a drive. I won't come back until I see that her car is gone."

He crossed the room and hunkered down in front of her, despite the sharp pain that shot through his poor old arthritic knees when he did it. He tilted her chin up with the tip of his finger, forcing her to meet his gaze.

"It's the only way, Lizzy. Whether I go or stay, it's the only way you'll be able to live with yourself."

She clasped his hand then. After a full minute while his hand slowly warmed hers, she seemed to gather her strength.

"Please don't go far, Brandon. I have a feeling I'm going to need you more tonight than I've ever needed anyone before in my life."

It was good that Brandon had forced her hand, Elizabeth told herself over and over as she sat with the phone cradled in her lap, willing herself to have the courage to dial. Only the certain knowledge that Brandon would be back in an hour or two or three forced her hand.

"Ellen," she said when her daughter finally answered.

"Mother, what's wrong?" Ellen asked at once. "Are you okay? You sound as if you've been crying."

"I'm fine, dear, but I would appreciate it if you could stop by."

"When? Now?"

"Yes, if it isn't inconvenient."

"I'll be right there," she said briskly, as if she'd guessed the urgency without her mother expressing it in words. Elizabeth made tea while she waited. A whole pot brimming with chamomile, which was supposed to calm the nerves. Then she couldn't even bring the cup to her lips, because her hands were shaking so badly.

It took Ellen barely fifteen minutes to get there, a miracle by L.A. standards.

"Mother, what's wrong?" she was asking even before she was inside the door.

Elizabeth kept a tight rein on her panic. Forcing herself to remain calm for Ellen's sake was the only thing keeping her steady at all. She studied her beautiful daughter's anxious expression, her troubled blue eyes and wished that this moment were past, that the truth was behind them and they were starting to rebuild their relationship.

"Mother," Ellen said again. "I'm starting to worry. Something must be terribly wrong."

"Sit down, darling. We have to talk." She reached behind her neck and unclasped the locket she hadn't taken off for weeks now. She took Ellen's hand and allowed the delicate gold chain to pool in her palm.

"Why are you giving me this?"

"I want you to open it and take a good look at the man inside."

"But why? I already know it's Brandon Halloran."

"Look again, darling. Even if you had never met Brandon, wouldn't he look familiar?"

Ellen studied the tiny photograph, then looked up, her expression puzzled. "I don't understand."

"You should recognize the eyes, darling. They're just like yours."

Ellen's expression was thunderstruck as she looked from her mother to the locket and back again. "What are you saying?" she asked finally in a voice that was barely more than a horrified whisper.

Elizabeth thought of the strong, caring man who was waiting somewhere out in the night and wished for just a little of his courage, just a little of his conviction that he could make anything turn out right.

"Brandon Halloran is your father."

The locket slid through Ellen's fingers and fell to the floor. "No," she said, oblivious to it. "I don't believe you."

"It's true, darling. Your father—that is, David—and I decided that you should never know. Maybe we were wrong, but there seemed to be no point in dredging up ancient history, especially when it seemed unlikely that Brandon would ever turn up here."

"You mean Dad knew all along?"

Elizabeth nodded, worried by her daughter's pale complexion. "You were just a baby when we married," she explained. "He could never have loved you more if you had been his own flesh and blood. He was so proud of you, so proud of being your father. And he was, Ellen. He was your father in every way that counted."

"But you lied to me, Mother. Both of you lied to me. Didn't you think I had a right to know? Maybe it would have helped me to understand why Kate and I are so different. Maybe it would have helped me to understand why she and Dad were always closer than he and I were."

"That's not true," Elizabeth said, shocked. "He loved you both." But even as she said it, she knew it wasn't true. He hadn't loved them equally. There had been a special bond between him and Kate, though he had done everything in his power to deny it. And her darling Ellen had recognized that bond and hurt for all these years because of it.

"Oh, darling, I'm sorry. I never knew how you felt. You never let on." She couldn't console her by explaining that Ellen was the child she had connected with— because she was the link to her lost lover.

"I suppose I never wanted to admit it out loud." She stood up then, picked up her purse and started for the door.

"Where are you going?" Elizabeth asked anxiously. "You must have questions."

"I do, but I can't deal with them right now. I have to figure out who I am." She glanced back. "Did Brandon Halloran know he was my father?"

"No. He never knew I was pregnant. Darling, none of this is his fault. Will you be back?" Elizabeth said, following her down the walk to her car.

Ellen turned toward her briefly, the tears on her cheeks glistening in the glow of the streetlight. "I don't know. It seems I don't know anything anymore."

Then, with her heart breaking apart inside, Elizabeth watched as her precious daughter drove away.

Elizabeth was still standing there, her arms wrapped tightly around herself as if she were trying to hold her-

self together, when Brandon came back. He emerged
from his car and walked slowly to where she stood.
He slid his arms around her and pulled her against his
chest, where she could hear the steady, reassuring beat
of his heart.

And for one brief moment she tried to imagine that
she was safe in a place where nothing would ever hurt
her so deeply again.

Brandon had grown tired of waiting, tired of watching Elizabeth grow increasingly pale, increasingly anxious as her daughter continued to avoid her day after
day. Though Kate called regularly, oblivious to the undercurrents that were tearing her family apart, it wasn't
Kate whom Lizzy longed for. She needed to hear Ellen's
voice. More, she needed Ellen's forgiveness.

"Lizzy, I think I'll go out for a while," he said a week
after he'd arrived in Los Angeles.

She barely spared him a glance.

"Is there anything you'd like me to pick up from the
store?"

"No, nothing."

He dropped a kiss on her forehead. "I'll see you soon
then."

He climbed into his rental car and drove straight to
Ellen's. She might slam the door in his face, but that
would be better by a long shot than this silence that was
destroying them all.

When Ellen opened the door and recognized him, her
eyes widened in dismay. "Why are you here?"

"I think you know the answer to that," he said quietly. "May I come in?"

Too well-bred to deny him, she stepped aside, and he found himself once again in the house where he'd come for Lizzy just a few short weeks back. It seemed as if that had been a lifetime ago.

Ellen followed him into the living room and stood nervously by as he chose a seat on the sofa. She kept sneaking curious glances at him, as if she weren't quite willing for him to know how badly she wanted to reconcile the man she had met so recently with the abstract title of father that she had thought belonged to another man.

He tried to imagine how Kevin would feel if some woman appeared after all these years and stripped him of everything in which he'd believed. Kevin was having difficulty enough simply accepting that there was a woman in Brandon's life who meant as much to his father as Grace Halloran had, a woman who'd preceded Kevin's mother in Brandon's affections.

"I think I have some idea of what you must be feeling," Brandon told Ellen finally.

"Do you? Then you're better off than I am. All I feel is numb. I keep trying to fit all the pieces together, but it never comes together right. My father, the man I've always known as my father, no longer fits. In his place there's this stranger. Worse, my mother never told me, never even hinted at it."

"So you feel as though your whole life has been a lie?"

"I suppose."

"In a way that's very much what I'm feeling. You see in my picture, there is a woman who looks nothing like your mother and there is a son. Later there's even a grandson. But there is no daughter. All of a sudden, I discover there is this beautiful woman who carries my blood in her veins. But try as I might, I can't make her fit in, either."

He regarded her steadily then, until she met his gaze and held it. "I want to, Ellen. I want more than anything to get to know my daughter, to become a part of her life. I don't expect that to happen overnight, but if we took it slowly, don't you think we might create a whole new family portrait?"

Her gaze slid away from his. Her lower lip trembled. "My mother says she loved you very much," she said in a low voice that begged him to confirm it.

"And I loved her with all my heart. You are the blessing of that love, Ellen. Don't ever believe anything less."

She blinked away fresh tears. "All my life I was told there was no sin worse than lying. The two people who told me that carried out the biggest lie of all."

"Why?" he said. "Why do you think they did that?"

She was silent for what seemed an eternity before she finally said, "I want to believe they did it out of love, not fear."

"Then believe that, because it's the truth."

"I can't."

"Why not?"

"Then I would have to forgive them," she said in a small voice, "and it still hurts too much to do that."

"Ah, Ellen," he said with a rueful sigh. "Let me tell you something I've only recently discovered about forgiveness. It's when it's needed the most that it becomes the hardest to give. You will never be happy until you forgive your mother, your father, even me."

"Why you?"

"Because I set it all in motion by searching for your mother. If I hadn't, you would never have known. Would that have been better?"

She hesitated, then finally admitted, "No. I think, if I give it some time, it might turn out that I'm luckier than anyone to have had the love of two fathers."

Brandon knew then that though it would take time for Ellen to accept him into her life, it would be all right. The healing really had begun. "Do you think you could tell your mother that?"

"Now?"

He nodded. "I think it's the only way I'll ever convince her to marry me."

A smile crept over her lips. "Better late than never, I always say," she said with more spirit. "Just let me fix my face."

"Your face is lovely just as it is."

"Only a father would say that," she said, then caught herself. Her smile broadened. "How about that? I can actually begin to laugh again. By the way, am I the only thing standing between the two of you?"

"Not the only thing," he conceded. "Just the most important."

"What else stands in the way? I knew weeks ago you loved each other."

"Time. Too much water under the bridge. Stubbornness."

"Yours or hers?" she asked slyly.

Brandon could tell his daughter had Lizzy's spunk from the twinkle in her eyes. "Maybe some of each."

Before Ellen could offer any advice, the front door

slammed open and Lizzy stood there, her expression wary. "Brandon," she said worriedly. "You didn't say you were coming here."

"Ellen and I were just getting to know each other," he said.

Elizabeth cast an anxious glance at her daughter. "Is everything okay?" Ellen hesitated, her expression indecisive. Then, after a glance at Brandon, she moved slowly toward her mother and put her arms around her. "Not quite yet," she said with the kind of honesty Brandon had come to respect. "But it will be. I'm sorry for shutting you out. I needed time to sort things out for myself."

"You had a right to be angry."

"Maybe. Maybe not." She glanced at Brandon. "It was…it was Father who made me see the light."

Lizzy turned to him, tears glistening in her eyes. "Thank you," she mouthed as she held her daughter.

Ellen gave her one last squeeze, then shot a pointed look at Brandon. "I think I'll leave you two alone now," she said. "There's tea in the kitchen, if you want some, Mother."

When she had gone, Lizzy crossed the room to him. "You worked a miracle here this afternoon."

He shook his head. "No, Lizzy, the miracle is you and me. We've got our second chance. I don't plan to let it pass us by. How about you?"

A smile spread across her face and her eyes lit with sparks of pure mischief. "You knew all along you'd have your way this time, didn't you?"

"Of course," he said. "You never could resist a story with a happy ending, could you?"

"Brandon, how will I be able to thank you?"

"By marrying me, Lizzy. By letting me become a part of your family, just as you'll become a part of mine."

She squeezed his hand. "I do love you, Brandon Halloran. I always have."

"And I you, my love. And I you."

"It won't be easy, you know. Kate and your family still have to be told."

"I think Kevin already knows, at least some of it. He may have guessed the rest."

"Then don't you think you should call him? He must have a thousand questions."

"I can't call, not about something as important as this. I'll stay here until you've had time to make things right with both your daughters, then we'll go to Boston together. I figure we can manage a June wedding, don't you?"

"Brandon, June is just around the corner."

He grinned at her stunned expression. "Then I'd say you'd better get a move on, woman."

Epilogue

"Ohmigosh," Dana murmured just as Brandon was about to cut the tiered wedding cake that was decorated with a frothy confection of white frosting and pink rosebuds.

"Sis?" Sammy said, an expression of alarm on his face as she clutched her belly.

Brandon heard the mix of anxiety and surprise in Dana's voice and immediately dropped the sterling silver cake knife. He shot her a look of pure delight. "Now?"

A grin split her face. "Now," she confirmed. "This great-grandchild of yours is definitely coming."

"By golly, I knew this was going to be a day to remember," Brandon said and started giving orders. "Jason, get the car. Kevin, you tell the guests they'll have to excuse us."

Dana looked him straight in the eye. "Don't you dare ruin this reception on my account."

"Ruin it! Hell, girl, this is the best thing that could have happened. Now I'll be able to leave on my honeymoon without worrying about missing the big event."

Forgetting that he'd just given the assignment to Kevin, he grabbed the microphone from the band-leader in mid-song and called for silence. "Well, folks, I guess you all know we wanted you with us on this special day because we care about you. It's a mighty big blessing to have so many friends and family around us on a day when we celebrate the true meaning of the wedding vows. There's been a little hitch in our schedule, though. I'm afraid you're going to have to excuse us. We've got a baby to deliver."

As a murmur of excitement spread through the room, he again asked for quiet. "While we get ourselves to the hospital, I hope you'll all stay here and enjoy yourselves and drink a toast to the newest Halloran, our fourth generation."

At the hospital it was difficult to tell who was more impatient Brandon, Kevin or Sammy. They paced the waiting room, while Elizabeth and Lacey exchanged looks of amusement. Ellen and Kate hovered nearby, still awkward around their new family but clearly wanting to be a part of this special moment.

"Why the devil don't they tell us something?" Brandon grumbled. "First babies generally take their own sweet time," Elizabeth reminded him. "I'm sure they'll let us know when there's anything to tell us. Why don't we go have a nice cup of tea to settle your nerves?"

"A stiff scotch couldn't settle my nerves," he said.

"I don't recall it taking this long for Kevin or Jason to come into this world."

"Probably because you were at work on both occasions," Kevin reminded him dryly. "Maybe you and Elizabeth should leave before you miss your plane."

"Not on your life." He stared down the corridor toward the delivery room. "Maybe I could get one of those gowns and just take a peek inside to see what's happening."

"Bad idea," Kevin said. "This is Jason's big day. There's no need for you to intrude."

"How would I be intruding? It's my great-grandbaby."

"Which puts you two generations away from the right to be in there," his son reminded him with a grin that had been a long time coming.

Though Kevin had taken the events of the past few weeks far better than Brandon had anticipated, it hadn't been easy. Once Kevin had been told the whole story, he'd swallowed any criticisms he might have had of his father or Elizabeth. He had not welcomed his new step mother as wholeheartedly as Brandon might have liked, but there had been no overt resentment.

Brandon suspected he could thank Lacey and Dana for that, just as he owed them for making both Ellen and Kate feel welcome under difficult circumstances. He was proud of all of them for trying to put the past behind them.

It had been most difficult of all for Kate, he suspected. She alone had no blood ties to her new family. But she was strong and independent, and a damned sight too cynical about romance from what he'd seen. Whatever hurts she'd suffered, it was time she let them go. She needed a new man in her life to spark things up. He might look around among the up-and-coming young men in Boston and see to that himself, once he and Lizzy got back from their honeymoon.

"Lizzy, have you seen the doctor?" he asked worriedly. "I didn't see him go in. Who ever heard of delivering a baby without a doctor?"

"The doctor probably slipped in the back way just to avoid you and all your last-minute instructions," Lacey teased.

Sammy sidled up to him. "Come on, Grandpa Brandon. Let's go get some cigars."

"I suppose we could," he said with a last grudging glance down the hall.

He looked at Elizabeth. "You suppose there's time?"

"More than likely," she told him.

"What's that mean?"

"It means I can't guarantee it," she said.

"Then I'm not budging. What do you suppose they'll name him? Did they tell anybody?"

"Not me," Sammy said. "I've been bugging Dana for weeks, but she wouldn't say a word."

"You seem awfully certain it's going to be a boy," Elizabeth said. "Last I heard girls were a possibility as well."

Brandon shot Lizzy a pleased look, then gazed for a moment at his new daughter. "I guess they are at that," he said, just as a nurse came out of the delivery room and started toward them.

"You're all here with Dana and Jason Halloran?" she asked. "Yes," Brandon said. "Everything's okay in there, isn't it?"

"Everything is just fine. If you'd like, you can come with me. Dana and Jason want you to see your new grandchild."

Brandon was the first one down the hall. This great-grandbaby of his was going to have a fine life. He'd personally guarantee that. He fumbled with the ties on the gown he'd been given, then struggled with the mask. He seemed to be all thumbs. He felt Elizabeth's fingers nudging his aside, then her sure touch at the fastenings.

Then the nurse was opening the door to Dana's private room. Brandon stepped inside, his gaze going at once toward Dana and his grandson. Jason was holding a tiny bundle cradled in his arms.

As they stepped closer, he could see Dana's radiant face and felt as though his own heart would fill to bursting with sheer joy at having a new little Halloran born on this day that would always be special to all of them.

"Dad, Granddad, Mom, Elizabeth, and Sammy," Jason said slowly, beaming with pride. His glance included Ellen and Kate, though he didn't mention their names. "I'd like you to meet our daughter."

"Oh, my," Lacey said softly, taking Dana's hand and squeezing it. "A girl. Darling, that's wonderful."

Dana looked at each one of them, then said, "If you don't mind, we'd like to name her Elizabeth Lacey Halloran… We'll call her Beth."

Brandon watched as his new bride and his beloved daughter-in-law exchanged a misty-eyed look. Truth be told, his own eyes seemed to be stinging just a bit.

"I would be honored," Lizzy said. "So would I," Lacey added.

Elizabeth Lacey Halloran, Brandon thought with a

sigh as he gazed into that tiny, precious face. A new generation, named for the old and made strong by their love.

Indeed, he thought, as he took Elizabeth's hand in his, the best was yet to come.

* * * * *

Visit her Author Profile page at Harlequin.com,
or patriciadavids.com, for more titles!

AMISH REDEMPTION

Patricia Davids

The book is lovingly dedicated to all my readers. Thanks for making my writing dreams come true.

Attend unto my cry; for I am brought very low: deliver me from my persecutors; for they are stronger than I. Bring my soul out of prison, that I may praise thy name: the righteous shall compass me about; for thou shalt deal bountifully with me.
—*Psalms* 142:6–7

Chapter 1

Joshua Bowman's parole officer turned the squad car off the highway and onto the dirt lane. He stopped and looked over his shoulder. "You want me to drive to the house or do you want to walk from here?"

The immaculate farmstead with the two-story white house, white rail fences and big red barn at the end of the lane had never looked so beautiful. It was like many Amish farms that dotted the countryside around Berlin, Ohio, but this one was special. It was home.

Joshua cleared his throat. "I'd rather walk."

It was kind of Officer Oliver Merlin to allow Joshua's family reunion to take place in private. It was about the only kindness he had received from the *Englisch* justice system. He struggled to put that bitterness behind him. It was time for a new start.

Officer Merlin leveled a hard look at him. "You understand how this works. I'll be back to meet with you in two weeks."

"I'll be here."

"After that, we'll meet once a month until the end of your sentence, but I can drop in anytime. Deliberately miss a meeting with me and you'll find yourself back in prison. I don't take kindly to making long trips for nothing." The man's stern tone left no doubt that he meant what he said.

"I'm never going back there. Never." Joshua voiced the conviction in his heart as he met the officer's gaze without flinching.

"Obey the law and you won't." Getting out of the car, Officer Merlin came around to Joshua's door. There were no handles on the inside. Even though he was on his way home, he was still a prisoner. The moment the door opened, he drew his first free breath in six months.

Freedom beckoned, but he hesitated. What kind of welcome would he find in his father's house?

Officer Merlin's face softened. "I know this is hard, but you can do it, kid."

At twenty-one, Joshua was not a kid, but he appreciated the man's sympathy. He stepped out clutching a brown paper bag that contained his few personal possessions. A soft breeze caressed his cheeks, carrying with it the smells of spring, of the warming earth and fresh green grass. He closed his eyes, raised his face to the morning sun and thanked God for his deliverance.

"See you in two weeks." Officer Merlin closed the door behind Joshua, walked around the vehicle, got in and drove away.

Joshua immediately sat down in the grass at the edge

of the road and pulled off his boots and socks. Rising, he wiggled his toes, letting his bare feet relish the cool softness beneath him. Every summer of his life, he had worked and played barefoot along this lane and through these fields. Somehow, it felt right to come home this way. Picking up his bag and carrying his boots in his other hand, he started toward the house.

Set a little way back from the highway stood his father's woodworking shop and the small store where his mother sold homemade candy, jams, jellies, the occasional quilt and the furniture his father and brothers made. The closed sign still hung in the window. His mother would be down to open it as soon as her chores were done.

Joshua had painted the blue-and-white sign on the side of the building when he was fifteen: Bowmans Crossing Amish-Made Gifts and Furniture. At the time, his father thought it was too fancy, but Joshua's mother liked it. The bishop of their congregation hadn't objected, so it stayed. The blue paint was fading. He would find time to touch it up soon. Right now, he had to face his family.

Joshua was a dozen yards from the house when he saw his brothers come out of the barn. Timothy led a pair of draft horses harnessed and ready for working the fields. Noah, the youngest brother, walked beside Timothy. Both big gray horses raised their heads and perked up their ears at the sight of Joshua. One whinnied. His brothers looked to see what had caught their attention.

Joshua stopped. In his heart, he believed he would be welcomed, but his time among the *Englisch* had taught him not to trust in the goodness of others.

Timothy gave a whoop of joy. He looped the reins over the nearby fence and began running toward Joshua with Noah close on his heels. Their shouts brought their oldest brother, Samuel, and their father to the barn door. Samuel broke into a run, too. Before he knew it, Joshua was caught up in bear hugs by first one brother and then the others. Relief made him giddy with happiness, and he laughed out loud.

The commotion brought their mother out of the house to see what was going on. She shrieked with joy and ran down the steps with her white apron clutched in her hands and the ribbons of her Amish prayer *kapp* streaming behind her. She reached her husband's side and grasped his arm. Together they waited.

Joshua fended off his brothers and they fell silent as he walked toward his parents. He stopped a few feet in front of them and braced himself. "I know that I have brought shame and heartache to you both. I humbly ask your forgiveness. May I come home?"

He watched his father's face as he struggled with some great emotion. Tall and sparse with a flowing gray beard, Isaac Bowman was a man of few words. His straw hat, identical to the ones his sons wore, shaded his eyes, but Joshua caught the glint of moisture in them before his father wiped it away. Tears in his father's eyes were something Joshua had never seen before. His mother began weeping openly.

"Willkomme home, *mein sohn."*

Joshua's knees almost buckled, but he managed to stay upright and clasp his father's offered hand. *"Danki,* Father. I will never shame you again."

"There is no shame in what you did. You tried to

help your brother. Many of our ancestors suffered unjust imprisonments as you did. It was God's will." He pulled Joshua forward and kissed him on both cheeks.

When he stepped back, Joshua's mother threw her arms around him. He breathed in the scent of pine cleaner and lemon. Not a day went by that she wasn't scrubbing some surface of her home in an effort to make it clean and welcoming. She had no idea how good she smelled.

Leaning back, she smiled at him. "Come inside. There's cinnamon cake and a fresh pot of *kaffi* on the stove."

"We'll be in in a minute, Mother," Isaac said.

She glanced from her husband to her sons and nodded. "It's so *goot* to have you back."

When she returned to the house, his father began walking toward the barn. Joshua and his three brothers followed him. "Do you bring us news of your brother Luke?"

"He is doing as well as can be expected. I pray that they parole him early, too." It was Luke's second arrest on drug charges, and the judge had given him a longer sentence.

Samuel laid a hand on Joshua's shoulder. "We never believed what they said about you."

"I was in the wrong place at the wrong time. My mistake was thinking that the *Englisch* police would believe me. I thought justice was on the side of the innocent. It's not."

"Do you regret going to Cincinnati to find Luke?" Noah asked.

"*Nee*, I had to try and convince him to come back. I

know you said it was his decision, Father, but I thought I could persuade him to give up that wretched life and return with me. We were close once."

In the city, Joshua had discovered his brother had moved from using drugs to making and selling them. Joshua stayed for two days and tried to reason with him, but his pleas had fallen on deaf ears. He'd been ready to accept defeat and return home when the drug raid went down. In a very short time, Joshua found himself in prison alongside his brother. His sentence for a first offense was harsh because his brother had been living near a school.

His father regarded him with sad eyes. "The justice we seek is not of this world, *sohn*. God knows an innocent heart. It is His judgment we must fear."

"Do you think this time in prison will change Luke?" Timothy asked softly.

Prison changed any man who entered those walls, but not always for the better. Joshua shrugged.

His father hooked his thumbs through his suspenders. "You are home now, and for that we must all give thanks. Timothy, Noah, Samuel, the ground will not prepare itself for planting."

Joshua smiled. That was *Daed*—give thanks that his son was home for five minutes and then make everyone get to work.

Joshua's brothers slapped him on the back and started toward the waiting team. Timothy looked over his shoulder. "I want to hear all about the gangsters in the big house tonight."

"I didn't meet any," Joshua called after him, wondering where his brother had picked up such terms.

"Not even one?" Noah's mouth fell open in disbelief.

"Nope." Joshua grinned at his little brother's crest-fallen expression. Joshua had no intention of sharing the sights he'd seen in that inhuman world.

"Come. Your mother is anxious to spoil you. She deserves her happiness today."

Joshua followed his father inside. Nothing had changed in the months Joshua had been away. The kitchen was spotless and smelled of cinnamon, fresh-baked bread and stout coffee. Standing with his eyes closed, he let the smells of home wash away the linger-ing scent of his prison cell. He was truly home at last.

"Sit," his mother insisted.

He opened his eyes and smiled at her. She wasn't happy unless she was feeding someone. She bustled about the kitchen getting cups and plates and dishing up thick slices of coffee cake. He took a seat at the table, but his father remained by the desk in the corner. He picked up a long white envelope. Turning to Joshua, he said, "Mother's *onkel* Marvin passed away a few months ago."

Joshua frowned. "I don't remember him."

His mother set a plate on the table. "You never met him. He left the Amish as a young man and never spoke to my family again."

"It seems Mother has inherited his property over by Hope Springs." His father tapped the letter against his palm.

"I didn't even know where he lived. His lawyer said he was fond of me because I was such a happy child. Strange, don't you think? Would you like *kaffi* or milk?" she asked with a beaming smile on her face.

"Coffee. What kind of property did he leave you?"

"Forty acres with a house and barn," his father replied. "But the lawyer says the property is in poor repair. I was going to go to Hope Springs the day after tomorrow to look it over, but you know how I hate long buggy trips. Besides, I need to get the ground worked so we can plant. Joshua, why don't you go instead? It would take a load off me, and it would give you a little time to enjoy yourself before getting behind a planter again."

Hope Springs was a day's buggy ride from the farm. The idea of traveling wasn't as appealing as it had once been, but doing something for his father was. "I'd be glad to go for you."

His mother's smile faded. "But Joshua has only just gotten home, Isaac."

Joshua rose to his feet and planted a kiss on her cheek. "You have two whole days to spoil me with your *wunderbar* cooking before then. I'll check out your property, and then I'll be home for good."

"Do you promise?" she asked softly.

He cupped her face in his palms. "I promise."

"Mary, I have just the *mann* for you."

Resisting the urge to bang her head on the cupboard door in front of her, Mary Kaufman continued mixing the lemon cake batter in the bowl she held. "I don't want a man, Ada."

Don't want one. Don't need one. How many ways can I say it before you believe me?

Except for her adopted father, Nick Bradley, most of the men in Mary's life had brought her pain and grief. However, the prospect of finding her a husband was her adopted grandmother's favorite subject. As much as Mary loved Ada, this got old.

"Balderdish! Every Amish woman needs a *goot* Amish husband." Ada opened the oven door.

"The word is *balderdash*."

Ada pulled a cake out using the folded corner of her black apron and dropped it on the stove top with a clatter. "*Mein Englisch* is *goot*. Do not change the subject. You will be nineteen in a few weeks. Do you want people to call you an *alt maedel*?"

"I'll be twenty, and I don't care if people call me an old maid or not."

Ada frowned at her. *"Zvansich?"*

"*Ja*. Hannah just turned four. That means I'll be twenty." Mary smiled at her daughter playing with an empty bowl and wooden spoon on the floor. She was showing her dog, Bella, how to make a cake. The yellow Lab lay watching intently, her big head resting on her paws. Mary could almost believe the dog was memorizing the instructions.

Ada turned to the child. "Hannah, how old are you?"

Grinning at her great-grandmother, Hannah held up four fingers. "This many."

Patting her chest rapidly, Ada faced Mary. "*Ach!* Then there is no time to lose. Delbert Miller is coming the day after tomorrow to fix the chicken *haus*. You must be nice to him."

Mary slapped one hand to her cheek. "You're right. There's no time to lose. I'll marry him straightaway. If he doesn't fall through that rickety roof and squish all our chickens."

She shook her head and began stirring again. "Go out with Delbert Miller? Not in a hundred years."

"I know he is *en adlichah grohsah mann*, but you should not hold that against him."

Mary rolled her eyes. "A *fairly* big man? *Nee*, he is a *very* big man."

"And are you such a prize that you can judge him harshly?"

Mary stopped stirring and stared at the cuffs of her long sleeves. No matter how hot it got in the summer, she never rolled them up. They covered the scars on her wrists. The jagged white lines in her flesh were indisputable evidence that she had attempted suicide, the ultimate sin. Shame washed over her. "*Nee*, I'm not a prize."

A second later, she was smothered in a hug that threatened to coat her in batter. "Forgive me, child. That is not what I meant. You know that. You are the light in this old woman's heart and your dear *dochder* is the sun and the stars."

Mary closed her eyes and took a deep breath.

God spared my life. He has forgiven my sins. I am loved and treasured by the new family He gave me. Bad things happened years ago, but those things gave me my beautiful child. She is happy here, as I dreamed she would be. I will not dwell in that dark place again. We are safe and that evil man is locked away. He can never find us here.

Hannah came to join the group, tugging on Mary's skirt and lifting her arms for a hug, too. Mary set her bowl on the counter and picked up her daughter. "You are the sun and the stars, aren't you?"

"*Ja*, I am." Hannah gave a big nod.

"You are indeed." Ada kissed Hannah's cheek and Mary's cheek in turn. "You had better hurry or you will be late for the quilting bee. I'll finish that batter. Are you taking Hannah?"

"I am. She enjoys playing with Katie Sutter's little ones." Mary glanced at the clock in the corner. It was nearly four. The quilting bee was being held at Katie's home. They were finishing a quilt as a wedding gift for Katie's friend Sally Yoder. Sally planned to wed in the fall.

"Who else is coming?"

"Rebecca Troyer, Faith Lapp, Joann Weaver and Sarah Beachy. Betsy Barkman will be there, of course, and I think all her sisters will be, too."

Betsy Barkman was Mary's dearest friend. They were both still single and neither of them was in a hurry to marry—something few people in their Amish community of Hope Springs understood. Especially Betsy's sisters. Lizzie, Clara and Greta had all found husbands. They were impatiently waiting for their youngest sister to do the same. Betsy had been going out with Alvin Stutzman for over a year, but she wasn't ready to be tied down.

"Sounds like you'll have a wonderful time. Make sure you bring me all the latest gossip."

"We don't gossip." Mary winked at her grandmother.

"*Ja*, and a rooster doesn't crow."

Shifting her daughter to her hip, Mary crossed the room and gathered their traveling bonnets from beside the door. She stood Hannah on a chair to tie the large black hat over her daughter's silky blond crown of braids. As she did, she heard the distant rumble of thunder.

Ada leaned toward the kitchen window to peer out. "There's a storm brewing, from the looks of those clouds. The paper said we should expect strong storms today. You'd better hurry. If it's bad, stay with the Sutters until it passes."

"I will."

"And you will be nice to Delbert when he visits."

"I'll be nice to him. Unless he squashes any of our chickens," Mary said with a cheeky grin.

"Bothersome child. Get before I take a switch to your backside." Ada shook the spoon at Mary. Speckles of batter went everywhere much to Bella's delight. The dog quickly licked the floor clean and sat with her hopeful gaze fixed on Ada.

Laughing, Mary scooped up her daughter and headed out the door. Bella tried to follow, but Mary shook her head. "You stay with *Mammi*. We'll be back soon."

Bella gave her a reproachful look, but turned around and headed to her favorite spot beside the stove.

Mary soon had her good-natured mare harnessed and climbed in the buggy with Hannah. She glanced at the rapidly approaching storm clouds. They did look threatening. The sky held an odd greenish cast that usually meant hail. Should she go, or should she stay home? She hated to miss an afternoon of fun with her friends.

She decided to go. She would be traveling ahead of it on her way to the Sutter farm and Tilly was a fast trotter.

Mary wasted no time getting the mare up to speed once they reached the highway at the end of her grandmother's lane. She glanced back several times in the small rearview mirror on the side of her buggy. The clouds had become an ominous dark shroud, turning the May afternoon sky into twilight. Streaks of lightning were followed by growing rumbles of thunder.

Hannah edged closer to her. "I don't like storms."

She slipped an arm around her daughter. "Don't worry. We'll be at Katie's house before the rain catches us."

It turned out she was wrong. Big raindrops began hitting her windshield a few minutes later. A strong gust of wind shook the buggy and blew dust across the road. The sky grew darker by the minute. Mary urged Tilly to a faster pace. She should have stayed home.

A red car flew past her with the driver laying on the horn. Tilly shied and nearly dragged the buggy into the fence along the side of the road. Mary managed to right her. "Foolish *Englischers*. Have they no sense? We are over as far as we can get."

The rumble of thunder became a steady roar behind them. Tilly broke into a run. Startled, Mary tried to pull her back but the mare struggled against the bit.

"Tilly, what's wrong with you?" She sawed on the reins, trying to slow the animal.

Hannah began screaming. Mary glanced back and her heart stopped. A tornado had dropped from the clouds and was bearing down on them, chewing up everything in its path. Dust and debris flew out from the wide base as the roar grew louder. Mary loosened the reins and gave Tilly her head, but she knew even the former racehorse wouldn't be able to outrun it. They had to find cover.

The lessons she learned at school came tumbling

back into her mind: *get underground in a cellar or lie flat in a ditch.*

There weren't any houses nearby. She scanned the fences lining each side of the road. The ditches were shallow to nonexistent. The roar grew louder. Hannah kept screaming.

Dear God, help me save my baby. What do I do?

She saw an intersection up ahead.

Travel away from a tornado at a right angle. Don't try to outrun it.

Bracing her legs against the dash, she pulled back on the lines, trying to slow Tilly enough to make the corner without overturning. The mare seemed to sense the plan. She slowed and made the turn with the buggy tilting on two wheels. Mary grabbed Hannah and held on to her. Swerving wildly behind the horse, the buggy finally came back onto all four wheels. Before the mare could gather speed again, a man jumped into the road, waving his arms. He grabbed Tilly's bridle as she plunged past and pulled her to a stop.

Shouting, he pointed toward an abandoned farmhouse that Mary hadn't seen back in the trees. "There's a cellar on the south side."

Mary jumped out of the buggy and pulled Hannah into her arms. The man was already unhitching Tilly, so Mary ran toward the ramshackle structure with boarded-over windows and overgrown trees hugging the walls. The wind threatened to pull her off her feet. The trees and even the grass were straining toward the approaching tornado. Dirt and leaves pelted her face, but fear for Hannah pushed her forward. She reached the old cellar door, but couldn't lift it against the force of the wind. She was about to lie on the ground on top of Hannah when the man appeared at her side. Together, they were able to lift the door.

Mary glanced back and saw her buggy flying up into the air in slow motion. The sight was so mesmerizing that she froze.

A second later, she was pushed down the steps into darkness.

Chapter 2

Pummeled by debris in the wind, Joshua hustled the woman and her child down the old stone steps in the hope of finding safety below. He had discovered the cellar that afternoon while investigating the derelict property for his father. He hadn't explored the basement because the crumbling house with its sagging roof and tilted walls didn't look safe. He couldn't believe anyone had lived in it until a few months ago. Now its shelter was their only hope.

The wind tore at his clothes and tried to suck him backward. His hat flew off and out of the steep stairwell to disappear in the roiling darkness overhead. The roar of the funnel was deafening. The cellar door banged shut, narrowly missing his head and then flew open again. A sheet of newspaper settled on the step in front of him and opened gently as if waiting to be read. A second later, the cellar door dropped closed with a heavy thud, plunging him into total darkness.

He stumbled slightly when his feet hit the floor instead of another step. The little girl kept screaming but he barely heard her over the howling storm. It sounded as if he were lying under a train. A loud crash overhead followed by choking dust raining down on them changed the girl's screaming into a coughing fit. Joshua knew the house had taken a direct hit. It could cave in on them and become their tomb instead of their haven.

He pressed the woman and her child against the rough stone wall and forced them to crouch near the floor as he huddled over the pair, offering what protection he could with his body. It wouldn't be much if the floors above them gave way. He heard the woman praying, and he joined in asking for God's protection and mercy. Another crash overhead sent more dust down on them. Choked by the dirt, he couldn't see, but he felt her hand on his face and realized she was offering the edge of her apron for him to cover his nose and mouth. He clutched it gratefully, amazed that she could think of his comfort when they were all in peril. She wasn't screaming or crying as many women would. She was bravely facing the worst and praying.

He kept one arm around her and the child. They both trembled with fear. His actions had helped them escape the funnel itself, but the danger was far from over. She had no idea how perilous their cover was, but he did.

He'd put his horse and buggy in the barn after he arrived late yesterday evening. One look at the ramshackle house made him decide to sleep in the backseat of his buggy while his horse, Oscar, occupied a nearby stall.

The barn, although old and dirty, was still sound with a good roof and plenty of hay in the loft. His great-uncle had taken better care of his animals than he had of himself.

Joshua hoped Oscar was okay, but he had no way of knowing if the barn had been spared. Right now, he was more worried that the old house over their heads wouldn't be. Had he brought this woman and her child into a death trap?

Terrified, Mary held Hannah close and prayed. She couldn't get the sight of her buggy being lifted into the sky out of her mind. What if they had still been inside? What if her rescuer hadn't appeared when he did? Was today the day she was to meet God face-to-face? Was she ready?

Please, Father, I beg You to spare us. If this is my time to come home to You, I pray You spare my baby's life. But if You must take Hannah, take me, too, for I couldn't bear to be parted from her again.

The roar was so loud and the pressure so intense that Mary wanted to cover her aching ears, but she couldn't let go of Hannah or the apron she was using to cover their faces. The horrible howling went on and on.

Make it stop, God! Please, make it stop.

In spite of having her face buried in the cloth, thick dust got in her eyes and her nose with every breath. Hannah's small body trembled against her. Her screams had turned to whimpers as her arms tightened around Mary's neck. The roar grew so loud that Mary thought she couldn't take it another moment. Her body shook with the need to run, to escape, to get away.

As soon as the thought formed, the sound lessened and quickly moved on. Was it over? Were they safe?

Thanks be to God.

Mary tried to stand, but the man held her down. "Not yet."

She could hear the wind shrieking and lashing the trees outside, but the horrible pressure in her ears was gone and the roar was fading. In its place, groaning, cracking and thumps reverberated overhead. A thunderous crash shook the ceiling over them and the old timbers moaned. Hannah clutched Mary's neck again. Mary glanced up fearfully. She couldn't see anything for the darkness and the man leaning over her.

He said, "Stay close to the wall. It's the safest place."

She knew what he meant. It was the safest place if the floor above them came down. She huddled against the cold stones, pressing herself and Hannah into as small a space as possible, and waited, praying for herself, her child and the stranger trying to protect them. After several long minutes, she knew God had heard her prayers. The old boards above them stayed intact.

"Is the bad thing gone, *Mamm*?" Hannah loosened her stranglehold on Mary's neck. Her small voice shook with fear.

Mary stroked her hair and kissed her cheek to soothe her. Somewhere in their mad dash, Hannah had lost her bonnet and her braids hung loose. "*Ja*, the bad storm is gone, but keep your face covered. The dust is very thick."

Hannah was only quiet for a moment. "Can we go outside? I don't like it in here."

Mary didn't like it, either. "In a minute, my heart. Now hush."

"We must let the storm pass first," the man said. His voice was deep and soothing. Who was he? In her brief glimpse of him, she had noticed his Amish dress and little else beyond the fact that he was a young man without a beard. That meant he was single, but she didn't recognize him from the area. He was a stranger to her. A Good Samaritan sent by God to aid her in her moment of need. She wished she could see his face.

"Is Tilly okay, *Mamm*?"

"I don't know, dear. I hope so." Mary hadn't spared a thought for her poor horse.

"Who is Tilly?" he asked.

"Our horse," Hannah replied without hesitation, surprising Mary.

Hannah rarely spoke to someone she didn't know. The current situation seemed to have erased her daughter's fear of strange men, or at least this man. It was an anxiety Mary knew she compounded with her own distrust of strangers. She tried to accept people at face value, as good, the way her faith required her to do, but her dealings with men in the past had left scars on her ability to trust as well as on her wrists. Not everyone who gave aid did so without an ulterior motive.

"I think your horse is safe. I saw her running away across the field. Without the buggy to pull, she may have gotten out of the way." There was less tension in his voice. Mary began to relax. The worst was over and they were still alive.

"But Tilly will be lost if she runs off." Hannah's voice quivered.

"*Nee*, a *goot* horse will go home to its own barn," he assured her. "Is she a *goot* horse?"

Mary felt Hannah nod vigorously, although she doubted the stranger could see. "She's a *wunderbar* horse," Hannah declared.

"Then she'll likely be home before you."

Hannah tipped her head to peer at the man. "Did your horse run off, too?"

"Oscar is in the barn. He should be okay in there."

Mary heard the worry underneath his words. In a storm like this, nowhere aboveground was safe.

Hannah rested her head on Mary's shoulder. "Are *Mammi* Ada and Bella okay?"

"They are in God's hands, Hannah. He will protect them." The twister had come up behind them. Mary had no idea if it had touched down before or after it passed over the farm. She prayed for her dear grandmother.

"I want to go home. I want to see *Mammi* Ada and Bella."

"Is Bella your sister?" the man asked.

"She's my *wunderbar* dog."

He chuckled. It was a warm, friendly sound. "Have you a *wunderbar* cat, as well?"

"I don't. Bella doesn't like cats. She's going to be worried about me. We should go home now, *Mamm*." Mary hoped they had a house waiting for them.

"We'll get you home as soon as the storm has moved on," the young man said as he stepped back.

Mary's eyes were adjusting to the gloom. She could see he was of medium height with dark hair, but little else. She knew that without his help things could have been much worse. He could have taken shelter without risking his life to help them. She had his bravery and quick action to thank for getting them out of her buggy before it'd become airborne. Just thinking about what that ride would have been like caused a shiver to rattle her teeth.

He gave her an awkward pat on her shoulder. "I think the worst is over."

She tried not to flinch from his touch. Her common sense said he wasn't a threat, but trusting didn't come easily to her. "We are grateful for your assistance. God was merciful to send you when He did."

He gave a dry bark of laughter. "This time I was in the right place at the right time."

What could he find funny in this horrible situation?

Joshua was amazed at how God had placed him exactly where he needed to be today to save this woman and child, and yet six months ago the Lord had put him in a position that sent him to prison for no good reason. Who could fathom the ways of God? Not he.

"I am Mary Kaufman and this is my daughter, Hannah."

He heard the hesitation in her words and wondered at it. "I'm Joshua Bowman."

"Thank you again, Joshua. Do you think it is safe to venture out?"

A loud clap of thunder rattled the structure over them. "I think we should wait awhile longer."

The thunder was followed by the steady ping of hail against some metal object outside and the drone of hard rain. The tornado had passed but the thunderstorm had plenty of steam left.

"I reckon you're right." Abruptly, she moved away from him.

"I'm sorry. I didn't mean to be overly familiar." Close contact between unmarried members of the opposite sex wasn't permitted in Amish society. Circumstances had forced him to cross that boundary, but it couldn't continue.

"You were protecting us." She moved a few more steps away.

She was uncomfortable being alone with him. He couldn't blame her. She had no idea who he was. How could he put her at ease? Maybe by not hovering over her. He sat down with his back against the old stone wall, refusing to think about the creepy-crawly occupants who were surely in here with them.

She relaxed slightly. "Do you live here?"

"I don't, but my great-uncle did until he died a few months ago."

"I'm sorry for your loss."

"*Danki*, but I never knew him. He was *Englisch*. He left the family years ago and never contacted them again. Everyone was surprised to learn he had willed the property to my mother. She is only one of his many nieces."

"He must have cherished a fondness for her."

"So it would seem. My father sent me to check out the place, as the letter from the attorney said it was in rough shape. *Daed* wants to find out what will be needed to get it ready to farm, rent out or sell. Unfortunately, it's in much worse condition than we expected."

That was an understatement. His father would have to invest heavily in this farm to get it in working order, and the family didn't have that kind of money. They would need to sell it.

"From the sounds of things, it will need even more repair after the storm passes."

He chuckled at her wry tone. "*Ja.* I think the good Lord may have done us a favor by tearing down the old house. I just wish He had waited until we were out of the way."

His eyes had grown accustomed to the gloom. He could make out Mary's white apron and the pale oval of her face framed by her black traveling bonnet. She sat down, too, pulling her child into her lap. Together, they waited side by side in the darkness. At least she seemed less afraid of him now.

The thunder continued to rumble, punctuating the sound of the wind and the steady rain. They sat in tense silence. Even the child was quiet. After a while, the thunder grew less violent but the rain continued. Was it going to storm all night? If so, he might as well find out what was left of the property and see if he could get this young mother and daughter home.

He rose to his feet. "Stay here until I'm sure it's safe to go out."

She stood, too, holding her little girl in her arms. "Be careful."

He made his way to the cellar door and pushed up on it. It wouldn't budge.

He pushed harder. It still didn't move. Something heavy was blocking it. He worked to control the panic rising in his chest. He couldn't be trapped. Not in such a small place. It was like being in prison all over again. His palms grew damp and his heart began to pound.

"What's wrong?" Mary asked.

The last thing he wanted was to scare her again, but she would soon find out what was going on. He worked to keep his tone calm. There was no point in frightening her more than she already was. "Something is blocking the door. I can't move it. Can you give me a hand?"

He sounded almost normal and was pleased with himself. If she knew differently, she didn't let on. Having someone else to worry about was helping to keep his panic under control.

"Hannah, stay right here," Mary said, then made her way up the steps until she was beside him. She braced her arms against the overhead door. "On three."

She counted off and they both pushed. Nothing. It could have been nailed shut for all their efforts accomplished. He moved a step higher and braced his back against the old boards. He pushed with all his might, straining to move whatever held it. Mary pushed, too, but still the door refused to budge.

This can't be happening.

"Help! Help, we're down here," she yelled, and beat on the door with her fists. He wanted to do the same.

Don't think of yourself. Think of her. Think of her child. They need you to be calm.

He drew a steadying breath. "There isn't anyone around to hear you. This farm has been deserted for months."

"There must be another way out."

He heard the rising panic in her voice. He forced himself to relax and speak casually. "There should be a staircase to the inside of the house. Hopefully, it isn't blocked."

"Of course. Let's find it. I don't want to stay down here any longer than I must. All this dust isn't good for Hannah."

She started to move past him, but he caught her arm. "You could get hurt stumbling around in the dark. Stay here with your daughter. I'll go look. I've got a lighter, but I'm not sure how much fuel is left in it. Shout if you hear anything outside. No one will be looking for me, but your family will be looking for you, right?"

"They will, but not soon."

That wasn't what he wanted to hear. "Maybe someone will see your buggy out there and come to investigate."

"My buggy isn't out there. Didn't you see it get sucked up and carried away?"

"I didn't. I had my eyes fixed on you."

"No one is going to know where to look for us, are they?" Her voice trembled.

"It won't matter once I find a way out. I'll be back as quick as I can." It was an assurance he didn't really feel.

He tried to remember the layout of the building he had surveyed for his father. Although he had looked in through the windows that hadn't been boarded over, he hadn't ventured inside to explore thoroughly since his father was more interested in the land and its potential. Joshua didn't remember seeing a door that might be an inside entrance to the cellar. Some older houses only had outside entrances. The most logical place for the stairs would be near the kitchen at the other end of the house.

As it continued to rain, water began pouring through cracks in the floorboards overhead. That wasn't good.

It meant a part of the house had been torn open, allowing the rain to come in. How sound was what remained? The steady rumble of thunder promised more rain. Would the saturated wood give way and finish what the tornado had started? He looked over his shoulder. "Mary, stay near the wall or in the stairwell, okay?"

"I will."

Joshua surveyed what he could in the darkness. The cellar itself wasn't empty. The only clear place seemed to be where they were standing. The cavernous space was piled high with odds and ends of lumber, boxes, old tires and discarded household items. His great-uncle, it seemed, had been a hoarder as well as a recluse.

Joshua had put a lighter in his pocket before leaving the farm in case he ended up camping out. It had come in handy last night and now he pulled it out, clicked it on and held it over his head. Gray cobwebs waved from every surface in the flickering light that did little to pierce the gloom. He couldn't keep the lighter on for long before he burned his fingers, so he quickly identified a path and let the light go out.

Stepping around a pair of broken chairs, he pushed aside wooden boxes of unknown items. When his shin hit something, he flicked on the lighter again. A set of box springs blocked his way. Most of the cloth covering had rotted away. Mice had made off with more. Skirting it as best he could without stepping on the springs, he continued along the cellar wall. A set of shelves on the far side was lined with dust-covered cans, jars and crocks, but he saw no stairs. He finished the circuit and moved back toward where Mary was standing. He flicked on his light.

"Have you discovered a way out?" Her voice shook only slightly, but he saw the worry in her eyes.

They weren't going anywhere until someone found them. He had no idea how long that might take. They could be down here for hours, days even. The thought was chilling. He stopped a few feet away from her and let the light go out. How did he tell a frightened woman she was trapped in a cellar with a man who'd spent the past six months in prison?

When Joshua didn't answer her question, Mary's heart sank. She knew he hadn't found an exit. She bit her thumbnail as she considered their predicament. Her friends would be concerned when she didn't arrive at the quilting bee, but they might assume she had stayed home to wait out the storm. When she didn't return home this evening, Ada would become concerned, but she might think Mary had decided to spend the night at the Sutter farm. Ada might not even know about the tornado if it had formed this side of the farm.

Mary hoped that was the case. Ada had a bad heart and didn't need such worry. It could be morning before she became concerned about them and perhaps as late as noon before she realized they were missing.

Mary's adoptive parents, Nick and Miriam Bradley would begin looking for them as soon as their absence was noted. Miriam stopped at the farm every morning and Nick dropped by every evening on his way home from work without fail. He would know about the tornado. He would stop by the farm this evening to make sure she and Hannah were safe. Would he go to the Sutter farm to check on them when he found they weren't home? She had no way of knowing, but she prayed that he would.

It might take a while, but Nick would find them. Mary had no doubt of that. But would he find them before dark? Or was she going to have to spend the night with this stranger?

Chapter 3

Mary shivered as she looked around the old cellar. If she had to spend the night in here, she wouldn't like it, but she could do it. She would depend on God for His protection and comfort. In the meantime, she had to be brave for her child and make the best of a bad situation for Joshua's sake, too. He was trying to hide his fear, but she saw it in his eyes.

"I noticed an old lantern hanging from a nail by the cellar steps. We should check and see if it has any kerosene in it." She spoke calmly, surprised to find her voice sounded matter of fact.

"Good idea. I'll see if I can find an ax or something useful to chop open or pry up the door." Joshua flicked his lighter on. He located the lantern, took it down from the nail and shook it. A faint sloshing sound gave Mary hope.

Hannah tugged on her skirt. "I'm hungry. Can we go home now?"

Joshua leaned toward her. "You mean you want to go home before our adventure has ended?"

Hannah gave him a perplexed look. "What adventure?"

"Why, our treasure hunt." He raised the glass chimney of the lantern and held his lighter to the wick. It flickered feebly for a second and then caught. He lowered the glass, wiped it free of dust with his sleeve and turned up the wick. The lamp cast a golden glow over their surroundings. It was amazing how much better Mary felt now that she could see.

"What kind of treasure hunt?" Hannah sounded intrigued by the idea.

"We're all going to hunt for some useful things," Mary said.

Joshua nodded. "That's right. Let's pretend that we are going to make this cellar into a home. What do we need first?"

"Chairs and a table," Hannah said.

"Then help me look for some on our pretend shopping trip." He glanced at Mary. She nodded and he held out his hand to Hannah. "I think I saw some chairs over this way. Don't you like to go shopping? I do. This storekeeper needs to sweep out his store, though. This place is as dirty as a rainbow."

Hannah scowled at him. "Rainbows aren't dirty. They're pretty and clean."

He held his lantern higher. "Are they? Well, this place isn't. It's as dirty as a star."

"Stars aren't dirty, Joshua. They twinkle."

"Then you tell me what is dirty."

"A pigpen."

"Yup, that is dirty, all right, but this place is worse than a pigpen. What else is dirty?"

"Your face."

Mary choked on her laugh. Hannah was right. His face was covered in dirt. There were cobwebs on his clothes and bits of leaves and grass in his dark brown hair. It was then she realized how short his hair was. It wasn't the style worn by Amish men. Joshua must still be in his *rumspringa*.

Mary had left her running-around years behind a few short weeks after Hannah was born. She had been baptized into the Amish faith at the age of sixteen, the time when most Amish teens were just beginning to test the waters of the English world.

Joshua seemed to notice she was staring at him. He rubbed a hand over his head in a self-conscious gesture and shook free some of the clinging grime.

Mary looked away. She wiped down her sleeves and brushed off her bonnet, knowing she couldn't look much better. Oddly, she wished she had a mirror to make sure her face was clean. It wasn't like her to be concerned with her looks, but she did wonder what Joshua thought of her.

That was silly. He would think she was a married woman with a child, and that was a good thing. She glanced at him again.

He wiped his face with both hands but it didn't do much good. He spoke to Hannah. "This isn't dirt. It's flour. I was going to bake a cake."

Hannah giggled at his silliness. "It is not flour."

"Okay, but this is a table and we need one." He held his find aloft. The ancient rocker was missing a few spindles in the back, but the seat was intact.

Hannah planted her hands on her hips. "That's a chair."

"It's a good thing I have you to help me shop. I'd never find the right stuff on my own. Let's go look for a donkey."

Hannah giggled again. "Joshua, we don't need a donkey in our house."

"We don't? I'm so glad. I don't know where it would sleep tonight."

His foolishness made Mary smile. He was distracting and entertaining Hannah. For that, she was grateful. Mary turned her attention to finding something to collect the rainwater. She had no idea how long they might be down here, but Hannah was sure to be thirsty soon.

She found a metal tub hanging from a post near the center of the room. It had probably been a washtub at one time. Using her apron, she wiped it out and positioned it under the worst of the dripping. Next, she found an empty glass canning jar and rinsed it out the same way. She put it in the center of the tub. Once the jar was full, the overflow would accumulate in the tub and leave her something to wash with later.

The plink, plink, plink of the water hitting the bottom of the jar was annoying, but they would be grateful for the bounty before morning. She refused to think they might be down here more than one night.

Taking off her bonnet, she laid it aside. Then she held the cleanest corner of her apron under a neighboring drip until it was wet and unobtrusively used it to scrub her face.

At the end of their shopping trip, Joshua and Hannah came back with two barely usable chairs, a small wooden crate for a third seat and another washtub with a hole in the side for a table, but no ax or tools. Joshua set the furniture up in their corner, allowing Hannah to arrange and rearrange them to her satisfaction in her imaginary house.

While her daughter was busy, Mary spoke quietly to Joshua. "I will be fine until we are rescued, but Hannah will be hungry soon. Do you have anything to eat?"

"Nothing. I'm sorry. Everything I have is out in my buggy in the barn. There are some cans and jars on the shelf back there. Want me to take a look?"

"*Nee*, you're doing a wonderful job keeping Hannah occupied. I'll go look." Normally leery of strangers, Mary didn't feel her usual disquiet with Joshua. She assumed their current circumstances made him seem like less of a stranger and more like a friend in need.

He pulled a candle stub from his pocket. "I found this along with a couple of others in a pan. It was the best one." He lit it, dripped a small amount of wax on the overturned washtub and stuck the butt in it to hold the candle upright. Then he handed Mary the lantern.

"Someone was probably saving them to melt down to reuse." She didn't have a mold to form a new candle, but she could make one by dipping a wick in the melted wax. A strip of cotton cloth from her apron or from her *kapp* ribbon would make an adequate wick. She would work on that before the lantern ran out of fuel. Sitting in the dark was the last thing she wanted to do.

Hannah began jumping up and down. "I hear a siren. Do you hear it? It's Papa Nick!"

Mary's spirits rose until the welcome sound faded away. Nick wasn't coming for them. He had no idea where she was. It might not even have been him. How much damage had been done by the tornado? Were others in need of rescue?

A few moments later, she heard the sound of another siren on the highway. Were they ambulances rushing to help people injured by the twister? She had been praying so hard for herself and for Hannah that she had forgotten about others in the area. This part of the county was dotted with English and Amish farms and businesses. How many had been destroyed? How many people had lost their lives? She prayed now for all the people she knew beyond the stone walls keeping her prisoner. It was the only thing she could do to help.

Lifting the lantern, she moved across the crowded room to the shelves Joshua had indicated and searched through the contents. She glanced back to see him placing the tub as Hannah instructed in her imaginary house. The lantern flickered and Mary turned up the wick. She hated being trapped, but at least she didn't have to face the situation alone.

A dozen times in the next half hour the eerie wailing of sirens rose and fell as they passed by on the highway a quarter of a mile away from the house. Each time, Mary's hopes sprang to life and then ebbed away with the sound. She met Joshua's eyes. They both knew it was a bad sign.

Joshua noticed the growing look of concern on Mary's face. It didn't surprise him. He was concerned, too. He had no idea when rescue would come. Would anyone think to search an old house that had been abandoned for months? Why would they? He racked his brain for a way to signal that they were here, but came up empty. Someone would have to come close enough to hear them shouting.

Hannah came to stand in front of him with her hands on her hips. "Joshua, we need a stove and a bed now. Take me shopping again."

She looked and sounded like a miniature version of her mother. He had to smile. "You are a bossy woman. Does your mother boss your *daed* that way?"

Hannah shook her head. "He died a long time ago. I don't remember him. But I have Papa Nick."

At first, Joshua had assumed Papa Nick was *Englisch* because Hannah connected him to the siren she heard. However, the siren could have belonged to one of the many Amish volunteer fire department crews that dotted the area. Was Papa Nick her new father, perhaps? He glanced to where Mary was searching the shelves and asked quietly, "Who is Nick?"

"He's my papa Nick," the child said, as if that explained everything.

"Is he your mother's husband?"

"Nee." She laughed at the idea.

He glanced at Mary with a new spark of interest. She wasn't married, as he had assumed. It was surprising. Why would the men in this community overlook such a prize? Perhaps she was still mourning her husband. Joshua rubbed his chin. He noticed a bit of cobweb dangling from his fingers and shook it off. He needed to concentrate on getting out of this cellar, not on his interest in Hannah's mother.

He patted Hannah's head. "We will go shopping as soon as your *mamm* returns. Let's wait and see if she brings us any treasures."

"Okay." Hannah sat on her makeshift chair, put her elbows on her knees and propped her chin in her hands. "I wish Bella was here."

Joshua sat gingerly in the chair with a broken arm. He sighed with relief when it held his weight. Remembering the black-and-white mutt that had been his inseparable companion when he was only a little bit older than Hannah, he asked, "What kind of dog is she?"

"She's a yellow dog."

Joshua smothered a grin and managed to say, "They're the best kind."

"Yup. She was *Mammi* Miriam's dog, but when I was born, Bella wanted to belong to me."

Mary returned with several jars in her hand. "These pears are still sealed and the rings were taken off so they aren't rusty. If worst comes to worst, we can try them, but they are nearly three years old from what I can read of the labels."

He grimaced. "Three-year-old pears don't sound appetizing."

"I wasn't suggesting they were, but I've known people to eat home-canned food that was older than this."

"Really? How can you tell if it's bad?"

"If the seal is intact, if the food looks good and smells okay, it should be okay…" Her voice trailed off.

He folded his arms over his chest. "You go first."

She rolled her eyes and he smiled. He could have been trapped with a much less enjoyable companion.

"Come on, Hannah. We're going shopping for a bed. I think I saw one earlier that might go with our decor."

"What's decor?" Hannah asked, jumping off her chair.

He gestured toward his clothing. "It means style."

"What is your style?" Mary asked with a gleam of amusement in her eyes.

"Cobwebs and dust. What's yours?" He leaned toward her. "How did you get your face clean?"

She blushed and looked down. "There is plenty of water dripping in on the other side. You could wash up if you'd like."

"Good idea. Come on, Hannah. Let's get some of this decor off of us."

"*Ja*, it's yucky."

Mary stopped Hannah. She lifted the girl's apron off over her head, tore it in two and handed him the pieces. "Use this to wash and dry with. It's the cleanest thing you'll find down here."

"*Danki.*" As he took it from her, his fingers brushed against hers, sending a tiny thrill across his skin. She immediately thrust her hands in the pockets of her dress and her blush deepened.

She was a pretty woman. He liked the way wisps of her blond hair had come loose from beneath her *kapp* and curled around her face. He liked her smile, too. Would he have noticed her if they hadn't been forced together? In truth, he wouldn't have looked twice if he saw her with a child. He realized he was staring and turned away. The last thing he wanted was for her to feel uncomfortable.

After washing Hannah's face and his own, Joshua returned to find Mary had put the candle stubs he'd seen in a small jar. She was melting them over the flame of the candle on the tub. Hannah had found a worn-out broom with a broken handle. She began using it to sweep the floor of her house. "We didn't find a stove, *Mamm*."

Joshua gestured toward Mary's jar. "Are you going to make me eat wax for supper because I don't want your ancient pears?"

Using a piece of broken glass, she cut the ribbons off her *kapp*. "*Nee*, I'm making more candles."

"Smart thinking." The lantern had been flickering. It would go out soon and he hadn't found more kerosene.

She flashed him a shy smile before looking down. "I have my moments."

He noticed she had opened one of the jars of fruit. "Did you eat some of that?"

She nodded. "If I don't get sick, it should be fine for the two of you."

"I'm not sure that was smart thinking. Were they good?"

"As sweet as the day they were canned, but kind of mushy. Would you like some?"

"I'll pass. I might have to take care of you if you get sick. Besides, I'm not hungry."

She glanced up. "I feel fine. Did you find a bed for Hannah?"

He sat down in the chair. "Just some rusty box springs and a pile of burlap sacks. I'll bring them over later. It's not much, but it will have to do. I'm sorry I couldn't find anything for you."

"The rocker will suit me fine." She dipped her ribbon in the melted wax and pulled it out. Letting it harden, she waited a little while and then dipped it again. Each time she pulled it out, the candle grew fatter. Hannah came over and Mary allowed her to start her own candle.

It was pleasant watching them work by lantern light. Mary was patient with her daughter, teaching her by showing her what to do and praising her when she did well. Outside, the sound of rain faded away. The storm was over. Would someone find them soon?

"You mentioned you were here inspecting the property. Where is home?"

He gingerly settled back in his chair. "My family has a farm and a small business near a place called Bowmans Crossing. It's north and west of Berlin."

"Do you have a big family?" Hannah asked.

"Four brothers, so not very big."

Hannah gave a weary sigh. "I want a brother *and* a sister, but *Mamm* says no."

Joshua chuckled.

Mary refused to look at him. "You have Bella. That's enough."

He couldn't resist teasing her. "Your *mamm* needs a husband first, Hannah."

Hannah's eyes widened and she held up a hand. "That's what *Mammi* Ada says. She says *Mamm* will turn into an old *maedel* if we don't find her a husband soon."

Joshua tipped his head to the side as he regarded Mary's crimson cheeks. "I think she has a few years yet. Tell your grandmother not to worry."

"I wish you two would stop talking about me as if

I weren't here. Your candle is thick enough, Hannah. I think Joshua should make up a bed for you."

Hannah looked at her in shock. "You mean we have to sleep here?"

Mary cupped her daughter's cheek. "I'm afraid so."

"I sure wish this adventure was over. Can I have supper now?"

Mary glanced at Joshua. He shrugged. "If you feel okay, I don't see why not."

Hannah enjoyed eating sticky pear halves with her fingers while Joshua fixed a makeshift bed for her. It wasn't much, but it would keep her off the cold damp floor. She made a face as she crawled onto the burlap bags. Mary checked the edge of her apron and found it was dry now. She pulled it off and used it to cover Hannah. It wasn't long before the child was asleep. The lamp died a few minutes later.

Joshua lit the candle that Mary had made and stuck it to the middle of the tub. It would burn out long before the night was over. Mary settled in the rocker, but he knew she didn't sleep any better than he did. The long night crawled past. He had no way to tell time. He simply had to endure the darkness, as he had done in prison.

The distant rumble of thunder woke him some time later. He lifted his head and winced at the pain in his neck. Opening his eyes, he realized he was still in the cellar. It was dark, but he could make out Mary's form in the other chair.

She sat forward and bent her neck slowly from side to side. "Is it morning?"

"I think so."

"It's raining again."

"*Ja.*"

"I was dreaming about bacon and eggs."

His stomach rumbled. "I was dreaming about three-year-old pears."

"Really?"

"*Nee,* I wasn't dreaming at all. If I was, I'd wake up and find I was at home in my own bed."

"Wouldn't that be nice?"

They both stood and stretched. She looked at him. "What's the plan for today?"

He rubbed his bristly cheeks with both hands. "I thought you had a plan."

"I'm sure it's your turn to come up with something. I thought of making the candles."

He nudged the broken rocker with his boot. "Which was good, but I thought of finding furniture for our snug little home. It's your turn to be brilliant."

"I've never felt less brilliant in my life. What would you like for breakfast? I believe we have more three-year-old pears or some four-year-old peaches."

"Peaches," Hannah said, sitting up on her makeshift mattress.

"Peaches," he agreed. "Provided they look safe."

After their meal, they spent more time exploring for a way out without success. By noon, the rain had moved on and a few narrow beams of sunlight streamed through cracks in the floorboards overhead, allowing them to see their dismal surroundings a little better.

Joshua studied the cracks for a while. "I think I might be able to knock some of the floor planks loose if I can find something sturdy to reach them."

"I knew you would have a plan." Mary began to search through the piles of junk and he joined her.

The best thing he could come up with was a post about five feet long and two inches thick. He chose a spot overhead, wrapped some cloth around one end of the wood to prevent slivers and began thrusting it upward. Mary and Hannah stood nearby watching him. After half an hour, his arms were aching, the end of the post was beginning to splinter and the floorboard above him had only been displaced by an inch. It was something, but it wasn't enough.

Mary reached for his battering ram. "Let me work on it for a while. Do you think we'd do better to try and knock a hole in the cellar door?"

He handed her the wooden post. "It's reinforced with metal straps and I didn't see any light shining in through it. There's no telling what's on top of it. I know it's open above me here."

They took turns working for several hours and had the ends of two planks above them loose when Mary suddenly grabbed his arm. "Wait. Stop. I hear a dog."

The barking grew louder.

Hannah got up off the floor and began jumping. "I hear Bella."

Joshua gave a mighty heave and the floorboard broke, leaving a narrow space open. They looked at each other. "Neither of us can fit through that," he said, his excitement ebbing away.

"Hannah might be able to."

The sunlight dimmed and Joshua looked up. The head of a large yellow dog was visible above him. The dog barked excitedly. Hannah rushed to Joshua's side. "I knew I heard Bella."

"I hear voices, too." Mary began shouting. A few moments later, the dog was pushed aside.

An English woman with brown hair knelt down to look in. "Mary, is that you? Is Hannah with you?"

Tears of joy streamed down Mary's face. "We're okay, Miriam, but we can't get the cellar door open."

"Thank God you are safe. We'll get you out. Don't worry. Nick, I found them!" She disappeared from view. The dog came back to the opening. She lay down and woofed softly.

Mary threw her arms around Joshua in an impulsive hug. "I knew they would find us. I just knew it."

Bella barked again. As if Mary realized what she was doing, she suddenly stepped away from Joshua and crossed her arms. "It's Miriam and Nick, my adoptive parents. Nick will get us out of here."

Joshua heard activity at the door and the sounds of something heavy being dragged aside. "Looks like our prayers have been answered."

Mary picked up Hannah. Joshua followed them as they hurried to the stairwell.

From the other side, a man said, "Everyone stand clear."

"We are, Nick." Mary replied. The sound of an ax striking the portal was followed by splintering wood. A hole appeared in the top of the door and grew rapidly. Through it, Joshua could see the leaves and limbs of a large tree that must have been holding the door shut. Mary's father was swinging the ax like a madman. Joshua ached to help, but he could only stand by and wait.

Finally, the top section of the door broke free and a man's hands reached in. "Give me Hannah."

Mary handed the child over and then waited until the opening was enlarged. Joshua boosted her up and then climbed out on his own. The sunshine and the fresh air was a blessed relief from their dark, dank room. He blinked in the brightness and focused on Hannah in the arms of a woman in her early thirties. Mary was in the embrace of a man in a brown uniform. It wasn't until he released her that Joshua realized he was an *Englisch* lawman.

Mary turned to him with a bright smile, but he couldn't smile back. "Joshua, this is my adopted father, Sheriff Nick Bradley."

A knot formed in the pit of Joshua's stomach as dread crawled up his spine.

Chapter 4

Mary's father was the *Englisch* sheriff!

It was all Joshua could do to stand still. He hadn't done anything wrong, but that hadn't made any difference the last time he'd had a run-in with the law. Cold sweat began trickling down his back.

"The storm came up so suddenly. I didn't know what to do when I saw the funnel cloud. Then Joshua stopped Tilly and pulled us into the cellar. God put him there to rescue us." Mary was talking a mile a minute until she turned to look at the house. Her eyes widened.

Joshua turned, too. Only part of one wall had been left standing. The rest was a pile of jagged, splinted wood, broken tree limbs, scattered clothing and old appliances. A small round table sat in one corner of what must have been a bedroom. There was a book and a kerosene lamp still sitting on it. The remainder of the room had been obliterated.

Hannah reached for Nick. He took the child from Miriam, who promptly drew Mary into her embrace.

"We're so thankful you're safe. God bless you, Joshua." Miriam smiled her thanks at him.

Hannah threw her arms around Nick's neck. "I'm so happy to see you, Papa Nick."

"I'm happy to see you, too, Hannah Banana," he said, patting her back, his voice thick with emotion.

She drew back to frown at him. "I'm not a banana."

He smiled and tweaked her nose. "You're not? Are you sure?"

She giggled. "I'm a girl."

"Oh, that's right."

It was apparently a running gag between the two, because they were both grinning. The sheriff put Hannah down and held out his hand to Joshua. "Pleased to meet you. My heartfelt thanks for keeping my girls safe."

Joshua reluctantly shook the man's hand and hoped the sheriff didn't notice how sweaty his palms were. "No thanks are necessary."

Nick's eyes narrowed slightly. "You aren't from around here, are you? I didn't catch your last name."

Here it comes. Joshua braced himself. "Bowman. My family is from over by Berlin."

"The name rings a bell. Who is your father?" Nick tilted his head slightly as he stared at Joshua intently.

"Isaac Bowman." Joshua held his breath as he waited to be denounced as a criminal. What would Mary think of her rescuer then? He wasn't sure why it mattered, but it did.

Miriam lifted Hannah into her arms. "Stop with the interrogation, Nicolas. Let's get these children someplace safe. We still have a lot of work to do."

"Is Ada okay?" Mary asked, looking to Miriam.

Nodding, Miriam said, "She's fine except for being worried about you and Hannah. The house was only slightly damaged, but her corncribs were destroyed."

"Oh, no. Who else was affected? We heard the sirens last evening."

Miriam and Nick exchanged speaking glances. Nick said, "A lot of people. The Sutters' house was damaged. Elam has minor injuries. Katie, the kids and the women who were gathered for the quilting bee are all okay. I'm sorry to tell you that Bishop Zook was seriously injured. They took him to the hospital last night and into surgery this morning. We're still waiting for word about him. He lost his barn and his house was heavily damaged, but his wife is okay."

"Oh, dear." Mary's eyes filled with tears. Miriam hugged her.

Nick cleared his throat. "The tornado went straight through the south end of Hope Springs. Ten blocks of the town were leveled. We're only beginning to assess the full extent of the damage in the daylight. I need to get back there. We've still got a search-and-rescue effort underway. As of noon, we had seven people unaccounted for, but that goes down to five now that we've found you and Hannah."

Mary took Hannah from Miriam. "How did you find us? We were supposed to be at the Sutter place."

Nick said, "When Ada saw your mare come home without you, she got really worried. She walked to a neighbor's house to use their phone to call me last night. We checked with Katie and learned you never arrived. Your buggy was found in Elam Sutter's field at first light this morning. When we saw you weren't in it, we picked up Bella in the hopes that she could locate you and tried to retrace your path. She led us here."

"She must have heard us pounding. She couldn't have followed our scent after all that rain," Mary said.

"I don't know how she knew, but she did." Miriam patted the dog and then began walking toward the road, where a white SUV sat parked at the intersection with its red lights flashing. The sheriff followed her.

Grateful that he hadn't been outed, Joshua caught Mary's arm, silently asking her to remain a moment. She did. Their brief time together was over and he needed to get going. "I'm glad things turned out okay for you and Hannah."

"Only by God's grace and because you were here."

"You were very brave, Mary. I want you to know how much I admire that. You're a fine mother and a good example for your daughter. I'm pleased to have met you, even under these circumstances."

She blushed and looked down. "I have been blessed to meet you, too, and I shall always count you among my friends."

"I need to get going. My folks are expecting me home in a day or two. When they hear about this storm they'll worry." He took a step back.

Mary's eyes grew round as she looked past him. "Oh, no."

"What?" He turned and saw the barn hadn't been spared. Half of it was missing and the rest was leaning precariously in hay-covered tatters. He'd been so shaken to see the sheriff that he had forgotten about his horse. He started toward what was left of the building at a run.

Mary was tempted to follow Joshua, but she knew he might need more help than she could provide. Instead, she ran after Nick. She caught up with him and quickly explained the situation.

Nick said, "I'll help him. Let Miriam drive you and Hannah home and then she can come back for me."

"Absolutely not," Miriam said before Mary could answer. "I'm not leaving until you and that young man are both safe."

He kissed her cheek. "That's why I love you. You never do what I tell you. Call headquarters and let them know what's going on. I don't want them to think I've gone on vacation."

"I will. Be careful."

As Nick jogged toward the barn, Mary said, "I'm going to see what I can do."

"No, the men can manage."

"More hands will lighten the load." Mary raced after Nick. When she reached the teetering edge of the barn, she hesitated. She couldn't see what was holding it up as she slowly made her way inside the tangled beams and splintered wood. Everything was covered with hay that had spilled down from the loft. It could be hiding any number of hazards.

Once she reached the interior, she no longer had to scramble over broken wood, so the going was easier. She saw the flattened remains of Joshua's buggy beneath a large beam. Ominous creaking came from overhead. Joshua and Nick were pulling debris away from one of the nearby stalls. A section of the hayloft had collapsed like a trapdoor, blocking their way. She reached Joshua's side and joined him as he pulled at a stubbornly lodged board.

He stopped what he was doing and scowled at her. "Get out of here right now."

"You don't get to tell me what to do." She yanked on the board and it came free. She tossed it behind her.

Joshua turned to Nick. "Tell her it isn't safe."

"It isn't safe, Mary," Nick said.

"It is safe enough for you two to be in here." She lifted another piece of wood and threw it aside.

"See what I have to put up with, Joshua? None of the women in my family listen to me."

Mary heard a soft whinny from inside the stall. "Your horse is still alive, Joshua."

He said, "We're coming, Oscar. Be calm, big fella."

They all renewed their efforts and soon had a small opening cleared. The gap was only wide enough for Mary to slip through. Joshua's horse limped toward her. He had a large cut across his rump and down his hip.

"Oh, you poor thing." Mary stroked his face. He nuzzled her gently.

"How is he?" Joshua asked.

"He has a bad gash on his left hip, but the bleeding has stopped. How are we going to get him out of here?"

Nick said, "Even if we free him from the stall, he can't climb over the debris to get out the way we came in."

"Can you cut through the outside wall?" To her, it looked like the fastest way out.

"The silo came down on that side and left a few tons of bricks in the way."

Looking around from inside the stall, Mary saw only one other likely path. "If you can get into the next stalls and pull down the walls between them and this one, we could lead him through to the outside door at the far end of the building."

"It's worth a look," Nick said.

He and Joshua headed in that direction. She heard Joshua call to her. "Mary, if the upper level starts shifting, I want you to leave the horse and get out as fast as you can."

"I will," she called back. She patted Oscar's dusty brown neck and said softly, "Don't worry. We'll get out of this together."

The sound of her father's ax smashing into wood told her they were starting. She looked up, ready to scurry through the gap if she had to.

She hadn't been waiting long when the chopping stopped. She heard voices but couldn't make out what they were saying. Oscar whinnied. From outside, more horses answered. The sound of a chain saw sent her spirits soaring. Someone had joined Nick and Joshua.

It took less than five minutes before she saw her new rescuer cutting through the adjoining stall. It was Ethan Gingerich, a local Amish logger. Oscar began shifting uneasily. She realized he was frightened by the sound and smell of the chain saw. He tried to rear in the small space with her. She barely had room to avoid his hooves.

"Ethan, wait! He's too fearful."

Ethan killed the saw's engine. Oscar quieted, but he

was still trembling. Mary patted his neck to reassure him and spoke soothingly.

"Use this to cover his eyes." Ethan, a bear of a man, unbuttoned the dark vest he wore over his blue shirt, slipped it off and handed it to Joshua. Joshua climbed over the half wall with ease and quickly tucked the vest into Oscar's halter, making sure the horse couldn't see any light. Although the horse continued to tremble, he didn't move. Without the roar of the saw, Mary could hear creaking and groaning from the remains of the hayloft.

Joshua kept his hold on Oscar and gave Mary a tired smile. "I've got him now. Thanks for your help. You would be doing me a great favor if you went outside."

His shirt was soaked with sweat and covered with sawdust and bits of straw. He'd been working to the point of exhaustion to get to her, not just to his horse. She nodded and watched relief fill his eyes. "I reckon I can do that."

He moved closer to the half wall and bent his knee. She stepped up and swung her leg over the wide boards. Nick caught her around the waist and lifted her down. She brushed off her skirt, straightened her *kapp* and went down the length of the barn through the openings they had cut. Behind her, she heard the chain saw roar to life again. She was tempted to stop and make sure all the men got out safely, but she knew they didn't need her.

Outside, she saw Miriam standing a few yards away beside the team of huge draft horses that belonged to Ethan. She had Hannah by the hand. When Hannah saw her, she dropped Miriam's hand and raced forward.

"*Mamm*, Bella chased a rabbit into the field and she won't come back. I called her and called her."

"That naughty dog." She swung Hannah up into her arms.

Miriam crossed her arms and glared at Mary. "Bella is not the only naughty member of this family. Go wait for us in the car, Hannah."

Mary put her daughter down and watched her run to the vehicle. Hannah loved to ride in Papa Nick's SUV. He often let her play with the siren. Smiling, Mary turned back to Miriam, but her adoptive mother's face was set in stern lines. Mary sought to defend herself. "I had to help. You would have done the same."

"No, I wouldn't have. They could have managed without you. You have a kind but impulsive nature, Mary. It's better to think things through than to rush into something only to find bigger trouble. You should know that better than anyone. Nick wouldn't have come out of there without you no matter how dangerous it became. He would have left the horse if he had to."

Miriam almost never scolded her, and she never brought up Mary's past. Chastised, Mary stared at the ground and whispered, "I'm sorry."

She felt Miriam's hand on her shoulder. "I know you are. I just want you to think with your head and not let your emotions rule you. Just be more cautious."

Mary heard trepidation in Miriam's voice. She was more upset than Mary's action warranted. "I'm sorry I frightened you. You must have been worried sick all night long."

Miriam pulled her close. "I was. Promise me you'll be more careful."

"I promise."

When Miriam held her tighter and didn't release her, Mary knew something else was troubling her mother. "What's wrong?"

Miriam sighed. "I didn't want to tell you this now after all you've been through, but there is something you need to know."

"What?"

"Kevin Dunbar is coming up for parole."

Mary's gaze shot to lock with Miriam's as dread seeped into her heart. "What does that mean?"

"If he is granted parole, it means he will be released from prison."

"But they sentenced him to ten years. It's only been four."

"I know, and Nick and I will speak at the hearing and object to his early release, but it may not be enough."

Mary crossed her arms tightly. "Will he come here?"

"He doesn't know where you live. He doesn't know your new name. He doesn't know that I adopted you or that I married Nick. I don't see how he could find you and Hannah."

"He said he would make me pay for speaking against him in court." She bit her lower lip, but it didn't stop the taste of fear that rose in her mouth.

Miriam laid both hands on Mary's shoulders. "He won't find you. Nick and I will see to that. We wanted you to know so it wouldn't come as a shock if he does get an early release, but we don't want you to worry. Here come the men. Why don't you join Hannah in the car?"

"I want to speak to Joshua first. His buggy was

crushed and his horse is injured. He has no way to get home. I'm sure Ada won't mind if he comes home with us."

"I'm sure she won't, but it wouldn't be proper for you to offer him a place to stay. You are a single woman. I'm married. I can suggest he stay with my mother."

"But—"

"No buts, Mary. Don't argue about this. An Amish woman is not outspoken. She is modest and humble. You need to cultivate those virtues or you will be perceived as prideful. Don't forget, your actions reflect on Ada, too. Nick spoils you. He's a good man, but he doesn't understand Amish ways."

Mary sighed deeply. Miriam had been raised Amish and knew what was expected of each member. While Miriam had chosen to live English, Mary had freely chosen the Amish way of life. It wasn't an easy path, but she felt called to follow it. The freedoms she enjoyed by having English parents shouldn't cause her to lose sight of what it meant to live a Plain life. She had placed her life totally in God's hands. She would remain His humble and obedient servant.

Ethan approached them with his chain saw balanced on his shoulder. Miriam said, "Thank you for your assistance, Ethan. Is your family safe?"

"Glad I could help. The storm wasn't bad at our place. I heard about the twister when Clara came home last night from the quilting bee. I went out this morning to see if anyone needed me, or my team. I've cut through a lot of trees blocking lanes and roadways and hauled them aside. I was on my way home when I saw the sheriff's SUV and thought I'd see what he was up to out here."

"I'm glad you did," Nick said as he and Joshua came up beside them.

Mary pinned her gaze to the ground. Joshua must think she was a frightfully forward woman after the way she had acted. "Have you heard if Betsy is safe?" she asked, knowing her friend, whose oldest sister was Ethan's wife, had been headed to the same quilting bee at Katie Sutter's home.

"*Ja*, she is fine. I took Clara and the *kinder* to Wooly Joe's first thing this morning. All the girls were at their grandfather's place. You've never heard such squawking as those sisters do when they have something exciting to talk about. They were getting ready to take food and supplies into Hope Springs."

Mary smiled at him. "I'm glad they're okay. God is *goot*."

"Indeed He is. I need to get my team home. They've had a tough day." Ethan bade everyone farewell and left.

Mary began walking toward Nick's vehicle. She tried not to look back to see if Joshua was watching, but she couldn't help herself. He was.

Joshua watched Mary walk away and a strange sense of loss filled him. This was probably the last time he would see her. He was shocked to realize just how much he wanted to see her again. Under normal circumstances.

Nick laid a hand on Joshua's shoulder. "You must be exhausted."

He tried not to flinch from the man's touch, but it

brought back the way the police and the prison guards had grabbed him in the past. "A little," he admitted. His strength was draining away now that the crisis was over.

Miriam glanced toward the car and then turned to him. "Unless you have other plans, why don't you come back to my mother's home with us? You can clean up and have a hot meal, spend the night and then decide what to do in the morning."

As much as he wanted to accept, he didn't want to spend any more time in the sheriff's company. "*Danki*, but I don't think so."

"Suit yourself," Nick said.

Miriam laid a hand on Joshua's arm. "You need a place to stay until you can sort things out and get home. My mother will welcome you. She is Amish, so I know you'll be comfortable there. Not another word—you're coming with us."

She walked away to join Mary and Hannah. Joshua stood rooted to the spot. He hadn't expected this kindness from outsiders. He swallowed hard and hitched a thumb over his shoulder toward the barn. "I have some clothes and a few things in what's left of my buggy that I need. Let me get those and see to my horse."

Nick said, "Leave him tied up here, and I'll have someone bring a trailer and take him to our vet."

"I would appreciate that, if it's not too much trouble." Joshua wasn't sure he had the money to pay for a vet, but his father would send more to cover the bill. Isaac Bowman never skimped on taking care of his animals. It was a lesson he had drilled into his sons.

"No trouble," Nick said. "I've had reports from all over about loose and injured livestock. I have nearly a dozen volunteers with stock trailers helping wherever they are needed and taking all sorts of animals to our vet's clinic. Doc Rodgers has already asked for help from other veterinarians in the state. He'll have someone to look after your horse."

After agreeing to the arrangement, Joshua tethered Oscar where he could reach green grass and water and covered him with a blanket to keep the flies out of the gash. Then he extracted his duffel bag and his few belongings from his crushed buggy and joined Mary's family in the SUV. Hannah greeted him with a big smile. "Bella came back."

Joshua glanced over his shoulder. The Lab mix was in the back of the vehicle panting heavily. "It looks like she had a good run."

"She was chasing a rabbit. She's not supposed to do that," Hannah told him in a low voice.

"Did she catch him?" Joshua asked in a whisper. He shared a smile with Mary, but she quickly looked away.

Hannah shook her head. "She never catches them. She's not very fast. What about your horse?"

"Nick said he'll have someone take him to the vet clinic."

Mary continued to avoid looking at him. He fell silent and remained that way. The sudden change in their circumstances left him feeling tongue-tied and awkward. Or maybe it was because her father kept glancing at him in the rearview mirror. Perhaps going to Mary's home wasn't a good idea.

He hadn't been able to think of a reason to refuse under the sheriff's steely gaze earlier. He didn't want to raise the man's suspicions.

Joshua's parole agreement said he couldn't leave the area without notifying his parole officer. Was he in violation of that even if he was still in the same county? He should have checked before he left home.

The radio crackled and came to life with a woman's voice. "Sheriff, do you read me?"

Nick picked up the mic. "I read you, dispatch."

"We found the missing Keim children. The boys are fine."

Nick grinned at Miriam. "That's great news. Where were they?"

"At their aunt's house. They had gone fishing. They ran to take cover there when the storm cut them off from home. It took her family a while to dig out afterward and gather their scattered horses and cattle before they brought the kids home."

"That only leaves the McIntyre family unaccounted for."

"Nope, they weren't home. They were out camping in the woods. They came back to town about an hour ago. That's everyone who was unaccounted for, and FEMA is now on scene."

"Good. Let Deputy Medford know. Lance is in charge until I return."

"He already knows, sir."

"Have you had any word on Bishop Zook?"

"He's out of surgery and is expected to make a full recovery."

"The blessings just keep coming. Thanks. I'll be at Ada's house in a few minutes. You can get me on my cell if I don't answer the radio."

"Roger that." The radio went dead.

Joshua glanced at Mary. With her eyes downcast and her hands clasped, she was a lovely sight. Even with the smudges of dirt on her face. Was there anyone special in her life?

He caught sight of Nick watching him in the mirror and looked away, but like a magnetic needle that was always drawn to the north, Joshua's gaze moved back to Mary's face.

He might be attracted to her, but he only had one option where the sheriff's daughter was concerned: go home and forget all about her.

Chapter 5

"Do I have dirt on my face?" Mary didn't look up. She could feel Joshua's gaze on her and wondered what he was thinking. Since entering the car he had been so serious, so worried.

"You do, but I was staring at the destruction out there." He gestured toward the view beyond with his chin.

She looked out the window beside her and gasped. They were driving parallel to the tornado's track. The land bore an enormous scar of destruction. Everywhere the twister had encountered trees, only denuded trunks with stripped and snapped limbs remained. Where the trees had been toppled whole, huge mats of roots stuck in the air. As the storm had passed through wheat fields, it was if an insane harvester had mowed down random sections. Even the grass had been torn out of the pastures, leaving a path of churned dirt in the funnel's wake.

"That's the Keim farm," she said as they rolled past the once neatly tended Amish home. The entire front of the building and the roof was missing. It resembled a dollhouse more than a home. She could see into the rooms of the upper stories, where beds sat covered in bright quilts and clothes still hung on pegs. Below, the stove was all that was left in the remains of the kitchen. Some two dozen Amish men and women were working to clear the rubble. It was one advantage of large Amish families—when someone was in need, there were lots of aunts, uncles and cousins to come help.

Mary pressed her hand to her mouth. "This is so terrible."

Nick said, "It's pretty much the same all the way into Hope Springs. The tornado stayed on the ground for five miles. At times, it was half a mile wide. I've never seen anything like it."

He slowed the SUV and turned in to Ada's lane. The tornado had missed the house by a quarter of a mile. Most of the wind damage was confined to the fields and the crops that had been planted by the young farmer who rented Ada's land. There were shingles missing from the roof of the house and many of Ada's flowers had been blown down.

Nick stopped the vehicle by the front porch, where Ada stood waiting for them. The worry on her face transformed into a bright smile when Mary opened the door and let Hannah out. The child raced up the steps straight into Ada's embrace. Mary followed her.

"I thank *Gott* you are both safe," Ada said as she hugged Mary. "You hadn't been gone more than twenty minutes when the storm hit. When I came outside and saw the twister had gone the same direction you were heading, I dropped to my knees and prayed for you."

"God heard you. He sent Joshua Bowman to help us. You must thank him, as well," Mary replied, turning to introduce her grandmother to him as he got out of her father's vehicle.

Miriam said, "Joshua's buggy was destroyed and his horse was injured. He's a long way from home. I'm hoping you can look after him until he has a chance to sort out what to do next."

Ada raised a hand and beckoned. "Of course. Everyone, please come inside. I've been keeping supper warm in the oven. I must hear what happened to you."

"I can't stay," Nick said. "I have to get back to the command post we have set up in Hope Springs."

"I can't stay, either," Miriam added. "The Red Cross needs volunteers. As a nurse, I know they'll have use for me. I don't know when I'll be back, *Mamm*."

Ada nodded. "I understand."

After another round of hugs from Nick and Miriam, Mary waved goodbye from the porch steps and then led the way into the house. The kitchen smelled of fried chicken and fresh bread. Hannah proceeded to tell her great-grandmother all about their adventure. Ada was shocked and amazed at their narrow escape. Finally, Hannah said, "And then Bella found us. I'm really hungry. Can we eat now?"

Mary laid a hand on her daughter's shoulder. "We should get cleaned up before we sit at the table. Come on. Let's find some decor-free clothes for you." She glanced at Joshua and saw him smile. Pleased by it, she led Hannah away to clean up and change.

When she returned, Joshua was coming in through the front door. He had washed up and changed, as well. His face was clean shaven and his hair was still damp. The house had only one bathroom, so she knew he must have washed at the pump outside. He had a blue plastic basin in one hand.

Joshua offered the basin to Ada. "Thanks for the hot water. It made shaving a whole lot easier."

"*Goot.* You are welcome to stay with us for as long as you like. I have a spare bed and you won't be any trouble. Now, sit and let me get some food on the table. Mary, slice some bread and fetch a jar of pears from the pantry."

"No pears," Mary and Joshua said together. They shared an embarrassed glance.

Looking confused, Ada said, "I have some peaches if you would rather."

Mary tried not to laugh. "Don't we have some plums?"

"*Ja,* we do."

Mary kissed her grandmother's wrinkled cheek. "Plums will be fine. It's so good to be home."

While Mary and Hannah were busy getting the table set, Ada began pulling pans from the oven. "Joshua, where is your family from?"

"A place called Bowmans Crossing. It's north and west of Berlin. About a day's buggy ride from here."

"I don't know it, but then I've only been in Hope Springs a few years. I moved here from Millersburg. Do you have someone special waiting back home?"

"Not yet."

"So you haven't met the right girl, is that it?"

Mary sent her grandmother a sour glance, but Ada

ignored her. Joshua grinned at Hannah. "I've met her, but she's not quite old enough to marry. I'm going to have to wait a few years."

"He means me, *Mammi*." Hannah put the last plate on the table. "I'm not going to be an old maid."

"At least one of my girls has some sense. What does your family do, Joshua?"

"They farm and run a small business."

"And how did you end up here?"

"He came to look over some property for his father. I think he has answered enough questions for one day." Mary took her place at the table.

"I'm just making conversation and trying to put the poor boy at ease." Ada carried her pan to the table and dished out the creamy potatoes.

When Ada was finished, she took her place at the table and everyone bowed their heads in silent prayer. Because Joshua was the only man at the table, the women waited until he signaled the prayer was finished. Mary hadn't realized how hungry she was until she dug into her grandmother's mouthwatering, crispy fried chicken. It was one of the best meals Mary had ever eaten.

When Joshua was finished, he leaned back in his chair and patted his stomach. "That was mighty *goot*, *danki*."

Ada smiled at him. "It does my heart good to see a man enjoy my cooking. Mary is a fine cook, too."

"I can help clean up," he offered.

Mary and Ada exchanged amused glances. Very few men offered to help with kitchen chores. "I can manage," Ada said. "It would please me if you would read from the Good Book for us when I'm done here."

"It would be my pleasure. Hannah, do you have a Bible story that you like?"

"Noah. I like the story about Noah and all the animals."

Ada smiled. "Very appropriate. As Noah and his family were delivered from a great storm, so were you and your mother. *Gott* is merciful."

Their evenings were often spent with Mary reading passages while Ada caught up with her needlework. It was a pleasant change to have someone else reading to her. Mary listened to the sound of Joshua's voice and realized once again how soothing it was. He had a strong, firm voice. He read with ease and with understanding, pausing occasionally to ask Hannah about something that he had read. She listened intently, seated on the floor in front of him with Bella at her side. He seemed to be a man devoted to his faith, but Mary knew not everyone was what they seemed to be.

When it was time for bed, Ada showed Joshua to the spare room while Mary took Hannah up to her room. She knelt beside Hannah as the child recited her bedtime prayers. Overwhelmed with gratitude for their deliverance, Mary gazed at her child and gave silent thanks. She would never again take moments like this for granted.

Hannah got into bed and pulled the sheet to her chin. "I like this bed much better. It smells *wunderbar*."

Mary tucked her in. "I agree."

"Will Joshua be here in the morning when I wake up?"

"*Ja*, he will be here."

"I'm glad. I like him. Don't you?"

Mary smiled at her daughter and planted a kiss on

her forehead. "I like him, too." Maybe more than she should.

"How old will I have to be before I can marry him?"

Mary bit her lower lip to keep from laughing. "Very old, I'm afraid."

"As old as you?"

Mary chuckled. "At least as old as me."

"Okay. *Guten nacht, Mamm.*"

"Good night and sweet dreams, *liebschen*." Mary stepped away. Bella took her usual spot on the blue rag rug beside the bed. Mary patted the dog's head. "And sweet dreams for you, too, Bella. You are a very *goot hund.*"

The following morning, Mary was up bright and early. By the time Ada came out of her room, Mary already had breakfast underway. Although she would have denied it if anyone asked, she wanted to impress Joshua with her cooking skills. Just a little. She pulled a pan of cinnamon rolls from the oven and set it to cool on the counter.

It wasn't long before he came in. "Something smells delicious. I hope it tastes as good as it smells."

"It will. How do you like your eggs?"

"Less than three years old." He tried to pinch off a piece of cinnamon roll, but she batted his hand away.

"Sit down and behave yourself or all you'll get is eggshells."

"Is there coffee?" He glanced hopefully at her.

"In the pot."

He helped himself to a cup and sat at the table. She could feel him watching her. It should have made her nervous, but it didn't. Somehow, it felt comfortable having him in the same room. It shouldn't, but it did, and she wondered why.

What was it about him that made him different from other men? She studied him covertly as she tried to put her finger on it.

His face wasn't particularly handsome, but he had a strong jaw and a square chin that made him look dependable. She finally decided his eyes were what made him so interesting. They were a soft, expressive brown. They crinkled at the corners when he smiled. She liked that. It proved he smiled often. And he didn't mind being quiet.

Ada and Hannah came in a few minutes later and Mary regretted the loss of her time alone with Joshua.

Did he feel the same? Or was he anxious to leave and get home? Of course he was. Why would he want to spend more time with her?

Ada poured some coffee and leaned her hip against the counter. "We will take food and supplies into Hope Springs when our chores are done. Our neighbors are in need. *Englisch* and Amish alike. We must do what we can."

Mary nodded, ashamed to admit she had forgotten for a little while the tragedy that had struck her community.

They had barely finished breakfast when Bella barked and trotted to the door, wagging her tail. Mary heard the sound of a buggy pulling up outside. Ada rose and went to the window. A bright smile transformed her face as she turned to Mary. "With all that has happened, I clean forgot Delbert Miller was coming by today. I must go out and make him welcome. Mary, you should come, too." Ada hurried out the front door.

Mary dried her hands slowly on a kitchen towel. "As if I had any choice in the matter."

After the women went out the door, Joshua leaned toward Hannah. "Who is Delbert Miller?"

"*Mammi* says he is the perfect *mann* for *Mamm*. He's going to fix the chicken house roof, but *Mamm* is afraid he'll fall through and squish our chickens."

The perfect man? Joshua rose to his feet and sauntered toward the door to get a look at the paragon.

The buggy in front of the gate was tipped heavily to one side. When the driver got out, Joshua understood the reason. Delbert Miller was a man of considerable size, with a jovial smile and a booming voice to match.

"Good morning, Ada. Good morning, Mary. I see the storm caught you, too."

"Not as bad as some, I hear. What about your place?" Ada asked.

"Not even a branch knocked down."

"You were blessed," Mary said quietly.

"Indeed, I am." Delbert gave Mary a bright smile. His gaze lingered on her face.

Joshua studied Mary closely, looking for her reaction. To his eyes, she didn't look happy to see the perfect man, and that pleased him.

A team of horses pulling a wagon came up the lane, driven by two young Amish men. The wagon was loaded with lumber.

"Have you brought help?" Ada asked.

Delbert gestured in their direction. "I met Atlee and

Moses Beachy on the road. They were on their way home from the Weavers' sawmill with lumber for the town. They insisted on following me in case you needed some repairs."

"That was mighty kind of them, but all I need is a few shingles on the porch roof."

"We have some with us," one of the twins said.

Hannah came outside, but the child stood behind her mother, peeking around the edge of her skirt.

The two young brothers, identical twins, got down from the wagon. "Has anyone seen Hannah Banana?" asked the one who had been driving.

"Could be she got blown away in the big wind," the other one said as they looked around pretending to seek her.

Hannah stepped out from behind Mary. "I almost got blown away. Did you see the tornado? It smashed Joshua's house, and we got stuck in the old cellar. *Mamm* and me and Joshua had to stay there all night. It was full of cobwebs and yucky."

"You don't say?" Delbert looked to Mary for more of an explanation.

Mary, her cheeks glowing pink, gave an abbreviated account to their visitors and introduced Joshua to the men. She sent Hannah back into the house before the little girl could repeat more of the story.

Ada spoke to the twins. "You can get out on the porch roof from the upstairs window. I'll show you. Delbert, I have some cinnamon *kaffi* cake I baked yesterday. Come up to the house when you're finished and have some."

"I'd love to, but it will have to wait. There's a lot of

people in need today and the twins and I should get going when we are finished here."

"I understand. Mary will show you what we need done to the chicken *haus*."

Joshua caught Mary's slight hesitation before she nodded. "Come this way."

"Why don't I give you a hand," Joshua offered. He was rewarded with a grateful look from Mary. It appeared that she didn't want to be alone with Delbert.

"I don't reckon I'll need any help." Delbert frowned at Joshua.

"Many hands make quick work," Mary said brightly. She led the way to the henhouse beside the barn.

The structure had seen better days. There was a hole in the roof where some of the shingles had rotted away. The red paint was faded and peeling from the walls. Joshua suspected a number of boards would need to be replaced. Mary pointed out where the chicken wire around the fenced enclosure was loose and sagging. She opened a gate to the enclosure and stepped back. The black-and-brown hens scurried past her and spread out across the barnyard in search of insects. A large rooster crowed his displeasure, but when all the hens were gone, he followed them and took up a post on the corral fence, where he crowed repeatedly until one of the twins shooed him away.

Delbert turned to Mary. "I'll need a ladder to get up on the roof. Do you have one I can use?"

She pointed toward the barn. "Of course. It's right inside the main door."

Delbert looked disappointed that she didn't offer to show him in person, but he went to fetch it alone.

"I think Hannah might be right," Joshua said, trying to hide a smile.

Mary frowned at him. "About what?"

"She said Delbert was the perfect man for you."

Her eyes narrowed in displeasure. "There's no such thing as a perfect man. Only God is perfect."

"True enough, but I think you were right about the rest."

"I have no idea what you're talking about."

"If he gets up on the roof of that chicken house, he's going to go right through it."

A reluctant smile tugged at the corner of her pretty mouth. "Why do you think I let all the hens out?"

Delbert returned, carrying the ladder under his arm. He propped it against the building, but before he could climb up, Joshua caught him by the arm. "Why don't you let me go? You and Mary can hand me the supplies I'll need once I am up there."

Delbert looked ready to argue, but thought better of it. "I reckon it would be better for a skinny little fellow like you to test those old boards."

Joshua slapped him on the back. "Exactly what I was thinking. Would you mind if I borrow some of your tools?"

Once he was on the roof of the henhouse, Joshua pried loose the rotted shingles with Delbert's hammer. A section of the plywood roof had to be replaced, but the underlying rafters were sound. Mary handed the new shingles to Delbert, who stood on the ladder and handed them over to Joshua. When Joshua came down, Mary excused herself and went up to the house, leaving the two men alone.

"I can give you a hand restretching the wire fencing," Joshua offered.

"Sure."

Joshua set to work pulling the old staples that held the wire onto the wooden fence posts. "Have you known Mary long?"

"Since she first came here. Four years now, I guess it is."

"Did you know her husband?"

"*Nee*, I'm not sure she was married. If that's the case, I don't hold it against her. We all make mistakes. She's a fine woman, and her little girl is as sweet as they come."

Joshua mulled over that startling bit of information. Did it change the way he felt about her? He wasn't sure, and that shamed him. "Hannah said her father has gone to heaven."

"That is what Mary told Bishop Zook when she joined our congregation. He was an *Englisch* fellow, and that's all I know about him."

Joshua stared at the house. "Does she mourn him still?"

"That I cannot tell you, but she doesn't go to the singings and she has turned down a lot of fellows who have tried to ask her out. Some people say she's too particular. I think she'll come around when the right fellow shows an interest."

Joshua glanced at his companion. "It could be the right fellow doesn't live around here."

Delbert stared at Joshua for a long moment, then he burst out laughing and slapped Joshua on the back hard enough to make him wince. "Only God knows the right one for each of us. If He has someone in mind for her, then that's the one she'll wed, and it won't matter where he's from. We should finish this pen right quick. Others need my help today."

The man had a big heart to match his big frame. "Delbert, I need to find a way to get to Bowmans Crossing as soon as possible."

"Why can't you get home the same way you got here?"

"My buggy was wrecked in the storm and my horse was injured."

"Sorry to hear that. I know a fellow in Hope Springs that drives Amish folks. I'll take you by his house. If he can't take you, well, you're handy with a hammer. You'll be most welcome to join the rest of us in the cleanup."

Joshua was ready to get home. He would miss his growing friendship with Mary, but it was better to leave before the attachment deepened. He had no illusions about his chances with her and the less he had to do with her father, the better. She wasn't the one for him. Joshua didn't believe Delbert was the man for her, either, but he wished the big fellow well in his pursuit of her.

Delbert looked around and lowered his voice. "I should warn you about the Beachy twins."

Joshua looked toward the porch roof, where the two young men were finishing the last of the repairs. "What about them?"

"They have a knack for playing pranks on folks. Harmless pranks for the most part, but beware. You might sit down on a chair and get up to find a red bull's-eye painted on the seat of your pants. It happened to me and I never did figure out how they did it."

Joshua laughed outright at Delbert's pained expression. "I'll beware of them. *Danki*."

"What can be so funny?" Mary stood at the window watching Delbert and Joshua out by the henhouse.

"What's that, child?" Ada asked. She was at the kitchen table wrapping sandwiches and packing them into boxes.

"Joshua and Delbert are out there slapping each other on the back and laughing like a pair of fools." It was an exaggeration on her part, but she had a sneaking suspicion that they were laughing at her expense.

"The Lord has blessed Delbert with a *wunderbar* sense of humor. The man likes to make other people smile. There's nothing wrong in that. Would you pack the plates for me? I expect there will be a lot of hungry people working in Hope Springs today. We'll need to fill some jugs with water, too."

Mary turned away from the window. If the town had seen the same kind of destruction she had witnessed, it would be bad. She was foolish and vain to be worrying about what Joshua Bowman thought of her. She put him out of her mind and began helping Ada prepare lunches.

A few minutes later, Joshua walked in the door. "I wanted to thank you for your hospitality. I'm going to ride into Hope Springs with Delbert and check on my horse, then I'm going to try and find a ride home."

The twins came down the stairs. Atlee patted Hannah on the head. "That should keep the rain from coming in, Hannah Banana. Take care." They doffed their hats and went out.

Joshua went to collect his gear. When he returned,

Ada handed him a large box. "Take this with you and tell Delbert to leave it at the Wadler Inn in Hope Springs. The twins said it is still standing. We don't have room for everything in our little cart and our pony Fred can't pull a bigger wagon."

Joshua nodded. "I'll be happy to do that for you. Anything else?"

"*Nee.* Bless you for all your help and for taking care of Mary and Hannah."

"It was my pleasure."

Mary didn't want to say goodbye to him. Not yet. Berlin wasn't that far away. He could find an excuse to return if he wanted to. Did he want to?

"Will we see you again?" she asked quickly, and then looked at her feet. That was too bold of her.

"I would like that," he said quietly.

Her cheeks grew warm. She knew she was blushing. Then she realized he didn't know anything about her. Not really. When he learned her history, he'd run the other way, and that was fine. She didn't need a fellow to like her. Only—wouldn't it be nice if he did?

Hannah ran and bounced to a stop in front of him. "Goodbye, Joshua. When will I see you again?"

"That's hard to say. I live a long way from here."

"But you could come for a visit. He's welcome to visit, isn't he, *Mamm*?"

"Of course he is," Ada said when Mary remained silent.

"*Danki*, Ada. Goodbye, Hannah. Goodbye, Mary."

"Goodbye." Clenching her fingers together until they ached kept Mary from saying anything else. She was a terrible judge of men. The ones she'd thought cared for her had hurt her unbearably. It was better to keep the memory of Joshua's kindness rather than count on him and have him fail her.

When she found the courage to look up, he was already out the door. Her spirits plummeted. Would she ever see him again?

"He was a nice young fellow," Ada said from behind her.

Mary crossed the room to look out the window. "*Ja,* he was."

"I'm gonna miss him," Hannah said and left the room with Bella on her heels.

Mary watched Joshua climb into the buggy with Delbert. The vehicle still tipped heavily to one side. She smiled at the thought of Joshua hanging on to the edge of the seat to keep from sliding into Delbert's lap all the way into Hope Springs. He would make Hannah laugh when he told her the story.

Only he wouldn't be back to share it with her.

And it was better that way. Wasn't it? She didn't want her daughter growing to depend on someone who would let her down.

That was true, but protecting Hannah from disappointment wasn't the whole reason Mary didn't date. The sobering fact was that she didn't want to like someone and then find out he wasn't what he seemed. She was terrified of making another mistake. It was better to depend on God and her family. It was enough. Although she was lonely sometimes.

Mary watched until the buggy was out of sight. She wasn't missing Joshua already, was she? That was ridiculous. They'd known each other for less than two days. A few extraordinary hours. It was foolish to think he'd return to see her and more foolish to wish he would. He surely had a girl waiting back home. He hadn't mentioned one, but it was the Amish way to keep such things private.

He'd been kind to her and to Hannah. It was silly to read anything else into that kindness.

"The Lord provides," Ada said.

Mary shot her grandmother a quick look. "The Lord provides what?"

"All that we need." Ada wore a self-satisfied smile. Humming, she returned to the table to finish packing supplies for their trip into town.

"You're right. He does." Mary joined her grandmother at the table. The Lord had supplied a kind man to come to her rescue in the storm and that was all there was to it. She was grateful, but she wouldn't expect anything more.

Chapter 6

As Joshua rode into town with Delbert, the extent of the destruction became increasingly evident. Where the tornado had reached the town, it had obliterated everything in its path. Houses had been leveled. Mangled cars had been rolled into buildings and trees lay everywhere. Pink insulation and articles of clothing fluttered from the remaining branches of denuded trees that were still upright. It was almost impossible to take in the scope of the damage.

A National Guard soldier had them state their business, and then allowed them to go on after warning them that the town would be closed at 6:00 p.m. and everyone would have to leave unless they were a resident with a habitable house.

A few blocks later, Delbert stopped his horse in front of a building that was little more than a pile of pale bricks. A single wall with an arched window remained standing. The grassy area around the building was covered with brightly colored books.

Delbert whistled through his teeth. "I heard it was bad, but I didn't know it was this bad."

"Was this the library?" Joshua had come to value books in his time behind bars. They'd become a solace during the long days and longer nights in his small cell.

Delbert nodded. "Across the street is the *Englisch* grade school."

That building was in the same condition as the library. A group of women and children were picking up books and papers off the ground and placing them in large blue plastic bins. Up ahead, Ethan Gingerich had his team of draft horses hitched to a fallen tree that had obscured most of a house. At a word from him, the horses leaned into their collars and pulled the massive trunk into the street. A battered white van emerged from the foliage. It had been crushed against the home. An elderly man moved to look it over.

Delbert sighed. "I reckon Samson Carter can't take you to Bowmans Crossing today."

"Why not?"

"Because that is Samson and that is his van. We can ask him if he knows anyone else who can give you a lift if you want?" Delbert waited for Joshua to make a decision.

An elderly woman joined Samson and the two of them stood with their arms around each other surveying the damage to the house and vehicle. She was crying. Everywhere Joshua looked, he saw people picking through the debris of what had once been a town but now resembled an enormous trash heap. Looking down, he noticed an open book on the sidewalk beside the buggy. Its pages fluttered in the breeze. He got out and picked it up. It was a second-grade reader that belonged to a girl named Ann. His mother's name was Anna.

He turned to Delbert. "I reckon I wasn't meant to go home today."

"I thought you had to get back?"

"I have to be home by next Thursday for certain, but my family will understand that I'm needed here until then. I'll write and let them know."

"I'll keep an ear out for anyone going that way."

"I'd appreciate it." Holding the book in his hand, Joshua crossed the street and joined the volunteers at the school.

Mary's eyes brimmed with unshed tears as she made her way past ruined fields and damaged farms to the outskirts of Hope Springs. Ada clutched Hannah close to her side and kept patting the child's back to comfort her. Mary knew her grandmother needed comforting as much as Hannah did. Ada loved the community that had welcomed her wholeheartedly when she first arrived.

Ada had once belonged to a strict, ultraconservative Old Order Amish congregation that didn't allow their young people a choice—they were expected to join the Amish faith. Because their daughter chose to live English, Ada and her husband were forced to shun Miriam. The split was painful for everyone. After Ada's husband died, she knew the only way she could have contact with Miriam was to leave the community she had lived in for sixty years. Hope Springs became a place of healing for both Ada and Miriam, and ultimately for Mary, too.

She loved the community for the same reason—unconditional acceptance from the gentle people who lived devout plain lives amid the rolling farmland and tree-studded hills. Now the village they both loved had been all but destroyed.

The closer they got to town, the more damage they saw. Broken tree limbs and whole uprooted trees blocked the streets and lanes. At the edge of town, houses and businesses were simply gone. Only rubble remained. They heard the sound of chain saws long before they saw the men working to clear debris. Several large vans with brightly painted letters on their sides were lined up along the road. A group of people stood beside them. Long black cables snaked around them and satellite dishes adorned the tops of the vehicles.

Two young men in military uniforms motioned for Mary to stop at the edge of town. Bella lay on the floorboards of the cart with her head on her paws, but she sat up when they stopped.

One soldier approached the cart. "I'm sorry, ladies. We've just been told not to allow anyone down this road. There's a gas leak. Until the utility company can get in to shut it down, it's too dangerous. You'll have to go around."

"We have food for the volunteers. Sheriff Bradley is expecting us," Mary said.

A helicopter buzzed low overhead. Hannah looked up. "What are they doing?"

"They're from one of the television stations. They're taking video of the storm damage."

Hannah gave him a puzzled look. "What's a video?"

He smiled. "Pictures for television."

"Why?"

"Because this is news." He pointed toward a side street. "The command post has been set up at the Wadler Inn. If you go two blocks west, you might be able to go north from there. There are still a lot of downed trees and power lines, but I think you can get your buggy through. The power is off to the whole town, so don't worry about touching the lines. Just be careful."

"We will. *Danki*." Mary started to turn Fred and head the way the young soldier had indicated. The group from the news van approached. One of them carried a large camera on his shoulder aimed in their direction. They were blocking Mary's way. A woman in a bright red dress came to the side of the cart and held a microphone toward Mary. "Vanetta Jones of WWYT News. Can you tell us how the Amish community is reacting to this disaster?"

The pony, frightened by the commotion, shied away. Mary had trouble controlling him. "We're here to help our neighbors however we can."

Ada turned her face away from the camera and held up her hand. "Please, no pictures." Mary struggled to control the pony, who was threatening to bolt. "Please, let us pass."

The cameraman and reporter stepped aside. Mary urged her pony forward, happy to leave the intrusive people behind her.

"I can't believe this is the same town," Ada said quietly. "I don't recognize it. I'm not sure which street we're on."

Mary wasn't, either. Nothing identifiable remained among the piles of debris. A sea of broken tree limbs blocked her way. Crushed cars were scattered helter-skelter among roofless and wrecked homes with large red *X*s painted on them. Halfway down the second block, an English family sat huddled together on concrete steps. A mother and father with three children, one a baby in the mother's arms. The baby was crying. The whole family wore dazed expressions. Their clothes were dirty, and only two of them had shoes on. A damaged van sat nearby. The house the steps once led up to was completely gone. Only the bare floors remained. All the nearby homes were in a similar state.

Mary stopped the buggy, handed the reins to Ada and got out. Although she was leery of strangers, she couldn't pass by these people in need. She pulled a box from the stack behind her seat and carried it to the young couple.

"We have some food and some water for you."

The man took the box. "Thank you. I don't know you, do I?"

"We've never met. Do you have somewhere to go?"

"We slept in our van last night but it doesn't run. We can't leave."

Mary's heart ached for them. "We're on our way to the inn. If they have room, I'll send word."

"We don't have the money to stay there. I don't know where my wallet is." He looked around as if expecting to see it on the ground.

"You won't need money," Ada said quickly. "God commands us to care for one another. There won't be any charge."

Bella hopped out of the cart and trotted up to the young boy and girl seated beside the man. Hannah followed her. The big dog sat and offered her paw to shake. The boy tentatively reached for her foot and shook it. He was rewarded with a quick lick on the cheek.

Hannah said, "This is my dog, Bella. She's sorry your house got blowed away." All the children began to pet her. Their faces slowly lost their hollow expressions.

Mary spoke to the young mother. "What do you need for the baby?"

She glanced around. "Everything. Diapers, formula, a crib."

"All right. We'll be back later. For now, I have some dry blankets and some kitchen towels you can use as cloth diapers until we return." Mary got the supplies from the back of the cart and gave them to her.

"Bless you." The young mother started crying and her husband pulled her close.

"Hannah, come on." Mary held out her hand.

"Can we help them look for their cat, *Mamm*? It ran away in the storm."

"We'll worry about Socks later," the father said to his children.

"There is an animal collection station being set up at the vet clinic north of town. Your cat may be there. If it is, someone will look after it until you claim it," Mary said.

The father gave her a tired smile. "Thanks. That's one less worry."

Mary returned to the cart and lifted Hannah onto the seat. Bella jumped in and lay down on the floorboards again. Ada kept the reins and clicked her tongue to get Fred moving.

They made their way toward the Wadler Inn, leaving the street in a few locations and traveling over people's lawns to get past downed trees. When they arrived at their destination, they witnessed a beehive of activity. Buggies and carts were lined up along the street next to pickups and cars. Amish and English worked side by side carrying in supplies and donations. A large Red Cross tent was being set up down the street at the town's small park. From here, it was easy to see most of the town remained intact, but the tornado had cut a path through the southwest end with merciless ferocity.

An Amish boy about ten years old ran up to the cart. "I'll take care of your pony if you're staying a spell." He pointed toward the outskirts of town. "We're putting them in Daniel Hershberger's corral."

"*Danki.* How did your family fare?"

"We didn't have much damage. Just a few trees down, nothing like here. God was good to us."

"Something good will come from all of this, too," Ada said, stepping down and handing him the reins. "Troubles are God's way of getting our attention. They remind us that this world is not our eternal home and our time here is not our eternal life. Tie the pony to the hitching rail, but leave him harnessed to our cart for now. We'll need him to bring another family here."

"Okay." The boy did as she instructed, then crossed the street to where another Amish buggy had pulled up in front of the hardware store.

Inside the lobby of the inn, Mary and Ada found Emma Yoder and her mother, Naomi Shetler, directing the placement of supplies and sending tired first responders and volunteers up to the guest rooms for a few hours of rest. Both women looked exhausted. Emma owned and operated the inn with her husband, Adam. Naomi had worked at the inn for years until her marriage to Wooly Joe Shetler, a reclusive sheep farmer and Betsy Barkman's grandfather.

Ada greeted each of them and said, "What can we do to help? We've brought water, sandwiches, cakes and extra bedding. Who needs to be fed?"

Emma swept a few stray hairs back from her forehead. "Bless you. Take the food around to the café entrance. Betsy and Lizzie are preparing lunches there. Give the bedding to Katie and Nettie. They're upstairs. We had forty souls sleeping on the floor in here last night. There won't be that many tonight. A lot of folks have relatives who are taking them in, but we will still have some with nowhere to go."

"Have you room for a family of five?" Mary asked. "We passed them on our way here."

Emma gave her a tired smile. "We'll make room."

"They have a newborn baby."

"I'll have Adam bring our son's cradle down from the attic. Where is that man?" She turned and went in search of him.

Mary caught sight of Betsy coming in from the café. When Betsy saw her, she raced across the room and threw her arms around Mary. "I'm so glad you're okay. You can't know how worried I was when I heard your empty buggy had been found. I didn't know you were safe until late last night when Ethan brought us word."

"It was quite an adventure. I'll have to tell you about it when we have the time."

Betsy nodded. "That may be a while."

She turned toward Naomi behind the front desk. "I've got six dozen cookies and sandwiches made along with three gallons of tea and lemonade. Shall I take it to the Red Cross tent or will we be serving people here?"

"Go check with the Red Cross and see what they want us to do. We'll be happy to serve people here if they need us to. Hannah, I know you'd like to see your friends. The Sutter *kinder* are upstairs with their mother helping fold linens and sorting donations. Would you like to join them?"

Hannah looked to Mary. "May I?"

"*Ja*, but I don't want you going outside. There is too much going on and too many things you could get hurt on."

"Okay." She darted up the stairs as fast as she could.

Ada and Mary went outside and brought in their contributions. After giving them to Naomi, Mary turned to Ada. "I'm going to go back and pick up that family."

Ada nodded. "*Goot.* I will see what I can do here."

Mary returned to the cart and retraced her way to the family without a home. They were still sitting on the steps, but the baby wasn't crying. She stopped the pony on their lawn. "There is room for you at the inn. I can take you there now."

The husband shook his head. "We can't take your charity. We will manage."

"How?" his wife asked.

He scowled at her. "I can take care of this family."

"Please," Mary said. "We have a place for you to

stay, but we are in need of many hands to help. It will not be charity. We will put you to work."

"This is very kind of you," the young mother said as she got up from the stoop. She handed the baby to Mary, got in and took the baby back. The father sighed and followed. He loaded the two older children in the rear of the cart and climbed up beside his wife.

When they arrived back at the inn, Mary turned the young family over to Emma's capable hands and went to the kitchen. Betsy was back from the Red Cross tent. She was packing sandwiches into a large box. "We are going to take half of these to the other end of the park and set up there. I'll take this basket. You grab a box and come with me. I can't wait another minute to hear about your adventure."

The two women walked side by side down the street and across the park. Mary gave Betsy a carefully edited version of her time with Joshua. Although she thought she had done a good job of downplaying the incident, Betsy wasn't satisfied.

"Tell me more about this young man. Wasn't it scary to be alone with a stranger?"

"I wasn't alone. I had Hannah with me. I was thinking about her, and about how to make things less frightening for her. He was, too. I wasn't thinking about myself."

Betsy peeked at Mary through lowered lashes. "Was he nice-looking?"

"I suppose he was. He was kind. That matters more than looks." He had been kind. And funny. And good with Hannah. All the things she dreamed a man should be. He had appeared in time to save them and now he was gone. She'd likely never see him again. She knew it was probably for the best, but it didn't feel that way.

"It's too bad that he left before I had the chance to thank him for taking care of my very best friend and her daughter."

Just then, Mary caught sight of Nick and Miriam. They were speaking to the woman in the red dress who had tried to interview her. Betsy said, "I heard that we made the national news."

"What a sad way for our town to become famous. They tried to interview Ada and me on our way into town."

"Did they? We'll have to find somewhere to watch the news. Maybe you'll be on it."

"We can't watch TV even if we wanted to."

"No one from the church will object if we happened to see it at an *Englisch* friend's home. Who has a television? The hardware store has one they keep on in the back."

"No one in town has electricity, Betsy. The power is out."

Betsey giggled. "That's right. I forgot. We're just used to being without it, so I didn't notice. I'm sure they'll have generators running soon. The *Englisch* can't do much without electricity."

Mary saw several members from her church setting up benches and tables. "I think that's where we're supposed to be."

She put her box on the nearest table. Betsy opened her basket and began setting out plates and a platter of cookies. Mary began unpacking the sandwiches and piling them on a plastic tray.

"I didn't think we would meet again so soon."

Mary looked up in astonishment. Joshua stood in front of her with a plate in his hand. "Joshua! What are you still doing here? I thought you were going home?" Her heart began fluttering like a wild bird in her chest.

"Delbert took me to Samson Carter's place, but his van is out of commission. It had a rather large tree on top of it. When I saw how much work needed to be done here, I thought I might as well stay for a few days longer. I dropped a note to my family in the mail so they won't worry about me. Happily, the post office is in one piece."

Flushing with pleasure at seeing him again, Mary continued setting out the sandwiches. "That's very kind of you to stay."

"Are you Mary's mystery man?" Betsy regarded him across the table.

"I'm not much of a mystery." He reached for a sandwich and a couple of cookies.

"Betsy, this is Joshua Bowman. Joshua, this is my friend Betsy Barkman." It was silly, but it felt odd introducing him to her friend as if he were an old acquaintance. They barely knew each other.

"I'm grateful you were able to rescue Mary and Hannah. I'm so glad I have a chance to tell you that. Oh, I see Alvin over there. I need to find out how his mother is doing. She was knocked down when a tree branch slid off the roof of a house and hit her this morning."

Betsy hurried away, but looked back with a wink for Mary before catching up with Alvin. The two of them had been dating for several years, although Betsy said she wasn't sure he was the one.

"This must be hard for you," Joshua said.

Mary ducked her head. How could he possibly know how confused and excited she felt when he was near? "Why would seeing you again be hard for me?"

"I meant it must be hard for you to see your community in ruins."

She felt like a fool. "It is sad, but look how everyone is working together. Friends are helping friends. Strangers are helping strangers. It will take a lot of work, but we'll get through this."

"I was wondering if your grandmother's offer of a place to stay was still open? If not, I'm sure I can find another family to put me up."

"Ada and Hannah will be happy to have you stay."

"And you, Mary? Will you be happy if I do?" His voice was low enough that only she could hear him.

She quickly looked down. She was excited at the prospect, but it also gave her pause. She already liked him too much. Her track record with liking and trusting the wrong men made her leery of repeating those mistakes. She chanced a glance in his direction. He was watching her with a small grin on his face that set butterflies loose in her midsection. She was trying to think how she should answer him when a group of volunteers arrived and began helping themselves to the food. Joshua moved aside. Maybe she should pretend she hadn't heard his question.

Someone called his name. Mary saw Ethan Gingerich gesturing to him from the back of a wagon. Joshua waved to acknowledge him.

Looking at Mary, he tipped his head toward Ethan. "I need to get back to work."

"But you haven't finished your lunch."

"I'll take it with me."

She tried for an offhand tone to make it seem as if she didn't care where he stayed. "Our cart is at the Wadler Inn. You can find us there when you're ready to call it a day. Unless you find someplace else you'd rather stay."

Joshua tempered his disappointment. He could hardly expect Mary to be overjoyed about spending more time with him. He was little more than a stranger, but at least she hadn't rescinded the invitation. That was something.

He wasn't sure what it was about Mary, but he was drawn to her in a way he had never been drawn to another woman. Maybe it was the circumstances of their first meeting. Maybe when their lives weren't hanging in the balance and the world wasn't smashed beyond recognition he would be able to see her in an ordinary light and this strange attraction would fade.

Or maybe she would always be special in his eyes.

For now, he was happy he hadn't been able to return home today. Seeing her again made the whole day brighter.

He glanced toward the command tent and found Sheriff Bradley watching him. A chill settled between Joshua's shoulder blades. If her father learned of his record, Joshua could kiss his chances of spending time with Mary goodbye. And maybe even his freedom.

Was he being a fool to risk it?

Chapter 7

Joshua caught sight of Mary several times during the day while he avoided being anyplace near where the sheriff happened to be working. Like many of the women, Mary manned the food stations and helped wherever she was needed. More than once, he saw her loading smashed lumber, chunks of insulation and broken Sheetrock into the waiting trucks lined up along Main Street. Late in the afternoon, he saw her with her arms full of dirty toys as she carried them toward the lost-and-found area. She worked tirelessly, as did most of the residents and volunteers who had flooded in to help the devastated town.

After a long, hard day of sorting books, cutting up trees and clearing the streets of debris so that vehicles could get through, Joshua was bone tired when he arrived at the inn for a ride to Mary's house. He found her sorting through papers and photographs that had been brought in by the volunteers. She looked up and caught sight of him. A smile brightened her face before it quickly became blank. She looked down and resumed her work.

Every time he thought she was glad to see him, she retreated just as quickly.

He crossed the lobby, stepping around people rolled up in blankets and sleeping bags. He spied Ada sitting in a large wing-back chair by the fireplace. She was asleep. Bella lay quietly beside her. He didn't see Hannah. When he reached Mary, he spoke quietly so as not to disturb the people trying to rest. "They told us to go home. The National Guard is locking down the town for the night soon. No one's going to be allowed in after curfew. They are asking only residents to stay."

"All right." Mary brushed the back of her hand across her forehead. "The rest of this can wait. I'm sure there will be more by morning. A woman from New Philadelphia brought in a photo album and a checkbook. She said she found them in her rosebushes. That's thirty miles from here. The checkbook belongs to Bishop Zook, but no one here knows who the photograph album belongs to."

"There are so many people trying to protect what is left of their homes that they haven't had time to search for missing items. We must have covered fifteen damaged houses with tarps this afternoon alone. Have you heard any more about your bishop's condition?"

"He's in intensive care, but he's improving. One of his ribs punctured his spleen."

"I'm sorry. Let us hope God speeds his healing. If

you want to keep working, I'll find a place to wait until the Guard makes us leave."

She shook her head. "Let me tell Emma and Miriam that we're going."

He looked around. "Where is Hannah?"

"She is out back with Katie and her little ones. I'll go get her and then wake Ada."

"Does she know I'm coming home with you?"

"I told her you might. I wish we could let her nap a little while longer. I'm afraid she did too much today."

"Maybe you can convince her to stay home with Hannah tomorrow."

"I'll try. Sometimes convincing Ada to do something that's for her own good can require delicate maneuvering."

He chuckled. "It must run in the family."

She rolled her eyes. "If you want to be helpful, go outside and find the boy who stabled our pony."

"Consider it done."

Joshua found a pair of boys sitting on the curb. One of them knew which pony belonged to Ada. He left at a run and returned a few minutes later with Fred. Joshua had the pony harnessed to the cart by the time Mary came out. He helped Ada up onto the seat. She was almost too tired to make it.

"*Danki*, Joshua. These old bones don't work as well as they used to. I'm glad you chose to stay with us."

He helped Mary up next, lifted Hannah up to her and then climbed in himself. Bella wanted on the floorboard but he made her get in back. It was a tight squeeze with all of them on the bench seat, but he didn't mind being pressed close to Mary. There was something comforting about her presence.

As he drove out of town, he was forced to stop as a police officer directed some heavy equipment across the road. A news van sat beside them on the shoulder of the road. The reporter, a man with gray hair, was speaking to the camera. "As you can see behind me, Amish families like this one have poured in to help this community in horse-drawn wagons, buggies and carts. Although very few Amish live in this town of two thousand people, it hasn't made any difference to them. Helping their neighbor goes far beyond the confines of religion and town limits."

Joshua ignored the camera that swung to include them. Mary and Ada turned their faces away. Hannah looked around him and waved. A woman behind the cameraman waved back. When the heavy equipment was safely over the road, they were allowed to go.

Something the reporter said stuck in Joshua's mind as he urged Fred into a trot down the highway. Joshua glanced at Mary and Hannah sitting beside him. The man had thought they looked like a family.

It was growing dark by the time they finally reached home. Hannah had fallen asleep in Mary's arms several miles back. Now her arm was numb from holding her daughter. Ada got down and headed for the house with lagging steps. Bella hopped out and loped toward the barn. Joshua noticed that Mary was having trouble.

"Here, let me take her." He lifted Hannah off her lap.

Mary rubbed some feeling back into her arm. "She's

getting heavy. I don't know how she has grown up so quickly."

"My mother used to threaten to tie a brick on top of my hat so I wouldn't grow so fast." Joshua settled Hannah over his shoulder and extended a hand to help Mary down from the cart.

"Did it work? Maybe I'll try it."

"It didn't work for any of her sons."

Mary hesitated to take his hand, but her common sense won out. He was just being kind. She had to keep reminding herself of that. She allowed him to help her down and then quickly stepped away from him, still rubbing her tingling arm. She reached for Hannah, but Joshua shook his head.

"I'll take her to bed if you'll show me the way."

"All right." She walked up to the house and held the door for him.

Ada was unpacking the baskets they had taken into town. Mary said, "Leave them, Ada. I'll take care of them as soon as I get Hannah into bed."

"*Danki*, child. I don't know why I'm so tired."

"It was an emotionally difficult day," Joshua said.

"It was. *Guten nacht*, all." Ada walked down the hall to her bedroom at the rear of the house.

Mary led Joshua up the narrow staircase to the second floor. She opened the door to Hannah's room and turned on the battery-operated lamp she kept on Hannah's bedside table. Joshua laid Hannah gently on her bed and stepped back.

He treated her daughter with such tenderness. If nothing else about him appealed to her that would. The trouble was *everything* about him pleased her.

Mary removed Hannah's prayer *kapp* and shoes and quickly changed her into her nightgown without waking her. Joshua crossed to the window and opened it to let in the cool night air as Mary tucked the sheets around Hannah and kissed her forehead.

"She's a sweet child," he said softly.

"She is the sun and the stars."

They left the room together. Mary closed the door quietly. Then it was just the two of them in the dark hall. His nearness sent a tingle of awareness across her skin like a soft evening breeze. He smelled of wood shavings and his own unique scent that she remembered from their time together in the cellar. She stepped back and crossed her arms. "I hope you are comfortable in the spare room."

"Compared to the backseat of my buggy and the chairs we tried to sleep in night before last, the spare bed felt *wunderbar*."

"Was it only two days ago? It seems like ages." She began walking down the stairs.

"A lot has happened since then. I got to meet Delbert."

Mary tried to smother her smile but it broke free, anyway. "Was the ride with him comfortable?"

"I wouldn't say it was comfortable. My arm was mighty tired of hanging on to the edge of the seat by the time we reached town."

"Delbert is a good man. I shouldn't make fun of him."

"He's a hard worker. Not fast, but he gets the job done."

Crossing to the stove, she stoked the coals and placed a kettle over the back burner when the embers flared to life. Although the *Ordnung* of their church allowed propane stoves, Ada refused to get rid of her wood-burning one.

"Would you like some tea?" Mary wanted to prolong their time together. She shouldn't. She should go to bed and forget he was even in the house.

Like that's going to happen.

"I would love some tea. *Danki*." He took a seat at the table.

Suddenly nervous, Mary finished unpacking the baskets, making a mental list of the things she would need to take with her in the morning. After putting out a pair of white mugs, she placed a tea bag in each one. She could feel Joshua's gaze on her as she moved around the kitchen. He didn't speak. Thankfully, the kettle began to whistle. She took it from the stove and filled the waiting mugs.

She carried them to the table and handed him one. "I would've thought you could have found a ride to Berlin with some of the *Englisch* volunteers."

"I did think of that, but by then I had seen the extent of the destruction and I wanted to help. I can stay a few days. The vet told me Oscar won't be fit to travel for at least a week unless I have him trailered home. You wouldn't believe the number of injured horses and cattle that have been brought in. To say nothing of the dogs and cats."

"So you're staying for a week?" A flicker of excitement shimmered through her.

"Oh, I don't have to stay here for that long. I can find somewhere else."

Don't make it seem important.

"I reckon the chair in your great-uncle's basement is still available."

Joshua chuckled. "As a last resort, I'll keep that in mind."

Mary took a sip of her tea. "You can stay with us. Ada won't mind and Hannah will love having you. I can ask Nick to have Oscar brought here. We can look after him for you. We have room in the barn. It's the least we can do."

"That would be great. I'll pay you for his keep."

"There are plenty of chores you can do. The corn-cribs are going to have to be rebuilt before fall."

"I'll see what I can do after I get back from Hope Springs tomorrow."

Mary sighed deeply. "This is not what I imagined I'd be doing a week ago."

"What do you mean?"

"Sorting through the wreckage of people's homes and lives, looking for something to salvage for them."

"It's not something anyone imagined. It's just what needs to be done."

"You sound very practical."

"Do I? My family often accuses me of being the dreamer. The fellow who always thinks he can make things better, help people change."

"Do I detect a hint of bitterness?"

He dunked his tea bag up and down without looking at her. "Sometimes people don't want to change."

"Sometimes they don't know how," she said gently.

"He knows how. He just won't."

"Someone in your family?"

Joshua shook his head. "I don't want to bore you with our problems."

"You saved my life. Feel free to bore me. Sometimes talking helps."

He hesitated, then said, "I have a brother who left."

"Left the Amish?"

Joshua hunched over his cup, staring at it intently. "*Ja.* Luke got in with bad company. He got into drugs."

"It happens." She rubbed the scar on her wrist. Her past was checkered with bad company and all the trouble it had brought her. Hannah was the only good thing to come out of that horrible time.

Joshua sat back. "*Nee*, Mary, it doesn't just happen. My brother made a choice. He hurt a lot of people."

"Including you?"

"Including me and everyone in our family."

"I'm sure he regrets that."

Joshua sneered. "Not that I can see."

"Where is he now?"

"Far away."

He looked so sad. She wanted to reach out and comfort him, but she held back. "I'm sorry."

"*Danki*, but it doesn't matter. He is my brother and I love him, but he is lost to us."

"Perhaps not. With God, all things are possible. I'll pray for him."

"You are a good woman, Mary."

The look he gave her warmed her all the way through. She basked in the glow of his compliment. When had she started needing someone's praise?

When he started giving it. When he called her brave outside the cellar.

Had it only been yesterday morning? It seemed as if she had known him for years.

He took a sip of tea. "Tell me how you ended up being adopted by two *Englisch* people? That's got to be unusual for an Amish girl."

She came back to reality with a thud. When he learned about her past, he would know she wasn't good and she wasn't brave. She took one last sip of her tea and carried the mug to the sink. "It's a long story. I think I will save it for some evening when I'm not so tired."

"Sure. I understand."

She left him sitting at the table and went to her room, but it was a long time before she fell asleep.

Someone was patting his face. Joshua cracked one eyelid. Hannah was bending close.

"Are you awake?" she whispered.

"Maybe." He glanced toward the bedroom windows. Only a faint pink color stained the eastern horizon.

"*Mamm* said I wasn't to bother you until you were awake."

He sat up stiffly and rubbed his face with both hands. "Okay. I'm awake. What do you need?"

"The wagon has a broken wheel."

Did they have a wagon as well as a cart? He didn't remember seeing one. How did a wheel get broken at this hour? "Do you mean the cart has a broken wheel?"

"*Nee*, my wagon does." She shoved a wooden toy in front of his face.

He took it from her and held it out where he could focus on it. The rear axle was broken and the right rear wheel was split in half. "This looks bad."

She held her hands wide. "I know. I can't take my chickens to market without it."

He heard the faint clatter of pans in the kitchen downstairs. Was Mary up already? He sighed heavily. He'd gotten out of the habit of rising early when he was in prison. There was no point. He stared at the broken toy. "How did this happen?"

Hannah spun to glare at Bella, sitting quietly behind her. "She got in it and she was too big."

The Lab perked up and wagged her tail happily.

The image of the eighty-pound dog trying to fit in a toy wagon that was only ten inches wide made Joshua look closely at Hannah. Something wasn't right. "Are you sure that's how this happened?"

Hannah stared at her bare feet. "I wanted her to get in, but she wouldn't. So I showed her how to jump in and the wheel broke."

"You jumped in the wagon?"

"Only because Bella wouldn't do it."

"I think the results would have been the same either way, but it's not right to blame Bella for something you did."

"I know. But can you fix it? *Mamm* says she can't."

He could if he was home and in his father's workshop. He didn't have the tools he would need to fashion the parts here. He hated to admit he couldn't help so he tried a different approach. "I'm afraid we'll have to take it to a wheelwright. Is there a buggy maker in these parts?"

"Levi Beachy makes buggies in Hope Springs."

"If his business hasn't blown away, I'll take your wagon in and see what he can do. It needs a new axle as well as a wheel. But Hannah, a lot of folks need their wagons and buggies repaired, too. Ones that aren't toys. It might take a while for it to get fixed."

"Okay. I guess I'll take my chickens to market next week."

"I'm sorry I couldn't be more help."

She picked up a cardboard box with paper cutouts of chickens in it and headed to the kitchen. "That's okay. *Mamm*, Joshua is awake!"

Mary peeked around the door frame. He managed a little wave. She gave her daughter the same look Hannah had turned on Bella. "Did you wake him up?"

"Bella did."

He couldn't let that slide. "Hannah, what did I tell you?"

Her little shoulders slumped. "That it's not right to blame Bella for things I do."

Mary frowned. "So you did wake him."

"Only because Bella wouldn't do it. Do I have to go to the corner in the kitchen now?"

"*Ja*, right this minute." Mary pointed toward the stairs. Bella followed Hannah with her head down and her tail between her legs.

Mary dried her hands on her apron. "I'm sorry, Joshua. You can go back to sleep for a while. She won't bother you again."

"I'm awake. I might as well see what can be salvaged of your corncribs after I take care of the horses."

"All right. Would you feed the chickens and the cow, too, while you are out there?"

"Sure. Do you want me to milk the cow?"

"Ada will milk her. They get along. She likes to kick everyone else."

"Ada does?"

Mary giggled. He adored the sound. "*Nee*, Rosie the cow does."

"Then I'll leave milking Rosie to Ada."

Mary turned around and left. Scratching his head and yawning, he headed for the bathroom. If he kept moving, he'd wake up. Every muscle in his body ached. It had been months since he'd done as much physical labor as he'd done yesterday, and it showed.

Twenty minutes later, he was wide-awake and pitching hay from the open door of the barn loft down to the horse, the pony and a doe-eyed brown-and-white Guernsey cow. His stiff muscles were loosening up and the fog had lifted from his brain. A decent night's sleep could do wonders for a man. As could walking outside without seeing high barbed-wire fences and guard towers.

He had stayed up late last night writing a letter to his parents. He wanted to share his thoughts, and he knew it would ease his mother's mind to hear more from him. It had been hard to describe the damage he saw and how the lives of people had been altered in Hope Springs, but it had been easy to write about Mary, Ada and Hannah. He might have written too much about Mary, but everything seemed to revolve around her.

He drew a deep breath as he leaned on his pitchfork and watched dawn break over the land. The springtime air was fresh and crisp. Thick dew covered the grass and sparkled where the sunlight touched it. If he faced south from the hayloft door, he could see fields of young corn just a few inches tall. By late summer, it would be higher than a man's head and by winter it would be stacked in rows of shocks waiting to feed the cattle. It was good land. A man could make a fine living for his family farming it. At the moment, it was green and brimming with the promise of new life.

"Joshua, breakfast is ready," Mary called from the front porch.

"Coming." He tossed one more forkful of hay to the animals and went down the hayloft ladder. When he came out of the barn, he saw the sheriff's white SUV coming up the lane.

Joshua's joy in the morning vanished as dread seeped in to replace it. The one thing he hadn't included in his letter was Mary's relationship to an *Englisch* lawman.

The vehicle rolled to a stop in front of the house. The passenger-side door opened and Miriam stepped out with a friendly smile on her face. "Good morning, Joshua. I thought you would have been well on your way home by now."

Nick got out, too. His smile wasn't near as friendly. Joshua fixed his gaze on the ground. "I thought I would stay for a few days and help with the cleanup."

"All help is appreciated," Nick said. He and Miriam both looked weary.

She sighed deeply. "Yes, it is, and sorely needed. I don't know how the town will ever recover from this."

Joshua couldn't think of anything to say. Fortunately, Hannah came flying out of the house just then. "Papa Nick, can you fix my wagon?"

He scooped her up in his arms. "What happened to your wagon?"

"Bella—" Hannah glanced at Joshua and lowered

her face. "I mean—I jumped in it and it broke. Bella didn't do it."

"You are just in time to eat," Ada said from the doorway. "Come in."

"I was hoping you'd ask." Nick set Hannah on the ground and they all went toward the house.

Joshua followed slowly.

Breakfast was a feast. Mary had prepared bacon and scrambled eggs. There were fresh hot biscuits with butter and honey and oatmeal with brown sugar and cinnamon. He picked at his food. It was hard to have an appetite when he was seated beside the sheriff. Every bruise, every humiliation Joshua had suffered during his arrest and time in prison came back to choke him. He rubbed his wrists at the memory of handcuffs chafing his flesh. Bile rose in his throat.

Ada poured coffee into the cup in front of him, bringing him back to the present. A rich, enticing aroma rose from the steaming liquid. He grasped the cup and raised it to his lips. It was hot, but the slightly bitter brew settled the nausea in his stomach. He looked up to thank her and noticed that she still had dark circles under her eyes.

Nick seemed to have noticed, as well. "Miriam and I'll head into town after we're done with breakfast. Ada, you and Mary don't need to come in today. There will be plenty of volunteers to help."

"I think I will remain here. I've gotten behind on my own work." Ada sat down at the table.

Hannah popped up. "Can I go to town with you, Papa Nick?"

"Nee." Mary shook her head. "Papa Nick has too

much to do to look after you in all that chaos. Besides, I need you to stay home and help *Mammi*."

"But how will I get my wagon fixed?"

"I'll see to it," Joshua assured her. She seemed content with that.

Miriam laid a hand on Mary's sleeve. "Are you going back today?"

"I am. Betsy and I have signed up for shifts at the food station."

"You can ride with us," Nick offered.

"That's all right. I know you need to get going, and I'm not ready. Joshua and I will take the cart."

Nick sent Joshua a sharp glance. "As long as you are both careful. The place is a zoo."

"We will be," Mary assured him. Joshua kept his gaze on his half-eaten eggs.

"May I have another biscuit? How long are you staying, Joshua?" Nick asked.

"I have to be home by Thursday so I need to leave by Wednesday."

Mary passed the plate of biscuits to Nick. "Can you have Joshua's horse brought here? We can look after him, and that will free up space at the vet clinic."

"Sure. I'll see to it. Will you be staying here, Joshua?"

He couldn't tell from Nick's tone what he thought about the idea. He glanced at Mary to gauge her reaction. She kept her eyes downcast. Joshua cleared his throat. "Yes, if it's not too much trouble for Ada and Mary."

"It's no trouble," Ada declared. "I'll put you to work. I need wood cut for the stove. I need my corncribs fixed. I have plenty to keep you busy."

Nick nodded slowly, but didn't say anything. Joshua had the impression he wasn't pleased, but there was little he could do about it.

Joshua shifted uneasily in his chair and took another sip of coffee. Had the sheriff noticed his nervous attitude? Hopefully he hadn't, but something in the man's intense gaze made Joshua doubt he missed much.

The sheriff and Miriam left shortly after that, much to Joshua's relief. Later, as he waited beside the cart for Mary to join him, his spirits rose with a growing sense of anticipation. The ride would only take thirty minutes or so, but it would give him thirty minutes alone with Mary, and he liked that idea.

That became the pattern for the next several days. Joshua took care of the animals in the mornings, then headed to breakfast, where Nick and Miriam joined them at Ada's insistence. She wanted to be kept apprised of the progress and needs in the community and she said no one was better informed than Nick. Miriam was able to pass along updates on Bishop Zook and the other injured people. Joshua strongly suspected part of Ada's plan was to insure her daughter was getting enough food and rest and not working herself into the ground.

After breakfast, Joshua would drive Mary into Hope Springs. They would go their separate ways in town, but they often found each other for a quiet lunch in the park. The work was exhausting and sad, but nearly everyone worked to keep each other's spirits up. One afternoon, an impromptu singing took place when five teenage Amish girls began a hymn in the park. They were soon joined by a group of young men, and for thirty minutes the cares of the volunteers and townspeople were lifted away by the sweet voices of the a cappella group.

In the evenings, Joshua rebuilt Ada's corncribs and read from the Bible after supper. Once Ada went to bed, he and Mary talked about their day over a mug of tea at the kitchen table. When he was alone in his room, he wrote to his family each night. He found himself writing more about Mary and Hannah than about the storm damage and recovery.

As he sealed the envelope of his current letter, he stared at it and wondered what his family would make of Mary if they met. Would they like her as much as he did? Would they approve of her adoptive parents?

He sighed as he realized he could easily go home now. There were plenty of helpers in Hope Springs, but he didn't want to leave.

Not just yet.

Chapter 8

Mary sat down on the cart seat beside Joshua on Saturday morning and worked hard to control her nervousness. It was another simple wagon ride into town just as they had done all week. It wasn't like riding with a young man in his courting buggy. They were on their way to help people affected by a disaster. They were not on a date. Yet a happy sense of anticipation gripped her.

Joshua had chosen to harness Tilly that morning. The mare stepped along brightly in the ground-eating trot that Standardbreds were famous for. Traffic along the rural highway was heavy for a Saturday morning. It seemed that people from all over were converging on the town in cars, pickups and wagons. Mary saw several license plates from neighboring states.

A large flatbed truck with a bulldozer on the bed followed them at a crawl for a half mile before it could pass on the hilly road. Joshua pulled over to give the traffic more room as it flowed by them. The large white van that passed them last was from Pennsylvania. It was loaded with young Amish men and women.

"It hasn't taken long for the word to get out among the Amish." He guided Tilly back to the center of their lane when the way was clear.

"The town will be grateful for the extra help. I heard yesterday that the Mennonite disaster relief people were on their way."

"They always find a way to help. I'm sure more Amish will be coming, too. The recovery will take months."

"So many groups rushing to help. It restores my faith in people."

He cast a sidelong glance her way. "Do you doubt there are good people?"

"Sometimes. I know it's wrong, but it's hard to accept people at face value."

"Our faith teaches us otherwise, but I know what you mean. It's hard for me, too."

"You are thinking about your brother and the people he became involved with."

"In part, but I was thinking about something else."

She waited for him to elaborate. He didn't. "Something that happened to you?"

He shook his head. "It's not important."

"Now you have made me doubly curious."

He glanced at her and smiled. "I see where Hannah gets it."

"Which is a polite way of telling me to mind my own business. Very well. Tell me about Bowmans Crossing. What's it like?"

"It's nowhere near as big as Hope Springs. It's more a collection of farms and small Amish-run businesses than a true town. When my family first settled in the area, they built a house by the river and ran a ferry crossing for their neighbors. That's how the place got its name. There is a bridge over the river now, but folks still call it Bowmans Crossing."

"You said your parents farm there."

"*Ja.* My *daed* was the youngest son, so he inherited the home farm. Two of his brothers own a buggy-making business. Another sells harnesses."

"Do they live nearby?"

"All within a mile. You can't throw a rock in any direction without hitting one of my cousins."

"It must be nice to have a big family."

"I guess it is. I've never known anything else."

"What will your father do with the land your mother inherited?"

"I'm not sure. My youngest brother will inherit the home place, so maybe one of us will take over my great-uncle's property here."

Would Joshua be sent to farm it? The idea that he might settle in the area brought on mixed emotions— happiness that he might remain close by, worry about what that would mean if her attraction to him grew unchecked.

"Delbert mentioned that you moved to Hope Springs a few years ago. Where was home before that?"

"I grew up near New Philadelphia." The edge of Hope Springs came into view and she quickly changed the subject. "I hope the television cameras are gone."

"I only see one."

A gray-haired man in the uniform of a county deputy stopped them. He held a large clipboard. "Are you residents?"

"We are volunteers," Joshua said.

"Names?"

He wrote down their information and then pulled two yellow bracelets from a box. He handed them to Joshua. "I know the Amish don't wear jewelry of any kind. You don't have to have this on, but you need to have it somewhere on your person so you can prove you are here legitimately. The numbers match your name, so be sure and check out with a sentry when you leave town. Please accept my gratitude for coming to help. I went to school here, way back when. It breaks my heart to see so much of the town in ruin."

"The town will recover." Mary tried to comfort him with her words.

"I know it will. There are some mighty fine, mighty strong people here. If we didn't know that before, we sure know it now." He waved them through.

She looked at Joshua. "I'm to meet Betsy and some of the other women at the Red Cross tent in the park. You can drop me at the inn. What will you be doing?"

"The volunteers were asked to meet in the park, too. Most of the streets have been cleared and all of the damaged roofs have been covered, so I think we're starting a house-by-house cleanup of debris."

"When our shift is over, Betsy and I will lend a hand."

He glanced at her feet. "Did you wear sturdy boots? You'll need gloves, too."

"I'm wearing Ada's work boots and two pairs of

socks so I won't get blisters. I have gloves in my pockets. I'll be fine."

"Where is the buggy maker's shop? I promised Hannah I would see about getting her wagon fixed and she reminded me this morning that I hadn't done it."

"Follow the street that runs behind the Wadler Inn to the west side of town. You can't miss Levi Beachy's place. I should warn you about the twins."

Joshua laughed. "I've already been warned about Atlee and Moses. I'll try not to fall prey to one of their pranks. The way folks talk, you would think the tornado was their doing." He pulled Tilly to a stop in front of the inn.

Mary got down before he could help her. "It wouldn't surprise me if they had something to do with it. Can you deliver these supplies to the Red Cross tent, too?"

"I sure can. See you later." He slapped the reins on Tilly's rump and drove away.

Betsy came out of the inn with a huge load of towels in her arms. "The two of you looked quite cozy riding together."

Mary knew she was being teased. "It's not a very big cart. I would look cozy if I'd only had a broom with me."

"Not that cozy. Is he still staying with you and your grandmother? What does she think about him? He's single, after all."

"Ada has her eye on Delbert Miller for me."

Betsy's eyebrows shot up. "You can't be serious."

"She's getting desperate. I'll be twenty next Sunday, so the pressure is on."

"I know that feeling." Betsy adjusted the load in her arms.

"How is Alvin's mother?" Mary took half the towels

from Betsy and they began walking toward the park. The persistent sounds of chain saws had been replaced by the rumble of heavy machinery and countless hammers boarding up windows and repairing roofs. The smell of diesel exhaust hung heavy in the air.

"She's getting as antsy as Ada. Lots of talk about the grandbabies everyone else is having while she may be in the grave before she has any. She told Alvin the tree branch that slid off the roof and hit her was God's way of telling him to speed things up."

"And is he?"

Betsy paused and looked around to make sure they couldn't be overheard. "He proposed last night."

Mary's mouth fell open. "He did? What did you say?"

"I told him I'd rather that he ask me because he loves me and not because his mother got hit by a tree limb. It wasn't that big a branch."

"You said no?"

"Not exactly."

"You said yes? You were going to stay single until you were twenty-five. I've heard you say that a dozen times."

"I know what I said. I told him maybe. It would be nice to have a home of my own. When I see my sisters Clara and Lizzie with their babies, I think it would be nice to have a baby, too."

"Take my advice. Don't make the same mistake I did. Have a husband first. It makes life a lot less complicated."

"Don't tell me you see Hannah as a mistake, because I won't believe you. No one could love their little girl more than you do."

"I never think of her as anything but the most precious gift God could give me. I made my share of mistakes, but she is my redemption. How did Alvin take your answer?"

Betsy sighed heavily and shook her head, making the ribbons of her *kapp* dance. "Not well. He has stopped speaking to me."

"He'll get over it. He's head over heels for you."

"I thought he was, but now, I'm not so sure."

They reached the tent. It was busy as volunteers manned stations of water, ice and food. The hum of a generator could be heard outside. Orange electric cords stretched across the floor, held down with strips of duct tape. A small television at a desk in the back flashed with images of the destruction taken by helicopters and reporters on the ground.

There was little time to talk as Betsy and Mary passed out food, water and hot beverages to a steady stream of volunteers. A few were merely sightseers, not interested in working. They had come to gawk. The rest, young Amish people from neighboring communities, college students and off-duty first responders from as far away as Kansas, were all there to give freely of their time simply because they wanted to help someone in need.

Moving tons of rubble was backbreaking work, as Mary learned after her four-hour shift at the tent ended. She was loading bricks from a collapsed chimney into a wheelbarrow when she saw Joshua approaching. She straightened and brushed her gloves together. "Did you get something to eat? They still have sandwiches at the food tent."

"I finished my break a few minutes ago. I'm on my way back to work, but I've been sent on a mission to find you."

"Me? What for?"

"I met a local fellow named Alvin. When he learned I was staying at your place, he enlisted my help to gather some information about a friend of yours."

"Betsy."

"*Ja.* He seems like a nice fellow, so I thought I would help him out." Joshua began picking up bricks with her.

"Oh, dear. What exactly does he want to know?"

"Is she seeing someone else?"

Mary threw a brick in the wheelbarrow and glared at Joshua. "Of course she isn't. She's been seeing Alvin for ages."

Straightening with a brick in each hand, Joshua tipped his head to the side. "Then I am a little confused. I thought he wanted to go out with her."

"He wants to marry her."

"Then he should ask her."

"He did."

"Now I'm even more confused. Did she give him an answer?"

"She said maybe."

"Now I get it." He tossed his bricks on top of hers. "He's wondering if she is waiting for someone else to ask the same question. Otherwise, she would've said yes or no."

The wheelbarrow was full, so Mary grabbed the handles. "She said maybe because she isn't ready to marry. She wants her freedom for a while longer."

"Can I tell him that?"

"Since he hasn't figured that out for himself, you can. And he should inform his mother." She began walking toward the street.

Joshua followed her with an armload of bricks. "I think I'll draw the line at telling him what he should say to his mother. I don't mind helping a fellow find out if a girl is interested, but this relationship sounds more complicated than I am equipped to handle."

She grinned at him. "It's a wise man who knows when he is in over his head."

Joshua stopped in his tracks. She had such a pretty smile. It made her eyes sparkle, and his heart stumbled over itself when she aimed it at him. He knew for a fact that he was getting in over his head because he sure wanted to see her smiling a lot more. At him.

He hurried to catch up with her. "What are we doing with these bricks?"

"We're stacking them on a pallet in the driveway. They'll be taken to be cleaned and reused to repair Mrs. Davis's chimney by a local bricklayer who has volunteered his services."

"Nice guy." Joshua began stacking the bricks tightly together.

"I think so, too. Mrs. Davis doesn't have family to help her. She is watching us from the window, by the way. I have heard she's afraid to leave her home and hasn't been out since the storm."

"It had to be frightening to see this destruction up close and then have the place overrun with strangers."

Joshua glanced toward the house. The curtain at the window fell back into place. A second later, it parted again as a yellow cat settled itself on the window ledge to watch them. Joshua casually bent to tie his bootlaces and glanced covertly toward the window. A small white-haired woman holding a gray cat in her arms pulled the curtain aside again.

A tall *Englisch* man came striding down the street toward them. "Let me give you a hand with those."

Mary straightened, put her hands on her hips and stretched backward. "This is the last of the unbroken ones. Joshua, this is Pete Metcalf. He's the bricklayer I was telling you about."

"Good to meet you." Pete held out his hand. Joshua shook it.

Mary pulled off her gloves. "How are your wife and family getting along?"

"It's still crowded at the inn, but we're really grateful that we have a place to stay. Thank you for insisting we go there. The baby is doing great. She is the center of attention when she's awake. It's like having two dozen babysitters. The only problem is that we can't find our cat. The kids have been all over town and they are brokenhearted. We even took your suggestion and checked at the veterinary clinic, but she wasn't there."

"You should have the children check with Mrs. Davis. She is a cat lover. I think she has taken in some strays. I noticed some open cans of cat food on her steps."

Pete hiked a thumb toward the house. "Mrs. Gina Davis, the lady whose chimney I'm fixing?"

"Ja."

"I'll go ask her now."

"*Nee*," Mary said quickly, stopping him. "Send the children."

"Why the kids?"

"They are less frightening than a strange man would be. When people are scared and anxious, small children can help them overcome that fear."

He shrugged. "Okay, I'll have them come over."

When he left, Joshua moved a step closer to Mary. "Why didn't you ask her if she had their cat?"

"I don't need a place to stay or someone to care for me or about me. Mrs. Davis and Pete's family both need those things. Maybe a cat can bring them together."

He tipped his head slightly and regarded her with a bemused expression. "You know she has their cat, don't you?"

"The children came by the Red Cross tent earlier. They were showing people a drawing of a gray cat with three white feet. The little boy drew it since they didn't have any photographs. They were hoping someone had seen her."

"And we just saw Mrs. Davis holding a cat like that."

Mary grinned. "It might not be the same cat. Then again, it might be. Or it might be another cat that needs children to love."

"And my family thinks I'm the optimistic dreamer. They should meet you. They would adore you."

Mary blushed a rosy red.

The moment the words were out of his mouth, Joshua regretted them. What was he doing? He wouldn't be in town for more than a few more days. He had no business implying he wanted her to meet his family. That wasn't going to happen. He was on parole. Her father was an *Englisch* lawman. His family wouldn't be comfortable with that.

The last thing he needed was to fall for this woman with a sweet daughter and an even sweeter smile. It couldn't work between them. As much as he liked her, he wasn't able to trust her father.

Maybe when his sentence was up. Maybe when he wasn't afraid of being sent back to prison. Maybe. All his life he'd been taught to avoid the *Englisch* and shun their worldly ways except when he had to do business with them. His time in prison had taught him to fear them. Mary's father was polite and it was clear he loved Mary and Hannah, but Joshua couldn't bring himself to trust the man. He avoided Nick when he could and stayed silent when he couldn't.

Stepping away from Mary, Joshua said, "I should get back to Alvin. I'm sure he's on pins and needles waiting to hear what I learned."

"Tell him Betsy needs time to think over his offer. I'm sure she loves him, but I think she's afraid to admit that. She isn't ready to settle down now, but she will be one day."

"I'll tell him that. *Danki.* How will I find you when I'm done for the day?"

"I'll be in the Red Cross tent with Miriam or Nick."

Joshua nodded. Hopefully, her father would be out working elsewhere.

Just then, Pete returned with his son and daughter. He waited at the foot of the steps while they went up to the door and knocked. When the door opened a crack, the little boy held up a piece of paper. "This is our cat,

Socks, and she's missing. Have you seen her? We miss her an awful lot."

The door opened a little wider. Joshua strained to hear the woman's reply. "I have seen a cat like that, but she's not so fat."

The boy turned his picture around to stare at it. "I'm not a very good artist. Where did you see her?"

"Wait here." Mrs. Davis closed the door. When she opened it again, she held the gray cat in her arms.

The little girl began jumping and shouting, "That's Socks. Socks, we found you." She held up her arms.

Mrs. Davis came out on to the porch and sat on a green painted bench. "She's been very scared. You have to be quiet so that you don't frighten her even more."

The little girl cupped the cat's face between her hands and rubbed their noses together. "I missed you so much."

The little boy stroked the cat who was purring loudly. "Thank you for taking care of her."

The little girl gathered the cat in her arms. "I'm going to take you home now."

"Except we don't have a home," her brother reminded her gently.

From the bottom of the steps, Pete spoke. "We appreciate you taking care of Socks. Our house was destroyed and we are staying at the inn. Could you continue to look after her until we find someplace more settled? We can pay you to board her, although it will be a few days before I have the money from our insurance settlement."

"But, Daddy, Socks wants to stay with me." His daughter looked ready to cry.

"I know, honey, but we don't have a safe place to

keep her. A lot of people are coming and going at the inn. She could get out and get lost again. You don't want that."

"No."

Mrs. Davis rose to her feet. "She can stay here. Why don't you children come inside and visit with Socks for a while? I have other cats. Would you like to meet them? If that's okay with your father," she added quickly.

"That would be great. Thank you. I'll get this mess in your yard cleaned up as soon as possible. Do you have other damage?"

"My attic window is broken."

"There's a fellow with glass and cutting tools over by the school. I'll let him know you need some work done."

Mrs. Davis opened the door and followed the children inside. Joshua gave Mary a wry smile. "You were right. Children can help."

"The way having Hannah with us helped you when we were in the cellar."

That surprised him. Had Mary noticed how fearful he'd been that day? "It did help. I hate small places, but knowing Hannah and you needed me to remain calm gave me a way to control my fear."

Mary fisted her hands on her hips. "I reckon I'll help Pete clean this yard so the children can play out here without getting hurt."

"I'm on my way to the Hope Springs Fellowship Church."

She smiled at him. "We'll meet up again later."

Joshua thought a lot about Mary as he walked toward the church. She had a knack for understanding people who were afraid. She saw ways to help them. His admiration for her grew. When he reached his destination, he saw a dozen men working on the roof of the white clapboard church that had sustained serious damage. The young pastor was the only *Englisch* fellow among the Amish men with their shirtsleeves rolled up. Joshua stepped into line and carried a bundle of shingles up a ladder to where Alvin was hammering them into place. He stopped working when he saw Joshua.

"Well? Is she seeing someone else? Did you find out anything?"

"Mary was very helpful. Betsy is not seeing anyone other than you. She isn't in a hurry to marry, and pressing her probably isn't the right thing to do." Joshua laid the bundle of shingles where others could reach them.

"I don't understand why she won't marry me. Her sisters are all married. That can't be the reason. Even her grandfather recently married, so it's not because she has to take care of him. I don't get it."

"Mary says to give her time." Joshua pulled his hammer from the tool belt Alvin had loaned him and began setting the shingles in place. The two young men, both the same age, were quickly becoming friends after meeting that morning at the command center, where they'd been assigned to the same tasks for the day. The rat-a-tat-tat of hammers filled the air around Joshua as he and the other men made short work of the project.

Alvin drove the next nail in with unnecessary force. "I'm tired of waiting. There are a lot of young women who would be pleased to go out with me."

"And yet none of them are Betsy."

Alvin put his hammer down. "That's the truth. I like

you, Joshua Bowman. You've got a good head on your shoulders."

"There are others who don't think so."

"How long are you staying?" Alvin positioned the next shingle.

"I need to be back in Bowmans Crossing before Thursday. I'll have to hire a driver or take the bus if one goes that way."

"With all the people that have showed up to help, I'm sure someone from your neck of the woods is here. There's a message board at the inn. You can put a note there asking for a ride."

"Good idea. *Danki*."

"Don't mention it. It's the least I can do after sending you to question Mary. I appreciate it. I could've asked one of my friends or cousins, but I thought since you knew Mary so well she might tell you something she wouldn't tell them."

"I don't know her that well. We only met the day of the tornado."

"Is that so? But you're staying with her and her family."

Joshua related the story of their night in the cellar while they worked.

Alvin slipped the last shingle in place. "She's a nice girl. She befriended Betsy when she and her sisters moved here. Have you got a girl back home?"

"I don't. You're blessed to have found the right one."

Alvin shook his head. "Only if she'll marry me."

"Don't give up. Looks like we are done here. What do we do now?"

"Go back to the command center and see what else they need us to do."

Would Mary be there by now? Joshua discovered he was eager to find out. It was sad—no matter how hard he worked at convincing himself he should stay away, he was ready to jump at the chance to see her again.

He followed the group of men back to the center of town to find where to go for their next project. He spied Mary standing by Miriam and Nick at the back of the Red Cross tent. Both women wore shocked expressions. Nick's angry scowl made Joshua hesitate, but Mary's distress pulled him to her side. "What is it? What's wrong?"

She looked at him with tear-filled eyes. "I was on the news. My face was on television and so was Hannah's."

Chapter 9

Mary noticed Joshua's perplexed expression. He didn't understand how serious this was. How could he? She hadn't told him anything about her former life. She was starting to like him too much. She didn't want him to know what a foolish girl she'd been.

What if Kevin Dunbar had seen her picture? Numbing fear made her heart pound. If he had, then he knew where she lived. Where Hannah lived.

"I'm going to have them stop airing it." Nick pulled his cell phone from his pocket and stormed out of the tent. As upset as she was, Mary couldn't help noticing Joshua's relief at Nick's departure. Did he dislike her father? Was it because he was the English law? Many Amish distrusted Nick in the beginning, but they soon came to see he was honest and sensitive to their ways even when those ways conflicted with the law he was sworn to uphold.

Miriam's phone went off. She read the text and shoved the phone in her pocket. She gripped Mary's hand. "I'm needed at the medical tent. I'll be back as soon as I can."

After Miriam left, Joshua took a step closer. His eyes were filled with compassion. "Your church members will understand that you weren't seeking notoriety. The news cameras must have captured many Amish people." He pointed to the television. "Look, there's Delbert helping clean out someone's house."

The camera was panning a particularly hard-hit area of homes. It wasn't a close-up of Delbert, but his size made him recognizable. There were several Amish men and women in the scene. Joshua believed she was upset because the Amish shunned being photographed. She wanted to explain but she couldn't. Miriam and Nick had decided years ago to keep her past and her old identity a secret. The fewer people who knew, the safer she and Hannah would be.

Besides, Mary didn't want to involve Joshua. This was her father's business. She needed to let him handle it.

"It isn't just you, Mary. I see the girls from the singing, too. Their faces are recognizable. You are worried for nothing."

She drew a deep breath. "You're right. It's foolish to be upset."

After all, what were the chances that Kevin had been watching? He was still in prison.

A few moments later, Miriam came back. "Nick said

he has taken care of it. The clip won't run again. Joshua, would you take Mary home? I'm sure that Hannah is missing her, and I'd like someone to check on Ada. I have to stay. I'm the only nurse on duty right now."

"I don't mind at all," he said quickly. He seemed relieved to have something to do. "I'll go get the cart and meet you out front in a few minutes."

Mary clutched Miriam's arm when Joshua was out of sight. "Do you think Kevin might have seen this? Would he have television in his cell?"

"Not in his cell, but there is a common room where the men can watch programing the warden deems suitable. This news channel is probably one of those. Even if he saw this, he's still behind bars. He can't hurt you."

"I'm afraid and I shouldn't be. My life is in God's hands. It has always been. I know that. He is my protection. He is Hannah's protection."

Miriam pulled Mary close for a quick hug. "I believe that, too, but I can't help worrying about you. Kevin may have friends on the outside. There is a multitude of strangers here. I think it would be best if you didn't come back to help."

Mary pulled away, shamed by her doubts. "These are our friends, Miriam. I can't hide when I see how much still needs to be done for our community. To remain at home would be cowardly."

"My Amish upbringing tells me you are right, but I've been married to a cop for too long. I know that evil exists."

"But it is not stronger than our faith."

"You are so brave."

Mary smiled at her adoptive mother. "I've had good examples to follow."

Miriam's phone went off again. She quickly scanned the text. "I have to go. More people have been hurt by nails and saws, falls and falling limbs in the last two days than were injured by the tornado itself. Let Ada know that Nick and I won't be by tonight or tomorrow morning. Nick is worn to the bone. He needs what little rest he can get. He's been going nonstop since this whole thing happened. If I can steal an extra half hour of sleep for him, I'm going to do it. He gets cranky when he's sleep deprived."

"I'll tell her."

"*Danki.* Give Hannah our love."

"I will." Miriam left and Mary went outside to wait for Joshua.

Betsy stood by a card table handing out donated gloves. She was pointedly ignoring Alvin standing nearby. Mary walked over to her and whispered an old Amish proverb. "Keep your words soft and sweet in case you have to eat them."

Shooting Alvin a sharp look, Betsy turned to Mary. "That's why I'm not talking to him. At all. Where are you going?"

"Home. Miriam thinks Ada needs a break from watching Hannah, but I'll be back Monday morning. What about you?"

"I'll be here. My sister Lizzie has decided the family needs something fun to do after all this work. She proposed we have a picnic by the lake next Saturday. I'd love it if you would join us."

"That's very kind. I know Ada is always happy to visit with your grandmother."

"*Goot.* I'll see you tomorrow at the prayer meeting. It's at Adrian Lapp's place. At least they didn't have any storm damage."

"Am I invited to the picnic?" Alvin asked. He had moved closer while they were talking.

"I reckon," Betsy replied without enthusiasm.

He stuck out his chin. "If I'm not busy, I might come."

"Don't fret about it. If you can't make it, you won't be missed." Betsy threw down the pair of gloves she held and marched away.

Joshua pulled up with the cart. Mary gave Alvin a sympathetic look. "Don't worry, Alvin. She'll come around."

He glared at Betsy's retreating back. "The question is will I be around to see it." He walked away in the opposite direction.

Mary climbed in beside Joshua and he set Tilly in motion. "Things are still not going well for them?"

"*Nee*, and I'm afraid Betsy is just digging in her heels now."

"That's a pity. Are you okay?"

She knew he was referring to the newscast. "I am. It's not likely that there will be trouble because of it. It was just a shock. I had already been scolded for being too forward and then to see my face plastered on the television screen was upsetting." It was true, but it wasn't the whole truth.

"I don't find you forward. Who scolded you?"

Mary folded her hands in her lap and kept her eyes down. "Miriam. She is right—sometimes I am too bold in my speech. She thinks that Nick is a bad influence on me, but he isn't."

"I don't find you bold at all. I find you refreshing."

She didn't know what to say to that. She noticed a cardboard carton beneath his feet and decided to change the subject. "What's in the box?"

"Hannah's wagon."

"I'm surprised that Levi Beachy had time to fix it."

"He didn't, but he let me use his tools."

"Did you?" How kind was that? In the midst of all this destruction, he'd made time to repair her daughter's toy. He was a good, kind man.

"It didn't take long. I had such a big breakfast that I didn't need a lunch break."

"I remember you just picking at your breakfast this morning. I thought maybe you didn't like my cooking."

That was the wrong thing to say. Now he would think she was fishing for compliments.

"Your cooking is good, but it's not like my *Mamm's*."

That put her firmly in her place. "I'll try to do better."

He grinned. "You don't have far to go."

Okay, that was nice. "Thanks again for fixing Hannah's wagon. She loves pulling that thing around."

"I noticed she had some paper chickens she wanted to take to market. Does she have other animals?"

"She used to have a cow, but its head was accidently removed by Bella."

He laughed. "Better a paper cow than the real one."

Mary smiled at him, her fright forgotten for a moment as she relaxed in his company. "You haven't tried to milk Rosie. You might change your opinion about that."

He laughed again and her spirits rose. Joshua Bowman was good company inside and outside of a cellar.

Seeing the worry fall away from Mary's face made Joshua happy. He still didn't understand why she had been so upset about appearing on the news. There had to be more to it than what she was sharing with him. He'd seen the flash of fear in Nick's eyes, too, before anger replaced it.

Joshua was curious, but it wasn't any of his business, so he kept quiet.

A car honked behind them. Joshua urged Tilly to a speedier pace. The road was still filled with traffic and many drivers grew impatient when they had to creep along behind an Amish wagon or buggy. He didn't want to cause a wreck. Unfortunately, it meant they arrived at Ada's farm that much quicker and his time alone with Mary was cut short.

And soon the rest of his time with her would be cut short, too. He would have to head home by Wednesday at the very latest. It wouldn't do to miss his first meeting with his parole officer, even for another day in Mary's company.

When they reached the farm, he stopped the cart by the front gate and got out. He held out his hand to help her down. Her fingers closed over his with trusting firmness. Hannah darted out of the house, letting the screen door slam behind her. Tilly flinched at the sound, jerking the cart. Mary lost her balance. She would have fallen if he hadn't caught her by the waist and pulled her against him. She clutched his shoulders to steady herself.

He gazed into her wide eyes as he slowly lowered her to the ground, reluctant to let her go. His hands spanned her tiny waist with ease. Color bloomed in her cheeks. An overpowering urge to kiss her hit him. What would she do if he tried?

Hannah shot down the porch steps. "Joshua, you're back. Did Levi get my wagon fixed?"

Joshua slowly released Mary. Her hands slid down his arms in a soft caress before she stepped away. He drew an unsteady breath and turned his attention to Hannah. Ada was at the screen door watching them with a knowing little smile on her face.

Feeling foolish, he gave Hannah his full attention and dropped to one knee to address her. "I went to the buggy shop, but as I suspected, Levi was too busy to work on your wagon."

Her hopeful expression fell and her lower lip slipped out in a pout. "Oh. Well, that's okay. Lots of people need their real buggies fixed. I can pretend my shoe box is my wagon for a little while longer."

"I'm glad to hear you say that, Hannah. It means you believe in putting the needs of others before yourself."

She tipped her head slightly. "It does?"

"It does. Thinking of others has its own rewards." He rose to his feet and withdrew the box from beneath the seat. Setting it on the ground in front of her, he waited for her to open it. Mary looked on with a pleased expression.

Hannah glanced up at him. "What's this?"

"A reward for putting others first."

She opened the flaps of the cardboard box. "My wagon! It did get fixed."

She pulled it out and then stared in the box with a puzzled frown. "Someone left their toys in here."

He grinned. "They are your toys. I made them for you."

"You did?" She reached in and came out with a handful of wooden animals.

"Look, *Mamm*, Joshua made me a cow and two horses and three pigs, and here is Bella!"

The toys were little more than crude wooden cutouts, but he'd had a chance to sand them smooth. They were recognizable animals even if they weren't detailed. "Do you like them?"

"They are *wunderbar*! Did you make some chickens?"

"I didn't because you already had some." And because they might have taken more skill than he could muster with Levis' jigsaw.

She loaded the animals in her wagon and ran toward Ada. "*Mammi*, look what Joshua made for me."

"They are very nice. Did you thank him?"

"*Danki*, Joshua."

"You're welcome."

Ada held open the screen door so Hannah could come inside. "Joshua is making both my girls smile today."

Feeling pleased with himself, he propped his arms on the gate. "Ada, you are the only Kaufman woman I want smiling at me."

"You are a flirt." She rolled her eyes and blushed before she disappeared into the house.

"Only because you tempted me with your fried chicken," he called after her.

He turned to put the horse away and found Mary watching him with her arms crossed and a tiny smile curving her lips. "How do you do that?"

"How do I do what?" He strolled back to stand in front of her with his thumbs hooked under his suspenders.

"How do you make us all like you so easily?"

Joshua leaned closer to gaze into her sky-blue eyes. He saw the chasm opening under his feet, but he was powerless to keep from falling in. Why did the first woman to turn him inside out have to be a sheriff's daughter? "Do you like me?"

"I can't decide."

"Guess that means I'll have to try harder." He leaned closer still, but instead of trying for the kiss he wanted, he slipped past her, grasped Tilly's bridle and led the mare to the barn. He knew Mary was watching.

Inside the barn, he found Oscar waiting for him in the first box stall. The big brown horse whinnied a greeting. He limped forward and Joshua saw the large dressing covering his hip. "Looks like the vet took care of you."

He led Tilly into an adjacent stall, unharnessed her and began to rub her down.

The barn door opened and Ada came in with a basket full of bandages and ointments. "Before you flustered me, I was going to tell you that your horse arrived."

"I'm sorry I teased you, but your fried chicken is the best. I mean that. Better than my mother's, and that takes some doing."

"Stop with the flattery."

"If I must."

"The vet sent instructions on how to take care of your horse's injury and some supplies. I'll leave them here." She put them on a workbench beside the barn door.

"Danki."

Her face grew serious as she walked toward him. "I know it is not our way to interfere in the lives of our young people, but I'm an old woman with a bad heart, so I hope you will forgive me."

"For what?"

"Are you a free young man?"

He stopped brushing the mare and stared at Ada. His stomach flip-flopped. Had she found out about his prison record? "What do you mean?"

"Don't flirt with Mary unless you are prepared for her to take you seriously."

Laying his currycomb aside, he came to the stall gate and leaned on it with his arms crossed. "I would never knowingly hurt Mary."

"I'm sure that's true, but she has endured many heartaches. I don't want to see her suffer another if I can help it. Do you know what I mean?"

"I like Mary. I think we can be good friends."

"But not more than friends?"

"I have to return home. It may be a long time before I can come back."

She sighed deeply. "I'm glad you are honest about it. You are a likable young fellow, but don't encourage her if you don't mean it with all your heart. I have never seen her smile at anyone the way she smiles at you. I don't want to see her get her heart broken. Supper will be ready soon."

"Can I ask you something, Ada?"

"Ja."

"Is Mary still mourning Hannah's father?"

"She does not mourn him. He did not treat her well,

but through him, God gave her Hannah, and for that gift we are all grateful."

"Why hasn't she gone out with some of the local fellows?"

"Because a man must win Mary's trust before he can win her heart, and she does not trust easily."

Ada left the barn and he mulled over her words as he finished taking care of Tilly. Was he being unfair to Mary? He liked her. He wanted to spend more time with her. If she felt the same, what harm was there in their friendship?

He wasn't prepared to admit his feelings were stronger.

He left the stall and picked up the supplies for Oscar. He briefly read through the vet's instructions. It was simple enough. He entered Oscar's stall with the intention of changing the dressing as per the vet's instructions. He noticed the grain in the horse's feed bucket hadn't been touched, but his nose was wet from getting a drink.

"What you doing?"

Joshua looked over Oscar's back to see Hannah had climbed to the top of the stall gate and was watching him. "I'm checking to make sure Oscar is comfortable. He's in a strange new place and he's had a lot of scary things happen to him."

"He looks okay to me."

"Looks can sometimes be deceiving. He hasn't eaten anything, but he has been drinking water, so that's good. I think he'll be okay in a day or two."

"*Mammi* says you are going to be leaving soon."

"That's right. I have to go home."

"You are coming back, aren't you?"

"I hope I can. Will you look after Oscar for me until he can come home?"

"I think *Mamm* should do that. He's pretty big."

"What is it that you think I should do?" Mary asked as she leaned on the gate beside her daughter. Joshua's heart jumped up a notch, as it always did when he caught sight of her. He was kidding himself. What he felt was much more than friendship.

"Joshua wants you to look after Oscar until he comes back because he's going to be leaving soon."

Mary met his gaze. "I reckon I can do that, if he will show me what needs to be done."

"I was about to change the dressing, if you want to watch. The vet left me detailed instructions."

She opened the gate and slipped into the stall, making Hannah giggle as she swung it wide and then closed it. Hannah grinned at her. "That's fun. Can we do it again?"

"After Joshua shows me what needs to be done." Mary moved to stand near him. She kept her arms folded tightly across her middle. He tried to keep Ada's warning at the forefront of his mind. He didn't want to hurt Mary. He would be more circumspect in his dealings with her.

"First thing is to remove the old bandage."

She stepped up beside Joshua to read the paper he held. Her nearness caused him to lose his train of thought. "Then what?" she asked.

He forced his attention back to the horse. "The vet stitched the wound, so you want to check and make sure none of the stitches look infected." He pulled the dressing off and revealed a swath of shaved skin with a neat set of sutures down the center. The cut itself was about eight inches long.

"It looks good to me."

"Me, too." He softly pressed along the wound. "You want to check for hot spots or lumps that would indicate an infection is forming deep in the tissue." Yellowish fluid oozed from the lowest stitch when he pressed beside it.

Mary placed her hand next to his and followed with an examination of her own. "I don't feel anything unusual. What about this drainage?"

"The vet says we need to wash it down with cool water and he suggests putting some petroleum jelly on the skin below where it is seeping. He sent along some ointment to put on the dressing to keep the edges of the wound moist. Mostly, I'm worried about Oscar rubbing it against the boards when it starts itching."

Mary rubbed her left wrist. "I remember how much they itched before the doctor took them out."

"You've had stitches? I never have. What happened?"

She looked away and tugged her cuff lower. "I got cut with a piece of glass."

"On your wrist? That could've been serious."

"I was fortunate." She folded her arms again and wouldn't make eye contact.

Something told him there was more to the story, but he didn't press her. "Other than a dressing change every other day, he shouldn't need anything special. The vet doesn't want him out where he can run, but I hate to see him confined to a stall."

"I can walk him."

"That would be great." He applied the ointment and a clean dressing, and then patted Oscar's shoulder.

"Do you know when you'll be leaving?" Mary followed him out of the stall.

He swung the gate wide several times, making Hannah laugh as she held on. He plucked her off and set her on the floor. "I must be home by Thursday. I'll stay as long as I can."

Hannah skipped out of the barn ahead of them. Mary walked slowly. "When do you think you'll be back?"

He had to be honest. He stopped walking and she paused beside him. "I'm not sure when I'll be back, or if I'll be back."

"I see." Some of the light in her eyes died.

"A lot depends on the man I'm meeting on Thursday. If I can't return, my father will send one of my brothers to collect Oscar."

"I hope you come back." She bit her lower lip and looked down, as if she were afraid she had said too much.

He lifted her chin with his fingers until she was looking at him. "I hope I can, too. But I can't make you any promises."

She laid her hand against his cheek. "I'm not asking for a promise."

The longing in her eyes was too much for him to resist. He leaned forward and gently kissed her.

Chapter 10

Mary knew she should turn aside, but she didn't. Joshua gave her a chance to do just that. He hesitated, only a breath away from her. She didn't move. She wanted to know what his mouth would feel like pressed against hers. She closed her eyes.

His lips were firm but gentle as he brushed the corner of her mouth. She tipped her head slightly and he took advantage of her willingness. His kiss deepened and it was more wonderful than she had imagined, than anything she remembered. Her heart raced. She gripped his shoulders to steady herself and kissed him back.

A few seconds later, he pulled away. She opened her eyes to stare up at him. His face mirrored her wonderment. She didn't know how to react or what to say.

Regret filled his dark eyes. "I'm sorry, Mary. I shouldn't have done that."

She pressed her hand to her lips. They still tingled from his touch. "Don't be sorry."

She turned and raced out of the barn, determined to regain her self-control. Something she couldn't do when he was near.

After all this time. After all the heartaches she had endured, the Lord had finally sent someone to make her believe in love again.

Only she knew it couldn't be love she felt. It had to be infatuation. She barely knew Joshua and he barely knew her, but for the first time in years, she believed it was possible to care about a man and have him care about her in return. A man who was kind and generous. Someone who could make her heart flutter with just a look.

When she reached the house, she paused and looked back. He was standing in the barn door watching her. He didn't look happy. Her common sense returned, pulling her silly girlish fantasy out of the clouds.

He was sorry he had kissed her. He was leaving. By his own admission, he might not come back. She was a fool to let her feelings get so far out of hand. Miriam had warned her to think with her head and not to let her emotions rule her. She hadn't listened.

It wouldn't happen again.

It couldn't happen again.

If Joshua had known how much a simple kiss would change his relationship with Mary, he would never have given in to the impulse.

Supper was strained. Mary wouldn't look at him. She barely spoke. She barely touched her food. Even

Hannah seemed to notice that something was wrong. She kept glancing from her mother to him with a questioning look in her eyes, but she didn't say anything.

Ada kept up her usual running chatter. Had Mary told her what he'd done? He didn't think so. If Ada thought he was trifling with Mary, he was pretty sure that she would sic Bella on him. He half believed that he deserved it. After professing that he would never hurt Mary, he'd gone right ahead and made a very stupid move.

The thing was, he didn't regret that kiss at all.

Mary's smile was sweet, but the taste of her lips was even sweeter. They were soft and delicate, like the petals of a rose.

And he had to stop thinking about it right this second. It couldn't happen again.

When he went into the living room to read the Bible after supper, Mary excused herself, claiming a headache, and went to bed early.

Hannah played quietly with her wagon and wooden animals for an hour, and then Ada took her up to bed. Joshua was left alone with his thoughts. They weren't happy ones. His impulsive gesture might have cost him a friendship he valued deeply. Was there a way to make it up to her? Would apologizing again help? Or only make things worse? He was afraid to find out.

He wandered into the kitchen. He missed having tea with Mary. He missed the quiet, intimate moments they shared across the red-and-white-checkered tablecloth. Leaving the kitchen, he climbed the stairs. He glanced at Mary's closed door, then kept walking until he reached his room. He didn't write home. Instead, he lay down on the bed and folded his arms behind his head as he tried to figure out his next move. The full moon rose and cast a bright rectangle of light through the window. He watched the moonbeams' slow crawl across the floor for hours and still didn't have an answer.

Sunday morning dawned bright and clear and Mary was thankful she could finally get out of bed. Attempting to sleep had been a futile exercise until the wee hours.

She saw Joshua's door was open when she stepped out into the hallway. His bed was neatly made and empty. He was already up, too. She paused at the top of the stairs. What would she say to him? What would he say to her?

Could they pretend the kiss had never happened and go back to being friends?

She was willing to try.

She had breakfast well underway by the time he came in from taking care of the animals. She smiled cheerfully. "Good morning. How is Oscar?"

A bemused expression flashed across his face before he turned to hang his hat on a peg by the door. "His hip is draining more. I changed the dressing again."

"Do you think we should have the vet out to look at him?"

Joshua washed up at the sink. "I don't think it's that bad. If it's not better by Monday, then maybe we should."

After drying his hands on a towel, he folded it neatly on the counter. "Is your headache better?"

"All gone."

"Mary, about yesterday. I'd like to explain."

Pasting a false smile on her face, she said, "It was just a kiss, Joshua. It wasn't my first one. In case you haven't noticed, I have a daughter."

"I just want you to know that I didn't mean to offend you. I value your friendship. I hope I haven't lost that."

"You haven't lost a thing. I'm still your friend." She turned away. It was too hard to keep up the pretense while he was watching.

"I'm thankful for that. It won't happen again."

Oh, but she wished it would. "Go ahead and pour your own coffee. I'm going to get Hannah and Ada up. We'll have to hurry if we don't want to be late for church." There was plenty of time, but she left the room, anyway.

Since they hadn't yet been able to purchase a new buggy, they journeyed in the cart to the home of Adrian and Faith Lapp about three miles away. The main doors of the red barn had been opened wide. Men were unloading backless wooden benches from a boxlike gray wagon the congregation used to transport them from home to home on the day of the services. A number of men recognized Joshua and called out a greeting. Atlee and Moses Beachy had been put in charge of the horses. They came up to the cart as Joshua helped Mary down.

Ada gave the young men a stern look. "No tricks from you boys today."

Atlee and Moses smiled at each other. Atlee said, "Everybody has been telling us that. A good joke is only funny when you least expect it. We couldn't get away with anything today. Everyone is watching."

Ada poked her finger toward them. "I'm keeping my eye on you just the same. Any funny business and you'll have to answer to me."

Mary tried to hide her smile, but she caught Joshua's eye and saw he was struggling to keep a straight face, too. A giggle escaped her. Ada could no more keep up with those two boys than she could fly, but that didn't stop her from giving them what for.

Joshua managed to cover his chuckle with a cough. He handed Mary the baskets of food from the back of the cart. "Find me when you're ready to leave. It doesn't matter to me how long we stay."

The service would last for at least three hours. Afterward, a light noon meal would be served. Afternoons were usually spent visiting with friends and neighbors while the children played hide-and-seek and the teenagers got up a game of volleyball. Families didn't normally leave until late afternoon. If the hosting family was having a singing that night, many of the young set would remain until dark.

Ethan Gingerich came up to Joshua. "How is your horse faring?"

"The wound is still draining more than I would like. Have you any suggestions?"

The two men walked away discussing equine medicine. Mary sighed deeply. Joshua seemed right at home among them. It was a pity he was leaving. She would miss him dreadfully.

Ada grasped Mary's arm to steady herself as they walked across the uneven ground. "What's the matter, child?"

"I just realized that Joshua is going to find out today that I've never been married."

"Why do you say that?"

"Because I will be sitting in my usual place with the unmarried women. He'll know I wasn't married to Hannah's father."

"And how will he know the women around you are single? He doesn't know them."

"He knows Betsy. We always sit together."

"Well, isn't it better that he finds out sooner rather than later?"

"I know, but I don't want him to think badly of me."

"Our mistakes cannot be undone, child. We face them, we admit them and then we strive to do better. The sins of your past were all forgiven when you were baptized. If Joshua thinks less of you, then he is not a man to worry over, he's a man to be forgotten. There are plenty of Amish men in this community who would prize you as a wife."

"I'm not sure that's true, but you are kind to say so. Only I don't fancy any of them."

Ada turned to face her. "And do you fancy Joshua Bowman?"

"I'm not sure, but I think I do."

Mary thought Ada would begin shouting for joy. She was always pressing Mary to find a man. To her surprise, Ada ignored her comment and said, "Let's take this food into the house and enjoy praising our Lord on this beautiful day. We have much to be thankful for. I wonder who will preach the service since Bishop Zook is still in the hospital?"

After delivering the food to the kitchen and chatting

briefly with the women gathered there, Mary, Hannah and Ada went out to the barn and took their places on the benches provided.

The sun shone brightly beyond the barn doors. They had been propped open to catch the warm rays on the cool spring morning. Rows of wooden benches in the large hayloft were filled with worshipers, men on one side, women on the other, all waiting for the church service to begin. Large tarps had been hung from the rafters to cover the hay bales stacked along the sides. The floor had been swept clean of every stray piece of straw.

Mary sat quietly among her friends with Hannah beside her. Glancing across the aisle to where the men sat, she caught Joshua's eye. He was near the back among the single men. He smiled at her and she smiled back shyly. If he realized the significance of where she was sitting, it didn't appear to bother him. Had she been worried about nothing? When would she learn to leave her fears in God's hands?

As everyone waited for the *Volsinger* to begin leading the first hymn, Mary closed her eyes. She heard the quiet rustle of fabric on wooden benches, the songs of the birds in the trees outside and the occasional sounds of the cattle and horses in their stalls below. The familiar scent of alfalfa hay mingled with the smells of the animals and barn dust as a gentle breeze swirled around her. She opened her eyes and saw a piercing blue sky above the green fields outside. It was good to worship the Lord this close to His creations.

The song leader started the first hymn with a deep clear voice. No musical instruments were allowed by their Amish faith. Such things were seen as worldly.

More than fifty voices took up the solemn, slow-paced cadence. The ministers, the deacon and the visiting bishop were in the farmhouse across the way, agreeing on the order of the service and the preaching that would be done.

Outsiders found it strange that Amish ministers and bishops received no formal training. Instead, they were chosen by lot, accepting that God wanted them to lead the people according to His wishes. They all preached from the heart, without a written sermon. They depended on the Lord to inspire them. Some were good preachers, some more ordinary and some, like Bishop Zook, were truly gifted at bringing God's word alive on Sunday morning.

The first song came to an end. The congregation sat in deep silence. The Lord's Day was a joyful but serious day. Everyone understood this. Many in the community had suffered, but God had spared many more. All of them were here to give thanks.

After a few minutes of silence, the *Volsinger* began the second song. When it ended, the ministers and the visiting bishop entered the barn. As they made their way to the minister's bench, they shook hands with the men they passed.

For the next several hours Mary listen to the sermons delivered first by each of the ministers and then by the bishop. They spoke of sharing the burdens that had been placed on the community. She tried to absorb the meaning of their words. There had been many times when she felt burdened by the vows she had taken, but today wasn't one of them. She belonged to a special, caring people.

She closed her eyes and breathed deeply. This day she felt the warmth of God's presence. She gave thanks for the goodness He had bestowed upon her and her family and begged His forgiveness for all her doubts and faults.

Facing the congregation, the bishop said, "Galatians, chapter six, verses nine and ten. 'And let us not be weary in well doing: for in due season we shall reap, if we faint not. As we have therefore opportunity, let us do good unto all men, especially unto them who are of the household of faith.'

"The Lord has made it clear that it is the duty of everyone present to aid our members in need. As you know, Bishop Zook was injured in the storm. He remains in the hospital, but by God's grace he will soon be released. We will be taking up a collection for the medical bills he can't meet. His barn was also destroyed in the same storm. I have met with other area bishops and we are planning a barn raising for him a week from Monday. Everyone is invited to help to the extent that they are able." He gave a final blessing and the service was over.

The scrabble of the young boys in the back to get out as quickly as possible made a few of the elders scowl in their direction, including Ada. Mary grinned. She remembered how hard it was to sit still at that age. It was harder still because the young people knew they would be spending the rest of the day visiting with their friends and playing games. Although the young girls left with more decorum, they were every bit as anxious to be out taking advantage of the beautiful spring day. She let Hannah follow them.

Mary happened to glance in Joshua's direction and caught him staring at her. All the other men were gone.

Betsy elbowed her in the side. "Will you stop looking at that man like you are a starving mouse and he is a piece of cheese?"

Mary rose to her feet. "I'm not a starving mouse."

"You could've fooled me." The two of them went out together and soon joined the rest of the women who were setting up the food. The elders were served first. The younger members had to wait their turn. When Joshua came inside to eat, Alvin was with him. Betsy saw him, muttered an excuse and quickly left the room.

Alvin put his plate down. "I reckon I've lost my appetite."

He left and Joshua looked at Mary. "Is there anything you can think of that would aid his cause? He's miserable. He's been talking about her nonstop for the last half hour."

"Betsy is miserable, too. I don't know how to help."

"I might have an idea. It's my turn to have a plan, right?"

She smiled. "I think it's my turn, but you go ahead."

"Is Betsy the jealous type?"

"I wouldn't know. Alvin has been stuck to her side ever since they met. She's never had to worry about him straying."

"Let's see how she reacts if he shows an interest in someone else."

Mary bit her lower lip. "I don't know. That doesn't seem right."

"If this blows up in our faces, it's your turn for a plan."

"Oh, make it worse and then hand it to me. *Danki.* What girl will go along with this? Don't look at me."

"Just make sure Betsy is where she can see the barn door on the south side in half an hour. Can I borrow your traveling bonnet?"

"What for?"

He gave her a big grin. "Because my helpers didn't bring theirs."

"I have no idea what you are talking about, but I left mine on the seat of the cart."

"Okay. Thirty minutes."

"South barn door."

"Right." He winked and went out.

Betsy returned shortly. When it was their turn to eat, they carried their plates outside and joined Betsy's sisters on several quilts spread in the shade of an apple tree. The alpacas that Adrian and Faith raised were lined up at the fence watching the activity. Mary found them adorable, especially the babies. The adults, with their freshly shorn bodies and fluffy heads, were comical. The south barn door was in easy view from where she was sitting.

"Betsy, where is Alvin?" her sister Lizzie asked.

"I don't know, and I don't care," Betsy declared.

Her three sisters shared shocked looks. Clara, the oldest, gaped at Betsy. "Since when?"

"Since ages ago. I don't have to share everything with you just because you're my sisters."

Greta touched Mary's arm. "Did you know about this?"

"I know she's been miserable since he stopped talking to her."

"I have not. And he didn't stop talking to me. I stopped talking to him."

Mary saw Joshua and Alvin standing just inside the barn door. The bottom half of the split door was closed, but the top was open. A tall woman in a black bonnet was standing with them. She was turned so Mary couldn't see her face. She appeared to be in an animated conversation with Alvin.

Lizzie noticed at the same time. "He's not having any trouble talking to that woman. Who is that?"

Betsy swung her head around to look. "I don't know."

Alvin laughed at something the woman whispered in his ear. Her bonnet dipped and her shoulders jiggled as if she were giggling. Clara said, "She's very tall. I don't know who it could be."

Joshua stepped out of the barn and came toward them. Alvin slipped his arm around the woman's shoulder and they disappeared from view inside the barn.

Betsy shot to her feet. "Who was that with Alvin?"

Joshua shrugged. "I didn't catch the name, but they seem to know each other well."

He sat down beside Mary. "Are you about ready to go?"

She tried to keep a straight face. "Not yet."

Betsy fisted her hands on her hips. "Is it one of those Pennsylvania Amish girls that came to help in town? She should stay in her own state."

Joshua shook his head. "That's unkind, Betsy. Alvin was just being nice."

"I saw how nice he was being. I'm going to give him a piece of my mind."

"But you aren't speaking to him," Mary reminded her.

"You're right. I'm not." Betsy sat down, but she couldn't keep her eyes off the barn. Alvin and his friend never reappeared.

Later, when they were getting ready to leave, Joshua was helping Ada into the cart when Atlee and Moses brought Tilly to them and hitched her up. Ada scooted to the far edge of the seat. "You boys were good today. I'm glad to see you've grown out of your need to play pranks."

Moses grinned at her. "I wouldn't say we've outgrown it."

Atlee handed Mary a bundle of cloth. "Thanks for the use of your bonnet. Alvin found it very becoming on my brother."

The boys punched each other in the shoulder and walked off laughing. Ada shook her head. "I'm glad they aren't mine."

Mary smoothed out her bonnet and took Hannah as Joshua handed her up. "Really? Moses, Alvin and my bonnet? That was your plan?"

He climbed in and took the reins. "I think it worked. Betsy was stunned. At least Alvin knows she isn't indifferent."

"You got her attention, I'll give you that."

"Now all Alvin has to do is keep it." He slapped the reins against Tilly's rump and the mare took off.

Relieved that his relationship with Mary seemed to be on the mend, Joshua was eager to return to work in Hope Springs. On Monday, he and Mary made the trip again. There were fewer volunteers in town. The initial storm and media coverage had brought in hundreds of people wanting to help. Now that the nitty-gritty of rebuilding was getting underway, there was less need for general cleanup and more need for skilled carpenters. The Amish and Mennonite workers remained as the backbone of the recovery effort.

After leaving Mary at the Wadler Inn, Joshua crossed the now barren blocks toward the church. He and several others would be rebuilding the portico that morning. As he passed by Gina Davis's home, he saw she was out pruning her rosebushes. Pete's children were playing in the yard. The front door of the house opened and a woman with a baby in her arms called for the others to come in. He saw Pete on the roof setting the last of the chimney bricks into place. Pete saw him and waved. "How's it going?"

Joshua stopped and tipped back his hat. "Not bad. And you?"

"I'm done here. I'll start at the school tomorrow. I've been hired by the school district to repair the building. It was an offer I couldn't refuse."

"The laborer is worthy of his hire. Are you still staying at the inn?"

Pete gathered his tools and came down the ladder. "Actually, we're staying with Mrs. Davis until we can get a new house built. It's working out for both of us."

Exactly as Mary had hoped it would. Joshua touched the brim of his hat. "Have a *goot* day."

He started to walk away, but Pete stopped him. "You might want to keep an eye out for anything odd. They told us in the town meeting this morning that some of the stores have been looted. The police have set up a tip line folks can call if they see something. Just when it seems the goodness of mankind toward one another is overwhelming, a few have to prove there are still miserable people out there."

Shaking his head in disbelief, Joshua walked on. Instead of following the winding street, he took a shortcut through a wooded area that surrounded the rocky outcropping behind the church. A small stream cut through the woods. It led to the bubbling spring that had given the town its name. There was a small bridge over the brook behind the church, but he had no trouble jumping across using a couple of convenient stones. He was about a block from the church when he saw two men slipping through the trees ahead of him. Something in their stealthy demeanor caught his attention. He watched as they entered the back door of a vacant house with faded paint and boarded-over windows that had fallen into disrepair years before the tornado arrived. He was tempted to walk on, but his curiosity drew him to follow them.

He approached the house and had his hand on the back doorknob when he heard voices coming from a broken basement window off to the side below him. "I stashed the weed here. Nobody's gonna check an old wreck like this place. How much do you want?"

"How much do you have?"

"Enough. If you want stronger drugs, I can get that too. I borrowed some from the pharmacy last night. The place was easy pickings. Their security system didn't even have power."

Joshua's skin crawled when he realized what was going on. He took a step back and his heel crunched a piece of broken glass.

"What was that? Check it out." The voice became a harsh whisper.

Joshua walked away quickly and hurried out to the street. At the corner, he saw Nick in his patrol car. Joshua hesitated. Should he tell Nick what was going on? Would Nick assume he was involved?

It would be better to say nothing. It wasn't Amish business. It had nothing to do with him. He hurried on toward the church. A few minutes later, he heard the sound of a siren behind him, but he didn't look back. He kept his head down and walked faster. He only slowed when Nick shot past him without stopping. Joshua blew out a long breath and waited for his racing heart to return to a normal pace.

It took him and his coworkers three hours to finish the new entryway for the church. Pastor Finzer came out of the rectory to view the finished project. There were tears in his eyes.

"Gentlemen, I can't thank you enough for your work here. It's wonderful to see the house of the Lord ready to welcome worshipers again. A little paint and elbow grease by yours truly and I don't think people will know the difference between the old and the new parts of the structure. It's beautiful."

He shook everyone's hand. "Please let me buy you lunch at the Shoofly Pie Café. It's the best Amish cooking for miles around."

Knowing that Mary was working at the inn that day, Joshua agreed and walked along with a group as they headed that way. Passing the section of woods where he had seen the men, Joshua slowed to see if Nick had gone that way. There was no sign of him.

The pastor noticed Joshua's interest. "That place belonged to the family that founded this town. It's a shame it was allowed to fall into ruin."

"I saw two men go in there earlier."

"Teenagers, perhaps. They've been known to hold parties there. I'll check it out."

The thought of the gangly young pastor stumbling into a dangerous situation forced Joshua to reconsider keeping silent. He stopped walking. "They weren't teenagers. I got the impression they didn't want to be seen."

Pastor Finzer stopped, too. Concern creased his brow. "Are you sure?"

"I heard there has been some looting around town."

"Sadly, that's true. Perhaps I should mention this to the authorities."

"You must do what you think is best. The fellow staying with Gina Davis said there is a tip line folks can call."

"That's right. I almost forgot. Go on to the café. I'll catch up with you." The minister walked rapidly back toward the church and Joshua breathed a sigh of relief.

At the inn, he checked at the front desk and learned Mary was running an errand. She wasn't expected back for half an hour. He found a seat at the café counter, ordered lunch and waited for Pastor Finzer to join him.

A hand clamped down on his shoulder. "Step outside right now," Nick growled.

Chapter 11

Joshua wanted to knock Nick's arm aside, but resisting would gain him nothing. He should have told Mary about his record when he had the chance. It would've been better coming from him than from her father. Now it was too late.

"I said, come outside."

Joshua turned on the bar stool. "Say what you need to say here. I am not ashamed."

"Outside!" Nick walked out of the building. Joshua followed slowly. He didn't have a choice. At least he wasn't being hauled away in handcuffs.

The sheriff didn't stop walking until he was half a block up the street. Then he turned on Joshua. "I knew there was something about you the minute I laid eyes on you. If I hadn't been so busy with this mess, I would have run a background check on you sooner. Not many

Amish men turn up in my database. Imagine my surprise when Joshua Bowman was at the top of the list when I checked this morning."

Joshua pressed his lips shut. Nick didn't want to hear anything he had to say.

Nick glared, but drew a deep breath. "Have you told her?"

"I thought I would leave that to you."

"Don't get smart with me. Have you told Mary that you're a convict?"

"That I was wrongly imprisoned? *Nee.*"

"I didn't think so."

"I was going to tell her. Not that I expect you to believe me."

"You were picked up for dealing drugs. What do you know about a burglary last night at the pharmacy?"

Joshua folded his arms and glared. "If I know something, I must be involved. If I'm involved, that means I violated my parole, and I'm on my way back to prison, which is exactly what you want, isn't it?"

"Where did you get that chip on your shoulder?"

"Your justice system gave it to me."

Nick reined in his temper with visible difficulty. "I skimmed through your case file."

"Then you know everything. I won't waste my breath explaining."

Folding his arms over his chest, Nick relaxed slightly. "It left me with some unanswered questions. I would've handled the investigation differently."

"My story would've been the same no matter who asked. I didn't do the things they accused me of doing."

"Just like that, I'm supposed to believe you? You

had a dozen chances to tell me you are out on parole. Why didn't you?"

"Because I knew exactly how you would react. Like this. Besides, I didn't see what difference it made. I came to look over some property for my father. I didn't choose to be trapped with Mary, but I started liking her. And this community. After I saw the extent of the damage here, I wanted to help these people rebuild."

"I think you're done helping. Hope Springs can get along fine without you."

"Don't you mean Mary will get along fine without me?"

"You're a smart fellow. That's exactly what I mean. Mary has had enough trouble in her life. She doesn't need to get involved with you."

"I happen to care for Mary a lot. If she were your *Englisch* daughter, I would say that you are right. But Mary is Amish. She knows that forgiveness comes first. She knows a thing that is forgiven must also be forgotten."

"You don't know anything about Mary."

Joshua reined in his own rising temper. "I know her better than you think. I also know you want to protect her."

"That's right. That's why you are leaving. I have a car waiting that will take you to Ada's place so you can pick up your stuff, and then my deputy will take you home. I'm also going to let your parole officer know that you were here without his knowledge. He's not going to like that, and he's going to keep a closer eye on you from now on."

Joshua strove to put his bitterness aside. He didn't

want this animosity between himself and Mary's father. Not if there might be a future with her. He hung his head, trying to be humbled before God and this man. "When my sentence is finished, may I come back?"

"I'd rather you didn't."

Joshua looked up. "Because you don't want the criminal element in your town? Or because you don't want Mary seeing some guy you don't like? It's her choice. The Amish understand that. They don't interfere in the courtship of their children."

"Someday when you have a daughter, remember this conversation." He pointed up the block where an unmarked white car was waiting. "There's your ride. Get going."

Mary learned that Joshua had been looking for her when she returned from her errand. She checked in the café, but he wasn't there. She combed the area she thought he might be working in several times without seeing him. When she spotted Delbert cutting lumber at the back of the grocery store across the street, she approached him and waited until he finished the cut and the saw fell silent. "Delbert, have you seen Joshua? He was looking for me a while ago and now I can't find him."

"I saw him talking to the sheriff. They went that way." He pointed up the block.

"Danki."

She walked in that direction and saw Nick at the drugstore on the next corner. He was standing with his deputy, who was busy writing a report. The store owner was gesturing wildly. There was no sign of Joshua. She walked up to Nick. "I'm sorry to bother you, but have you seen Joshua?"

"He's gone home," Nick said without looking at her.

"Back to the farm?"

"Back to Bowmans Crossing."

"I thought he wasn't leaving until Wednesday."

"Something came up and he caught an early lift."

"What came up?" She tried to wrap her mind around the fact that he was gone.

Nick looked at her then. "You knew he was going to leave sooner or later."

Sooner or later, yes, but not without saying goodbye. Mary turned away to hide her distress. What a foolish woman she was to think she meant something special to him. "You're right. I knew he was leaving. I just didn't want him to go."

Tears stung her eyes as she walked away from Nick. When she turned the corner and there was no one to see, she broke down and sobbed.

Joshua received a heartfelt hug from his mother when he arrived home. No one had expected him until Thursday. His father and brothers were all out working in the fields. He looked forward to doing the same. To getting back to a simple life with plenty of hard work and little time to mourn the loss of Mary's company.

His mother gestured toward the table. "Sit down. I've just made some brownies. We have been reading about the damage at Hope Springs in the newspapers. It must be terrible."

"It is. The community is making progress, but a third of the homes were destroyed. Electricity has been restored to many of the English businesses and homes that are left, but some of them are still living Amish."

That made her chuckle. "It's good to have you home. Will the town recover?"

"The people are determined. There's still a lot of cleanup that needs to be done. Mary thinks it will take years for the place to look normal again. I think she's right."

"Mary is the woman you wrote about? The one you were trapped in the cellar with?"

"She's the one." He tried to remember exactly what he'd said about her. Probably too much. She occupied a central place in his mind.

His mother got down a plate and began cutting her brownies. "Is she pretty, this girl you couldn't leave behind?"

"Not as pretty as you, and I did leave her behind." He bitterly regretted that he hadn't been allowed to tell Mary goodbye. Would she think he didn't care enough to find her, or would Nick tell her the truth? Was she grieving or was she relieved to have Joshua Bowman out of her house and her life? Would he ever know?

His mother put a plate in front of him. "What will you do now?"

"I want to go back to Hope Springs. There is still so much work that needs doing." And Mary was there. Mary and Hannah, the two people who had come to mean the world to him.

His mother took a seat across from him. "Your father and I have been talking about that."

"You have?"

"Our bishop made a plea for supplies and money to

aid the Amish folks there. You know they will share the financial burdens among themselves, but the expenses will be high and some families will suffer because of it. We must help if we can. Your brothers have agreed. I wish I could go along, but your father and your brothers could not do without me. I would like to meet your Mary."

"She's not my Mary and there is something I haven't told you about her."

"So serious. What is it?"

"She is adopted. Her parents are *Englisch*."

"That is not a terrible thing, although it is unusual."

"The woman that adopted her is married to Sheriff Nick Bradley."

Sitting back, his mother stared at him with wide eyes. "Perhaps we should not mention this to your father just yet."

"As much as I want to go back, it isn't up to me. I'll need to convince Officer Merlin it isn't a risk to let me go there. I don't think he'll agree. Nick Bradley doesn't want me seeing Mary."

"Is she a good Amish woman?"

"She reminds me a lot of you."

"I could be a better Christian."

"Mary isn't perfect, but she has an Amish heart. She is a good mother. She cares for her elderly grandmother with tenderness. She is sometimes outspoken, but she repents when she steps over the line. She would do anything for her friends and neighbors in need. *Ja*, she is a good Amish woman."

Better than he deserved. Maybe he shouldn't go back.

Maybe this was God's way of telling him that she was better off without him.

"Let us pray about this and wait to see what the Lord wills. Your father can be a very convincing man. I should know. He convinced me to marry him when I had three other perfectly good offers."

Joshua laughed. "*Mamm*, were you a wild girl with a string of fellows?"

"I was. Until I wed. Eat your brownie and don't fret. God has a plan for us all. We must have faith in that."

"Why wasn't I informed that you were away from home?"

Officer Oliver Merlin sat at the kitchen table in the Bowman home on Thursday morning as promised. He finished the last bite of a cinnamon roll and licked his lips. Joshua's father and mother sat with him. Joshua was too nervous to sit in one place. He leaned against the spotless kitchen cabinets. He knew his brothers would be hovering nearby outside.

"My son was only doing what dozens of other young Amish people were doing. He was helping those in need. It was God's will that he was in Hope Springs when this disaster struck. He was not involved in any crime."

Officer Merlin dabbed his face with a napkin, then folded his hands together and leaned on his forearms. "I am not your son's enemy, Mr. Bowman. Nor am I your enemy. I am required to keep detailed records of my parolees' activities. My job is to see that Joshua can become a functioning member of society and stay out of trouble."

"Would you like another cinnamon roll, Oliver?" Joshua's mother pushed the plate in his direction.

"Don't mind if I do. These are just about the best I've ever had."

"*Danki.* You are too kind."

Isaac frowned at his wife before he leaned forward, too. "You can put my son back in prison with a word."

"My opinion can sway the court for him or against him, that's true, but it's his behavior that forms my opinion and that is what a judge will evaluate."

"My son is already a good member of our Amish community. He adheres to our ways. He needs no judge but God."

"I appreciate your religious convictions. I admire the Amish. I don't want to be intrusive, but I don't have the all-seeing eye of God. I need to observe Joshua at home as well as at work. I may show up at any time. I can even visit his friends to make sure they aren't involved in criminal activities. Joshua is motivated to do well, but he has a chip on his shoulder where law enforcement is concerned."

"Can you blame me?"

Joshua moved to brace his arms on the edge of the table and glare at his parole officer. "I didn't do anything wrong. I was there to convince my brother to come home. The police who arrested me wouldn't listen. No one believed me. The prosecutor made it sound as if I had been making drugs for months. The woman who said I did this, under oath, did it to get her own sentence reduced. People acted like we were freaks. I saw the papers—Amish Brothers Arrested for Cooking Meth by School. Buggies Used to Smuggle Drugs to Rural Teenagers. I wasn't with my brother until two days before I was arrested. Do I have a distrust of English law enforcement? *Ja*, I do."

It wasn't until his father laid a hand on his shoulder that Joshua realized he was shaking with anger. His father spoke quietly in Pennsylvania Dutch. "We forgive them. We forgive them all as our Lord forgave those who persecuted Him unto death."

Joshua nodded, shamed by his outburst. "Forgive me."

"I'm not here to retry your case, Joshua. Do innocent men go to jail? Yes, they do. Do guilty men go free? All the time. I'm here because I don't want you to go back to prison. I want your family and your friends to understand that. They may think they are protecting you by clamming up when I ask questions, but they aren't. If we can't be honest and forthcoming with each other, this may not work. I don't want that. I like it when my people stay out of trouble."

Joshua's mother placed her folded hands on the table. "What about Luke? Can he come home soon?"

"I can't make that determination. I can report that he has a stable home environment waiting and his family will be supportive if I'm called on to testify."

Joshua walked to the window. He stared outside without seeing his father's farm. It was Mary's face he envisioned. "Will I be allowed to return to Hope Springs and continue with the recovery efforts?"

"Do you have an address where you will be staying?"

"I'm not sure. There's a place called the Wadler Inn. They are giving rooms to workers. I'm sure you can find their telephone number. They will know how to reach me if I find lodging elsewhere."

"I'd like a little more concrete information."

Joshua turned away from the window. "The town was nearly leveled. Some people still don't have electricity. They don't have water. Many don't even have a roof over their heads. I'm sure I'll be staying with an Amish family, but the Amish don't have telephones. The phone number for the inn is the best I can do. If you say I can't go, then that is that. But know there are people in desperate need there."

He wouldn't be able to stay with Ada and Mary. He was sure Nick wouldn't allow it. Joshua turned back to the window. How could he miss them all so deeply after only a few days? He missed Hannah's energy and Ada's cooking and teasing. He missed everything about Mary, but mostly he missed her smile.

Officer Merlin folded his black notebook and zipped it closed. "All right. You can return to Hope Springs. Check in with Sheriff Bradley when you get there. If I decide to drop in and see how you're doing, I'll expect the people at the inn to tell me where you're staying."

"Sheriff Bradley doesn't want me in his town. I was... I was seeing his daughter."

Oliver rose to his feet. "I noticed he was quite sharp on the phone."

"He can be more so in person."

"It's a free country. You have limits because of your parole status, but Sheriff Bradley can't stop you from returning to Hope Springs if I give my approval. However, I would suggest you give serious thought to avoiding his daughter. I'll be at the inn in Hope Springs on Saturday evening. You will be there."

"I will." Joshua hoped his face didn't reveal his relief. He would see Mary again. He would explain everything and pray that she understood and forgave him. He would find out if the Lord had a plan for the two of them. He prayed it was true. All he wanted was to see her again.

When Officer Merlin drove away, Isaac sighed heavily. "I wished only the best for my children. How have I failed them?"

Joshua came and laid a hand on his father's shoulder. "You did not fail us. We have failed you."

"Life is long. I pray I will see all my sons around this table again one day." He rose to his feet. "I made arrangements with the *Englisch* horse hauler to get your animal brought home, but he can't pick him up until Saturday. Would you write to Ada Kaufman and tell her that?"

"I will." Could he explain what happened in a letter to Mary? No, it was better to see her face-to-face.

After his parents went into the living room. Joshua stayed in the kitchen. Samuel came in carrying the mail. "Was the *Englischer* satisfied with your behavior?"

"Well enough, I reckon. He'll be here again in two weeks and he will check on me in Hope Springs."

"*Daed* and I have loaded a wagon with furniture and lumber for you to take with you. It's not a lot, but we have some to spare for those less fortunate." His voice trailed away as he stared at the envelope in his hand.

"What is it?" Joshua asked.

"It's a letter from Luke. He's never written before."

"That will please Mother."

Samuel held it out. "It's not addressed to Mother. It's addressed to you."

"To me? Why would he write to me and not to *Mamm* or *Daed*?"

"You'll have to open it and see." Samuel laid the letter on the counter. "I've got a rocking chair to finish and a harness to repair. I could use your help."

"I'll be out in a minute." Joshua picked up the letter and tore it open. It was short and to the point—Luke needed to see him. There was no other explanation. Something was wrong.

"You'll get over him. Men can't be trusted. Women are better off without them."

"You don't mean that, Betsy." Mary looked up from the supplies she was restocking in the Red Cross center and glanced around. The temporary tent had been taken down and the relief center now occupied the basement of the town hall. A new truckload of donations had arrived that morning. The first boxes contained much-needed necessities like soap, toothpaste and shampoo. Some of the men, including Alvin, were setting up tables and folding chairs in the room down the hall that would serve as a place of relaxation and a meeting room when needed.

"Maybe I do mean it. Just a little. Some men can't be trusted. And those are the ones we are better off without."

Mary didn't feel better off without Joshua and she didn't want to talk about it. The ache was too new, too raw. She prayed that he would write and tell her why he left without a word. There had to be an explanation. "Does that mean you haven't made up with Alvin?"

Betsy glanced down the hall. It was empty. "He was flirting with another woman. You saw it."

"Betsy, you turned him away. He has been faithful to you for two years and you turned him away because you are afraid to commit to marriage. You tell him to go away, and when he does, that makes you angry? Do you know how ridiculous you sound?"

Betsy snapped the lid closed on a cooler filled with water bottles. "Okay. I didn't like seeing Alvin interested in someone else, but I don't know what I want. Do you?"

Oh, yes, she did. Mary wanted to see Joshua again. She wanted to know that the friendship and affection she thought they shared wasn't one-sided. She wanted to believe she could have a chance at a normal life and not have to live out her days alone. Joshua had opened her eyes to that possibility, but now he was gone.

"We aren't talking about me, Betsy. It doesn't make any difference what I want. Alvin is still here. You are the one who has a choice."

"But what if it's the wrong choice? How can I tell that I'll like him in ten years, let alone still love him in fifty years?"

"Ada says marriages are made in heaven, but husbands and wives are responsible for the upkeep."

"It's a wise Amish proverb, but what does it really mean?"

"It means you won't love him in fifty years if you aren't determined to love him every day from now until then. Answer me this. Can you see your life without him in it?"

"I don't know. I just don't know."

Alvin came around the corner with a set of folding chairs in his hands. He dropped them on the floor with a clatter. "I know what I want, Betsy Barkman. I want to have children with you and grow old with you and lie down in the earth beside you when my time comes. That's what I want. That won't change in ten years and it won't change in fifty years. Maybe you can see a life without me, but I can't see one without you. I love you, and I don't care who knows it!" He turned to look at the room but it was empty.

Mary hid a smile and picked up the supplies. "I'm going to take these to the closet."

Betsy snatched the box from her hands. "I'll take them. Alvin, would you give me a hand?"

His face turned beet-red and he rushed around the end of the counter to take the box from her. Together, they vanished into the supply room that was so full of donations there was barely enough room for one person, let alone two.

When they came out ten minutes later, Betsy's lips were puffy from being kissed and her cheeks were bright red. Alvin wore a look of bemused satisfaction. He picked up the chairs and hurried down the hall with them.

"Well?" Mary knew the answer. Betsy's eyes sparkled like stars in the night sky.

"A fall wedding. He loves me." She whirled around once and hugged Mary.

As happy as she was for her friend, Mary couldn't

help the stab of jealousy that struck her. Would she ever find that kind of love?

Nick walked in through the front door, pulled off his sunglasses and came over to the two women. "How's it going?"

Betsy composed herself and gestured to the counter. "Two boxes of much-needed things like soap, and one box of shoes that contained two pairs of red high heels and six pairs of flip-flops. Not the best footwear for working in a disaster zone. What are people thinking?"

He chuckled. "We'll never know. Mary, I thought I would see if you'd like to join me for lunch. We haven't had a chance to spend much time together lately. I'm sure Miriam can join us."

Shaking her head, Mary said, "I'm not really hungry. You go on."

"Mary, you have to eat. He isn't worth getting this upset over."

She knew he meant Joshua. She looked down. "I'd rather not talk about it."

"He wasn't who you thought he was," Nick muttered.

She looked up quickly. "What do you mean by that? What aren't you telling me?"

Chapter 12

The following afternoon, Joshua once again faced the gray walls and high wire fences of Beaumont Correctional Facility. The driver his father had hired for the day agreed to be back to pick Joshua up in an hour. Although Joshua dreaded walking in the doors, it was considerably better to come as a visitor than it was to be a prisoner. He was searched and led into a small waiting room. A second door opened and Luke came in. His brother was all smiles, but Joshua knew something was up.

"It's good to see you, little brother. Mother's home cooking agrees with you."

"You're looking thin." Joshua sat down at the table.

"The food here stinks. You haven't forgotten that so quickly." Luke paced the room.

"What's up, Luke? Why am I here?"

"Maybe I wanted to apologize for getting you in trouble in the first place."

"I appreciate that. You know you have been forgiven. The family will welcome you—surely you know that."

Smirking, Luke said, "I know the Amish forgive sinners. I've heard it all my life."

"It's not something we say. It's something we do." Something Joshua was learning to do.

Luke looked at him sharply. "You're really beginning to sound like our old man."

"I pray that is true. Our father is devout and wise."

"Mom wrote that you've been working in Hope Springs."

"I've been helping with the tornado cleanup. There's still a lot to be done."

Luke brightened. "Are you going back?"

Joshua nodded. "Our family is donating some lumber and furniture and *Mamm* is sending canned goods. I'm headed back tomorrow with the wagon."

He hoped that Mary would forgive him for his sudden departure when he explained why he'd left without saying goodbye. She had the right to be upset that he hadn't told her about his prison time, but he believed she would understand. He was anxious to see her again. He dreamed of her at night and thought about her every hour of the day.

Luke sat down at the table. "That's just great. I was wondering if you met a woman there named Mary Shetler."

"*Nee*, the name isn't familiar."

Luke's left leg tapped up and down. There was a hollow look in his eyes. Joshua scowled at him. If he didn't know better, he would suspect Luke was using drugs again, but how could he get them in here?

Luke frowned and bit thumbnail. "That's too bad. I need you to do me a favor when you go back. I need you to find her."

"Why?"

"I've got a friend in here. His name is Kevin Dunbar. Joshua, he saved my life. There was a fight in the yard and I would have been stabbed if Kevin hadn't knocked the knife out of the guy's hand. I owe him. You understand that, don't you?"

"If he saved you, he was an instrument of God's mercy. I'm grateful for his intervention, but what does this have to do with finding someone in Hope Springs?"

"Kevin had a girlfriend, an ex-Amish girl. She was pregnant with his baby when he was locked up. She hasn't contacted him. His letters have all been returned unopened. He thinks she returned to the Amish. Her name is Shetler, Mary Shetler. He wasn't sure where she went. He had some friends looking for her in her hometown, but they never found her. He about gave up hope until he saw her on the news about Hope Springs."

"If she didn't answer his letters, maybe she doesn't want to see him."

"He still loves her. He respects her decision. He doesn't hold it against her. He just wants to know that they are both okay. Joshua, the man doesn't know if he has a son or a daughter. He's made mistakes, but he deserves to know his child is okay."

"She might not be living in Hope Springs. Many Amish came from other places to help. I don't know,

Luke. The fellow is *Englisch*. His business is none of ours."

"You know it's important in here to have someone who can watch your back. This isn't Bowmans Crossing. Things can get ugly in here. This guy is my friend. He's helping me out."

"How?"

"He's taking care of me. Making sure I'm okay."

"Is he getting you drugs?"

"That's not a very Amish thing to say. He's going to get me a job with a couple of his old pals in Cleveland when I get out of here."

"Making meth again?"

"You are the suspicious one now. They run a salvage yard. I want to help a friend just the way you want to help the people in Hope Springs. Some of them are *Englisch*, too, aren't they? This is no different. All you have to do is ask around quietly and see if you can locate her. You don't even have to speak to her. He just wants to know that she's okay."

Joshua thought of Mary. He longed to know how she was. He hungered for any word of her. He could understand a man wanting to know his child and the woman he loved were safe and happy. "Okay, I'll ask around."

"Great. That's all you have to do. You are doing me a big favor. I owe you for this, little brother. When I get out of here, we are going to have some good times together, you and I."

"Does this mean you'll come home?" Joshua asked, fearing he already knew the answer.

Luke rubbed his face with his hands, shot to his feet and began pacing again. "You know the Amish life isn't for me. I don't want to be stuck in the Dark Ages. I want to be surrounded by life and fun."

"We Amish have life and fun all around us, Luke. We aren't stuck in the Dark Ages. We work hard and live a simple life so that we may be close to God and to each other."

"Like I said, you sound like *Daed*. So tell me about this girl you're seeing in Hope Springs. What's she like?"

"How do you know about her?"

"*Mamm* forwarded all of your letters. You know how she loves to keep circle letters going in her family. You sound quite taken with Mary Kaufman and her daughter, Hannah. Is Mary pretty?"

"She's very pretty and very sweet." His heart ached to see her again.

"And Amish. *Mamm* must be over the moon about it."

Joshua sobered. "Not as much as you might think."

"Why not?"

"It's complicated."

"What's complicated about love? It's spring. It's in the air, unless you're locked in this place."

"In my case, a lot. Mary is Amish, but she was adopted by an *Englisch* couple when she was a teenager."

"So?"

"Her father is the sheriff."

Luke burst out laughing and slapped the tabletop. "My ex-convict brother is dating the daughter of a sheriff. That has to be the funniest thing I've ever heard. What does her *daed* think about you?"

"Nick Bradley doesn't care for me."

"I can imagine. Are you going to call him Papa Nick

after you marry his little girl, or will it always have to be Officer Nick? You might have been better off taking a ride in the tornado."

"I'm glad it's a joke to you. For me, it's serious."

"I'm sorry. I don't mean to tease you. All you have to do is ask around for Mary Shetler when you get back to Hope Springs and let me know as soon as you hear anything. Kevin is going to be paroled soon. You don't even have to come see me. Just call. Do this favor for me and I'll come home when I get out. I promise. What do you say?"

It was late in the afternoon by the time Nick turned into Ada's lane. Mary sat beside him quietly. Their relationship had become strained over the past few days and Joshua was the reason. Nick knew something about Joshua's sudden departure, but he wouldn't talk about it. Mary never doubted how much Nick loved her and Hannah, but somehow, his feelings about Joshua were driving a wedge between them. She hated it, but she didn't know what to do about it.

In the yard, she saw a wagon piled high with lumber. Two gray draft horses stood with their heads down at the corral fence. They looked as weary as she felt.

Nick stopped the car. "Looks like more Amish contributions are on their way to Hope Springs. It must be someone who knows Ada."

They opened the car doors and got out. Hannah came flying down the steps and threw herself into her mother's arms. "*Mamm*, guess what? Joshua is here. He came back."

Mary's heart stopped for an instant and then raced

ahead as joy welled up inside her. He was back. He had come back.

It was hard to breathe.

She looked toward the porch and saw him standing with Ada. Mary choked back a sob. She was so happy she was ready to cry.

Joshua came down the steps with his hat in his hand. It was then she noticed that he didn't look happy to see her. He looked worried. Her joy ebbed away.

Nick moved to stand beside her and crossed his arms as he glared at Joshua. "I'm surprised to see you here."

"I just stopped to rest the horses and to let Ada know a horse hauler will be here Saturday to pick up Oscar. I'll be heading into town after I speak to Mary. If that's okay?"

The men were staring daggers at each other. Mary's confusion grew. "Of course you can speak to me, Joshua. What's going on?"

His expression grew puzzled. "I wasn't sure you would want to see me after the things Nick told you about me."

"Things? What things? Nick, what's he talking about?" Something was going on, and she had no clue what it was. She didn't like the feeling. She put Hannah down. "Run inside and tell Ada to put on some tea, will you, dear?"

"Sure." Hannah dashed away.

Mary glanced at Joshua and saw confusion in his eyes. He was staring at Nick. "You didn't tell her."

"I thought I would leave that up to you if you had the courage to come back."

Mary fisted her hands on her hips. "Someone had better tell me what's going on?"

Nick looked down at the ground. "Don't make me regret this, Joshua. She is a pearl beyond price and more dear to me than my life. I don't know what I would do if anyone hurt her." He kissed Mary's cheek and walked to his vehicle.

He opened the door, but paused and looked back at Joshua. "I arrested a couple of guys on suspicion of burglary yesterday. We got a tip from Pastor Finzer about where they were staying. He said you had seen something suspicious. I appreciate it when citizens look out for each other. It makes my job easier." He got in and drove away.

Joshua looked ready to fall down. Mary rushed to his side. "Are you okay?"

"I believe I would like that tea now. I have a few things to tell you, Mary, and Ada should hear them too."

"Finally. Come inside." She took his arm and led him toward the house.

When they were settled in the kitchen, Mary sent Hannah to play in the other room. Ada glanced back and forth between Mary and Joshua without comment.

He drew a deep breath. "The reason I had to get home was so that I could meet with my parole officer."

Mary sucked in a sharp breath. Of all the things she expected him to say, this wasn't among them. Ada frowned. "What is a parole officer?"

Joshua gave her a lopsided smile. "He watches over people who have been released from prison early to make sure they are walking the straight and narrow."

Ada's mouth fell open. "You were in prison?"

Mary was equally stunned. "Why?"

"Do you remember me telling you about my brother? The one who left the Amish."

Mary nodded. "His name is Luke."

"Luke had been in and out of trouble for a while. His first arrest for drugs nearly broke my mother's heart. He went to jail and we thought when he got out that he would come home. But he didn't. My parents believed that he was lost to us. I couldn't accept that."

"Of course not. You love him," Mary said softly.

"I went to see him. I went to try and convince him to come home. He had gone from using drugs to making and selling them. I couldn't make him see how much he was hurting everyone. I couldn't get through to him. After two days, I gave up. Before I could leave, there was a drug raid. Luke had sold meth to an undercover cop. I was there when it happened. I wasn't making drugs. I wasn't using drugs. I wasn't selling drugs, but that didn't matter to the men who arrested us. The house was across the street from a school. I don't know how my brother could have been so stupid."

"Why would being near a school make a difference?" Ada asked.

"The penalty for endangering children is much higher."

Kevin had always made sure he stayed far away from them when he was selling drugs. Mary looked at Joshua. "Didn't your brother tell them you were innocent?"

"He did but no one believed him. No one believed me. The district attorney was eager to get a double conviction. One of the women Luke supplied was arrested on another charge. In exchange for a lower sentence, she testified that I had been helping Luke for months." He took a sip of his tea.

"She lied?" Ada stared at him in disbelief.

He set down his mug. "Drugs are a powerful and evil master."

Mary leaned toward him. "Why didn't you tell me this to begin with?"

"If you remember, you were trapped in a cellar with a total stranger and you were scared to death."

"And later? When we got out of the cellar?"

He stared into his tea as if it contained some important information. Suddenly, she knew the answer to her own question. "Nick."

Joshua nodded. "It seemed the wisest course was to keep silent. I wasn't sure if I had violated my parole by coming here. I *was* sure Nick wouldn't like the idea of a convict staying with you."

"He found out and that's why you left early."

"It was Nick's...suggestion."

Ada sighed and gave him a bright smile. "Well, you are back now and things are as they should be. I'll get fresh sheets for your bed."

Joshua shook his head. "There's no need. I won't be staying here. I'll come by to visit often, but I'm going to stay in town."

Mary reached across the table and laid a hand on his arm. "You can stay with us. I can handle Nick."

Joshua could barely believe the blessings the Lord had bestowed on him. Nick had not turned Mary against him. Joshua was guilty of misjudging the man. Mary and Ada accepted his explanation and were still willing to open their home to him. It was more than he had dared hope for. Until now, he'd cared for Mary and valued her friendship, but seeing the determination in her blue eyes sent a rush of deeper emotion through his chest. He was in love with her. It didn't matter that he hadn't known her long. He wanted to spend a lifetime getting to know her, earning her trust, providing for her and caring for her for the rest of his days.

That was his goal, but he knew he had to start with small steps. She liked him, but Ada had warned him that Mary grew to trust people slowly. "I'm sure you can handle Nick, but I don't want to cause friction between you. I would love to stay, but it's best if I go on into town. Besides, my parole officer will be checking in with me at the Wadler Inn."

He loved that she looked disappointed. "Okay, but you are staying for supper tonight."

"I can't, but I will be back tomorrow morning to do the chores and to finish fixing your corncribs, Ada. After that, I'll be working in town. But first, I have to deliver this lumber to your bishop's home before dark."

Mary pulled her hand away. "Your family's contribution is most generous."

He wanted to be alone with her. To show her how much he had missed her. He rose to his feet. "I should go check on my team. How is Oscar getting along?"

Mary shot to her feet with her hands clenched in her apron. "I was just going to change his dressing."

Ada smiled. "I thought you did that this morning?"

Mary blushed. "Did I? That's right, and I felt the drainage was worse, so I was going to check it again.

Joshua, why don't you take a look and tell me what you think. It's your decision if we need to call the vet."

"Sure. I'll take a look at him." He followed Mary to the door.

Ada chuckled. "That's going to be the most pampered horse that has ever lived in my barn."

Joshua made a pretense of checking over his team before he entered the barn. As soon as Mary came in behind him, he held out his hands. "I missed you so much."

She took his hands and squeezed them. "I missed you, too. I was so afraid I would never see you again."

He drew her into his embrace. She rested her cheek against his chest. For a long time, they simply held each other. He had never known such happiness. Unfortunately, he couldn't hold her forever. He lifted her chin and brushed a kiss lightly across her lips. "As much as I want to stay, I had better get on the road. I don't want to be driving my big wagon after dark."

"Promise me you won't vanish again without telling me where you're going."

"That's an easy promise to make."

"Thank you for your honesty in the house. I should be honest with you in return. There are things about me that you need to hear."

"They won't change how I feel about you."

"You won't know that until I'm finished."

Hannah came through the barn door. He and Mary quickly stepped apart. "*Mammi* wants to know how Oscar is."

He shared a knowing smile with Mary. "*Mammi* wants to make sure we are behaving ourselves." He tweaked Hannah's nose. "Oscar is fine. You have been taking good care of him. I missed you."

"I missed you, too. *Mammi* says we're going to have a picnic at the lake tomorrow for *Mamm's* birthday." She hopped up and down with excitement.

"That sounds *wunderbar*. I'm sure you'll have a good time."

"You can come with us." Hannah clapped her hands.

"Happy birthday, Mary. That's awful nice of you to invite me, Hannah, but I think the picnic is just for your family."

"Nonsense," Ada said as she came into the barn. "I expect you to join us. We aren't leaving without you. Not after all the work you have done in this community. There will be several families there, not just ours."

"Please say you'll come," Hannah begged.

"I don't see how I can refuse such a kind invitation." He caught Mary's eye. Maybe he could find some time alone with her.

She looked away first. "You don't have to come if you would rather do something else."

"I can't think of anything I'd rather do than go on a picnic with you. I'd love to take a long stroll around the lake."

Ada laughed. Mary didn't smile.

When Ada and Hannah left the barn, Joshua took Mary's hand again. "I'm listening now. What did you want to tell me?"

She stepped away from him. "It can wait until tomorrow. You should leave before it gets too late."

"I'm not in a hurry, Mary."

"Tomorrow. We'll talk tomorrow." She hurried out of the barn, leaving him puzzled.

Was she that worried about what she had to tell him? What could be so bad?

Chapter 13

On Saturday morning, Joshua picked up Mary, Hannah, Ada and Bella for the short wagon ride to the Shetler farm. Mary sat quietly beside him. He'd spent the night wondering what she needed to tell him, determined to convince her it didn't matter. He hoped he wouldn't have to wait long to get her alone.

At the Shetler farm, they joined Joe and Naomi Shetler, along with all the Barkman sisters and their husbands and children on the shore of a small lake in Joe's pasture. The green hillsides around the lake were dotted with white sheep and playful lambs. After helping Mary and Ada out of their buggy, Joshua joined the men standing in the shade of a tall oak tree. Hannah and several of the children ran to the water's edge and threw a stick for Bella. The Lab raced in, splashing the children urging her on. When she came out, she put the stick down and shook from head to tail. While she was busy, a large black-and-white sheepdog darted in and stole the stick and the chase was on.

Mary produced a bottle of soap and some wands and the children were soon blowing bubbles. The dogs gave up chasing each other and launched themselves at the orbs floating in the air. The other women, chatting and bustling about, were busy setting out the quilts and chairs and arranging the food on the tailgate of Joe's wagon.

Joe stroked his gray beard. "I've learned it's best to stay out of their way until they tell us it's ready."

Joshua surveyed the lake. "Is the fishing any good here?"

Nodding, Joe gestured toward the north end. "There's some mighty good fishing all along this side. Would you like a pole? I have several extras."

"I might take you up on that later." Joshua was watching Mary laughing with the children. It was good to see her so carefree.

"After you've had time to walk out with Mary, you mean." Joe chuckled.

Joshua gave him a wry smile. "Am I that obvious?"

"You forget that I've had a houseful of granddaughters all finding mates in the last two years. I know the look of a man who is smitten. Alvin and Betsy are slipping away now. You should take Mary in the other direction."

"I will. Speaking of granddaughters, I've been meaning to ask if you're related to a girl named Mary Shetler?"

"I've no relative named Mary. Why do you ask?"

"My brother knows an *Englisch* fellow who is looking for a girl by that name. Apparently, she was an old girlfriend. He thought he saw her on the television here in Hope Springs helping after the tornado."

"I'm the only Shetler in this community, but there are plenty of them over by New Philadelphia, although they are only distantly related to me. Maybe she's from one of those families. Mary is a common name. I don't know how to help you find her."

"New Philadelphia. I'll let my brother know."

"If she is Amish and left this *Englisch* fellow, it may be best that he not find her."

"I've thought of that, but they had a child together that he never met. A man should know his child."

"Perhaps this woman had a good reason for leaving him."

"Perhaps. *Danki*, Joe." Joshua saw Clara had taken over supervising the children. Mary was strolling toward the water's edge. He left Joe chuckling behind him and went to join her.

She smiled shyly when he stopped beside her. He gazed out over the lake. Fleecy white clouds in the blue sky floated above their flawless reflections in the water, as if the beauty was too great for the heavens to hold. "This is a pretty place, don't you think?"

"*Ja*, it's peaceful here." She began walking and he fell into step beside her. He could tell she was nervous.

They strolled for a while until a bend in the shoreline took them out of view of the others.

He found a fallen log beside a blooming dogwood tree and sat down. Mary joined him.

He glanced at her sitting beside him. He wanted to kiss her more than he wanted anything else in his life.

He wanted the right to hold her in his arms. In the depths of his heart, he believed she was the woman God had fashioned for him alone. It didn't matter that he wasn't her first love. It only mattered that she loved him now. He took her hand. It was small and soft and it fit his perfectly. "Mary, I have come to care deeply for you. I need to know that you feel the same."

She pulled her hand away and stood. "There are things I need to tell you before you say more. You aren't going to like hearing them."

He tried to take her hand again, but she pushed away. "Please, don't touch me. If you do, I may falter."

"I'm sorry. Mary, I don't know why you are afraid of me. I would never hurt you. Nothing you can say will change my feelings for you."

Mary wanted so much to confide in him, but she was scared. Scared it would matter. "I'm not afraid of you, Joshua. I'm afraid of the way I feel when I'm with you."

He took her hand and squeezed gently. "And how is that?"

"I feel like there might be a chance for me. A chance at happiness."

"That's how you make me feel. Why does that scare you? You deserve happiness."

"I'm afraid I'll reach for it and it will burst like one of Hannah's soap bubbles on the grass."

"There's more to it, isn't there? Is it me? Do you think I won't be back the next time I have to leave?"

"Maybe. I'm not sure."

"Why would you think that?"

"Because it has happened to me before. Hannah's

father left me. The next man who took me in betrayed me, too. I've been with more than one man. I was never married, Joshua. Hannah is an illegitimate child."

"I know that."

Mary frowned. "You do? How could you know this?"

"Delbert mentioned it the first day I met him. I asked him if he knew your husband and he said he didn't think you'd ever been married but he didn't hold that against you. It is a grave matter, but it is in the past. We will never mention it again. I love you and I love Hannah."

"You've known since then?" A sob escaped her and suddenly she was crying as she hadn't cried in years. She had been so afraid and all this time he knew.

"Don't cry. It doesn't matter. I love Hannah. She is the daughter of my heart." Joshua drew Mary into his embrace and held her. He gave her his handkerchief and she cried until she didn't have any tears left.

When she grew calm, he knelt in front of her. She dried her eyes and blew her nose.

"Are you okay now?" he asked.

She had a headache and her eyes were burning as if they were full of sand, but she ignored those minor discomforts. "I'm better than I have been in a long time."

"If you are ready to go back, I'm sure they have a birthday cake for you."

"*Nee*, stay. I'm ready to tell you what happened."

"You don't have to do that."

"I do. I want you to understand what I was going through when I made some horrible decisions."

He took a seat on the tree trunk beside her. "Okay, I'm listening."

She gazed up into the beautiful sky and prayed for

courage. "My father died when I was only six. I vaguely remember him. My mother remarried when I was ten. My stepfather was a good man, but he wasn't an affectionate man. He needed a wife to help him raise four sons and my mother fit the bill. I was an extra mouth to feed. My mother died in a buggy accident four years later. My stepfather didn't waste time remarrying. I never felt like I was part of the family after that."

"I'm sorry you were left alone."

"I found a job as a live-in maid with a family in Canton when I was fifteen. The husband was so nice to me. I just wanted to be loved. He saw how vulnerable I was and took advantage of that. He seduced me."

"Is he Hannah's father?"

She nodded. "When I suspected I was pregnant, I told him and I was promptly fired. He was terrified his wife would find out. I went back to my stepfather, but I wasn't welcome there. I was alone and out on the streets. I turned to my church for help, but the bishop called me terrible names. I was shunned. That's when I met someone who said he wanted to take care of my baby and me. I was so naive. You'd think I would have been smarter about men at that point, but I wasn't."

"We are taught to trust in the goodness of all men. Who was he?"

"A truly evil person. He took me in and took care of me. I thought I loved him. I began to suspect he was dealing drugs on the side, but I didn't want to believe it. I couldn't be that wrong about another person I wanted to love."

"What happened?"

"I overheard him making arrangements to sell my

baby when it was born. He knew someone who would pay a lot of money for a white child. They would pay more for a son, but they would take a girl. I was sick with fear for my baby. I had nowhere to go. He made me believe I couldn't escape him."

"But you did."

"I couldn't let them have my baby. God was watching over her. I went into labor one night when he was gone and delivered Hannah by myself. I had nothing for her. I stole a quilt off the clothesline of a neighbor and wrapped her in that. I knew I had to hide her. I knew he would be back at any time. There was a convenience store not far from our place. I used to see Amish buggies parked there. There was one in the parking lot that night. I put Hannah in the basket on the backseat and I left a note begging the Amish family to take care of her. I told them to meet me in the same place in a week. I needed time to gather enough money so we could get far away from him. I believed he would find us and take her if I didn't."

"That was an incredibly brave and unselfish thing to do. Did the buggy belong to Ada?"

"*Nee*, it belonged to Levi Beachy. His brothers, Atlee and Moses, had taken it without his knowledge and met up with some girls to see a movie. They didn't know Hannah was in the backseat until they were almost home. She started crying and they panicked. They couldn't take her back. They couldn't take her home with them or their brother would know they had sneaked out without his knowledge. They were passing Ada's farm and it occurred to them that she didn't have grandchildren, so they left Hannah on her doorstep. They never saw my note. They never told anyone about her. She was found by Miriam. She saw an Amish buggy leaving and thought some unwed mother didn't want her baby. Miriam and Ada found the note and waited for me to show up at the farm. I didn't. I was in the parking lot of a convenience store praying the people I left Hannah with would bring her back. When they didn't return, I knew I'd lost her forever."

"What about the man who wanted to sell her?"

"I told him the baby was stillborn. He was furious, but he believed me. He still thought I was in love with him, but I knew I was nothing to him. I was nothing to anyone."

"That is never true. We are God's children. He is always with us, even in the dark times."

"I know that now, but I didn't believe it then. Nick and Miriam were investigating and trying to discover the identity of Hannah's family when I was taken to the hospital. I was…sick."

She wasn't ready to tell him that she had tried to end her life. She didn't have the courage. Not yet.

"Eventually, they figured out who I was and they gave Hannah back to me. I couldn't believe it. I had my baby in my arms and I had people who cared about us. Nick and Miriam were amazing. They gave me a home when they took me to live with Ada. They gave me protection and security by adopting me. God saved more than my life. He gave me a family. How can I expect anything more than that?"

"I think you are selling God short. I think He gets to decide how much joy and how much sorrow comes into our lives. His love is limitless."

Did she doubt God's mercy and goodness?

"Does Hannah's father know he has such a beautiful daughter?"

"He died in a small plane crash when she was eight months old."

"What happened to the man who wanted to sell her? I can't believe Nick would let him go unpunished. It is not the *Englisch* way to forgive."

"He was arrested for the drugs and then charged with second degree kidnapping, too, because I was a minor. It was then he learned my baby was still alive. I testified against him in court. If I hadn't, he would have gone free. I know it is not our way, but I believe he would've found another girl in trouble and sold her baby. I could not be a party to that. He made many threats against me. After only four years, he's getting out on parole. Nick and Miriam are worried that he will try to find me. That's why I was so upset about seeing my face on television." Emotionally drained and exhausted, Mary closed her eyes.

"Do you believe he will?"

"I do. That's why I changed my name to Kaufman when Miriam adopted me. It was at Nick's urging. He knew it would make it harder for Kevin Dunbar to find me. There are a lot of Mary Kaufmans among the Amish."

"Did you say Kevin Dunbar?"

The strain in Joshua's voice caused Mary to open her eyes. "Do you know him?"

Joshua rose to his feet and walked a few feet away. He raked a hand through his hair. "No, but I've heard my brother mention someone by that name. It might not be the same man. There could be more than one Kevin Dunbar in the world."

"The Kevin Dunbar I know is in the Beaumont Correctional Facility."

Joshua stared at her in shock. This could not be happening. Mary could not be the woman he had been sent to look for. He paced back and forth in front of her.

"Joshua, what's wrong?"

How much information about her had he shared? He racked his brain trying to recall all the times he had mentioned her in his letters and spoken of her when he was with Luke. Had Luke shared that information with Dunbar? Was it enough for Dunbar to figure out it was the same Mary? Maybe.

Luke was waiting for Joshua to contact him with more information. His brother needed to know Dunbar wasn't being honest with him. Joshua needed to find out exactly how much the man knew about Mary Kaufman, if anything. What if he had put her in danger?

"I know it's a lot for you to take in, Joshua. I understand that. I wouldn't blame you if you packed up and went home. I'm not exactly the kind of girl you want your parents to meet." She rose to her feet.

He stopped pacing and reached for her. "Mary, you're the only woman I'd like my parents to meet. I *am* going to pack up and go home, but I'll be back. I want you to believe that. I love you. I want us to be together, but I have to take care of something else first."

"Does it have to do with your parole?"

Joshua's jaw clenched. He had a meeting this evening with Officer Merlin at the inn. He would have to miss it.

The man would be furious, but Mary was more important. Joshua had to make sure her identity was still safe.

"It's family business. It could take a couple of days. After your party, I'll catch a ride home with the man that's picking up Oscar." From there, he could get a ride with a local man to see Luke.

"But you will be back. I believe that. I love you."

He saw the soft glow in her eyes as she spoke. He pulled her into his arms and kissed her gently. "I love you, too. God willing, we will have many years to whisper those words to each other."

Joshua was shocked at the change in his brother when he visited him the following morning. Luke was hollow-eyed and shaking. "You look terrible."

"So do you. So what? What do you want?"

"I found the woman you asked me to look for. I found Mary Shetler, but you can't tell Dunbar anything about her."

Luke laughed but there wasn't any humor in it. "I didn't have to."

"What are you saying?"

"All I did was tell him my brother was courting the *Englisch* sheriff's adopted Amish daughter. I thought it was a *goot* joke considering you're on parole. Does she know that? It turns out Dunbar knows Sheriff Bradley rather well."

"Oh, Luke. You have no idea what you've done."

"I helped a friend find his daughter. Not that he turned out to be much of a friend."

"You're using again, aren't you?"

"I'm going cold turkey this time, thanks to my *goot* buddy."

"Dunbar was supplying you drugs in here? That's the kind of man you helped find an innocent woman and child?"

"Hey, keep your voice down. Do you want the guards to hear? I'm not a rat."

"Dunbar isn't Hannah's father. He tried to sell her on the black market when she was born. Mary was fifteen and homeless when he found her and took her in. Not because he cared about her, but because she was pregnant. Apparently, some people will pay large sums of money for a white baby."

Luke lost his smug look. "I don't know what you're talking about. Kevin said he was her father."

"He lied to you. Hannah's father died in an accident months after she was born. Kevin is looking for Mary because she testified against him. She's the reason he's in here."

"I didn't know any of this."

"You know what kind of man he is. You know he is dealing drugs and you would do anything for them. Did he see my letters? Does he know where she lives?"

"I'm sorry, Joshua. You have to believe that I'm sorry. He saw your letters. He was paroled two days ago."

"What is Bella barking at?" Ada looked up from her needlework.

Mary laid down the book she was reading. "I'll go see. Did Hannah come in?"

"I don't think so."

Rising from her chair, Mary went to the window to look out. There was a black car parked on their lane. Was it a driver bringing Joshua back? "I see a car at the end of the drive."

"Are they coming to the house?" Ada rose to join Mary at the window.

"*Nee*, it's just sitting there."

"Perhaps someone is lost."

"Maybe Joshua has come back." She was so eager to see him. Eager to explore the future with him.

Ada remained at the window. "I thought he said it would be several days. Now they are coming this way. You might be right."

"I'll go see." Mary hurried through the house to the kitchen door. She paused before opening the screen to still her racing heart. It might not be him. But it might be.

Bella's barking intensified, then she yelped once and was silent. Hannah screamed. Mary pushed open the screen door and rushed out. Her heart dropped to her feet when she saw Kevin standing beside the car. He had Hannah in his arms. She was struggling to get free and crying. There were two men with Kevin. Bella lay sprawled on the ground at the feet of one of them.

Mary ran toward Kevin. "Don't hurt her. I'm begging you, don't hurt my baby."

"You should have kept your mouth shut. None of this would've happened if you had just kept your mouth shut."

Mary reached Kevin's side but one of the men stopped her when he wrapped his arms around her. She tasted the salty tears that streamed down her face.

Clutching her hands together, she pleaded with Kevin, "Please, if you ever had any feelings for me at all, don't do this."

"That's just it, Mary. I never did have feelings for you. The baby was all I wanted and now I've got her. She's still worth money, although not to the same people. Tell your boyfriend I appreciate him finding you for me." He looked at his men. "Let's go."

The man holding Mary threw her to the ground. Before she could get up, they were all in the car. She grabbed the door handle, trying to reach Hannah. Her baby was screaming. Her baby needed her, but she couldn't hold on as the car drove away.

She fell to a heap in the driveway screaming Hannah's name.

Chapter 14

Joshua jumped out of the van before it pulled to a stop in Ada's yard. Bella lay on the porch with her head on her paws. There was blood on the left side of her face. As soon as he saw Mary walk out of the house, his heart leaped. She was safe. He ran toward her. "Mary, I have to talk to you."

She didn't speak. She didn't move. His steps slowed as he approached her. Her face was streaked with tears. It twisted with agony. "Why did you do it? Where is she, Joshua? I can forgive anything else. Just tell me where she is."

"What are you saying? Oh, please, God, don't let it be Hannah." He caught Mary by the arms. The raw pain in her eyes was unbearable.

"He took my baby. I couldn't do anything to stop him. Why did you tell Kevin where we were?"

"I didn't, Mary. You have to believe me. I never told him anything."

Nick Bradley came out of the house. "Mary, get inside."

She ducked her head and turned away. Joshua reached for her, but Nick grabbed his arm, twisting it behind him and forcing Joshua up against the side of the house. "Joshua Bowman, you are under arrest for violating your parole and for conspiracy to commit kidnapping. You have the right to remain silent. If you give up that right, anything you say can and will be used against you in a court of law."

Joshua knew his rights. He ignored Nick as he continued to recite them and focused on Mary where she stood only a few feet away. "Mary, let me explain."

Nick jerked Joshua around. "You were in on this with Dunbar from the beginning. Where is she? Where did he take Hannah?"

"I'm not working with Kevin Dunbar. I don't expect you to believe me, but Mary, you have to believe me. I would never hurt you. I would never hurt Hannah."

"Then tell us where he took her," Nick bellowed, anger blazing in his eyes.

Joshua recoiled from the sheriff's rage. What would Nick do if he learned of Luke's part in this? Joshua didn't believe Luke had known Kevin would harm Hannah or Mary, but he had given away their location in exchange for drugs. That alone would add years to Luke's sentence. Joshua struggled with his need to protect his brother and to find Hannah.

"I don't know where he took her." He bowed his head. He didn't expect Nick to believe him.

"Wrong answer." Nick yanked Joshua toward his SUV.

"Wait." Mary touched Nick's arm.

He stopped. "I'm not Amish. I don't get to forgive and forget. I have to uphold the law."

"I need to hear what he has to say."

Nick shook his head, but took a few steps away.

Mary placed her hand on Joshua's chest. Her heart was being torn to pieces by her frantic grief, but she knew—she knew in her soul that he was telling the truth. He loved her and he loved Hannah. She had to trust that love. If she couldn't, then she truly was a broken human being. Joshua had kept things from her, but she had kept things from him, too.

"I believe you when you say you didn't have a part in this, Joshua. I trust you. I'm sorry I accused you."

When she looked at him, his eyes were filled with tears. She loved him so much. "God sent you to save us once before. Can't you help save her now?"

Nick came to Mary's side. A tense muscle twitched in his cheek, but he had his anger under control. "Tell us what you know. I don't want to make this harder for you. I just want our little girl back."

Joshua had no choice. Hannah and Mary needed him. He had to put aside his distrust and fear of the *Englisch* law and believe that God was in charge of his fate and of Luke's. He faced Nick knowing his words might condemn his brother to more years in prison.

"I wrote home about Mary and about Hannah and their lives here. I wanted my family to know what an amazing woman she is. My mother forwarded all my letters to my brother Luke the way the Amish do with their circle letters."

Nick crossed his arms. "How did he know you were seeing Mary Shetler?"

"He didn't. Kevin saw Mary in one of the news reports about the tornado. He knew she was in Hope Springs. Luke knew I was here, too. He wrote that he needed to see me. When I went there, he told me about his friend, a guy who had been in love with an Amish girl before he went to jail. He said she was pregnant and went back to her Amish family. He saw Mary on the news. He knew she was in Hope Springs. He wanted to make sure she and his child were okay. I said I would ask around. Something about Luke's behavior bothered me. I thought he might be using drugs again, but I had no idea how he could be getting them."

Mary wiped at the tears on her face. "You never asked me about Mary Shetler."

"The only person I asked was Wooly Joe. He said what I was already thinking—that it was better to let Mary Shetler's child grow up without knowing he or she had a drug dealer for a father."

Nick pushed his hat up with one finger. "Do you think Dunbar was supplying your brother with drugs in exchange for information?"

"I can't be sure, but I think he was. I told Luke that Mary had been adopted by you. Luke thought it was hilarious—I was fresh out on parole and dating the sheriff's daughter. He shared the story with Dunbar. The man figured out that Mary Kaufman and Mary Shetler were one and the same. When Mary told me about her relationship with Dunbar, I was sick with worry that my letters would lead him here. I went to see Luke. That's why I missed my meeting with Officer Merlin. As soon as Luke told me Dunbar had been released, I came to warn you."

"Why didn't you call me?' Nick demanded. "I could have stopped him."

"Because I didn't trust you. I was afraid if you knew about Luke's dealings with Dunbar, you'd make sure he stayed in prison."

"So now Dunbar has Hannah and we're still no closer to knowing where he took her."

"Luke once mentioned Dunbar was going to set him up in business when he got out. With some of his friends in Cleveland. They're brothers who run a salvage yard."

"There are a lot of brothers in Cleveland. You're gonna have to do better than that.'"

"That's all I know. Luke may know more."

"You had better hope he does. He's going to tell me everything."

Joshua understood Nick's anger. "He might not talk to you, but he'll talk to me."

Nick turned to Mary. "Get your things together. You and Ada are leaving this afternoon. Miriam has a safe place for you. I want you out of harm's way in case that maniac comes back." Nick pulled open the rear door and pushed Joshua in.

"I'm coming with you. I'll be as safe with you as I am with Miriam. If Joshua's brother knows where Hannah is, maybe I can convince him to tell us."

"All right, get in."

Joshua remained silent on the long ride to the correctional facility. Mary didn't speak to him. She didn't even look at him. He could hardly blame her. She had to be terrified. The handcuffs were cutting into his wrists by the time they arrived, but he didn't complain. It was nothing more than what he deserved. Nick was right. If Joshua had only trusted Nick enough to call him, Hannah might be safe.

Mary and Joshua were seated at a wooden table when they brought Luke into the interview room. Nick leaned against the cinder-block wall. Luke wore a defiant look. "So you couldn't keep your mouth shut, little brother," he said in Pennsylvania Dutch. "You had to involve me."

"Sit down and speak English." Nick pushed away from the wall and shoved Luke into a chair. Luke glared at him.

Mary clasped her hands together on the table. "Please help us. Kevin has taken my daughter. Her name is Hannah. She is only four years old. I know she must be so frightened. I only want to get her back. Anything that you can tell us may help us find her."

Joshua added his plea. "Please, brother. I know you would never hurt a child. I know you didn't mean for any of this to happen."

Some of Luke's bluster slipped away. "I thought he was the kid's father. A father has a right to see his child."

Nick struck the table with both hands, making everyone jump. "Do you know where he took her?"

"I don't."

Joshua said, "You told me Kevin had friends in Cleveland who would set you up with a job when you got out."

"He probably lied about that. He lied about everything else. He said he'd take care of me but the minute he got out, the supply dried up."

"Was he smuggling drugs to the inmates here?"

Luke hunched forward and rubbed his arms as if he were cold. "He still has friends inside. I can't tell you anything."

Nick pulled up a chair and sat beside Luke. "Hannah is the sweetest child you have ever met. Her eyes are as blue as the sky. She doesn't deserve to be punished because Kevin Dunbar wants to make Mary suffer. She did the right thing when she testified against him."

"I forgave him for what he tried to do to me, but I could not let him do it to someone else," she said.

Nick patted Mary's hand and then looked at Luke. "I know it will take courage to tell us what you know. Do you have as much courage as this woman does?"

Luke sat back. "The name is Sanders. They own an auto salvage lot on the west side. They've been helping Dunbar smuggle drugs into here. I don't know how. That's all I know.

"Thank you." Nick jumped up from his seat and left the room.

"Danki," Mary said, and followed him.

Joshua gave his brother a tired smile. "You did a good thing."

"It doesn't make up for all the wrong things I have done."

"Maybe not. But it's a start."

"This means I'm going to be in here for a long time."

Joshua stared at the door. "Maybe they will give us a cell together."

Perched on the end of his cot in the county jail in Millersburg, Joshua prayed, not for his release, but for

Mary's and Hannah's safety. The last thing he wanted was to hurt them, and yet he had led a vicious man to their door. He didn't know how he could live with himself if anything happened to Hannah. All things were according to God's plan, but it was hard to see that when his heart was breaking.

He heard the cell-block door open. He looked up as Sheriff Bradley paused in front of his cell. Joshua jumped to his feet. "Did you find her?"

The sheriff looked tired and worn. "My family is no concern of yours."

"I just want to know that she is safe. Please, can you tell me that much?"

Nick sighed heavily. "We found her. She's frightened but safe. We arrested two men, but Dunbar got away."

"Where is Mary now? Can I see her?"

"She and Hannah are safe with an Amish family in another community."

"Thank God." Joshua gripped the bars and laid his head against the cold steel. It didn't matter what happened to him now. He would go back to prison and finish out his sentence, but he could face that knowing they were safe.

Sheriff Bradley unlocked the cell door and held it open. "You're free to go home if you agree to follow the conditions of your original parole."

"I don't understand."

"You had a valid reason for missing your meeting with your parole officer, but it can't happen again. Do you understand?"

"Why are you doing this?"

"Because I think you love my daughter."

"I do. I love her more than life itself and I love Hannah like she was my own child."

"Then I'm sorry, but you are going to have to forget about them. They are no longer your concern. The only way to keep Mary and Hannah safe is to keep them hidden."

"If I could just say goodbye to them. That's all I'm asking. That's all I'll ever ask of you."

"No."

Hope died in Joshua's chest.

"There's a car waiting outside that will take you home."

"What about my brother? What will happen to him?"

"I'm not at liberty to talk about an ongoing case. Go home. There's nothing you can do for them."

"You have to eat something. You're going to dry up and blow away. Who will take care of Hannah then?" Ada pushed a plate piled high with meat loaf, green beans, mashed potatoes and gravy across the table to Mary.

Mary pushed it aside. "I'm not hungry, and I'm not about to dry up and blow away. I will always take care of Hannah. You should stop worrying about me."

"How can I stop worrying when there is such sadness in your eyes?"

"If you're worried that I'm going to do something stupid, don't be. I was very young and very foolish when I tried to commit suicide. I have learned that I can bear all things if I trust in the Lord. This too shall pass." They were hard words to say while her heart was breaking, but she spoke the truth.

Her daughter was safe. Bella was making a good recovery from the blow to her head. Ada hadn't suffered any ill effects from the fright and stress. It had been two weeks since Hannah's abduction and Mary had no idea if she would ever see Joshua again. She missed him dreadfully.

The outside door opened and Miriam came in. "They caught him."

Mary jumped to her feet. "They caught Kevin Dunbar?"

"He was trying to cross into Canada."

Ada patted her chest. "The goodness of the Lord be praised."

"Amen," Mary and Miriam said together, and smiled at each other.

"Does this mean we can go home?" Hannah was sitting at the table eating her green beans and dropping a few to Bella, who was on the floor at her feet.

Miriam grinned at her. "According to Papa Nick, you can."

Mary laced her fingers together and squeezed hard. "When can I see Joshua?"

"Nick is going there tomorrow. He wanted to know if you would like to go, too?"

Mary squealed in delight. "I do. I do want to go."

"Me, too," Hannah shouted.

"Me, three," Ada shouted, and they all laughed.

Miriam looked over the table. "We're to meet him there at ten o'clock. This looks good. Can I join you?"

"I will get you a plate." Ada hurried to the cupboard.

Mary sat back and gave silent thanks. The dark clouds covering her days had been blown away. If only

Joshua could accept her family and her family accept him. It was a tall order, but nothing was impossible in the sight of God.

Joshua was cleaning Oscar's stall when he heard a car drive in. He put aside his pitchfork and headed to the door. It wasn't his day to meet with Officer Merlin. Who was here?

He recognized Nick Bradley's SUV and his heart thudded painfully. Were Mary and Hannah okay? Had Dunbar found them again?

Nick got out and opened the back door on the passenger's side. Joshua couldn't believe his eyes when Luke got out. He glanced toward the house. His father and mother had heard the vehicle, too, and had come outside. The joy that spilled across their faces took his breath away.

He hurried forward and held out his hand. His brother was still pale, but his eyes were clear. "Luke, I can't believe it's you. What's going on?"

"I got an early parole."

"How?"

Nick closed the door and folded his arms over his chest. "Your brother is cooperating with our investigation into drug-smuggling activities at the Beaumont Correctional Facility. In the interest of his safety, the judge has granted him parole. You might also want to know that Kevin Dunbar was arrested this morning trying to cross into Canada. He's going away for a long, long time, without the possibility of parole."

Another car turned into the drive. It was a blue

sedan. Joshua didn't recognize it. By this time, all of Joshua's brothers were standing behind his parents.

Luke rubbed his palms on his pant legs. "Reckon it's time to get a tongue lashing from dear old *daed*."

Joshua slapped him on the shoulder. "It won't be as bad as you think."

As his family went into the house with Luke, Joshua stayed behind. "Was this your doing, Nick?"

"A little. I thought your family deserved a break after what happened to you."

The car pulled up behind Nick's vehicle. Joshua went weak in the knees when Hannah burst out of the back-seat and came running toward him. He crouched down and gathered her in his arms. "Hannah Banana, it is so good to see you."

She squeezed his neck in a huge hug, then leaned back and patted his face with both hands. "I'm not a banana."

"I guess you aren't. You're getting to be a very big girl." Joshua put her down. He saw Miriam get out of the driver's side and open the back door. Ada got out. Then the beautiful woman he was dying to hold in his arms stepped out, too.

"Mary." He breathed her name into the air.

She slowly approached him. He'd thought about her so often, agonized over what he might say to her. Wondered what she might say to him. Now that she was standing in front of him, words failed him. He wanted to drop to his knees and beg her forgiveness.

"Hello, Joshua." Her voice was tentative, hesitant.

"Hello, Mary." He wanted to tell her how beautiful she looked in the morning light. He wanted to tell her how much he had missed the sound of her voice, the curve of her lips when she smiled, the soft blush that stained her cheeks so easily.

Miriam took Nick by the elbow and Hannah by the hand. "Let's go inside and meet Joshua's family. I'm sure they have a lot of questions for us."

Joshua shoved his hands in his pockets. He had no idea where to go from here.

Mary couldn't believe how nervous she was. Once she had Hannah safely in her arms, the only thing she'd wanted was to tell Joshua how much she missed him. Now that he was standing in front of her, she couldn't think of a thing to say. She just wanted to be in his arms. Why was he just standing there? Couldn't he see how much she loved him?

He raised his face to heaven. "When you look at me like that, I can't think straight."

"How am I looking at you?" she asked softly, stepping closer.

"Like you need me to hold you."

"I do, Joshua. I need you to hold me all the days of my life." He groaned as he pulled her close and her joy filled her to the brim. He was strong and solid—this wasn't a dream. She wouldn't wake and find she was alone in her bed in a strange house. She was finally where she belonged. She was afraid to breathe, afraid he would pull away and she would never feel this complete again. She cupped his face with her hands and gazed into his eyes. "You are a wonderful man. I don't deserve you."

He gave her a wry smile. "I'm the one who doesn't

deserve you. I understand if you would rather have Delbert Miller."

Mary's heart soared as she realized her life was about to take an amazingly wonderful turn with this amazing and wonderful man. She grinned happily. "He's a fine fellow, but I think Hannah likes you better."

"What will she think about having me as a father?" His voice was hesitant. Didn't he know Hannah already loved him, too?

"She will be delighted."

"Are you sure?"

"I'm very, very sure. There's no one in the world who will be a better father than you, Joshua. I believe that with all my heart."

He brushed his lips tenderly over hers. She raised her arms to circle his neck as he crushed her close. She wanted to be held by him this way for a lifetime. When he drew away, she missed his warmth and the feel of his heart beating against hers.

Drawing a shaky breath, he said, "That still leaves one obstacle."

"I don't see any." She needed his lips on hers. She tried to pull him back, but he resisted.

"What about your father?"

"Nick? What about him?"

"Mary, my brother and I are felons. Your father is a sheriff. He's not going to like having ex-cons for in-laws. Neither will your mother."

"Oh, Joshua, you underestimate Nick and Miriam. They fell in love young, but theirs was not an easy path. Nick was English, Miriam was Amish, but there was much more. Nick was responsible for the death of Miriam's only brother."

Joshua's eyes widened with shock. "How?"

"Miriam's brother had stolen a car. He was desperate to reach the English girl he loved before she left town. Nick gave chase, not knowing who was driving the stolen vehicle. He ran the car off the road in an attempt to stop it and Miriam's brother was killed in the crash. It took a long time for Nick to forgive himself and much longer for Miriam to forgive him. A baby left on Miriam's doorstep years later brought them together."

"Hannah?"

Mary slipped her arms around Joshua's waist and laid her head on his chest. "*Ja.* It was Hannah. The baby I gave away."

When his arms closed around her, she knew he was the one God had chosen for her. "Isn't it amazing how the Lord uses us to reach others in ways we can't imagine? Nick and Miriam understand that people make mistakes, but those mistakes do not define who we are. What we do with each new day that God gives us defines who we are in His sight."

"In that case, Mary Kaufman, will you marry me? I love you. I don't want to face a life without you. Every morning and every night I want my love for you to define who I am in the sight of God."

Sweet bliss filled her heart and surged through her veins. She hated doing it, but he had to know one more thing before she gave him her answer. She stepped back and pulled up her sleeve. Her scars stood out puckered and white on her wrists. "You know what these are from?"

"I don't, but it must have hurt you very much."

"I don't remember it hurting. I did it to myself, Joshua. I tried to kill myself with a broken piece of bathroom mirror. I cut my wrists open and waited to die."

She expected the shock she saw in his face, but she hadn't expected how quickly his expression changed to compassion. "You must have been terribly alone."

It was so long ago, but she could feel the cold creeping over her even now the way it had as she lay dying. "You can't know what it's like to reach the point where you believe in your soul that you and everyone else will be better off if you're dead. After I lost Hannah, I had nothing to live for. I wasn't sick when Nick and Miriam found me in the hospital. I tried to commit suicide."

He caressed her cheek with his fingers. "I'm sorry you went through such a terrible ordeal, but I rejoice that your life was spared. Mary, it doesn't change the way I feel when I'm with you."

"Truly?"

"Truly."

She let out the breath she had been holding. "In that case, I would love to marry you."

He pulled her close and kissed her again, with infinite tenderness and passion. Mary saw just how wonderful their life together was going to be.

The door to the house opened and Hannah came out with a cookie in her hand. "Joshua, your mother is a *goot* cook."

"I'm glad you think so." He picked her up and sat her on the hood of Nick's SUV. "Hannah, I have a serious question for you."

"I haven't blamed Bella for anything she didn't do."

He glanced at Mary and chuckled. "I'm glad to hear that. I need your permission for something important. I would like to marry your mother. What do you think about that?"

Her mouth fell open. "I thought you were going to marry me?"

"I love you dearly, but your mother is already twenty. This might be her last chance to get a husband."

Hannah thought it over, and then nodded. "Okay. Can I get another cookie?"

Laughing, Joshua took one of her hands and Mary took the other. They swung her off the hood and walked into their future together.

* * * * *